Secrets

Volumes 1 and 2

~❧~

The Best in Women's Sensual Fiction

Secrets

Volumes 1 and 2

❧

The Best in Women's Sensual Fiction

Red Sage Publishing, Inc.
P.O. Box 4844
Seminole, FL 33775

ISBN: 1-56865-484-7

Contents

Secrets

Volume 1

A Lady's Quest

by Bonnie Hamre

To my reader:
  Have you ever wondered what it would be like to experience exquisite lovemaking with the perfect lover? Antonia Blair-Sutworth did and look what happened! Enjoy along with Antonia…

Chapter One

Antonia heard the breathless murmurs and glanced beyond her dance partner's shoulder. Across the crowded Wolfington ballroom, guests gathered at the foot of the sweeping staircase to watch a man descend.

Head erect, broad shoulders straight, he made his leisurely way down the steps, seemingly at ease with being the center of attention. Even the dancers slowed to observe the tall man with the regal bearing. Like the dominant lion whose coloring he shared, he moved with the sinuous, controlled grace that spoke of might held under strict restraint.

He reached the bottom of the steps. The crowd parted before him. Ladies dipped in welcoming curtsies, men lowered their heads as he made his way between them, ignoring the sussuration that encircled and flowed in his wake.

As he joined her, Countess Wolfington all but swooned. She rose from her curtsy, puce skirts puddling from her broad hips, clasping the hand he extended.

He lifted her fingers to his mouth. "Countess. Beautiful as always."

More than twice his age, she simpered like a young girl in her first Season. "Your grace, such an honor to have you attend our simple entertainment."

Dougal MacDonald, seventh Duke of Sutherland, lifted an eyebrow. The Wolfingtons were known for their extravagant and ostentatious parties and this one promised to be no exception. He glanced around at the gaudy ballroom, at the scores of flickering silver candelabras, and the elaborately dressed hordes milling about hoping to catch his attention.

"We heard you were back from the north, your grace," the

countess ventured.

"Aye. I rode hard to be here tonight."

She raised a fan to cover a coy titter. "Oh, you flatter me."

Let the woman think what she wanted. Covertly, Sutherland searched the faces of the guests. Even on his isolated estates, he'd heard the news that Lady Blair-Sutworth had dismissed Effingdale and he had wasted no time returning to London. Now that she was free, he meant to make her his.

Immediately.

His gaze traveled past an ensemble dancing a quadrille, then snapped back. There. No mistaking that glorious chestnut hair piled atop that slender neck. Her gown, a deep blue, clung to her figure, subtly revealing the curve of her hip, the tantalizing hint of her thigh. She wore no adornment other than the glowing gems at her throat and ears, yet her simplicity drew him far more than the ornately decorated gowns of the other women.

For an instant their eyes met, then she looked coolly away from the interest he let show on his face. He frowned. The lady was no blushing virgin, but a sophisticated woman well aware of her own sensuality. Why then did she look away in a deliberate snub?

He accepted a glass of champagne from a passing footman and moving out of the way of the dancers, he took a position where he could watch her without interference.

She moved gracefully through the steps of the quadrille, her fingers just resting on those of her partner. Though she smiled as she danced, and nodded and acknowledged acquaintances who shared the floor, she showed no particular preference for any man that Sutherland could discern. That pleased him. However, she steadfastly refused to look his way, which did not.

When the music ceased, she smiled at her partner, rested her fingertips on his arm and allowed him to escort her from the floor. Sutherland straightened his shoulders and made his way to her side.

He intercepted her as she turned to join another group. "Lady Blair-Sutworth."

Antonia glanced up and stiffened. "Your grace." She made him the smallest curtsy imaginable.

He hid a smile. "Have I offended you in some way?"

Casting her emerald gaze somewhere beyond his shoulder, she murmured, "I cannot imagine why you should think so."

"Almost the cut direct should do it, wouldn't you agree?'

She slanted her head in inquiry.

"A few moments ago, while you were dancing?"

She paused, as if in reflection. "I don't believe I noticed you."

"I am wounded."

Her gaze flicked up and away. "Is there not a sufficient number of women here to fawn over you? Perhaps our hosts would be good enough to import some additional female guests."

He laughed. "One will do. Shall I tell you who?"

"That is not necessary, your grace. If you will excuse me?"

"Not yet."

Her mouth tightened. Sutherland studied the set look to her face, Why was she so eager to rid herself of his presence? Though he found it more irritating than complimentary, he couldn't pretend he knew nothing about the usual reaction of women to his attention. He didn't flatter himself that it was for himself alone, for Dougal MacDonald, that some women flirted and chatted gaily to attract his attention to their charms. It was common knowledge that he would have to marry soon to protect the title and fill his nurseries. More than one woman hoped to become his very wealthy Duchess.

But not yet. Marriage and children would have to wait. First, he would lay claim to Lady Antonia Blair-Sutworth. Anticipating the outcome of his intentions, he studied the tender flare of her lips and wondered how they would feel under his. His loins tightened at the thought.

The music began again. A waltz, perfect. He turned to her, but she took a step back.

"I've promised this dance to Talbot." She looked past his shoulder. "Here he is, now."

Sutherland turned his head and waited until the other man, a young fop by the looks of his intricately tied neckcloth, approached. Calmly, he said, "Lady Blair-Sutworth has pledged me this dance."

She caught her breath. "Oh, but I didn't—"

The younger man cast her a startled glance and bowed. "My error, your grace."

"Wise of him," Sutherland commented as the younger man retreated. He turned to lead Antonia to the floor.

"Do you always get what you want?"

"Always. Make note of that, my lady."

"I do not wish to dance a waltz with you, sir."

"Why not?"

Antonia knew he knew exactly why she did not want to dance with him. The waltz, only recently accepted by the patrons at Almacks, would allow him to put his hand on her waist, to hold her facing him, to command her steps. How could she maintain a distance between them when he held her? "I prefer to choose my own partners," she said firmly.

"As do I." He looked into her eyes. "I have chosen you. Will you waltz with me or cause a scene? Already people are staring at us."

"They look at you, your grace. They always do."

She tensed as he took her into his arms and held her much too closely. She withdrew immediately to the acceptable distance between partners. His grip loosened, but she heard the slight rumble of laughter deep in his chest.

"Jealous?" He took the first slow, graceful steps, immediately establishing his mastery of the dance. "You are beautiful, witty, always in demand. Surely you are used to people watching you? Particularly men?"

"As the women watch you, your grace? Your reputation far exceeds mine."

He laughed, a low sound meant for her ears alone. "Perhaps we shall add to our reputations."

The implications of his statement whirled in her head as he moved her around the dance floor in flawless rhythm. She had no trouble following him. He performed the scandalous dance as though it were invented to show off his lean physique, his manly command of his partner's body. Even with the proper space between them, she knew intuitively that their bodies would fit perfectly.

The music swirled through her. Closing her eyes, she let the melody and the man sweep her in wide, circling turns. Her body throbbed to life as the thought of the sensual possibilities this man offered.

Indeed, for a moment, she allowed herself the pleasure of imagining a far more intimate dance. Once or twice, as their thighs brushed together, she felt the hard muscles and envisioned his phallus, rigid and ready. Desire, heated and heavy, rushed through her. She felt her limbs go limp, knew only that his arm supported her, and savored the feeling.

But only for an instant. Abruptly, she forced the pleasure away. She knew only too well the risk of allowing her desire to govern her head. She could not allow this dance to be any more than it was, a brief moment out of time, an exquisite interlude.

Much as she would prefer to let the passion sweep her along, she could not allow an instant of weakness to threaten her liberty. If she allowed her heart to interfere with her head, if she let herself relax the vigilance that had served her well, she'd lose all that she had gained. In the three years of her widowhood, she'd become used to managing her own affairs and being in control of her inherited income.

Though there was nothing to say that Sutherland would be anything other than a passionate liaison, she knew herself too well. If she once allowed herself to indulge in the pleasure of making love with him, she wouldn't be content with a mere affair. She would want everything, the man, marriage and a life together. In return, she would be expected to surrender everything to him. The thought of submitting that authority over herself to a husband was enough to discourage any idea of matrimony.

She longed for the music to end, to release her from this sensual torment of being near him, yet she dreaded the moment when she would have to move out of his arms. She shivered at the touch of his hand on her waist. Through the material of her gown, and the delicate undergarments, she felt the warmth of his palm. The heat insinuated itself through her skin, to flicker like fire through her body. It penetrated her defenses. She longed to move closer, to lay her head on his broad chest and feel whether his heart thundered as hers did.

"I believe I knew your husband, madam. Died at Waterloo, didn't he?"

His voice, deep with the rolling resonance of the Highlands, brought her to her senses. She collected her wavering defenses and gathered them closely about her. Her only hope lay in discouraging him, of being so cold that he would seek feminine company elsewhere. "Yes."

"A hero. No doubt you miss him greatly?'

"As any woman grieves for her husband, your grace."

This time he didn't hold back the laughter. It boomed out, drawing attention to them. She grit her teeth in frustration, resenting the intrusion into her brief moment with him. Why hadn't he the good sense to keep silent until the dance ended?

She started to withdraw from the circle of his arms, but he tightened his grip on her gloved hand. "My apologies," he stated as he twirled her around. "In my observation of the ton, grief is the last thing young wives feel when their elderly husbands cock up their toes."

"Perhaps you have been observing the wrong people," she said, a crisp edge to her voice.

"Perhaps. I would rather observe you. Those sapphires about your neck become you. They enhance the smoothness of your throat. Like fresh, sweet cream. I wonder, will it be as delicious to my tongue?"

"Your grace!" Her gaze darted up to meet his intent brown eyes. Once again she was reminded of the lion stalking his prey, all sinuous stealth and deadly determination. She felt impaled on that gaze, unable to move, to run, to protect herself.

"Yes? Surely men have complimented you before?"

She made herself speak lightly. "Not quite that way. At least, not in public."

"Quite so. When we are alone together, I shall compliment you in great detail—"

"There will be no opportunity for you to do so."

He smiled slightly. "Make no mistake, madam. You and I shall become intimately acquainted."

"I have no wish to continue this discussion, your grace. Pray release me."

"When the music is over."

She glanced up at his steely tone. She saw the predatory expression on his rugged face and despite her wish to escape the enticement of his arms, her heartbeat faltered. Temptation made her feel faint. She had to escape from his sensual lure before desire made her lose her good sense.

With relief, she heard the closing strains of the waltz. Sutherland could not expect another dance without causing speculation and that would protect her, at least for this evening. She would take care that they did not dance again.

They came to a halt not far from the grand staircase. He released her with a slight nod.

"Until we meet again."

A moment later, to her surprise, he was halfway up the stairs, leaving her feeling strangely abandoned. The buzz of gossip surrounded her as her fellow guests discussed the Duke's extraordinary departure and directed their curious glances at her. Holding her head high and her shoulders back, she, too, ascended the stairs, and called for her wrap and her carriage.

* * *

"Clarry! You must help me!"

The older woman paused as she carefully placed Antonia's jewelry into their velvet lined case. "What's the matter, milady?" She scrutinized Antonia. "You look all flushed and shivery like. Did you forget your shawl?"

"I must find a lover. There is no time to waste!"

Clarry bustled to her side and touched Antonia's forehead as if checking for fever.

"What's amiss?"

"Sutherland intends to make me his mistress."

Clarry's eyes lit up. "Sutherland? Now there's a man to keep you warm at night. I've heard that the women he beds wear smiles for a week—"

"This is no jesting matter," Antonia protested.

"What's wrong with his grace, I ask? I've heard he's a tiger—"

"Not a tiger," Antonia corrected. "A lion. He intends to make me his next meal."

"And about time, too."

"Clarry!" Antonia couldn't help smiling at her servant's plain spoken ways. The old woman had been her maid for many years and knew every one of her secrets and sins, yet sometimes Clarry still managed to surprise her. "Never him."

"And why not, milady? Now there's a real man for you—"

Antonia shut her eyes to avoid seeing the look on her servant's face. If Sutherland could make even elderly serving women look that rapturous, what more damage could he do to her heart? To her hard-won control over her own life?

"I will not have that man. Any but him"

Clarry's lips set firmly. "You are a fool, milady."

Antonia took no offense. "No doubt. You must help me find a new lover."

"Me?" Clarry all but squeaked.

"You've never failed me yet, Clarry. I count on you to help me." To take my mind off Sutherland, to assuage my need, to submerge myself in all the pleasure I can stand so that I no longer wonder what it would be like to make love with that Scot.

"You're sure about this, milady?"

"I am," Antonia stated. Her blood quickened at the memory of the duke's body so close to hers. "There is no time to lose."

Clarry sighed. "On your head be it."

"Oh, no," Antonia murmured to herself once Clarry had left her alone. "It's my heart that will pay the price."

Chapter Two

Antonia removed her hat and veil and gazed around the salon in the suite of rooms Clarry had secured. "You've done well, Clarry. You and the footmen will wait here while I am otherwise engaged."

Clarry nodded. "It's not too late to change your mind, milady. The first of the lot isn't due for another half hour."

"No. I must do this. For my own sanity, if nothing else," Antonia murmured, her mind filled with the erotic dreams she'd had of Sutherland ever since the Wolfington ball. He wouldn't let her sleep. Now, more than ever, she needed a lusty lover to replace the thoughts of him.

She moved forward and opened the door leading to the bedroom. She studied the dimly lit room, the wide bed draped in gold brocade hangings, the thick Oriental carpets under her feet and the plump pillows piled invitingly on a well-upholstered chaise. "Oh, Clarry. This is beyond description!"

A low fire warmed the room, while aromatic candles provided just enough light to set a sensual mood. The room promised seduction. At the end of the bed, an emerald silk robe, richly embroidered in gold thread, lay next to a matching emerald silken scrap. Antonia picked it up and saw that it was a full head mask, with openings for the nose and mouth delicately outlined in matching gold floss. She smiled and lifted it to her face. "I can't see through it. Good."

"Nor be recognized," Clarry commented, her voice betraying her misgivings.

"Everything's just as you said, milady. There's your bell, there, if you need us. Ring, and we'll come running."

"I hope that won't be necessary."

"You never know, I say. Though I picked them carefully, some of these men aren't what you're used to. Some of them aren't gentlemen," she sniffed. "Why you can't stick to your own kind—"

"Because they are too full of themselves," Antonia said. "We've been over this before."

Clarry sniffed. "These men are common!"

"Just so they satisfy my requirements," Antonia reminded her. "I want no one who will remind me of Sutherland."

"No chance of that. Only thing these 'applicants'," she said in a voice laced with scorn, "Have in common with his grace is a yard."

Antonia frowned at the vernacular for a man's penis. "No need to be crude." She dropped her reticule on a small table and studied her servant's face. "You are sure you know what to tell them?"

"I know. Nothing more foolish I've never heard, but I'll tell them right enough."

"Good." Antonia removed her pelisse and started to undo the buttons of her high-waisted walking dress. "I had best get ready then."

She paused when Clarry drew it from her. A sudden chill swept across her, leaving her shivering. It's just nerves, she reassured herself. She'd come this far, she could go through with it.

Before she could change her mind, Antonia hastily undressed and donned the emerald robe. It fell over her breasts in a silken shimmer to sweep to her feet. She placed the mask over her face, adjusted the mouth and nose openings and tied the strings at the back of her head. She experimented with the mask until she was comfortable. "There. That should do it."

Clarry drew back the perfumed sheets. "You'd best get into bed, milady. That is if you insist on doing this."

Antonia said nothing as she arranged herself artfully on the soft mattress. "I'm ready."

She heard Clarry's rustles as the maid bustled about, tweaking a blanket here, plumping a pillow there, placing Antonia's clothes in the armoire. Antonia composed herself against the oversized pillows, until at last, they heard a knock on the outer door.

She sat up, her backbone straight.

"Shall I send him away, milady?" Clarry sounded hopeful.

"No." Antonia made herself relax back against the pillows. "When you are ready, allow him in."

Clarry left the door partially open. From her position on the bed, Antonia could hear the murmurs as Clarry spoke with the applicant. The voice was rough edged with none of the cultured tones of the peerage, but it was young and enthusiastic.

"First off," Clarry stated, "You are not to ask milady's name. You are to know nothing about her unless she tells you. If you are rough with her, or if you hurt her, heaven help you, for these two won't."

Antonia envisioned her two footmen bristling at the young man. She and Clarry had chosen them for their absolute loyalty to her, for their strength and ability to protect her.

"If milady says enough, or if she rings her little bell, you are to stop at once and leave her. If you do not, then it's that sorry I am for you." Clarry's voice carried the threat of what would happen to him if the applicant ignored her instructions.

"Aye. When do I meet the lady?"

"You understand what you are to do?"

"I'm to pleasure the lady—"

"That's all. You are not to do any more, do you understand?"

"I can't—"

Clarry interrupted him, her voice firm. "No."

"But, that's not natural, like. It's the man who's to say when and how—"

Antonia tensed. "Those are milady's rules," she heard her servant state. "No questions.

If you go in that room, you do as she says."

"And if I pleasure her, and she likes it, then I get to—?"

"Not this time. If she likes you enough, she'll tell you to come again."

"But if I do all that, when am I to—?"

Clarry snorted. "If you can't control yourself, man, then when she's done with you, you can go into the room beside hers and do what you must."

"Crazy fool notion," he grumbled, then his voice brightened."I can do what I please with her?"

Antonia held her breath until she heard Clarry reply, "You may touch her to give her pleasure. You can do whatever she lets you do. But you're not to harm her, you understand?"

"All right. Where do I take my clothes off?"

"You don't. Your jacket and those great hob boots is all."

Antonia heard the heavy boots drop to the floor, one after the other. Her breath quickening, she lay back against the pillows and waited.

The young man came through the doorway and closed the door behind him. "Milady?" he whispered.

Now that the moment was upon her, Antonia felt nerves overtake her, then remembered that this was her plan. She was in control. If necessary, she had only to call out and her servants would rush to help her. With that reassurance, she remembered why she had to take a lover. How else would she subdue her desire for Sutherland? Perhaps this applicant would be lusty enough to drive the thought of the Duke from her mind. She beckoned. "Come closer."

His footfalls muffled by the thick carpet, he approached the bed and stopped at the edge of the draperies. Antonia could hear the slight rustle of the draperies and his breathing change as he waited for instructions.

"Do you know what to do?" she murmured.

"Pleasure you," he said after a moment. "But how?"

"How do you usually do it?"

"Kiss her 'til she says she wants me."

"Kiss her where?"

"On the mouth, o'course."

"But you may not kiss my mouth. Where else would you kiss me?"

She felt the bed jiggle as he edged closer.

"Can I touch you?"

"Yes." She felt the tip of a callused finger against her nipple. "That would be nice, but a little later. Where else could you start?"

His fingers trailed down her body to the chestnut curls. He hesitated, then dipped between her legs, looking for her little bud.

She closed her thighs. "Too fast," she corrected him. "Think again."

This time, his fingers trailed down her legs to her knees. She felt him drop beside the bed and then felt first his warm breath, then his lips hover over her knee. "That would be a good place to start," she agreed.

His mouth was warm, his tongue agile as he pressed kisses to her calf, her knee and then licked his way up her thigh. "That's the right idea."

His kisses grew hotter the closer he got to the juncture of her thighs. She relaxed, but not enough to give him access. Taking his cue from her, he bypassed that area and moved his mouth across her hipbones, down into the hollow of her stomach, then nudged his way past her ribs. He nuzzled between her breasts, and when her nipples began to peak, he lapped at one, then took it firmly between his lips and suckled.

As the tugging at her breast grew stronger, she sighed and relaxed. With this encouragement, he climbed on the bed with her and lay at her side. He continued to feast on her nipple.

She lifted a hand to stroke his shoulder. "That's very nice," she murmured. "Don't forget the other one needs attention, too." He let the one go and turned obediently to the other as her hand drifted over his corded muscles. "How old are you?"

He lifted his mouth just enough to say, "Three and twenty."

His endurance wouldn't be a problem, then. "You're very strong."

He nodded. The motion pulled at the breast, making her feel the sensation deep down inside. It felt good to concentrate only on her own feelings, without having to worry about pleasing her companion.

Gradually, she let the strangeness of the situation be forgotten as she delved deeper into the pleasure. While his technique lacked polish, his willingness to take direction satisfied her. Now that he had an idea of what she wished, he seemed determined to fulfill her requirements.

With his mouth still busy at her breasts, his hands roamed her body, learning the curves and indentation of her hips and buttocks. He trailed a warm finger between the half moons of her derriere until it eased into the moist heat between her legs. She moaned and flexed her thighs, opening herself to his inquisitive touch.

With a gentleness that surprised her, he caressed her inner flesh, his breath quickening as he felt the dew of her desire. Seemingly spurred on by the evidence of her acceptance, he eased a finger into her, stroking softly, then harder as her hips lifted to him.

"Yes," she whispered. "That's it. More."

He obliged, fitting himself more securely on the bed that his hand might pleasure her more deeply. He maintained the stroke, alternating that with a flicking motion of his thumb on her nub. His breath came harsher, hotter, as she responded to him.

Against her thigh, Antonia felt his erection grow and strain against the coarse material of his trousers. The length of it pleased her as she thought of the depths he could reach and caress with his hard manhood. All at once, the memory of Sutherland's body, so close to her in that unforgettable waltz, spurred her into her a mild fulfillment.

When the inner contractions stopped, she lay on her bed, unsatisfied. The young man had done as she bade him. It wasn't his fault that the thought of Sutherland intruded at such an awkward moment, yet it was apparent to her that this applicant would be incapable of banishing Sutherland.

She sighed with disappointment. "Go now."

"But, I pleased you." He eased into a sitting position. "You know I did. What about me?"

"You may take care of yourself elsewhere."

"Aye, but next time?"

"You will be informed if there is to be a next time."

She felt him hesitate, as if debating with himself whether he should press the issue. Then with a muttered curse, he heaved himself away from her. She listened to his heavy footfalls as he left the room, then heard him draw on his clothing.

She heard the clink of coins, and imagined the look on his face as Clarry paid him.

"That's it, then?"

"If my mistress wants to see you again, I'll let you know."

Moments after the outer door closed, Clarry wasted no time in going to Antonia.

"You're all right then? He didn't hurt you?"

Antonia pulled the mask off and shook her head to free her hair. The chestnut tresses tumbled to her shoulders. "No, but he won't do."

Clarry put her hands on her ample hips. "He didn't satisfy you, then?"

Regret tingeing her voice, Antonia said, "No, not enough."

"You want to go on with this, then?"

"I must," Antonia said simply.

Clarry muttered under her breath all the while she helped Antonia refresh herself and dress. She took a moment to tidy the room, then ushered Antonia, in her veil once more, down the stairs to the waiting carriage.

Antonia hid a yawn behind her black lace mitt as she sat in the ornate salon of the Howard's town house. Feeling the strain of interviewing potential lovers by afternoon, and maintaining her social calendar by night, she longed to put an end to the intimate testing.

Though each of the applicants had pleasured her, some more so than others, none measured up to her requirements.

Tensing her jaw against another yawn, she noticed movement to her side then glanced first at a pair of trousers barely skimming the hard muscled thighs beneath them, then up at the man wearing them. Not again!

"Hate these musicales, myself," Sutherland murmured as he took the gilded white seat next to her. "Hear Lady Howard has them weekly. Poor Howard."

She said nothing.

He leaned closer and lowered his voice. "You are yawning, my lady. Perhaps you are fatigued by your busy days?"

She froze. Could he know? Feverishly, she thought over the arrangements. Clarry had vowed secrecy. Sutherland could not possibly know anything. Reassured, she kept her eyes on the trio of musicians. "My days are always busy."

"More so lately."

She shot an alarmed glance at him. He regarded her with casual ease, but she didn't miss the narrowed brown eyes, the craggy cheek bones made more pronounced by the muscle ticking at his jaw. He was angry? With her?

Antonia looked around None of the other guests seemed interested in them. She kept her voice low and forced a polite smile. "My activities are no concern of yours, your grace."

"And if I wish to make them mine?"

"There is no reason to do so."

His mouth tightened. "Let us discuss this more privately."

"There is nothing to discuss. Pray do not disturb me any longer."

He hooked his hand under her elbow, and forced her to rise with him. Stepping carefully past the people seated next to them, he drew her to the aisle, then out into an adjoining foyer. With one grim look, he dismissed the footmen.

Once they were alone, she tugged her elbow free. "What do you think you are doing?"

"Merely ensuring you listen to me." His voice softened and he looked at her with something like amusement. "Did you know I came haring to London when I heard you had ousted Effingdale?"

Antonia shrugged. "Gossip travels exceedingly fast, your grace.

What does that prove?"

"Do you know why I came so quickly?"

She shivered at the intent look on his face. His amusement had faded, replaced by a look more akin to possessiveness. He stood so close that she could feel the warmth of his breath upon her cheek, feel the heat of his body next to hers. Once again she felt like his quarry and stared back, mesmerized, into his predatory eyes. Her blood began to simmer. She moved away, hoping her casual manner betrayed none of her inner turmoil. She gestured with her fan. "I'm sure your reasons have no interest for me."

He moved closer. "On the contrary, they concern you."

"How odd. I can think of no reason why you should involve yourself with me."

"No?" He took another pace closer. "Shall I tell you why?"

She edged behind a small round table. "I am not interested, your grace." She cocked her head as the music floated to her. "Lady Howard will wonder what has become of us."

He came forward, rounding the table after her until she found herself with her back against the wall. Though several inches remained between them, Antonia felt surrounded. His body blocked out the sight of anything behind him. She was conscious only of him, of the heat of his body, of the determined way he stared at her, eyes narrowed and intent. Her heart beat faster beneath the low décolletage of her evening gown.

Desperately, she tried not to let him see how his nearness affected her, but her body sensed the lure of his and responded. She told herself she was susceptible only because she had thought of him at a critical time only that afternoon, but what she felt now made her earlier feelings tepid and dull.

The warmth spreading through her softened her, making her moist and ready. Her breathing became jerky under his intent and powerful gaze. Her breasts expanded as her nipples bloomed against the delicate lace of her chemise. The tiny chafing made her wonder how Sutherland's mouth and tongue would ease the small hurt.

"I can tell you what will become of us, Antonia. We shall be lovers."

"How absurd." She tried a laugh, but it sounded more of gasp. "I choose my own liaisons."

"And so you shall. You shall choose me." Bending slightly forward, so that his voice reached only her ear, he asked, "Can you imagine what it will be like between us? Pure flame. You are a passionate woman, not in the least afraid of your womanly desires. Do you know how rare that is? I am a man who appreciates and rewards sensuality in a woman. We shall do wonderful things together."

He smelled of rare and marvelous spices and ointments, of aroused masculinity held rigidly in check. Antonia wanted nothing more than to put out the tip of her tongue and trace the underside of his jaw and his throat, to sample him, to see for herself if he tasted as she imagined.

She eyed the tanned flesh of his neck above the snowy white cravat and wondered if his skin would be as tawny everywhere else. Would the pelt on his chest be as silk to her hand, or the rougher fur of the lion he resembled? Would he be as dominant, as forceful in bed as he appeared to be out of it?

She swallowed past the dry lump in her throat. "Nonsense," she demurred though the heat rose in her blood and melted her resistance. She swayed on her feet, leaning toward him in an irresistible longing to feel even more of his warmth, to feel his body next to hers, to savor the pleasure his few words had conjured up. More than anything, she desired to put his claim to the test. Would they indeed go up in flames together?

"You are in need of a lover, Antonia. Even now your body is ready for mine. Why not accept me?"

His words cooled her faster than an icy bath. In another instant, she would have succumbed to desire and ruined everything. "I...no."

"Be warned, Antonia, I am not a patient man."

Chapter Three

"How many more applicants are there?" Antonia peered over her morning cup of chocolate as Clarry brushed crumbs away from the bedcovers.

Clarry jumped and tipped the silver pot. She fluttered with a napkin, mopping up the few drops that had stained the pristine white cloth.

"Is something the matter?"

"No, not so's you'd notice, milady."

Antonia studied the older woman's face. She appeared uneasy and strangely reluctant to speak. "Then, what is it?"

"Don't go on with this any more. You'll regret it."

"What ever is the matter with you this morning, Clarry? You look like you're going to collapse. Sit down, here, next to me." Antonia moved her legs to make room for Clarry's ample rump. "Now, talk."

Clarry fidgeted with a fold of her skirt. "I don't want you to go back to that place. Not again. No telling what'll happen if you do."

"I have to," Antonia murmured. "Are there any more applicants, then?"

Clarry looked away. "Just one."

"That is all? I thought you'd said that you had to turn them away."

"I did." Clarry faced Antonia, her old face indignant. "I turned dozens of them away, all of them with their tongues hanging out."

Antonia winced. "I don't understand. What has changed?"

Clarry devoted her attention to her skirt again. "Maybe the word's out that the masked lady is too particular like. That no one can please you."

Her words reminded Antonia of Sutherland. Despite herself, warmth coiled low in her abdomen. She lifted the cooling chocolate to her lips and sipped.

Clarry continued, "Why don't you choose one you've already tried out and let it go at that?"

"I can't." Antonia replaced the cup on the tray and sank back against her fluffed pillows. "None of them will do." She thought of the fumbling applicant she'd last interviewed and without volition, her mind instantly compared him to Sutherland. Until she found someone who could erase Sutherland from her mind, she had to continue. "Perhaps this last one will do the trick."

"He'd better," Clarry muttered.

"Is everything arranged?"

"Your bath is ready."

"That is not what I'm asking, Clarry, and you know it."

Clarry turned away from her ladyship's gentle voice. At the knock at the door, she opened it and took a folded note from the footman. She saw the ducal seal and took it to Antonia with trembling fingers.

Antonia broke the seal and read the few words. Admiration for his perseverance and dismay that he persisted warred within her. She glanced up at Clarry. "It's from Sutherland. He wants me to ride with him this afternoon."

"Good idea, that. You could use some fresh air."

"I will be busy at that time, Clarry. Remember?"

Clarry pursed her lips. "Wouldn't hurt to cancel."

Antonia rose and went to her small desk where she penned him a polite refusal. "Send this back, will you?"

"Why are you refusing the duke? He's perfect for what you want."

Antonia's shoulders slumped against the desk chair. "That's the trouble. He's too perfect. Oh, Clarry, he could ruin me."

"How?" Clarry asked bluntly. "He's got enough of everything. More than enough, if you can believe the gossip. Pots of money. An income to make the Prince his best friend. And he's not half bad to look at, either."

"How do you know all that?"

"It's no secret that the Prince of Wales is always short in the pocket. Borrows from all his friends, he does, but not much chance of his ever paying them back."

"No, I mean about the Duke."

Clarry hesitated. "I hear things. That's why you wanted my help with all this foolishness, isn't it?"

"That's true." Antonia looked thoughtful. "What else have you heard?"

"About his grace?"

Antonia nodded.

Clarry sat and settled her weight comfortably, as if preparing for a cozy chat. "Well, he's got estates in Scotland. Way north, where the sun never shines."

"He is brown from the sun," Antonia demurred.

That didn't stop her maid. In full swing, Clarry continued. "Pots of money, like I said. He's good to his household staff. Only one mistress at a time. He's faithful, like."

Antonia laughed. Somehow the description Clarry offered didn't resembled the tawny lion she knew. She made him sound like a trusty hound, content to lounge at her feet in front of a warm winter fire, while the man she knew was all lion, roaming his domain, intent on maintaining his rule. Her laughter faded as she considered her situation. She couldn't afford to see him again. She didn't dare, never knowing when she'd swoon at his feet and hope that he'd pick up and care for her heart as well as her person.

"Well, let's get on with it, then." Antonia shrugged out of the lace and satin gown and

let it drop to her feet.

After her bath and a simple coiffure that wouldn't be mussed later, Antonia donned an elegant afternoon gown and pelisse. She picked up her heavily veiled hat.

Clarry opened the door. "You don't have to go," she offered on a hopeful note.

Antonia shot her a thoughtful look. Clarry was up to something, but she didn't have time to find out. Later, after the afternoon interview was over, then she'd get to the bottom of this. An hour or so later, once more wearing only her emerald silk robe and the matching mask, Antonia reclined on the bed in the boudoir of her rented rooms and waited for the last applicant to arrive. She heard the knock at the outer door, then muted voices as Clarry instructed him. After a few moments, Clarry knocked and entered.

"He's here."

"Show him in, then."

Antonia heard Clarry close the door and waited. Knowing that this man was her last applicant made her all the more aware that everything must go well. The strident calls of street vendors hawking their wares, the heavy wagons and carriages passing by were muted by the thick drapes at the windows and seemed very far away.

A log shifted in the grate. Antonia heard the hiss of new flame, then the steady flames and imagined them licking eagerly at fresh fuel. The man, if he had indeed entered the bed-chamber, was so still that Antonia began to wonder. Senses straining for some indication that she wasn't alone, she shifted position on the bed and wondered why he waited. "Is someone there?"

There was no answer, but she became aware of a presence, no more than the barest hint of another person breathing. A curious anticipation filled her as she detected the slightest disturbance in the air and then the soft footsteps. He approached the bed and stood silent beside it.

As though it was already her lover's touch, she felt his gaze on her body, nude except where the emerald silk artfully revealed her. She couldn't repress the warmth suffusing her skin.

"You may begin," she whispered.

He dropped on his knees beside her. Now she could hear him breathe, a slightly ragged sound that reassured her. He paused, as if contemplating what his first move would be. Antonia waited, excitement building. He exhaled, as if calming himself. His warm breath wafted over her. She shivered.

With a forefinger, he touched the tender skin of her bent elbow, then traced the delicate curve to her wrist. He bent and touched his mouth to the pulse there. Her throat went dry at the feel of his warm, firm lips on her skin. With just that simple beginning, she knew that this was no ordinary applicant.

He lifted his head. Linking his fingers with hers, he brought her hand to his mouth and pressed tiny kisses over the back of it, then turned her hand and repeated the kisses, nibbling now and then again, on the soft palm and each of her fingers.

They quivered in his. He took one into his mouth, sucking gently, twirling his tongue around the tip of it, then nipping. He laved the tiny hurt with his tongue, and suckled harder. Antonia sighed blissfully, anticipating how that would feel on her breasts.

He left her hand to trail kisses up to her elbow, until the sleeve of her robe stopped him. He switched his attention to her other arm, repeating the same kisses and nips until Antonia squirmed and changed her position on the plump pillows.

He undid the sash at her waist. With one hand, he parted the sides until the gap revealed her breasts and the curve of her waist and abdomen. His breathing told Antonia that he liked what he saw. She expected him to push the robe farther out of the way, but instead he left it where it was and with a touch so light that she imagined she barely felt it, he smoothed his fingertips over the soft down of her body. The tiny hairs, invisible to the eye, quivered at their passing. Antonia felt the slight stroking caress all the way to her bones. She trembled, waiting for more.

Only when he had caressed all the skin visible to him did he nudge the robe out of the way, an inch at a time. He continued his massage, fingering now the curves and planes he had left un-touched before, making her aware as never before of the sensitive arch where arm met chest, of the tenderness of the sides of her breasts. He traced each of her ribs from side to front, learning her, until her eyes closed and her breath came shallow. He feathered her breasts and nipples, making her arch against his hands, mutely asking for more. Instead, he moved the robe out of the way and lightly touched her armpits. Ordinarily ticklish, Antonia felt no desire to laugh. She gasped when he turned her, removing the robe in one swift motion.

On her stomach, she felt vulnerable and exposed to him, but the instant his fingertips returned to her body, she forgot her qualms. She wanted more. With the tip of his finger, he followed the curve of her back to her buttocks, stopping to explore the indentation of her spine. By the time he reached her buttocks, she was moaning.

The delay was excruciating. Antonia wanted more, and she wanted it all at once. That he made her wait while he pleasured every inch of her skin was unbearable, both thrilling and frustrating. She heard his breathing change as he varied his method and replaced his fingertip with his tongue.

She stiffened at the first moist touch on the swell of her hip. Her shoulders came up off the bed as her head lifted. He pressed her back down into the mattress with both hands, a gentle inexorable pressure, until she subsided and lay supine for him.

With long, slow strokes of his tongue, he covered every inch that he had previously massaged with his fingertips. Antonia felt ready to scream. He followed his moist lapping with a gentle exhalation. The cool air on her skin after the warmth of his mouth almost drove her out of her mind. She gripped the pillows at her head and hung on.

He moved away only long enough to shift her to her back again. Antonia lay with her eyes closed, waiting expectantly for what he would do next. He didn't keep her waiting long as he bent his head to her and continued laving her, until he had attended to every inch of her except her most intimate feminine recesses. She waited for him to caress her there as well, but he skirted her mound, to move on to her belly, which quivered under his ministrations.

She felt stretched on the rack of sensuality, unwilling to stop and equally unwilling to have it end. Heat pooled deep within her, building to an inexorable ache. She was afraid that if he continued, she'd burn alive under his touch, yet she feared with an equal dread that if he stopped, she'd hang quivering, nerves stretched to breaking point. He was the most imaginative, tender and stimulating man ever to provoke such a response from her, and all he had used was his hands and his mouth!

She moaned softly as she stretched under his touch. Her legs parted, inviting him, but he nuzzled at her neck through the silken mask and made her earlobes the focus of his attention. After a few moments, Antonia realized that she'd never put on another pair of earrings without thinking of this man. Vaguely she wondered where he had perfected his lovemaking technique, but her curiosity ended abruptly when he withdrew and sat by the side of the bed. She waited, barely breathing, for what he would do next.

His hand stroked her from throat to mound. Antonia knew he waited for permission to continue. She hesitated. He had shown her things about herself that she'd never known. How much more could he teach her?

"Please continue." Her voice sounded low and sultry even to her own ears.

Immediately, he bent his head and touched the tip of his tongue to a nipple. Already hard and ripe, the nipple ached and grew even more swollen. He eased his lips around it, sucking gently, etching circles around it, then suckling. A red hot burst of desire shot through her. She clutched his shoulders.

Even with her attention occupied by the marvelous sensations at her breast, she felt the hard muscles beneath his skin and gripped harder, her nails biting into him. When he raised his head to attend to the other breast, she eased up on him enough to smooth her palm over her back.

"Take your shirt off," she whispered.

He complied. She put her hand on his chest, smiling beneath her mask at the feel of him, all hard muscles rippling and the thatch covering him from flat male nipple to belly. She circled his nipple and murmured her pleasure in how quickly it hardened under her touch.

Her hand traced the silky curls until they disappeared under his waistband. He drew in his breath but said nothing. She let her hand follow the flat planes of his belly until it came to the unmistakable hot length of his turgid shaft. She cupped him through the material of his trousers, entranced by the unseen promise of his erection. It pulsed, hot and heavy, in her hand, as if eager to be free of the confines of his clothing. Through the delicious haze, she wondered how it would feel to have him enter her, to stroke her, first slowly and provocatively, then fast and furiously.

She smiled, a slow satisfied smile at the knowledge that she wasn't the only one affected by his lovemaking. "You like that?" she murmured.

He said nothing but the way his member grew, harder and longer, in the palm of her hand told her everything she needed to know. "What would you like to do next?"

In response, he moved his palm, cupping her mound in return. He toyed with the curls, drawing them through his fingers as the skin of her belly contracted. He stroked her muff, his finger at first gentle and slow, then moving faster as her body responded. He slipped a long finger into the moist warmth, gently separating the plump outer lips until he found her bud. He stroked it once or twice, then circled it, and traced the opening to her inner passage. She clawed at the sheets as pleasure shuddered through her. Sensation centered in that one throbbing bloom.

She moaned when he took away his hand, but as his mouth replaced his fingers, Antonia breathed out, a long shuddering exhalation. She sighed in relief, then felt the inner contractions that surrounded his finger even as he did. He had to know it.

Instead of continuing, he withdrew. She moaned in distress. He palmed her once again, drawing her moisture into his hand, then spread it in sensuous circles around her navel. He followed his hand with his mouth, licking every drop away from her quivering skin. She arched under him, offering him more, begging for more.

As if he had heard her plea, he returned to her privities, licking and nipping in tiny bites. She thrashed on the bed, head tossing from side to side, strung out on a rack of desire and aching for release. She lifted her knees and parted her thighs to make room for him between her legs, but he ignored the blatant invitation and stuck to his instructions. Her breath came in short pants and the flames threatened to consume her.

"Now," she cried. "Oh, please, now!"

He pushed one long finger within her, then two, stroking hard, mimicking the thrusts his body would make. He put his mouth to her breast and suckled one while his hand attended to the other. Wracked with pleasure, every susceptible nerve in her body hummed with passion. She closed her inner muscles around his fingers, pulsing around them, milking them, until her last shivering cry died away.

His breath coming as harshly as hers, he pulled free. She barely noticed how he arranged her lax body and rested briefly beside her. They lay quietly together until their breathing calmed.

When she turned her head to thank him, he pressed his lips to hers. Sated, exhausted and pleasured beyond belief, Antonia had no strength left to protest. She felt the desire, fiercely controlled, within him, and pushing the mask aside, she opened her mouth to him.

He refused the invitation, and left her.

Chapter Four

That evening, Antonia hid a yawn behind her hand as she waited for her partner to draw another card. Though she had slept for two hours after the applicant left her this afternoon, her body was still lax and exhausted. She would have sent her regrets to Lady Fox's whist party, but that would have disarranged the numbers, and Maude Fox was unforgiving when it came to disrupting her card evenings.

She gritted her teeth against the need to yawn again. The man, whoever he had been, had satisfied her like no other lover. His touch had made her body come to life and go up in flames before he had finally allowed her release. Just thinking about the way he had pleasured her made her legs go limp. Thank goodness she was sitting down.

If he could make her feel as she did without his body entering hers, what could he do when their bodies were joined? She felt a flush creeping up her breasts to her throat and placed a hand over her bosom to cover it.

"Are you feverish, Lady Blair-Sutworth?"

Her hand dropped as her gaze flew upward to the man standing by her table. Dougal MacDonald, that insufferable seventh duke of Sutherland, looked down at her with a quizzical smile on his leonine features. With his tawny hair perfectly in place, his evening attire clothing his body like a lover's caress, he appeared to be very much in control.

She stiffened. "I am quite well, your grace. How kind of you to inquire," she added cooly when she saw the curious looks cast their way.

"Not kind at all," he denied. "Your skin is quite flushed." He bent closer and studied her. "Your eyes have a strange look to them. Quite dreamy. Are you sure you are not ill?"

She leaned away from him. "I am not ill. It is a shade too warm in here."

He straightened but didn't take his gaze from her. "Perhaps a breath of fresh air?"

Though she hadn't noticed the temperature of the room before now, it was suddenly unbearably close. A few moments out on the terrace would be just the thing to clear her brain. Excusing herself, she rose from the card table and took Sutherland's arm. He guided her through the mass of tables to a set of doors open to the night air.

She tried to ignore the feel of his muscled arm beneath her hand, but the heat rose through his clothing and added to her feverish sensation. Though he was the soul of discretion as he moved her through the crowded room, acknowledging acquaintances and friends, she knew he was intent on getting her alone. It didn't bother her this time, since she was now immune to his sexual lure. After all, with a lover like the man she'd tested this afternoon, she had no reason to succumb to Sutherland's masculine allure.

She confidently stepped outside and she the cool evening air into her lungs.

"Better now?"

She glanced at the man at her side. "Very much so."

Grateful for the dark that hid his intense interest, he turned slightly away from her and gestured to a couple strolling off a path into the darkened arbor. "Those two have the right idea. They'll come to an agreement in the shrubbery. He'll emerge with a satisfied look on his face, I wager, while she will come forth with her hair and clothing awry and an equally satisfied expression."

She had to laugh. "You are far too observant."

"Perhaps we should find our own bit of greenery," he offered in an off-hand voice.

"I have no desire to be mussed, thank you."

An image of her body sprawled in sensual pleasure whipped through him. Her lush body, slender and yet voluptuous, would tease and arouse him until his control threatened to snap under the weight of just a murmur, or one movement of silken limbs. Her legs, long and shapely, enticed him. He imagined them clasped around his waist as she begged him for release. Her breasts, full and just the right size for his hand, made him sweat.

He would muss her, he vowed. And she would love it.

"Pity," he drawled. "I would make sure you emerged from the bushes with more than a satisfied look on your beautiful face."

"You have a vivid imagination, your grace."

He hid a grin. She'd had only a taste of his inventive mind. He could hardly wait until their next meeting. "Do I?" he asked in a languid voice though his body was taut and hardened with desire. "Shall we compare our fantasies, then? I'll tell you one of mine, then you shall tell me yours."

She flicked him a small, seductive smile. "I think not, sir. I have heard of your legendary prowess with the ladies. I am afraid that I could not compete."

"I don't want your competition, madam," he said in a voice suddenly harsh. ""I want you."

Chapter Five

Sutherland entered the dim bedchamber and paused while his eyes adjusted to the dark. The sumptuous room lured him in with promises of sensual delight. The mingled aromas of fresh flowers, subtle perfume and the lingering scent of sexual release made his nostrils flare.

He made his way to the reclining figure on the bed. Wearing the emerald green mask and gown she hid behind, Lady Antonia Blair-Sutworth presented a most delicious sight. She rested on an elbow, the gown slipping off her shoulder to reveal pale skin that gleamed like vanilla satin in the candlelight. One knee was drawn up, the other leg extended with the gown draped just so, enough to tantalize him with glimpses of her shapely legs and the merest hint of the chestnut curls between her thighs.

His mouth went dry with anticipation of the things he would do to her this afternoon. He'd come prepared. As he neared the bed, he saw that the green mask fluttered as she breathed. The cloth rose and fell with her bosom. So, she, too, was eager. That made his task all the more pleasant and rewarding.

He'd vowed he'd keep his mind cool and uncluttered, that he would delve the depths of sensuality with her without he himself becoming affected. In short, he vowed he'd teach her a lesson, a dangerous lesson, about the depths of depravity and decadence. After today, she would know better than to allow anyone but himself into her bed.

Without waiting for her permission, he stripped off his fine linen shirt and tossed it carelessly on a nearby chair. In his buckskin trousers, he placed one knee on the bed and allowed himself

one tender touch, just for his pleasure, before he steeled his nerve
to carry out his plan.

Her skin was warm, smooth to his fingertips. She quivered at
his touch, telling him wordlessly that she was already aroused.
Good. By the time he was done with her, she'd know all there was
to know about arousing unfulfilled desires. He almost smiled at the
thought of himself, Dougal MacDonald, randy seventh duke of
Sutherland, so besotted with her that he'd stoop to playing stud for
her.

"Good afternoon," she murmured in the low and throaty voice
that enchanted him. "Are you going to speak today?"

When he said nothing, she continued, "No? Then I shall speak
for us both. I was content with yesterday's interview. Have you
something new to show me today?"

He grinned. Taking her hand, he held it to his cheek as he
nodded yes.

"M'mm, that's good. Would you like to begin?"

Again, he indicated he would. He kissed her hand, then replaced
it on her hip. She settled more comfortably into the plump pillows
at her back as she waited for him to start making love to her.

He considered, then reached for the small leather case he'd
placed on the table next to the flickering candle. He opened it, eyed
the contents, and withdrew a plume with soft, eider down feathers.
He tested it on his neck then drew it slowly along hers.

"What is that?" she gasped.

In response, he drew the feather down the edge of her robe, now
tracing the gold embroidery, now skirting the edge of the material
to brush her bare skin. She shivered.

He feathered every inch of exposed skin, making her skin
tremble under his touch, until he reached her toes. She laughed as
he tickled the soles of her feet, but her laughter changed to a
pleased murmur when he found the sensitive spot behind her knee.

"You are a devil, aren't you?" she all but moaned when the
feather reached the back of her thigh and teased the chestnut curls.

Sutherland grinned. She had experienced only the beginning.

With the tip of the feather, he drew the robe back slowly, caressing her as he exposed her. She parted her legs for him, inviting more, but he ignored the offer and drew the robe back up over her thigh. He paused to exchange the soft downy feather for a stiffer one, a fine egret. With that, he traced the enticing curve of her hip, pushing the robe back as he went, until her entire hip and the swell of her buttock was his.

She murmured, low in her throat.

He pulled the robe from her in slow motion, using the silken fabric as an additional caress on her skin, until she lay open and naked for him. He moved her to her stomach, positioning her the way he wanted her, with one leg slightly bent and the other extended. Satisfied with the way she was open to him, he ran the egret feather from ankle to thigh. Her skin, soft and finely textured, quivered as he passed, increasingly so as he reached the curve of her blind cheeks. He ran the feather between the twin mounds, first up toward the base of her spine, then back again, slower this time, lingering, tantalizing, making her moan, until he reached the softest flesh of her outer lips.

He withdrew the feather and brushed it over the back of his hand. The feathers were damp with her dew. Gratified, he placed the feather back in the case and while one hand rested on her hip to keep her in place, he selected a small jar of lotion.

He uncapped it, sniffed it and replaced it. Choosing another, he tested it again and pleased with this one, he left the cap on the table while he poured a small amount of the lotion into the hollow above her buttocks.

She tensed at the feel of the cool lotion, then relaxed as he began to smooth it in slow circles, kneading away any remaining tension. The scent of almonds filled the air about them as the lotion warmed under the combined heat of his hand and her back. He felt her muscles go limp under his ministrations and nodded with satisfaction.

He loved the way she responded to him. Granted, he was using all the seductive tricks he knew to batter her senses, but as she responded so willingly and wholeheartedly, he found his determination not to feel anything weakening. His rigid cock chafed against the confines of his clothing. He gritted his teeth against the ache and set his mind again to ignore his own lust.

He continued the sensual massage until every inch of her back, shoulders and legs had been covered with the scented lotion. He eased her over on her back and paused to view his handiwork. In the candlelight, he saw her full breasts and the dark aureoles surrounding her already hard and extended nipples. Pouring more lotion into her navel, he began his massage again.

When he had covered every inch but her breasts, he sat back on his haunches a moment to contemplate his next move. By the way she moved against the sheets, he knew she was eager for more. Her skin was flushed, warm from his ministrations, aromatic with the scent of almonds, her own perfume, and the scent of aroused woman, what the French called *cassolette*, perfume box.

"Don't stop now," she pleaded.

Smiling, Sutherland bent his head, placed his open mouth on one breast and did nothing for a moment but inhale her fragrance. His head reeled with the seductive, sensual scent of a woman who was not afraid of her own sexual nature, who even now was urging him on to greater heights of sensuality.

Obliging both her pleas and his need to make love to his woman, he traced the aureole, gently at first, then varying his touch, loving the firm texture and the way her skin puckered and her nipple grew even harder and longer in his mouth. He nipped gently, small love bites that increased her sensitivity and her pleasure. He sucked, gently at first, then harder as he suckled, taking what he vaguely understood and then accepted as both lustful and a more enduring nourishment from her.

He turned to the other breast, giving it the same dedicated, thorough attention while his hand caressed the breast he had just left, keeping it satisfied and the nipple hard under his palm.

Her breathing grew heavier.

He left her breast for a moment to nuzzle the sweet, tender flesh of her armpit. He inhaled deeply, aroused by her femininity, then showered her with kisses and drew her skin into his mouth, leaving faint marks behind on her skin. She arched her back, giving more of herself to him, and he couldn't help the low growl of possession with which he accepted the gift of herself.

She lifted a knee, drawing his attention to her parted thighs. Smiling to himself at her responsiveness and eagerness for more, he now followed her hint and traced with his tongue a lingering, teasing path to the curls between her thighs. He nipped at her skin as he went, easing the tiny hurt with kisses, as he inched his way around her navel to the satiny skin below it. He followed with his hand, pulling gently at the curls, until she moaned as he cupped her mound.

He caressed the fleshy outer lips for a moment, while he positioned himself, he slipped an elbow under her raised knee, and then kissed his way up to her muff. He placed gentle, open mouthed kisses on the closed lips as though she were an inexperienced virgin he was initiating, enjoying the way she chafed under his restraint, until she reached for his head and holding him by the temples, grated, "More!"

He chuckled and obeyed.

He gave her deeper tongue strokes, parting the lips with his tongue until he came to the treasure within. She moaned with pleasure and came immediately. Her orgasm pleased him immensely. Lifting his head, he took the heady moisture and smoothed it on her belly, then lapped it up, enchanted by both her response and the fragrance of her moist perfume. She lay still under his mouth, yet her skin rippled and quivered, telling him without words that she was still aroused and ready for more.

He gave her more. Bending his head to her once more, he put his mouth on her still quivering bud and licked. When that wasn't enough, he inserted his tongue into her intimate recesses and then withdrew. She tightened her legs about him. He penetrated her again and again with his tongue, deliberately controlling his almost frantic need to replace his tongue with his yard, until she came, again and again, in great flooding orgasms.

She lay limp under him.

When he took his mouth away, she moaned and attempted to curl up on her side. He prevented her by placing a hand on her hip, keeping her in place, while the other hand cupped her mound. With a finger, he traced the path his tongue had taken earlier.

"No more," she whimpered. "I can't stand any more"

He ignored her just as he ignored his own desperate need. Wanting, needing, aching to thrust into her and relieve his own painful arousal, he penetrated her, finding the silken inner walls still contracting around his finger. He added another finger and placed his thumb on her bud, arousing her with strokes and gentle pressure until she cried out and convulsed around his fingers.

He left them there until the last shudder died away and she slept.

He stood and studied her as she lay, arms and legs tangled in the mussed sheets. Instead of feeling satisfied that he'd beaten her at her own game, he had to admit that it was he who had surrendered. He'd succumbed to her womanly sensuality and wanted her more than ever. She was everything he could ever hope for. Passionate, comfortable with her own sexual need, she'd match him in bed and demand more and more. He'd die happy trying to satisfy her.

Though he'd come haring to London to make her his mistress, knowing full well that they'd tire of each other eventually, that was no longer enough. Now that he'd tasted her, experienced how she responded to him, he'd be damned if he'd release her to move on to another liaison. From now on, no man but he would share her bed.

Like it or not, Lady Antonia Blair-Sutworth was his, forever.

Chapter Six

Late that evening, Sutherland saw Antonia going into midnight supper on the arm of the Honorable Edward St. John. A moment of fury passed through him before he regained the rigid control he cultivated. How could she look so radiant, so damned beautiful on the arm of another man after he had wracked himself to bring her pleasure this afternoon?

Jealousy, hot and violent, followed his footsteps as he strode, barely slowing to acknowledge the other guests of the Baroness of Rockingham's ball. Though she tried to detain him with thanks for gracing her home, and thus making her a name to be reckoned within the *haute ton*, he barely spoke two words to her on his way to Antonia.

He reached her side just as St. John seated her. Sutherland grasped the back of the chair the other man had intended for himself and seated himself before St. John could protest.

He nodded to the startled man. "Thanks, St. John, for allowing me to take your place."

With nothing to do but bow gracefully before the peer, St. John did just that and murmured an apology before he disappeared into the crush.

"That was very rude of you, your grace. Perhaps you should have inquired if I desired your company before you acted so rashly."

"And good evening to you, my lady. You are more beautiful than ever." He meant every word. She was truly exquisite this evening, her green eyes sparkling and her skin the color of pale porcelain, barely tinged with a subtle warmth. Her chestnut hair, burnished from the light of a hundred candelabra, was piled high in an intricate style that accentuated her slender neck and beautiful shoulders. If he looked closely, he could just detect the faint markings of the love bite he had given her that afternoon.

Gratified, he sat back in his chair and watched her. Her gown, a deep red that brought out the creaminess of her skin, had a low décolletage that emphasized her bosom. He remembered the feel of her skin, the texture of the aureoles and the way her nipples had hardened to little kernels in his mouth. He was instantly aroused.

She looked like a woman who had been loved well and long. She had that languid, sated air that kept the men surrounding her frantic to know who had bedded her and why that man had not been himself. Sutherland smiled. They might not know it, but the luscious lady was going to torment them in just that manner quite often. He would see to that.

He smiled at the thought.

She saw his smile, satisfied and proud, and frowned in return. How dare he, no matter that he was Dougal MacDonald, the utterly masculine beautiful seventh duke of Sutherland who had stolen her heart, how dare he interrupt her supper with St. John and burden her with his presence. Why wouldn't he leave her in peace!

"Has something displeased you, my lady? Perhaps the lobster patties are not to your liking?"

She scanned the plate of food she had not yet touched. Though it displayed a tempting assortment of the delicacies the Baron's chef was famous for, she had no appetite.

She glanced at the man beside her. Clad as all the other gentlemen in faultless evening attire, on him the severe black and snowy white cravat were outstanding. The fit of his coat across his broad shoulders was perfection, leaving no one in doubt that he needed no padding to enhance their breadth. The white of his impeccably tied neckcloth against his tanned skin was almost blinding. His brown eyes in his chiseled face were fixed only on her.

He didn't even look at the women, all gowned in the latest fashions, who flitted by, décolletages so low that the bodice barely covered their breasts. His gaze was fixed on her, as if he could see through her clothing to her nakedness beneath. Her throat went dry. She lifted the crystal glass to her lips and took a sip of champagne. The sparkling wine soothed her throat and calmed her nerves.

She smoothed her white silk evening glove over her wrist. "Is it your exalted rank that makes you feel you can do as you please without regard to other's wishes?"

Her cool tone, disdainful and not quite hiding her pique, interrupted Sutherland's study of her. No man spoke to him thus. He waited a moment until his pride settled down. He cocked an eyebrow at her. "If being a Duke doesn't allow me to have what I want, what good is it?"

She gasped. Sutherland smiled at her reaction to his trifling dismissal of the responsibilities and duties that accompanied the privilege of his position.

"Do not jest with me, your grace."

"Then do not speak foolishly, my dear."

"I am not your dear."

He smiled at her denial. "I would speak less quickly, if I were you."

She frowned, a tiny narrowing of her eyes. "What do you mean?"

"I shall tell you at the proper time."

Antonia's frown deepened. This smacked of the authoritarian control her husband had exerted. She had no intention of submitting to anything like it ever again.

"There will be no time, proper or otherwise, for you, your grace."

"I am afraid you are going to be most surprised. I can only hope it will not be an unpleasant shock."

She cast a quick glance at his face. His eyes glowed and his face was lit by an odd smile. What could he find so amusing? Unnerved that he should know something she did not, she wracked her brain for an explanation. She came up with nothing. He could not possibly know of her afternoon interviews.

If he but knew! She thought of the lovemaking she had experienced this afternoon, and only wished she had stayed awake long enough to inform the man of her decision. Whoever he was, she would have him for her lover.

As she thought of the final interview, the one in which she finally allowed him to take her, anticipation filled her with moistness between her thighs. This man, whoever he was, was just the one to dismiss Sutherland from her thoughts.

"Something amuses you?" Sutherland queried.

She spared him a questioning glance.

"Your smile," he explained. "It reminds me of the cat at the cream."

She laughed. How astute he was. Suddenly she was enjoying herself in his company. Now that she no longer had to worry about her heart, she could allow herself to enjoy his quick wit. "The word is about, your grace, that you are in need of a wife."

His rapidly cocked eyebrow was his only reaction to the change in subject.

"Yes. Have you thought of your requirements yet? Perhaps a wife who will keep you pleasantly occupied at home—"

"Pleasantly occupied?" he interrupted. "By that do you mean cozy evenings before the fire?"

"However you wish to enjoy yourself," she murmured, a small teasing smile on her lips. "However, I would imagine that it is time you saw to establishing your nurseries for your heirs."

"Indeed? And have you chosen my future duchess?"

"H'mm." She smiled at his serious tone. "I shall have to give that some thought. Perhaps Caroline, Lady Arbuthnott's niece. You recall, you met her at the opera one evening."

"The young lady just making her come out? She seemed interested enough," he admitted with a modest smile.

"It would appear so. She is very beautiful, don't you think?"

"Is she? I didn't notice. I shall have to make that observation myself."

Antonia stomach clutched at the thought of Sutherland looking at and enjoying other women. Evidently she had been premature in thinking she could speak like this with him and not suffer the penalty. She made herself keep her tone light. "She is of good family. Not as distinguished as your own, of course, but well established. She would be a good match."

He nodded. "She is certainly young enough to fill the nurseries with no problem, but would she have the proper conversation to keep me entertained?"

"Ah." She paused as if giving thought to his questions. In truth, she struggled with the temptation to offer herself for his consideration. "That complicates matters. Entertaining conversation is a requirement, then?"

"Most definitely. I should hate to be bored by a wife with only one talent."

"That talent would be—" she questioned delicately.

"Providing my heir."

She exhaled. "What else would you require? Perhaps I could be of some assistance in finding the right wife for you."

He laughed. "You might at that."

"Well, come then, tell me what you want in a wife, and I shall endeavor to help you."

"Very well. Let me see. I want a woman with passable good looks—"

"Just passable?" she interrupted.

"More would be preferable, but so long as she is not a gargoyle—"

"Your grace! Very well," she managed through her laughter. "No gargoyles."

"To continue, then. A woman who I enjoy looking at, a woman with intelligent conversation, someone who will not bore me before the month is out."

"You are serious?"

"Absolutely."

She didn't know what to say. Clearly Sutherland was made of different cloth from other men.

"I should also like a woman to be well attired, but that is up to me. I shall dress her well."

Antonia took exception to that. "And if the woman you choose to dress prefers her own taste in clothing?"

"If it is satisfactory to me, I should allow her to continue. No billowing flounces or lace up to her ears."

Antonia glanced at the sleek lines of her gown and hid a smile at the image his words presented. Without trouble, she could visualize a woman smothered in lace and furbelows, with only her nose and eyes visible. At that, it wouldn't matter if she were less than passable.

"Share the jest with me," he suggested.

She did. Their laughter mingled and drew curious glances. Antonia ignored them.

"What else would you like in a wife?"

"Let's see. We have looks, heirs, intelligence, the outer wrappings. What else is there?"

"Ah," she sagely. "What about the inner woman?"

"The what?"

She gathered her thoughts. "Have you never envisioned what kind of woman? So far, we have discussed all the exterior things, but what about the qualities that must wear well to last a lifetime together?"

His gaze sharpened. "And what would those be?"

"Patience. Good humor, tolerance for one another. A loving disposition. Fidelity. Anything you would want specifically?"

"Ah. I see what you mean. Indeed, those are admirable qualities. Yes, I should want all those, and more."

"And what are they?"

"Loyalty. A spirit of adventure," he said with a private smile Antonia found intriguing. "Faith in me. An acceptance of me as the man I am, of my heritage."

She listened to his Scots burr. "You would want your wife to live on your estates in Scotland? I hear it is very cold."

"It can be. It is also wild, rugged, beautiful country. My wife would not spend all her time in the Highlands, but I would expect my children to be born on land I inherited from my ancestors."

She nodded. "That is reasonable. Is there anything else your wife would have to do in Scotland?"

"Perhaps she could learn to fish?"

Her eyes widened. "I understand fishing is a solitary, silent activity. Would you want her chatter to scare away the fish?"

"Ah, but remember, my wife would have intelligent conversation." He grinned, his teeth gleaming in his tanned face. The candlelight accentuated the interesting hollows in his cheeks and flattered his manly looks. "It follows that she would also know when to refrain from speaking."

"I see. So while you are fishing together, she is to keep silent and save her conversation for the drawing room."

"And elsewhere."

"Where?"

"Bed," he said bluntly.

She felt her eyes widen. "Bed?"

"Aye. I like a woman to tell me what she likes, what pleasures her. I should expect my wife to do no less."

Antonia swallowed. "Yours will be a most unusual marriage, your grace. Quite the exception to stylish marriages."

"My marriage will be not be a Society alliance for the usual reasons, but a lifelong union. There will be no others for either of us."

"How can you be so sure, your grace?"

"You have forgotten the most important ingredient to a successful marriage, Antonia. It is my chief requirement."

She hesitated to ask, but could not bear not to know the answer. "And that is?"

"Love. My wife shall love me beyond everything."

"Oh," she said faintly. "Is that not one-sided? Will you not love your wife in return?"

"I already do, Antonia."

"It sounds as though you have already chosen your wife, your grace."

"I have."

Chapter Seven

Antonia lay sleepless. By all rights she should be sleeping soundly after her late night and the most satisfying way she had been pleasured by her anonymous lover, but her conversation with Sutherland kept her awake.

She hadn't known before how enjoyable conversing with him would prove to be. She'd reveled in their verbal sparring for the lift it gave her spirits. It had made her feel as if she danced on the edge of a cliff.

To fence with him with words always made her feel that she'd come away from a perilous encounter with all her parts in place. She'd enjoyed the danger, the element of risk in dueling with a man reputed to be as good with a blade as he was a lover. Their conversation over the delicious midnight supper had been entertaining, suggestive, and had allowed her a glimpse of what she had renounced.

She envied the woman he had chosen to be his wife. Whoever she was, she was an extremely fortunate woman. To have won his love, to have him forswear his mistresses to be faithful to her alone was singularly rare. And for him to have done this without the gossips of the *ton* at his heels was another extraordinary feat. He had them all buzzing with his pursuit of her while he was actually courting another.

Whoever the unknown woman was, she had much to be thankful for. Sutherland would kept her identity secret until he was ready to announce their engagement, protecting her privacy and her good name until he was ready to give her his.

Clever, clever man. She admired his strategy so much that she could forgive him using her as a blind for his true activities. She should resent the attention he'd paid her, the unbelievable tale he'd told of hastening back to London when he'd heard she was free of Effingdale. She should be furious for making her a laughingstock with his public pursuit of her.

Many gentlemen of the *ton* had placed wagers on the outcome of the chase. The betting books in Whites and the other clubs had page after page of entries that the Duke of S would make Lady B-S his mistress before the Season was over. She'd heard the tremendous sums being wagered on the outcome of Sutherland's public hunting her through the ballrooms and drawing rooms of their acquaintances.

She should be angry and plotting his set-down, but instead she was envious of the woman he had chosen. Envious, and more than regretful that she would have to relinquish Sutherland's company. It would be too painful to meet him when he had his duchess on his arm.

She tossed restlessly. Much good it did her now to wonder what it would be like to have Sutherland love her. For all she'd renounced marrying again, she couldn't help but wonder what it would be like to be his duchess, to share his life. Sighing, she turned on her side and drew her legs up. At least she had her wonderfully imaginative lover to console her. She'd content herself in his arms.

When she woke late the next day, Clarry was already bustling around her bedchamber. Steam from a tub of water curled up through sunshine streaming in the opened windows. The scent of roses from her garden perfumed the air as freely as the bath salts Clarry poured into the bath.

Antonia stretched. "Good morning, Clarry. How late have I slept?"

Clarry turned and placed her hands on her hips. "It's not morning any longer, milady, and if you intend to keep your appointment this afternoon, you'd better get up out that bed and into the tub."

Antonia blinked at Clarry's tone, but didn't have the heart to scold her. "What's the matter with you?"

"It's that tired I am of this constant traipsing over to that rooming house and you carrying on while I wait with the footmen. Aren't you done yet? How much longer do we have to twiddle our thumbs?"

"Today is the last time, I promise. Today I'll tell him that I've chosen him to be my lover." Antonia stretched, feeling energy rush through her body as she thought of the way she would inform him. Now he was just "him," but later, she would know his identity and have a name to put to that magnificent male body. He would be pleased, and proud, that she had chosen him out of all the others, but determined to make her happy with her choice. "I can hardly wait to see his face."

Clarry turned her back, all at once quite busy laying out Antonia's clothes. "What if you don't like him once you see who he is?"

"Why should I not like him? Is there something wrong with him?"

"Not that I know, milady, but you never can tell. He might be not what you want, after all."

"You're acting very strange, Clarry. If I weren't late, you can believe we'd have all this mysterious behavior out."

"You can ask me anything you want later, milady. I'll tell you everything."

Antonia wondered at Clarry's words while she rushed though her bath and her dressing ritual. She had nothing planned for this evening, and she would not go to bed until she had cleared up the reason for Clarry's puzzling manner.

She dressed quickly, in a simply cut afternoon gown of a deep blue that flattered her pale skin and hair. As she placed a small drop of perfume behind her ears and between her breasts, she eagerly waited her lover's reaction to her preparations for him.

She donned the veiled hat, knowing it was the last time she'd do so, and was soon on her way to her last interview. Eagerly, she rode through the streets of London until they reached the now familiar street and rooming house. Only the barely concealed smirks on her footmen's faces kept her from lifting her skirts and running up the stairs in her impatience to meet her lover. He hadn't arrived yet, which disappointed her, yet she used the time to prepare herself for one last anonymous encounter.

Moments later, reclining on the sofa instead of the bed, she heard his footsteps coming up the stairs, then the murmurs in the outer room. She stopped breathing until she heard the door open and close behind him.

She breathed again as she heard him approach the bed. Today she'd had Clarry leave the heavy drapes slightly open and the windows open to the warm afternoon. The street scents and sounds mingled with his. Together, they made a heady, earthy combination.

"Will you speak today?"

He said nothing.

"That will be acceptable for now, but later," her voice dropped as she promised, "later, you will speak with me."

She waited excitedly for him to begin. She had left off the robe, keeping on only the mask. She heard his breathing, then felt his body as he stood over her. She felt his heat and trembled with anticipated passion.

Watching her, Sutherland stripped off his shirt and trousers, leaving himself nude. He was already erect, his cock hard and aching. Willing himself to ignore his own desire, he took a deep breath and began as he had begun before, with soft, delicate touches on her skin that soon had her craving more.

Her skin heated under his touch as the fine hairs quivered under his fingertips. He'd brought none of his seductive toys in his box of sexual tricks, wanting to rely only on himself and her ardent response to his lovemaking.

Her skin was smooth and silky, delicately perfumed by both a floral fragrance and her own personal musk. The heady mixture swamped his senses, increasing his hunger for her and his determination to make their lovemaking so perfect that she'd have no cause for complaint when he drew the mask from her and she discovered his identity.

She would have no reason to refuse him.

He placed little kisses on every inch of her skin, beginning with her toes and working up to her mouth. By the time he reached it, she was panting. The silken mask presented only the flimsiest barriers, but he managed, by the merest thread, to control the urge to tear away the mask and plunder her soft recesses.

He kissed her as he had been longing to, with nips at her lips, tracing the outline of her lips with his. He savored the taste of her mouth as he had relished the taste and texture of her everywhere else. The silk mask tore at one corner of the mouth opening. He pulled it further apart to reach more of her.

She didn't protest. Instead, she opened her mouth to him and he swept in, conquering and being conquered at the same time. She was delectable and heady, like the strongest whiskey and the sweetest meadow flower. Like honey, he lapped at her until she moaned and dueled with his tongue, circling it with her own and darting into his mouth to taste him.

At last they broke apart, breathing heavily, stunned by the emotions they'd aroused in each other. Though he knew she was as lusty and passionate as he, to feel her become aggressive with his mouth stimulated him and made him crave more. He wanted everything with her.

He reached for the mask.

Antonia forestalled him. "No, not yet."

He stopped. So his lady was still unsure of him. Very well. That would be rectified. He removed some of the plump damask pillows behind her and repositioned her so that she lay sprawling against the cushions, her satiny thighs open to him and her feet resting on the thick carpet.

He dropped to his knees between her thighs and caressed her legs from ankle to thigh. When she moaned and shivered, he lowered his mouth to drink from her. She cried out as his tongue entered her, she convulsed immediately. Her orgasm delighted and spurred him onward. He kissed her repeatedly, using his tongue on her intimate folds, tasting, savoring. teasing, learning her tastes and textures and always demanding greater passion from her.

"More," she moaned, unknowingly echoing his hunger. He increased his pace, his tongue now flickering on the swollen tissues, now entering her slick passage, varying his technique until her hands clutched his bare shoulders, her nails buried deeply, as she urged him upward to enter her.

"Please, now, I need you now."

He sat back on his heels, breathing heavily, his mouth full of the taste of her as he contemplated how he would take her. He could rise on his knees, pierce her and thrust until they shattered together. If he did that, he could suckle at her breasts at the same time. The thought tempted even as he considered other positions. Draw her to the carpet with him, turn her over and enter her from behind? Stretch her out on the sofa and cover her?

While he debated which would afford them the most pleasure, she reached down and took his stiff yard in her hand. He bucked and almost spent his seed until he gritted his teeth and commanded himself to resist the fierce ecstasy.

With soft fingers, she measured and pleasured him. She played with him, alternating featherlight strokes with harder ones, then cupping his sac and rolling his testicles gently in her hand. He closed his eyes, willing himself to remain motionless, gripped by passion, until he though he'd lose control. He grasped her hand, stilling the motion, until she released him and lay back.

He stood and scooped her up into his arms. With a few long strides, he reached the bed and kissing her, leaned over to place her the way he wanted her. She let him do as he would with her. Triumphantly, possessively, he lowered himself beside her, stretching his longer length next to hers and he bent his head to take her nipple in his mouth.

Antonia trembled. Fire surged through her. She arched under his mouth, begging, pleading for him to take her. He had stretched her on a rack of sensual pleasure so keen she thought she'd fly apart. Every inch of her body was attuned to his. Each of her muscles strained to hold him closer, to urge him to rise above her, part her thighs and make her his.

His long legs, muscled and strong, enclosed hers. She felt the hair on them as a furry pelt and moaned. She traced the line of the hair on his chest as it tapered in a wide vee from his nipples to his navel, then extended down to luxuriantly cup his sex. She gasped when he lowered his chest to hers and caressed her with his body hair.

He took first one nipple, then the other in his mouth, taking as much of her rounded breast as he could until she felt as if she were being devoured by him. Passion poured through her with each pull of his lips. She moaned, "No, it's too good. No more."

Yet he did not desist. Instead he maintained his control by pushing her beyond pleasure, into the realm of rapture. He lowered his body to hers, and with one supreme thrust, entered her. She responded with instinctive tightening of her muscles around him. Her orgasms came, one after another, with such force that she cried and gripped him harder.

Once, twice, a dozen times he thrust, each lunge more powerful and deeper than the one before, until at last, with a mighty roar, he claimed her as his.

When he collapsed, breathing heavily, his body resting on hers, searing her with his heat, she lay with her eyes closed, holding him near. With one hand she stroked his back in slow, easy caresses, sated and grateful. She had been right to search for a new lover. This man more than fulfilled her every requirement.

At last, his breathing evened out and he rolled to his side, pulling Antonia with him. She went willingly, wanting this closeness as much as she had earlier hungered for the passion.

Sutherland kept one hand on her hip, and with the other, caressed her throat. He pressed a kiss on each eyelid, closing them. When she didn't protest, he slipped a finger under the material at her throat. The green silk, moistened by her perspiration, clung to her skin. The moment he drew it away on one side, it clung to the other. She made a sound in her throat, part laugh and part moan, as if she enjoyed his struggle to unmask her.

He persisted, cursing his suddenly fumbling fingers, until he managed to loosen the strings that kept the mask in place. One by one, he undid the knots at the back of her head and lifted the fabric away from her face. Feature by feature, her beautiful face was revealed to him.

He dropped the mask to one side, relieved that the masquerade would soon be over. He bent and pressed kisses on her closed eyes, on her temples, down her cheek until he came to her mouth. He gave her a kiss of promise, of welcome.

He drew his mouth away. "Open your eyes, Antonia."

Chapter Eight

Drugged with pleasure, it took Antonia a moment to focus her eyes, and then they popped open in disbelief. Dougal MacDonald, that unmitigated cad of a seventh duke of Sutherland, gazed down at her.

She sat bolt upright and grabbed a sheet to cover her breasts. "What on earth are you doing here?"

He laughed. "Surely that should be obvious, Antonia."

"Why are you here? What have you done with—" she fell silent when she noticed his nudity. "Oh, no. Not you."

"Without a doubt."

"You mean to tell me that you, that you—"

"It isn't often I have seen you a loss for words, my dear. What happened to your gift for conversation?"

She drew the sheet closer to her throat. Her pulse pounding, she closed her eyes. She had to be dreaming. When she opened them a few moments later, he was still there. "I had hoped I was having a nightmare."

He lifted a finger to stroke her cheek. She leaned away from his touch. "Come now. You can not deny that you and I have just experienced one of the most wonderful moments together."

"I do not understand. Why have you done this?"

"Ah, Antonia, where is your sharp wit? I can only hope that I have worn it to a frazzle by my lovemaking. And as to why I am here, I repeat, that should be obvious. I am to be your next, and I might add as a small warning, your only lover."

"No."

He sat upright. "You wish to renege on the arrangement, Antonia? I'm afraid I will not allow that."

She cast him an annoyed glance and then pointedly looked away from his broad shoulders and muscled chest. "You are here under false pretenses. The arrangement does not apply to you. I specifically do not want another peer in my bed."

"Could you not forget my title for a moment and consider me as any other man?"

She refused to be drawn. "I will not consider you at all."

"You have no choice," he said briskly. "You yourself set up the rules. You would allow only the man you intend to take as your lover to enter your body. I have done that. Ergo, I am your lover."

"You are quite wrong. I refuse you."

"You would change the rules that easily?"

His voice, soft with unspoken threat, made her throat go dry. She swallowed and gathered her wits. "This is not a game. Nor a duel. I alone set the rules."

"A man would be held accountable for such dishonor."

She hitched the sheet up to her throat. "Please clothe yourself and leave. Immediately."

"Not quite so fast, my lady. We have yet to set the conditions for our new arrangement."

She exhaled. "There is no arrangement between us. How often must I tell you that?"

"I have heard you." His voice turned hard, as if he would brook no further disagreement. "Now you are to listen to me."

"If I cry out, my servants will eject you immediately."

He blinked, then smiled. "If you do that, my servants will thrash your servants and I shall return in triumph."

His sense of humor worried her more than his authoritarian tone. It made her weak, vulnerable to the man as well as the lover. In some desperation, she cried, "This is not a jesting matter! Please leave me."

His voice lost its teasing tone. "You are quite right, on that score at least. This is not a humorous situation. Allow me to tell you what this is."

"And if I refuse?"

He hooked a finger under her chin and lifted her face to his. "You will not refuse."

She shuddered but she kept her gaze steadily on his.

"This, my dear Lady Antonia Blair-Sutworth, is an offer of marriage. You would do me great honor by becoming my wife."

Her mouth dropped open. With his finger, he gently closed it.

"You are mad," she breathed.

"About you, yes. I am besotted, insane with love for you. I would grovel at your feet, but I am afraid in your present mood you would take the opportunity to do me damage."

"Why? Why are you doing this?"

"Antonia, I should have thought my motives perfectly clear. I want you to be my duchess."

"Last night you said you had already chosen one."

"I was quite honest with you. I just didn't mention that I had chosen you."

She shook her head. "No. I will not marry you."

"Why not? As you yourself mentioned, the *ton* has decided that it is time I take a wife." He paused, as if reflecting on the *ton* managing his affairs, then continued. "For the first, and no doubt the only time, I am in agreement with Society. You need not worry about your future. I have wealth to support you and our children many times over. I have lands and houses at your disposal. I will shower you with jewels and whatever fripperies you wish—"

"There is no need to catalogue your material advantages, your grace."

"Many mothers have set their daughters at me, but I have held out," he continued as though she had not interrupted him. "Refusing many a tempting morsel for a chance at—"

"At the entire pie?" she asked, smiling despite herself. "Your words are not very complimentary, your grace."

He laughed. "I do admire your quick wit, my dear. Even when I am the butt of your joke."

"It is flattering to be asked to be your duchess, but I must refuse."

"Are your affections engaged elsewhere?"

Startled by the abrupt change in his manner, she paused before answering him. "No."

"Are you suffering from some dreadful disease?"

"Of course not."

"Are you already married?"

"I am a widow, as you very well know."

"Then I find no impediment, unless you find me distasteful."

She touched his cheek. "You know that I do not."

He smiled at her. "You find me attractive?"

"Very much so."

"We already know that we suit quite well together in bed. What keeps you from accepting?"

"I have my reasons."

"You do not love me?"

She sighed. "I fear that I love you to distraction, your grace."

"Call me Dougal."

She smiled at the intimacy he offered with his given name. "Dougal."

"Good." His smile was fierce, proud and possessive. "Now repeat that last sentence."

"I love you to distraction, Dougal."

He bent his head and kissed her. His lips told her he loved her. He'd cherish her to their last days.

When he lifted his head, Sutherland saw the tears in her lustrous green eyes. "Why do you cry, Antonia?"

"I cannot marry you, or any other. I have sworn so."

"A religious vow?" he asked, confusion in his voice.

"No, not that." She wiped her cheeks dry. "A vow to myself."

"I don't understand. Why do you not want to marry again?"

"It's not something a man would understand."

"Try me," he urged, his voice low and encouraging.

She studied him, her gaze lingering on each of his beloved features. "Since my husband died three years ago, I have discovered several things about myself. Things that many would consider unsuitable in a woman."

"Such as?"

"I prefer being a widow to being a wife."

"You do?" He leaned forward to rest an elbow on his knee. "Why is that?"

"I do not have to answer to a husband, for one."

He sat up. "I can see where that might discomfit a husband or two."

She smiled at his wry tone. "Shall I continue?"

"Please do. This is fascinating."

"I am my own mistress, as I said. I control my own means."

"That is point two," he observed. "Is there more?"

"Quite a bit more, but it can be summarized easily. In short, I am independent."

He was silent for a moment, as if considering the meaning of her words. "If you had all of those things, and you could be married at the same time, would you consider it then?"

"It is not possible, your grace—"

"Dougal."

"Impossible, Dougal. It is a contradiction in terms. How can a woman be married and independent at the same time?"

"Let me think on it. I shall come upon a way."

"You are too confident of yourself."

"Should I not be? Do you not like it when I am sure of what I am about?"

She knew they no longer spoke of her wish for independence. She pressed a kiss on his shoulder. "How could I deny it?"

"You cannot," he agreed with satisfaction.

She continued with her kisses, making her way slowly along the musculature of his chest until she came to a nipple. She flicked her tongue on it, once twice, then sucked on it in imitation of what he had done to her.

He grasped her head in both hands and gently raised her face to his. "If you do that, I shall not be able to think straight."

"Do not think," she murmured. "Let me make love to you." One last time, she added silently. Once more to last me the rest of my days and nights.

"If you think to distract me—" he warned.

"I think you are a most wonderful, imaginative, powerful lover. Your stamina is truly impressive."

He rose to the occasion immediately. His arousal grew against her hip and she smiled with satisfaction. He lay back, putting his body at her disposition. She toyed with the hair on his chest, running her fingers through the silky hairs, pulling and tugging gently as her mouth continued its foray down his belly. She felt his heart pick up speed, his breathing grow shallow even as she felt his stomach muscles contract under her questing touch.

She pressed kisses all over his face and throat, then settled down and kissed him seriously. His mouth opened under hers when she traced his lips with the tip of her tongue and probed deeper. He tasted of sweet passion, now heady and frantic, now soft and languid. She lingered, testing every bit of his mouth, dueling with her tongue, aping the thrusts he would make soon.

By his passivity, he gave her the freedom to explore his body as he had explored hers. With every touch, she expanded on what she had learned from him. He groaned but made no move to stop her.

His chest rubbed against hers, the hair caressing her breasts. They were already sensitive from their earlier lovemaking and peaked instantly against him. She arched to feel more.

"Dougal," she whispered. "I want—"

"Yes? What do you want?"

"You, just you. Love me."

He could refuse her nothing. Complying with her whispered request, he moved closer, shifting his weight to rub against her. His cock, already hard and eager, throbbed against her thigh. She moved her hands to his shoulders, then to the back to play with his hair and stroke his neck. He responded by nuzzling her neck, leaving kisses in his wake. She murmured and lifted her chin to give him greater access.

He shifted to reach her breasts, and followed the line of her shoulder to her arm, kissing and nibbling as he went. He pushed her arm out of the way and licked his way to her elbow, then up again, blowing gently at the moist path he'd made until she moved restlessly beneath him. His hands clasped her breasts and she moaned with the joy of it as he left her arm and concentrated on her nipples.

Everything he had done to her before in the name of seduction, he did again with love. Where before his technique had evoked raw lust from her, now his tenderness and emotional approach wrought intense passion all the more lustful and ardent for being caring and tender.

She lay under his hands, coming alive in every pore, as euphoric and avid as though they had not already indulged themselves to exhaustion. Wherever she could reach him, she stroked and petted him, nipping at his skin, breathing in the scent of aroused male. She licked him, tasting the salt of his earlier exertions, and left bites of her own on his broad chest.

When he pushed himself down the bed to rest between her legs and placed his mouth on her intimate flesh, made extra sensitive by his earlier ministrations, she cried, "Oh, no more! I can't bear it."

He gentled his embrace but did not move away. His tongue barely touching her, he laved her soreness away until it was replaced by need. Her orgasm was his reward.

He moved up on her again, and rising to his knees, he lifted her legs and placed them around his waist. When he did not move, she lifted her eyes in confusion. "When I come into you now, I come as your husband."

She bit her lip, wracked with unbearable passion, yet wanting him more than she had ever wanted anything before, or would ever want anything again.

He probed at her entry with the tip of his member. "Decide now, Antonia."

She felt the velvety smoothness of the skin stretched over hard muscle and wavered. She knew it was emotional blackmail to force her to choose when she was unable to think straight, but oh, Lord, how good he felt against her!

"You mean this?" she gasped.

"I do not lie. You should know that by now." He penetrated her, barely entering her, and withdrew.

She moaned at the loss.

"Decide, Antonia, before I go mad," he ordered in an aching whisper.

She arched against him, her hips moving restlessly. The silken feel of her was more than he could bear, yet he forced himself not to move. Muscles straining, sweat beading his forehead and chest, he held himself immobile above her.

She stared up at him with wild eyes. She tossed her head back, her mouth gasping for breath. At last, she surrendered. "Yes, yes, damn you, yes!"

With a groan he penetrated her in one long thrust. They moaned together as he rested, deeply imbedded, for just a moment before he began a long, slow rhythmic stroke.

It was madness. It was sheer bliss. It was heaven.

It seemed hours that he maintained a steady rhythm, propelling them forward. She begged for release. He increased his pace and with his thumb, found her bud and stroked it. Madness overtook her. With each movement of his body he propelled her further into passion until her orgasms overtook them both and provoked his. He cried out her name as his back arched into one spasm after another. He poured himself into her.

She wept.

She raised her head to look at him. "It will be difficult for me to forget you."

"Forget me?" He forced an eye open. "How are you going to forget me when I intend to make love to you every day and most of the night?"

"You will not have the opportunity."

"I thought we had settled this. You agreed to marry me."

"You forced me to say so under duress."

"Duress?" he repeated, his tone severe.

"How could you expect me to think, much less make such an important decision, under those circumstances?"

"Listen to me, Antonia." He sat up against the pillows and made himself comfortable, then drew her into his arms. "I have no intention of letting you get away from me. I have thought of a way to satisfy us both."

"Impossible."

"You shall keep your independence, I swear."

She laughed. "And how shall I do that if I am married?"

"Do we agree that we are both imaginative, intelligent people?"

She nodded cautiously.

"Then, if we both agree to live in a certain way, who is to say us nay?"

"I don't understand."

"It's simple, my lady duchess-to-be. We shall agree, in a marriage contract if you wish it, that what you now possess shall be yours alone, to do with as you please."

Her green eyes opened wide. "You would do that?"

"I would," he stated. "And more."

"More? How could you do more?"

He cleared his throat. "Well, I admit it will take a considerable amount of adjusting on my part, but then, it's in a good cause."

"What are you saying?"

"If you had a husband who did not demand obedience, but instead requested agreement, would you still be adverse to marriage?"

"That is unheard of."

"But not impossible," he countered.

"Rather than have to answer to a husband's every whim, I am to be consulted and my wishes considered?"

He reflected. "Perhaps the proper theory is compromise. A husband and wife ought to be able to agree on the important decisions, wouldn't you agree?"

"I would," she said, cautious again.

"And if they agreed, in advance, that there were certain decisions only one would make, and the other agree to without argument, do you think that would work?"

"I think your imagination is running away with you, your grace."

"Dougal," he corrected. "Now, if this same couple had the agreement I mentioned, they should get along famously."

"Of course," she agreed with an airy gesture. "So long as she made the decisions such as what to serve for tea and which polish to use on the staircase, and he made all the other decisions—"

"You malign me, Antonia. I am speaking of a partnership."

"A business partnership?"

He winced. "I wouldn't like to think it was a cold business partnership, with hereafters, wheretofores and penalties."

She stroked the frown from his forehead. "What would you call it then?"

"A loving partnership between two people who want only the best for each other."

"Could there be such a thing?"

"We shall make it so."

"I fear you are too optimistic. What about the first time I over-spend on gowns?"

"If you don't wish to pay for them yourself, I shall do so gladly."

"May I have that in writing?" she inquired politely.

He roared with laughter and pulled her closer to him. They settled back, resting comfortably. Antonia fell into a light sleep. A knock at the door interrupted his thoughts about Antonia. "What is it?"

Clarry poked her head through the half-open door, "Begging your pardon, your grace, but it's gone seven and—"

He pulled a sheet up over their nakedness. "And what, Clarry?"

"Well, it's the footmen, you see. They're wanting their supper."

He laughed. Nothing could daunt his good humor, not disre-spectful servants nor recalcitrant ladies. "You may congratulate yourself, Clarry. You have done well."

"It's over, then?"

At his nod, Clarry entered the bedchamber, closed the door behind her and approached the bedside table with a fresh candle.

"Do not wake her ladyship," he warned as the light fell over Antonia.

"Humph, she sleeps like she's exhausted. You did right by her?" Sutherland blinked. "You might say so."

"I could hear the two of you in here. Had to send the footmen below."

"Very discreet of you, Clarry."

"I see to her, you know."

"And very well indeed. There'll be a little something extra for you. Is everything ready?"

"It is, but it's so late—"

Antonia opened her eyes and stretched. "What are you two talking about?"

"It's time to get up, my love. Your servants are hungry."

Antonia glanced at the window, at the dusky light coming in through the gap in the draperies. "Oh, we shouldn't have slept so long!"

"Just out of curiosity, you understand, but are we going to let the servants' stomachs govern our lives?"

"Your lives?" Clarry asked, her eyes growing big.

"Her ladyship has consented to be my wife, Clarry. You may be the first to wish us well."

Clarry bustled closer and swept Antonia up into her arms. "Oh milady, this is wonderful news." She sent Sutherland a severe warning glance. "I hope you will be very happy."

"As happy as I can make her," he assured Clarry.

Antonia returned Clarry's hug. "Not so fast, you two. There are a number of questions to which I want answers, and I want them now."

"You could wait until we get home, milady, all cozy like," Clarry suggested.

Antonia watched the glances fly between Clarry and Sutherland. "Now. And don't leave anything out."

Clarry kneaded her skirt.

"Do not blame Clarry, my love. If you wish to cast fault at anyone, sling it at me."

"You shall have your share, I promise you that."

He laughed at the threat. Plumping the pillows behind them, he lay back with her in his arms. He didn't seem to mind that Clarry gawked at his naked chest. "I am properly abashed."

She glared at him. "Get on with it, then."

"Well, you will recall that I told you I wanted you?"

At her wary nod, he continued, "I enlisted Clarry's help. The long and short of it is that she agreed to let me pose as another applicant."

"Did she now?" Antonia slanted a long look at her maid.

"Only for your own good, milady," Clarry hastened to explain.

"Indeed." Antonia turned to gaze Sutherland.

He gave her a bland look in return. "So, you see, all is explained."

"Not quite."

"What is left to resolve?"

"A simple matter. How could you be here in the afternoons with me and then bedevil me at night?"

"With the greatest difficulty, Antonia." He leaned closer. "You have had your revenge, and all without knowing it."

"I have?"

"Aye," he whispered. "I all but expired from the ache of wanting you."

"A fitting punishment," she announced, though she couldn't help the smile tugging at her lips. "Are there to be any more of these surprises?"

"Perhaps one," Sutherland admitted. "A small one," he added.

Clarry coughed and hurried over to the armoire. Keeping her back turned to the couple on the bed, she removed Antonia's clothing.

Narrowing her eyes to see through the rapidly failing light, Antonia said, "Those are not the clothes I came in."

"I know milady. I thought you'd be wanting fresh."

"But, Clarry, that's my cream satin. Why now?"

"Just thought you'd like something pretty, milady."

Antonia started to protest again.

Sutherland silenced her with a kiss. When he moved back, Clarry had finished laying out Antonia's clothes and left the room. "She'll be back to help you dress, my love, but I imagine she thought the rest had better come from me."

"Rest of what?" Antonia asked suspiciously.

He glanced at the gown, then back at her. "If you agree to marry me immediately, those will your wedding clothes. I shall dress in the next room. No doubt my valet is also wanting his supper," he added, attempting to lighten the frown that wrinkled her lovely forehead.

"Wedding, valet? Your grace, what is going on here?"

"Dougal." He rose from the bed. "We could be married as soon as you dress."

"Impossible!"

"Not at all. The minister is waiting in the other room. I have a special license with me."

"But why the rush? I mean, what if I want a proper wedding?"

He hesitated. "Do you?"

"Well, no," she said after a moment. "I had all that with Blair-Sutworth, and look what it got me."

"Good. There is another reason for the haste, you know."

She raised her eyebrows. "Surely you don't think I would change my mind after being so uniquely coerced into saying yes?"

He drew on his trousers and his shirt before he bent down and kissed her again.

"What?" she gasped when he let her up to breathe.

"You may already be pregnant, my love. I want no one counting on their fingers when my heir is born."

She could say nothing. She'd never thought of it, but of course he was right. Once more, she was reminded of his thoroughness.

"I shall leave you now to dress. If you come through that door wearing that gown, you shall leave these rooms as my wife."

She watched the door close behind him. For a moment she couldn't move, stunned by all that had happened in the last few hours. She, Duchess of Sutherland—it wasn't to be believed!

She lay still, allowing herself time to become accustomed to the idea, then all at once energized, she rose and called for Clarry. With her help, she bathed in the warm water Clarry provided and then dressed in her elegant cream satin.

"I brought your pearls, milady, and I thought your hair down—"

"I am not a blushing virgin, Clarry."

"Maybe not, but I think the duke brought a blush or two to your face." she sighed. "Ah, he's a fine figure of a man. He'll keep you happy."

"I hope so." Antonia's legs felt weak. She sat unsteadily. Clarry picked up the silver backed hair brush and began brushing Antonia's hair.

"Oh, Clarry, am I doing the right thing? All along I've said I would never marry again and here I am preparing to go out there and —"

"Now don't you be getting all nervy on me, milady. The Duke is a fine man, and he'll make you a fine husband."

"But, Clarry, all I wanted was a lover!"

"And didn't you get one?" Clarry's face settled into a wide, self-satisfied smile. "Couldn't ask for a better end to this foolish plan of yours."

"It seems to me that I had some help with it," Antonia reminded her.

Clarry went on brushing. "It was all his idea, I swear. He came to see me and invited me to sit down, all proper like, and we had such a nice chat."

"About me?"

"Well, of course about you. Why else would the duke be sitting in your parlor chatting with me?"

"It makes me feel faint to think of it," Antonia murmured.

"Do you need your vinaigrette?" Clarry asked, a worried expression on her face. "I didn't think to bring it."

"No, no, I'm quite all right. Are you finished with my hair?"

Clarry fidgeted with one last tendril before pronouncing herself satisfied. "Now I am."

"Go and tell them I'm ready. I'll be out in a moment."

Clarry eyed her. "You make a beautiful bride. First time, you were all innocent and nervous, now you know what to expect, and you're like a blooming rose."

They hugged and Clarry left the room.

Antonia stood and paced slowly through the sumptuously appointed bedchamber. The room had served her well, but now the furnishings seemed overblown and somewhat tawdry. She glanced at the bed, still undone, with sheets and pillows strewn to the floor and the aroma of heated passion still lingering in their folds.

The room had been perfectly prepared for sex and seductions, but it suited her no longer. Now that she had found love, she wanted all the furnishings to be fresh for the two of them. She wondered what Sutherland's bedchamber was like, and what he would say when she informed him that they would not be sleeping apart. Would she need to change the furnishings?

Maybe all the furniture in his bedroom was old and meaningful to his family history. She reflected on that. Would she be able to sleep in a bed in which the first six dukes and slept? Wouldn't it be awfully lumpy by now?

She smiled at herself. She was procrastinating, she knew, postponing the moment when she would go through that door and face a new life. For just a few more minutes she wanted to relish the successful completion of her quest, with a reward far greater than she had ever expected.

For all that Dougal had promised her that she would remain independent and his partner, she knew that the promise could never be fully kept. While a small part of her regretted that, the greater part of her, her heart and mind and soul, loved him. She loved him for listening to her, for caring enough to make that pledge to her.

She threw open the door and advanced to meet her bridegroom, Dougal MacDonald, the masterful, exciting, utterly virile seventh duke of Sutherland.

About the author:

Born in Ecuador and raised in Chile, Bonnie Hamre was edu-cated there and in the United States. She has also lived in Italy, England and Scotland, where she gained an appreciation for her Scots heritage. She now makes her home among the coastal red-woods south of San Francisco. Published also in book-length women's fiction, Bonnie finds there is nothing as satisfying as an emotionally gripping tale of two people making a commitment to each other. She writes with sensitivity, with passion and with the tough of humor that makes sensuality fun.

The Spinner's Dream

✦⊱⋆⊰✦

by Alice Gaines

To my reader:

    The most romantic worlds are the ones that live in your imagination. I've created one here, and now I can share it with you.

Chapter One

Solitude and contemplation. Cool fog and the shade of giant trees. The goddess-mother's balm for a fire in the heart. It should have been enough.

Kareth sa-Damil selected an arm's length branch of wood from the dwindling pile and tossed it onto her small hearth-fire. The wood in the forest was plentiful. With no other human soul living in this part of the forest, Kareth had no competition for the abundance of downed timber that lay everywhere. Even if that weren't true, she was young and healthy enough to take the ax from its hook on the wall, find a log, and split it. But the perpetual chill suited her one-room cottage far better than a raging fire.

Some might choose sun and heat to burn their sins away. Kareth had run instead to the silent company of ancient trees and swirling mists. The goddess guided her here to purify herself. Why did she still ache inside?

She sat, cross-legged at her hearth and envisioned the fog seeping under her door, around the window pane, through cracks in the walls to envelope her. Cool, detached, dispassionate. She closed her eyes and sighed. *Dendra take me, school me. I am yours.*

A crashing sounded nearby—as someone raced through the underbrush just outside. Then wood slammed against wood, as her door flew open and banged against the wall. Kareth opened her eyes and found the cause. A man stood on the threshold, not much more than a silhouette in the shadows—a large figure, filling the doorway with shoulders, arms, legs—but indistinct nevertheless. She scrambled to her feet to confront him.

"So, there is someone here," he said. "With the meager smoke from that fire I couldn't be sure."

"Who are you?" she gasped.

He stepped into the room, a long woolen cape swirling around him, and shut the door. "I should think that would be obvious."

And suddenly it was, from the glint of metal around his throat. Nothing gleamed quite like a churl's collar—slick and smooth and inexorably attached to the poor soul who wore it. This man's owner had chosen brass and sapphire blue to mark his property.

"What do you want?" Kareth demanded.

The man looked at her then, really looked at her, his eyes flashing emerald fire from under brows the color of sun-bleached sand. "There are eight or ten catchers close behind me. What I want is to kill a handful of them and escape the rest."

"You'll not kill anyone here."

"Without a weapon, I won't." He glanced around him, and his gaze fell on the ax. "Ah, this will do."

He headed toward the wall where the ax hung, but Kareth blocked his path. "No," she said, staring upward into his face. "You'll not kill anyone here."

"And who's to stop me?"

"I will," she answered. "Dendra will."

"Dendra," he repeated. He slipped a finger under the chain around her neck and pulled the amulet from inside her bodice. His fingers toyed briefly with the crescent-cut crystal. "A priestess."

"A novice," she corrected.

"All the same. Only a true believer would be stupid enough to live in a wilderness like this."

From outside came shouts and the sounds of people blundering through the forest—branches breaking, ferns being trampled underfoot, a flock of curo-curas rising up on noisy wings and cackling out their alarm.

"Blast." The man grabbed her arm and pushed her toward the window. "What do you see?"

She glanced outside. As he had said, nearly ten men were

making their way toward her home, hacking a path through the trees and ferns with long, ugly knives. They came to within several yards of the cottage and stopped. A large, barrel-chested man at their head motioned the others to fan out, and the rest of the party disappeared back into the woods to encircle the cottage.

"You're right," she said quietly. "Catchers, a whole patrol of them."

"Get me that ax."

"No."

"Curse you, woman. Do it."

She glared up into the murderous green of his eyes. "No," she repeated.

He dropped her arm and ducked low to crawl under the window. He made his way to the far wall and grabbed the ax from its hook. He took a wide stance, the ax handle clutched in his fists, the blade gleaming in the flickering firelight. "Let them in," he snarled. "One at a time."

"I'll not let you kill anyone."

He stared at her, his eyes wide, as much from terror as exertion. "Do you know what they'll do to me?"

She did. Dendra guide her, she well knew those knives weren't used only to cut the forest apart. They also served to slice through flesh and even to cleave bone. No wonder he wanted to carve the catchers to pieces before they could do the same to him. And from the look of desperation in his eyes, he'd do it, too. She had to find some way to save him without allowing bloodshed in her sanctuary.

She held up her hands to him in a gesture of reassurance. "I'll send them away."

"Easily said, my little brown-eyed believer. But if they smell blood, they won't stop for you or Dendra or anything else." He brandished the ax. "This is all they know."

"Hide," she ordered. "I'll protect you."

He barked out a mirthless laugh. "You? You'd blow away on the first good gust of wind."

"I'm your only hope," she answered. "Hide now, or I'll run out and leave you to their mercy."

His eyes widened ever further. "You'd do that?"

Of course, she wouldn't. But he couldn't know that. So she simply stared back at him, giving him a choice between trusting her and facing ten or so blood-thirsty churl-catchers with only an ax for protection.

At that very moment, a heavy knock sounded on the door. "Open up, in the name of Lord Rabal."

Breath of the Beast. She had to do something, now. Her intruder churl still held the ax in strong hands, the muscles of his arms and shoulders bunching, clearly visible even beneath his flowing cape. If one of his pursuers got inside alone, the catcher would likely end up in pieces.

The knocking turned to pounding. "Open up."

"Lord Rabal rules not here," Kareth called back.

"Of course my lord doesn't rule here, woman," the voice grumbled outside. "We've had to travel these four days to get here from his province."

"Then you can travel four days back. I obey no one but Dendra."

"We're chasing an escaped churl. A dangerous man," the catcher shouted through the door. "You'll want us to stop him, or who knows what he'll do to you? Now, be an obedient female and open this door."

Obedient female, indeed. No man referred to a priestess of Dendra as an obedient female, even if she was still a novice. She'd show these males—all of them—who obeyed whom in her own private haven. She glared over at the churl and waved her arm toward the wardrobe. He opened it silently and slipped inside, taking the ax with him.

She walked to the door and lifted the latch. The door flew open, pushing her back toward the center of the room. One of the catchers, the leader, strode in, his long-knife raised. "Where is he?"

"He's not been here."

The man's gaze traveled slowly around the room, taking in

every corner. "We saw him come this way, and he hasn't left, or one of my men would've found him."

She folded her arms over her chest. "I've seen no one."

He leered down at her. "Then you're blind as well as deaf, little mother. That churl was making enough noise to raise my grandam from the dead."

She stood tall and lifted her chin. "I must ask you to leave."

"I must decline." He sketched a sarcastic imitation of a bow. Then he straightened and headed toward the only place in the room where a man could conceal himself—the wardrobe. She backed up to intercept him then stood her ground.

The man continued until he stood nearly on top of her, until she could easily make out his stubble of beard and the grease stains on his shirt, from Dendra knew how many dinners. In a moment he'd push past her to the wardrobe. And when he opened the door, he'd be greeted by a swinging ax.

She rested her hand on his chest and let herself sway into him. Then she let out a loud cough. He caught her shoulder in his free hand and shoved her away from him, staring down into her face. "Here, what's wrong with you?"

She covered her mouth with her hand and coughed some more. More emphatically this time, long and hard, giving him her best imitation of someone fighting for breath. "Nothing," she wheezed. "Only..."

She wavered again and made as if to lean into his chest, but he backed away. "I've not been well," she muttered. "Nothing. A fever. I'll cure myself soon."

His eyes went round. "The pestilence."

"No. Only a fever," she said. "But there are some soiled things in there," she added, nodding toward the wardrobe. "Not pestilent, not at all." She took a gasp of breath. "Still, I wouldn't have another person see them."

He backed up another step, staring at the wardrobe as though it imperiled his very life. And indeed it would, if she were pest-ridden, if her wardrobe did contain unclean bedclothes and dressings.

"I'll leave you then, mother." He lifted his knife as if for protection and backed toward the door. "To cure yourself."

She coughed again and nodded, following along to be sure that he took not an extra moment to leave. She needn't have worried. He made it to the door and jumped across the threshold, nearly knocking down one of his cohorts.

"Easy, Brath." The other catcher reached out and steadied his leader. "Did you find him?"

"No," Brath answered. "You?"

The second catcher shrugged. "Nothing back there but a privyhouse. Empty." He made as if to enter the cottage, but Brath caught his arm.

"Don't go in there."

"But we haven't found him out here," the second man protested. "He must be inside."

"He got past us somehow," Brath said.

"Impossible," the other one replied, again moving to step over the threshold. Brath held on, now almost throwing the man back down the path they had carved through the forest.

"What's got into you, man?"

Brath gave him another shove. "We've disturbed the mother enough." Brath nodded toward Kareth.

She coughed one more time and nodded back.

"Round up the others," Brath ordered. "We'll continue the search."

The second man let out a loud whistle, and the two catchers headed away. Kareth closed the door, turned, and leaned against it.

The wardrobe door opened slowly, and a blond head peeked out, followed by broad shoulders and then the head of the ax. "Are they gone?"

"Yes," Kareth answered. "And now you can go, too."

The churl sidled to the window and peeked outside. "A clever bit of deception, the pestilence tale." He glanced over his shoulder at her. "That was a deception, wasn't it?"

"I'd not have let you into that wardrobe if it wasn't." She glared at him. "Pest-soiled linens would kill you faster than those men would."

"Thank you."

"I'm not in the habit of lying, and I don't thank you for forcing me to it."

He turned to peer out the window again. After a moment he set down the ax, leaning the handle against the wall. Then he ran his hand over his eyes. "They are gone."

"Now your turn has come."

He slumped against the wall. "In a moment."

"No." He couldn't stay, not with his shining golden hair and flashing green eyes. Not with that jaw and those hands and the muscled thighs that filled his breeches. He'd bring it all back if she let him—the urges, the weakness that had led her astray. He wasn't Jahn, but still...he was so..so male. He couldn't stay.

"Four days." He sighed. "Little sleep, less food." He yanked on the tie that held his cape, and it dropped to the floor. "And this..."

Dendra guide her. A rust-red stain colored most of one shoulder of his shirt. Blood. "How..." she gasped.

"Lord Rabal himself." He laughed through gritted teeth. "Got a dirk into me on my way out of his wife's bedroom window."

"His wife?"

"A long story." He closed his eyes and swayed. "For later."

"We have no later. You have to leave, now."

He didn't answer but brushed past her and walked to the room's sole chair. Sighing deeply, he dropped onto the seat, tipped back his head, and closed his eyes.

She crossed to him and stared down into his face. She took one look at the pallor of his skin and the tiny lines of pain around his mouth, and her fingers itched to touch him. To brush the platinum hairs from his face and stroke his brow. Soft feelings, these urges, but they would lead to others. "You can't stay here," she whispered.

"You can't make me leave," he answered, his eyes still shut. "As a priestess you can't turn me away. Or does your goddess' kindness only go to the powerful of this world?"

"No," she protested. "Dendra cares most for the helpless, the hungry."

He opened his eyes and smiled at her, stealing her breath with his beauty. "I'm helpless, little mother. I'm hungry. Care for me."

She stood and stared at him, lost in the heat of his gaze.

He reached out slowly and took her hand in his. He brought it to his face, studying her fingers, caressing them with his own. "Heal me."

His words, his breath fanned over her skin—warm and sweet. No, not sweet. She couldn't taste him, wouldn't let her imagination run in those directions.

She jerked her hand back. "Very well. I'll heal your wound. Then you'll have to go."

He sagged against the back of the chair. "Fine."

She reached to his shirt to ease it away from his wounded shoulder. The fabric whispered under her fingertips, impossibly smooth shalisse—far too elegant for a churl. And his buckskin breeches had been tanned to a butter-softness that molded around him. No common slave, not even one who served in the household, merited such finery. And yet, slave he was, as his collar garishly proclaimed.

What had he said? The lord's wife's bedroom. Oh, Dendra, a handsome-man. She couldn't help herself, she took a step backward.

"So," he gritted. "You know what I am."

"I don't judge."

"Liar." He glared at her. "You can't get away from me fast enough."

"You startled me...I hadn't known..." That much was true, at least. She'd heard of such doings but hadn't credited the stories. That a man would allow himself to be thus used—a noble lady's carnal plaything.

He stared at her a moment more, his gaze boring into her. "Now that you do know, will you still help me?"

"Of course." She approached him again and slid the fabric of his shirt away from his wound. "This doesn't seem deep. You've lost some blood. And you'll need to rest for a time."

"Here?" He glanced around the room. "And where will you put me?"

"In the bed, of course."

He laughed, but the sound had little amusement in it. "In your bed, little mother?"

"I'll sleep elsewhere." She pushed his shirt off his shoulders. "As soon as I've cleaned the wound, I'll help you to bed."

He nodded and sighed, slumping in the chair again. Growing smaller, if that was possible for a man of his size. Like it or not, she'd have to heal him before she could again ask him to leave. Only, please Dendra, let him heal fast.

�֍⟊⟊⟊⟊֍

A groan awoke Kareth—for the third time. She rolled onto her back on the hard floor and stared up into darkness. Maybe the man was just muttering in his sleep this time. Maybe he'd fall silent, and she could rest for a few more hours before the sun came up. But no, he moaned again, louder this time. A cry of pain, of fever. He needed tending, again.

She threw back her makeshift bedding—his cape—and turned toward the hearth. The fire had dwindled down to embers, so she picked up a stick of wood and tossed it onto the top. It caught instantly, sending more heat and light into the room. That would have been enough for herself, but the man had had chills more than once after falling into a deep sleep. She sighed and added a few more logs. She'd have to gather firewood tomorrow.

He groaned again—a strangled, helpless sound. He'd robbed her of her bed and then her rest. Now he'd used up her fuel, too. And she had no choice but to go to him.

She scrambled to her feet and approached the bed. He'd thrown back the blanket and lay curled up on the side of his good shoulder.

A sheen of sweat coated his naked shoulders and back. She'd helped him take off his boots and stockings, but his breeches would have to stay on, no matter what.

Poor fellow. He'd come to her for help, and all she could see in him was danger—a threat to what little inner peace she had managed to find here. She had feared him so much, in fact, for what he was she hadn't bothered to find out who he was.

But enough of fearing him, or pitying him, either. She took a deep breath and focused her mind on her goal—getting him well so he could go. At least his sweat promised healing. Perhaps his fever had broken.

She sat on the edge of the bed and checked the bandage on his shoulder. It appeared secure, still holding the herbal poultice tightly against his wound. Now she need only make him comfortable and trust in Dendra.

She reached to the basin of cold water she'd placed on the bedside table earlier. Keeping her gaze on the man, she swished the cloth around and then wrung it out. His face twisted into a grimace, and one leg lashed out, almost sending her flying to the floor. She resumed her seat and pressed the cloth to the back of his neck where his collar rested just below the nape. He arched, and a hiss escaped his clenched teeth.

"Hush," she crooned to him, all the while dabbing at his neck with the cool cloth. "Hush."

He sighed, and some of the tension seemed to ease out of him. She continued down his spine. He had a beautiful back—broad and smoothly muscled. The sort of back that would offer shelter, warmth—an anchor. But his scent didn't comfort, no matter how pleasant it might be. She could just make it out now—a spicy perfume that tickled her nostrils and haunted the back of her mind. But she couldn't mistake it, not after spending the night wrapped in his cape and surrounded by the smell of him.

Dendra guide her, she had to rid herself of such thoughts. She reached again to the basin and replenished the cloth. With her free hand, she brushed stray hairs from his eyes. As delicate as the shalisse of his shirt, the strands slipped through her fingers and back over his forehead. Odd how they could be so soft when the rest of the man was so hard. She placed the cloth against his cheek and dabbed at his temple.

He let out a soft "ahhhhh," and rolled onto his back, revealing his chest. The broad expanse glistened with moisture, outlining sinew and muscle, two tawny male nipples, and a furrow down the middle. Sleek and hard it was, naked and vulnerable, with not a hair to mar its beauty.

But that was what he was, after all—a man cultivated for beauty, kept for a woman's pleasure. She ought not to expect the scars of hard work on the chest of a man who crept in and out of his lady's bedroom window. She ought to expect exactly what lay before her, a man so flawless her breath froze in her chest at the sight of him. A man whose perfection caught the fire's light and held it in shining glory.

She let her fingers trail over the length of his throat to his shoulders and then along his collar bone. The man was a test—one that would be all to easy to fail. No intellectual challenge this, no bookish debate of good versus evil, but far more dangerous than that. The goddess knew her, had searched out the weakest part of her soul and had sent this man to undo all her cool contemplation. And if she let down her guard for an instant, she'd be lost.

She moistened her cloth and brought it to his chest. She stroked him quickly, trying to give no heed to the smoothness of his skin where her fingers brushed it accidentally. Forcing herself not to notice the heat of his flesh that penetrated through the cloth as she worked. She'd be finished soon. Her duty performed, she could get away from him. Even if she did have to sleep in his cape, cloaked in his scent, she'd be rid of the vision he made in the glow of the fire.

Finished, she put the cloth back into the basin and lifted the blanket to cover him. One glance downward, and she dropped it again, a tiny cry escaping her lips.

There, straining at the front of his breeches—a bulge, long and thick. He was hard in that animal way of men. Impossible but true. And large, so large.

Dendra, give me strength. She couldn't be tempted by this man, a stranger, as she had been by Jahn. She wouldn't let herself be. No matter how sleek he was...how beautiful...how...

He grabbed her then. His hand came up, and his fingers curled around her arm, pulling her down. Down until she rested against the width of his chest, her face inches from his, his breath burning against her cheek.

"No," she cried. And she struggled against him. But he held her fast, his fingers like iron bands around her flesh. "No," she said again, a plea this time.

His eyes opened, and the light of the fire played in their emerald depths. He studied her as if he'd never seen her before. Then his gaze focused, and his features softened. "You," he whispered.

She swallowed hard and nodded.

His grip loosened, but he still held her. His fingers played over her skin, soothing now where they had crushed before. He lifted his head slowly, as if the movement cost him.

"Thank you," he said, his voice as soft as a spring breeze.

She nodded again, helpless to do anything else. He closed his eyes and parted his lips as if to kiss her. She couldn't allow that, didn't dare let his mouth touch hers. But, as strong as he was, how could she prevent it without struggling so hard she'd open the wound in his shoulder again? Breath of the Beast, she'd have to find some other way to free herself.

She pulled back, firmly but cautiously. "Let me go."

He gave a twist with his hips, and suddenly she found herself flat on her back, looking up at him. His eyes were open, flashing sparks of firelight at her. The hardness she had seen before now pressed into her thigh—more tempting that she could have believed possible. This wasn't Jahn, wasn't the man she had loved. Why did the feel of him make her so weak and fluttery inside?

"Please, let me go."

His lips curled into a seductive smile as he gazed down at her.

"Not until I've thanked you properly."

"I don't need any..."

His mouth came down on hers, stealing away her words and dismantling any protest. His lips moved slowly, softly along hers, in a gentle exploration that pleaded for an answer rather than demanded it. And answer she did, helpless creature of the flesh that she was. She took the urgings from his mouth, amplified them, and gave them back until the kiss burned hot and sweet enough to singe the edges of her heart.

"That's it, my little one," he murmured against her lips. "That's it."

"You can't do this," she whispered.

He raised his head and gazed into her eyes. "Do what?"

"Make me feel like this."

"How do you feel?"

She couldn't answer. Didn't dare answer. Had not the words. She shut her eyes and turned her head on the pillow.

He laughed softly. "Does it feel good?"

She said nothing but lay as still as she could, counting her heartbeats, measuring out her breaths.

His lips slid along her jaw and then down the length of her neck—nipping, teasing, setting fire to her skin. His hand brushed aside the light fabric of her shift and reached inside to cup her breast. Her breath caught on a gasp.

"Does that feel good?" His mouth followed along the path his fingers had taken. "Does this?"

His lips closed over her breast, and he sucked gently, as his tongue flicked at the nipple. She cried aloud, and her back arched. He didn't stop but continued the pressure, on and on until she ran her fingers into his hair, catching handfuls of it in her fists.

"Please," she gasped.

His hand trailed over her hip, bunching up her shift and then dipping beneath to stroke the outside of her leg. A fire kindled inside her—the forbidden flame that had burned at her as she had lain so many nights alone and dreamed of Jahn. As she had imagined his caress until the need grew past her control and she had to touch herself to find peace.

No—more. Those nights, that fire, that hunger paled next to this. Even the final reality of Jahn's loving came nowhere near this. Feather soft, his hand slipped over her leg—now over her calf, now inside her knee, and then between her thighs. Close to the throbbing, so close.

"Please."

"Please? Please what, little one?" he repeated. "Please stop? Please more?"

"Please." The word was all she had, all she could hold onto in a world gone mad with throbbing.

"Please here?" he asked finally. Then his fingers found her most feminine spot, parted the petals, and slipped inside to rub her.

She cried aloud, all language gone.

"Yes, here," he whispered. "You're burning."

He stroked her firmly and then gently, until she floated, hovering outside of reality, ready to explode. Then he hesitated just long enough for her to take a gasp of air. And he started again. A maddening rhythm that took her to the brink over and over. She cried out, pressing herself against his fingers, begging with her body for release.

He granted it. His touch quickened, pushed her steadily toward ecstasy and then past it. She rode the crest, her body convulsing. Violent spasms of pure delight. One wave on top of another until she fell, weak and trembling, back onto the mattress—a mere mortal again.

He sighed and rested on top of her. "And now, my little one," he murmured into her ear, "now you have been properly thanked."

Chapter Two

A cold breeze woke Kareth. It grazed her cheeks and blew stray hairs into her face. She opened her eyes and found herself on the floor next to her hearth. The previous night flooded back to her in one humiliating, cheek-burning, stomach-churning wave. What she'd seen. What she'd done. What she'd let the man do to her.

Dendra forgive her, she'd succumbed again, and this time to a man she'd just met. A man who didn't have a name—only smooth muscle, shining eyes, and persuasive lips. And fingers. Oh Dendra, his fingers.

The cool air floated to her again. She clutched his cape around her and glanced across the room. No wonder she was shivering. The cottage door hung open, and tendrils of mist curled inside, incited by early morning light that made the fog shiver like fingers of ice. She looked toward the bed and found it empty, the sheets turned back. The man himself was gone.

She heaved an enormous sigh of relief and hated herself for it. As a healer, she ought to care about him and his wound. He was hurt, perhaps delirious again. And she had his cape, so he couldn't keep himself warm. But instead she only wanted to be rid of him and his temptation. Better he leave her in peace. She wished him well.

He appeared then—filling the threshold, backlit by the mist. The fog touched him only tentatively, brushing against the shalisse of his shirt and then retreating as if frozen. But the light—that was another matter—the morning light shone on him as though the distant sun recognized him as one of its own.

A smile warmed his features, amused and indecent and breathtaking. "Did you sleep well?"

She sat and looked at him, near blinded by the light. Her heart danced a few steps in her chest—turning her earlier relief at his absence into excitement at finding him still here. Traitorous heart.

He stepped fully into the room. In his hand he held the ax, shaft in hand, and he leaned on it for support. "Why is it so blasted cold in here?" he demanded.

She found her voice finally. "Because you left the door open, for one thing."

He grunted and closed the door behind him. Then he walked slowly, haltingly toward the bed, using the ax to anchor his movements. He reached the bed and sank onto it, letting out a deep sigh as he did.

So, back he was. And injured. And still in need of her help. She couldn't turn him away. But she could take charge of things in her own cottage, and she would. She threw back the cape, rose, and walked to him. "Where have you been?"

"I had to go out." He set the ax on the bed beside him.

"If you had awakened me I could have helped you," she answered.

He smiled again, mischief now crinkling the corners of his eyes. "There are some things a man doesn't want help with."

She glared back at him. "Open your shirt."

He laughed but did as he was told. Kareth pushed the shalisse away from his shoulder and lifted the bandage carefully. The redness and swelling of the joint had eased, and the wound itself had lost its angry look.

"Why did you leave me last night?" he asked, his voice soft in her ear.

"You needed your rest."

"I needed your warmth."

She held the cloth of the bandage tightly in her fingers and took a steadying breath.

He moved his lips closer to her face. "Didn't you like what I did?"

Strict obedience forbade lying. But her faith did not demand that she answer him. So she continued her inspection of his shoulder and remained silent.

"I can do much more," he added. "If you'll let me."

"That won't be necessary," she said. "This will heal completely in a few days, and then you can leave."

"Ah, no. Then I'll cut you some firewood, and we can make this cottage warm, you and I."

"I can gather my own firewood, thank you."

"I would have done so today, but I found I wasn't quite up to hard work."

As if he ever had been. "That's very kind of you, Sir..."

"Sir?" he repeated. Then he laughed again, heartily this time. "No one calls a churl 'sir.'"

She replaced the bandage and put her hands on her hips, looking down into his face. "Then, what is your name?"

"Thiele."

"Only Thiele? No sa-name?"

"A churl takes his sa-name from his master. When my lady made a gift of me to Rabal on the occasion of their marriage, I became Thiele sa-Rabal to the world. To myself, I'm Thiele."

"Very well, Thiele. I'm Kareth sa-Damil."

He put his hands over her own, circling her waist with his long fingers. "As soon as I'm well, Kareth sa-Damil, I'll chop you enough wood to build a hot fire—one that will let you go naked in here."

"Why would I want to do that?"

He shrugged. "To amuse me?"

She pushed his hands away from her. "I'll heal you and that only. Then you can leave."

The gleam in his eye grew cold, his mouth tense. "But I can't."

"Of course you can. The border's not far. You can make good your escape."

He slipped his fingers under his collar and gripped the metal in his fist. "With this I'll never get across the border. My lord's magician has conjured up a barrier. No one wearing Rabal's collar of ownership can cross the border undetected."

"That's nonsense. Faith can't be used that way—to throw up a pen to hold people inside like animals."

"Rabal's man has done it somehow." He released the collar and dropped his hand to his lap. "The news went through the churl quarters like wildfire."

"Put out by someone in Rabal's pocket, no doubt," she replied. "To keep you all under control by fear."

"It's true, I tell you."

"And I tell you it's impossible."

He glowered at her, and his hand clenched into a fist again, this time against his thigh. "I can't take the chance. I'd be caught at the border."

"Listen to me. I know something of spells, and the one you describe doesn't exist. Nor would Dendra allow such a perversion of her powers to exist."

His eyes widened again. "You? You know magic?"

"I know something of it, and that only a little."

"Then you're my solution." He took her hands in his. "You'll work the spell to get this collar off me."

"I know nothing of such spells. You must remove the collar yourself."

"I can't. I've tried everything—files, saws, even prayers."

"I can't help you. You have to leave. You have to leave me in peace."

He gripped her fingers, now so tightly the pressure hurt. "Kareth sa-Damil, you will get this collar off me. I won't leave here until you do. Do you understand?"

She looked down into his eyes, into the fire of determination there. Determination and something more. Stay he would, and she would confront that something more. Over and over.

Dendra, give me strength.

"Sun."

Kareth turned and found Thiele standing, looking skyward with his hands shading his eyes. Ferns that came up to her own waist barely reached the middle of his thighs. But the large basket he carried, nearly full now of firewood, still disappeared among the leafy, green fronds. "Finally, some warmth," he added.

"The sun's been out since morning."

"Not so that you'd notice."

She crossed her arms over her chest. "What's wrong with you, anyway? You've done nothing but complain about the fog and the cool air since you got here."

"The spinner's dream," he said.

"Ah, yes," she replied. "For roast meat, a hot fire, and..."

"...and an even hotter lover to warm her bed," he finished.

"I know the proverb. What has that to do with you?"

He looked at her, his gaze even but definitely not tranquil. "My mother was a spinner."

"Spinning is done in mills, with waterwheels to do the work."

"Perhaps in towns where you lived before you became a slave to your goddess," he said.

"A priestess of Dendra," she corrected.

"In grand houses churls still do the work," he went on, "women with long, agile fingers."

"Why?"

He lifted his arm from his side, and the shalisse of his shirt billowed around him, catching the sun's rays and fracturing them into sparks of light and shade, highlights of different hues. "The thread is finer if spun by hand."

She turned and proceeded down the path. "So," she said over her shoulder, "your mother was a spinner."

"A churl like myself."

She pushed aside a fern frond and found a good bit of wood—a branch nearly as thick around as her wrist and yet not too long to fit into the basket. She picked it up, walked back to him, and tossed it onto the pile they had already gathered. Then she raised her eyes and looked into his face. "What has that to do with your complaints about the climate?"

"I spent my time with my mother when I was small," he answered, gazing back down at her. "I understand the spinner's dream."

"Of meat, of fire, and lover?"

"Of warmth." He stared at her in silence for a moment. "And I think you do, too."

"Dendra, how could I?" She turned to search for fuel. "I don't know what you're talking about."

"Shalisse fibers have an oiliness to them."

She pushed aside another fern but found nothing of import underneath. "So I've heard."

"They must be kept cold until they're woven into cloth and the cloth is cured, or they'll go rancid. The churls who work the fibers—the spinners—are kept cold, too."

"How?"

"Unheated rooms in winter. Underground chambers in summer. Sixteen hours a day, seven days a week."

She straightened and turned toward him. "All that time in the cold?"

He stood there and looked straight at her. "In winter, their quarters are underheated, too. To save fuel."

"That's cruel."

He shrugged. "A churl expects no better."

"I always thought the spinner's dream was..." She let her voice trail off, not sure exactly what she had thought. All those women going cold. And all their children, like the one standing before her. Grown now, but once a little boy shivering with cold.

"I thought it was just a saying," she said. "A warning about caring too dearly for the comforts of the flesh."

"Easy enough to rail against the comforts of the flesh when you have enough of them. Harder when you're always wanting."

"I'm sorry."

He smiled, a cockeyed sort of expression that might charm but didn't reassure. "It isn't your fault. You've never worn that sort of shalisse, I'm sure."

"But you have." She raised her hand to point toward his shirt. "You're wearing it now. When you know what it cost the women who spun the fibers."

"This is what I was given to wear," he snapped. "My lady Eria always wanted me in shalisse. She said it felt good against her naked skin."

"I see." Kareth turned away from him, facing down the path into the forest.

"Especially in her most sensitive places—her throat, her breasts, her..."

"I see," she repeated. She strode off, leaving their little pool of sunlight to step into the shade of an ancient emperor tree.

Soft laughter followed her. "There's no disgrace in taking pleasure where it's offered. Not even your Dendra condemns what goes on between men and women."

"I know that."

"And yet you're ashamed of what I did for you last night, aren't you?"

She didn't look at him but continued around the massive trunk of the tree, her attention fixed on the ground.

"Aren't you?" He grasped her elbow and turned her around to face him.

She couldn't avoid his gaze. But instead of mockery, anger, or even a seductive smile, all she found was puzzlement in his deep, green eyes. He didn't understand her confusion over what had happened between them the night before. After all, touching was a simple act for him—something he did because he was supposed to do it. Something he did as an uncomplicated thank-you. But for her, intimacy was a very complicated thing, indeed. It had driven her here, to solitude where she had hoped to arrive at some understanding of herself. She had never expected a man like Thiele to appear and tempt her back into the hunger, the madness.

He set the basket onto the ground and lifted his hand to her face. "You've done nothing wrong, little mother," he murmured, caressing her cheek with his thumb. "You did me a kindness by saving me from the catchers. I paid you back the best way I knew."

"I don't require payment," she whispered. "I'm supposed to help the afflicted. I don't want anything in return."

"But you did." He lowered his hand to her throat and stroked its length, feather-light pressure that set her skin on fire. "You wanted the touching very much. I've never seen a woman respond like that."

"Please don't..."

"Your body came alive in my hands."

She took a step backward, but he followed, his fingers still brushing the length of her neck. She took another step and another until her back met the trunk of the tree and there was no more escape. He stayed with her—so close he towered over her and his chest pressed against her bosom. Her heart raced, and her breath came in a labored, erratic rhythm, crushing her breasts against the rock hardness of him in bondage too sweet to resist. "Thiele, you mustn't," she gasped. "I can't."

"Yes, you can. And yes, I must," he murmured. "Your fire excites me. That doesn't happen often to a man whose business is loving."

"No," she sighed. But the sound came out as a plea, not a command. A plea for him to continue—not to stop, but to press himself against her harder. And he did until the rough bark scratched against her back and her face buried itself into the crook of his neck and she had to taste him.

She pressed her mouth to the base of his throat and felt his pulse beating under her lips. His skin gave off that wonderful perfume of spices and wood smoke she had slept in the night before, and she sipped at him greedily.

He groaned and bent to take her mouth in a searing kiss—hot and honeyed and intoxicating. His tongue opened her lips and entered her, at the same moment that his knee parted her legs and slid between them. He moved his body against hers, the hard ridge of his manhood rubbing her hip—beseeching and commanding, inciting and demanding her response.

She wound her arms around his neck and pulled herself against him, plundering his mouth with her tongue, taking his breath to feed her hunger. He caught her buttocks in his hands and kneaded them. The action brought her even harder against the thick ridge of his arousal, and she answered with her own movements, until her body measured every inch of him. Until she knew exactly how it would feel to have him inside her, rocking, thrusting, pushing her to the edge of herself.

She was going to have him. Now. Here among the ferns, with leaves clinging to her hair and the breeze playing over their bodies. She was going to open the front of his breeches and take out his sex and stroke it until he growled and roared and yanked up her skirts so that he could take her like the animal she was.

Animal. A blind, groping, hungry animal. And she didn't care. She had to have him now, and she didn't care.

Overhead a loud, shrieking cackle sounded. He pulled back from her and lifted his head, scanning the branches. She rested her fists against his chest for support and felt his breast rising and falling in a struggle for air.

An answering call came, every bit as ear-splitting as the first, and Kareth finally recognized it.

"What is that?" he demanded.

"Curo-curas," she answered.

"What?"

"Birds." She took an unsteady breath. "One seldom hears their call so close."

With a fluttering of wings, the curo-curas flew into view. The large cock settled on a branch twenty feet above them and smoothed an errant scarlet feather with his curved beak. His smaller, less colorful hen swooped down next to him and studied her mate with an adoring eye.

"Birds?" Thiele ran his fingers through his hair. "I was distracted from you by a pair of birds?"

"Very loud birds," she answered. And very welcome ones. One more minute and...Dendra, that didn't bear thinking about. "I've seen these two often. They're almost pets."

"Then they won't mind if we resume." He reached for her.

She caught his hands and pushed them away. "But I'll mind."

"Kareth," he chided.

"There's something between us, I'll admit."

"Something?" he repeated. "Something?"

"There's a madness between us."

"Why must you call it madness? It's normal for a man and woman to make love to each other."

Not for me. She leaned against the tree and closed her eyes, digging her fingertips into the cracks in the bark. The touching, the kisses, the sighs had never been normal for her. Her drive was too strong. It robbed her of all reason, made her want people she couldn't have. It made her do things she shouldn't do.

His fingers brushed her shoulder. She jumped and pushed them away. "I can't," she cried. "I can't make love to you. I can't."

"Very well." He sighed. "I won't make love to you. But I will stay until we've found a way to rid me of this collar, and I will give you comfort while I'm here."

She turned and stared at him. The indecent smile had returned to his face. With the sunlight forming a golden halo around his head and sandy brows lifted in amusement, he looked for all the world like a naughty little boy. But the heat in his eyes belied any resemblance to innocence. Comfort her, would he? How would he do that without raising the fire again in her blood? He couldn't, of course, which he knew very well.

Somehow she'd have to convince him to leave. And until he did, she'd have to keep him at arm's length. But how? Dendra, how?

゚゚ヽ(ꞋꞋꞋ)ノ゚゚

The moon was high in the sky by the time Kareth led Thiele to the pool to bathe. She held a lantern in front of her, although she'd already memorized the path. If Thiele tripped and fell, he might reinjure his shoulder, which would delay his leaving. She hadn't yet arrived at how she would convince him to leave when he was healed. He truly seemed to believe the story about the magic barrier at the border. But convince him she would, and then she'd be rid of him.

He crashed behind her now, just as he had when running through the woods the day before with the catchers after him. Everything about the man was an intrusion, from his power and his size to his scent and his wicked smile. She would have given him the lantern and sent him out alone, but he might have ended up lost, blundering through the forest bringing grief to ferns and wildlife alike.

No matter. She'd sit by while he bathed, looking safely off into the darkness until he finished. Then she'd take him back to the cottage. She'd have her bath after he had fallen asleep.

They turned a corner in the path, and a small shape scurried past her and disappeared into the undergrowth. Behind her Thiele gasped and stopped in his tracks. "What was that?"

She laughed softly. "No need for secrecy. There's no one here."

"Then what was that?"

"Only an animal."

"But what type?"

She turned back to face him. He glanced around, his eyes darting from one shadow to the next. For such a big man, he frightened at very small things. "A woodlar, perhaps, or a scimp. Little creatures. They won't hurt you."

"Little, eh?" he answered. "The vermin that lived in the grand house walls were little enough, and pest-ridden."

"There's no pest here. The forest is a healing place."

He looked down at her, skepticism clear in his gaze.

She reached out and took his hand. "Come."

She turned and led him down the path again, the lantern held before them. "Why did we wait until dark to bathe?" he asked.

Why, indeed? Because she couldn't bear to look at him naked, and yet she wanted to be nearby. Wanted to hear his body enter the water. Wanted to smell him when he'd finished rinsing the saarflowers from his hair.

"We spent most of the day gathering wood so the fire would be big enough for you," she answered. "Then I was hungry and wanted supper after all that work."

"Gave you an appetite, did it?"

She glanced at him out of the corner of her eye and found that smile again. The one he'd teased her with all afternoon. "I was hungry for my supper and that only."

Now it was his turn to laugh softly. "Of course."

"We're here now, and you'll thank me when you've done."

"For plunging me into frigid water?" he grumbled. "I don't think so."

"Did I say the water would be cold?"

"What else could it be?"

She lifted the lantern high, showing him the pool and the clouds of steam rising from it.

"Mercy, woman," he gasped. "How did you do this?"

"I didn't. It's only an underground hot spring."

"It looks like a saint's afterlife." He charged toward the pool, stripping off his shirt, dropping it beside the path as he went. She set the lantern down and turned to look into the forest. Behind her more clothing dropped into the undergrowth. Then water splashed, and he let out a loud "Ahhhh."

She put her fingers over her mouth and giggled. More splashing sounded and more animal noises of contentment. "Ah, little one. Of all the kindnesses you've done me, this must be the greatest."

"I'm glad you like it."

"The water's perfect, as though you heated it for me. Are you sure it isn't magic?"

"Absolutely certain."

"Thank you, anyway." Splash, splash, splash. "Thank you a hundred times."

"You're very welcome. Now I'll pick you some saarflowers for you to wash with." She walked to a spot a few yards away where a saarbush grew, draped in rays of moonlight that had managed to slip between two emperor trees. She picked a few branches and walked back with them to the pool. Keeping her eyes averted from Thiele, she reached down to hand him the herbs.

"What's this?" he asked, taking them.

"Saarflowers. Moisten them and rub them into a lather to wash your hair."

"I know this scent. The potion I used on my lady's hair smelled like this."

"The essence is made into a soap."

"Yes." He splashed some more and crushed the flowers between his palms, releasing the fragrance of saar into the night. "Aren't you coming in?" he asked after a moment.

"I'll bathe later."

"Please, Kareth, there's plenty of room."

"I don't think..."

"Let me wash your hair, as I did for Eria," he said. "You have very beautiful hair."

She tugged at her braid, and the gentle pulling let her imagine how it would feel to have his fingers in her hair, pressing against her scalp. It would feel wonderful to have him wash her hair, to sit in that deliciously hot water with Thiele and let him minister to her.

"Please," he entreated. "Let me do that for you."

"All right." She unlaced the bodice of her gown and lifted it over her head. Her shift went next, dropping beside the gown. She stood for a moment, naked except for her crystal amulet, and the cool night air washed over her, warring with the steam from the pool to raise little bumps on her flesh. She looked directly at Thiele. He smiled an innocent invitation and extended his hand. She took it and lowered herself into the pool, finding her favorite rock and sitting on it.

"That's better," he declared. He rubbed some flowers between his palms, making a thick lather. "Eria loved for me to wash her hair."

She unplaited her braid and turned her head, offering her hair to him. He massaged the herbs into it in a hot, soapy balm.

"She had nice hair," he continued. "Bright red and curly. But yours is much softer."

"How did she..." She hesitated, searching for the right word. Find you? Get you? Buy you? "How did you come into your lady's service?"

"I was fourteen and working in her father's granary. She saw me and felt stirrings." His fingers made lazy circles over her scalp, soothing and invigorating all at once. "Eria called me a pretty child, even though she was only sixteen herself. She asked her father, and he gave me to her. He gave her everything she wanted."

"How terrible," Kareth said. "To be chosen like a prize animal."

"Not at all. She took me into the house, found a position for my mother so that she could be warm in her last years, at least. Rinse."

Kareth dipped her head back, bringing the hot water up over her ears. He stroked her hair, pulling it back and spreading it out between his fingers. Then he guided her back to a sitting position and lathered his hands again.

"Eria was a stunning young woman—all elegance and bright colors." His fingers slipped into her hair for a second time. "Copper hair, sapphire eyes, alabaster skin. After I first saw her in the granary, I couldn't take my eyes off her. The first sight of her naked, waiting for me in her bed almost unmanned me."

"Did you love her?" Kareth whispered.

He sighed. "At first I did. We had a game of our own—if I were in love with you, we called it. We made up stories of how we'd run away and live together, just the two of us. I half believed them...then."

"What happened?"

His fingers stopped their motion through her hair. "One night she sent me to pleasure a friend of hers who was visiting. I was to share our intimacies with a stranger."

"Did you...that is...could you?" Dendra, how could she even ask such a question? It was certainly not her concern.

"Was my manhood up to the job?" He laughed and resumed his massage of her scalp. "Not really. But I still had my hands and my tongue. She was satisfied."

"Thiele, I didn't mean..."

"I've schooled my cohort since then. He performs when I want him to."

"What about your pleasure?"

"My pleasure? Who would care about my pleasure?"

"Why, you, of course."

He laughed again. "What odd ideas you have, little one. You've lived alone in this forest too long."

"Still..."

"Rinse."

She ducked her head into the water. He smoothed his fingers through her hair, rinsing away the flowers and their fragrant oil. She pushed back up, and he caught her around the waist and pulled her into his lap. She ought to object, to move away. But it felt so right to float in his arms, looking into the moonlight, listening to the breeze rustle through the emperors, smelling saarflowers and warm, clean man.

He moved his hips and, unhindered by clothing or any other barrier, his hardness pressed into her back.

"Have you commanded your cohort to perform now?" she whispered.

"You're different, my little sorceress. He has a mind of his own where you're concerned."

"I've told you—I'm no sorceress. I know no magic."

"You've worked your charms on me. I've never been so continually, so maddeningly hard and ready."

At that she did try to pull away. But he held her firmly. "Let me show you how it feels," he murmured into her ear.

His hands moved from her waist, up and over her ribs, finally catching her breasts in his palms. Her breath came hard on a gasp, as he kneaded and tugged softly—using just the right pressure to heat her blood to the same temperature as the currents of water that lapped at her collar bone and slid between her thighs.

"Yes," he whispered, his thumbs now playing over her nipples, making them hard. Achingly hard. She bit her lip, but a cry escaped from between them before she could stop it.

"Yes," he repeated, as his hands moved lower. Back over her ribs in a slow caress. To her hips and down to her buttocks. He smoothed his palms over the outside of her thighs and pulled her against his hardness. She melted inside, tipped her head back against his shoulder and sighed and rubbed herself against him. If she made just the right move—it wouldn't take much—she could rise up and lower herself onto him. She could take him inside her. And he would...he would...he would...

He rose abruptly, setting up waves of hot water around her and leaving her bereft. She glanced up to find him beside the pool, moonlight spilling over his shoulders and reflecting out of his eyes, his manhood standing erect. He reached his hand down to her. "Come, Kareth sa-Damil. It's time."

Chapter Three

Kareth stood in her little cottage and looked around her as though seeing everything for the first time. And indeed, this was the first time the room had been so brightly lit by a fire. The first time a man had stood by that fire, piling wood onto it until the flames jumped high, their tops disappearing up the chimney. The first time in this place that she would lose herself in a man's embrace. The night before had been only a sample, that she knew. Tonight her body would reveal how deep her passions ran, and this man—Thiele—would know how to play them.

He finished building the fire and turned to her, stretching out his arms. "Come, little one, let me make you warm."

She went to him. No point in resisting—he'd only bring her to the hearth if he had to. She stood only a foot away from him, staring up into his face. The light of the fire captured his beauty as the moonlight had before. The long shadow of eyelashes against his cheek, the angle of his jaw, the seductive curve of his lips. Those lips could move softly over hers, or they could burn against her skin. They pursed now, as he took her face in his hands. He tipped it upward and planted a soft kiss on her forehead.

How did one resist such tenderness, even knowing the madness that would follow? Kareth had not the strength, so she leaned into him and sighed. He lowered his mouth to hers and took her lips, softly again. He lingered at her mouth, his lips and tongue tasting her, tempting her, daring her to come to him for more honey, more heat. She tried to embrace him, but he held her away, drawing out the kiss for heartbeat after thundering heartbeat.

His hands moved to the closure of her bodice and unlaced it.

One last little voice of sanity sounded in her brain. This hadn't gone too far yet. She could still stop. "Thiele, no," she whispered.

"Yes." He moved his mouth to her ear and nibbled at the lobe.

"You promised," she breathed. "You said you wouldn't make love to me."

He lowered his head further and kissed her neck. "I lie sometimes." She caught his arms, digging her fingertips into his flesh.

He straightened and looked down into her face, his own expression drugged with passion. His eyes hung sleepily half-open, his lips moist and parted. "You want this, Kareth. You need this."

"Thiele..."

"If this were only for me, I'd resist. As hot as you've made me, I'd still hold back. But you—you're trembling, vibrating in my hands."

"The cold," she tried.

"It's not cold in here." He pulled her into his arms and buried his face into her neck. "And you're hot, too. You're burning. Let me put the fire out."

He held her against him, and she felt his hardness again. He crushed her to him, and a moan escaped his throat. He wanted her, and, Dendra help her, she wanted him. She would have him before he left. So, why not now?

"Yes," she whispered. "Yes, Thiele, take me."

He swept her up in his arms and spun her around, letting out a triumphant whoop. When he stopped, the room continued to swirl around her. Only his face stayed in focus—beautiful and radiant with passion. "Ah, woman. How you make me work to have you. I'll have my revenge. Wait and see."

"Take it now. Please, take it now."

He headed toward the bed. He laid her down softly and reached for her gown. She offered no resistance but instead lifted herself to allow him to slip it and then her shift over her shoulders and head. When she lay back again, her crystal slipped smoothly into the valley between her breasts.

Thiele sat back on his heels on top of the coverlet and gazed at her, his eyes wide.

"Mercy, woman. You're beautiful."

She brought her hands up and over her nakedness. But he reached out and pushed them away. "I want to look at you," he said.

"You've seen me."

"It was dark last night and again tonight when we bathed. I never would have believed that under your loose clothes I'd find a form so perfect."

"Don't flatter me."

"It's not flattery." He reached out to run his fingertips over the length of her throat and then along her shoulder. "You don't have a glass here. You have no idea how you look."

Perhaps not, but she knew how she felt. And right now the gentle pressure of his fingers made her skin come alive. She lay perfectly still, watching him. Watching his gaze follow the progress of his hand, along her side down to her breast.

"And these," he sighed, covering one globe with his palm. "So full and round."

He flicked his thumb over the nipple, and it grew hard, standing erect for him. A charge of pure pleasure shot through her, from the point of contact to her core. The restlessness started in her belly and below. Soon it would be a throbbing, and she would have to use her all the air she could fit into her lungs to beg him to take her. For now, his fingers trailed along her ribs to the flare of her hip.

"And your thighs." He stroked the outside of her leg. "So soft, so warm. So vulnerable I'm tempted to nibble on them."

His hand moved to the inside of her leg and slid up and down slowly. Up and down. Until the throbbing started and built.

"I think I will nibble on you here," he murmured, his voice growing dark and husky. "I'll start here." He touched a spot just inside her knee. "And move along here." His fingers slid up her thigh. "Until I get here."

He touched her at her most sensitive spot, where her legs came together, and her hips began to move. He rubbed her, and the pleasure grew into a hot flame, its center at her core.

"Ah, yes. I like this part of you best. Your sex, so hot and sweet. So little, it's bound to grip me tightly. I swear I could come just thinking of it."

"Take me," she whispered.

"In a moment. First—while I still have some control—I'll do what I promised." He lowered himself to the mattress and slid his arms under her hips, lifting them and pulling them toward his mouth. Dendra, he meant to do it, he meant to kiss her there. He pressed his lips to her inner thigh. Then he stroked her with his tongue and nipped at her with his teeth. Heavenly and gentle. Incendiary and irresistible. If he did that at the juncture of her thighs, at the center of her femininity, she'd splinter into so many fragments she'd never put herself back together. She'd die with the joy.

But she didn't.

He buried his nose into the curling hairs of her sex and breathed hotly on her. She gasped, and her hips rose, but she didn't die. He gripped her tightly, even though she moaned and tossed about. But she didn't die. When his lips closed over the throbbing nub and sucked, she was very much alive. She cried his name and dug her fingers into his hair, holding his face against her.

"Thiele! Oh, Thiele. I'm going to...it's on me. I can't stop it."

He rose above her, taking away the pressure. The caresses that had her ready to burst. She whimpered in disappointment and moved her hips again. Searching, searching for something to ease the ache.

"Not yet, little one. I can take you still higher."

"Now, please. Now."

"Undress me."

She took a shuddering breath and tried to slow her heart. The fire still raged in her loins, but she did as he asked, tugging the tails of his shirt out of his breeches, pulling the shalisse over his head, and tossing it to the floor. She reached to the buttons of his breeches and fumbled with them. Just under the ruckskin, his sex strained to be free. As she twisted first one button and then another, he moved his hardness against her hands. She curled her fingers over the thick ridge of flesh, and he took a sharp inward breath.

"Hurry, little one. I want to feel your fingers around me."

The fury of his passion helped her bank her own need—to keep her own lust at the simmer, demanding and hot. Ready to run free the moment he could join her. She worked at the buttons more calmly now, savoring his every moan, his every movement. Finally, she had the ruckskin open, and she could reach inside and take his sex into her hands. It was heavy and swollen into an impossible hardness, smooth and hot. She curled her fingers around the shaft and stroked its length.

He gritted his teeth in an expression of desire that approached pain. "Ah, Kareth...I never...ah, Kareth...stop now. You have to stop."

She dropped her hands to her sides and looked up at him, waiting. She didn't have to wait long. He stripped out of the breeches, nearly ripping them at the seams in his haste. Then he parted her legs and positioned himself between them.

She slipped her arms around his neck and pulled him down to her. He moved his hips, and the tip of his sex touched her own. She jerked up to rub herself against him, and in an instant she was lost again. The fire, the hunger, the need came over her again, stealing her breath. The universe centered at the point where his hardness pressed against her throbbing. She dug her fingertips into his back and held on as he moved against her. She couldn't hold out much longer. She was going to shatter, any moment now. Just one more movement. Just one.

She shifted, only a few inches, but enough to bring him to the entrance of her core. She took the tip of him inside her, and a shout tore from her chest. He thrust—deep, so deep inside her. She did die then, after only one thrust. She shuddered and convulsed. She grasped at him, over and over. Pulling at his manhood, milking him with her spasms.

He held absolutely still as she floated back onto the coverlet, her hands still clutching his back. He bent his lips to her ear. "Was it good, little one?"

She took a few gasping breaths. "Yes," she finally managed.

"I nearly came, too. Feeling you around me like that was almost more than I could bear."

She opened her eyes and found him smiling down at her. Not with mockery but tenderly. "Truly?" she whispered.

"Truly." He kissed her gently. "We'll just wait now until you're ready again."

She moved her hips and felt him inside her—still so big and hard. "Now," she said.

"Now?"

She lifted her hips, sliding herself over the length of him. "Now."

"Mercy, woman." He let out a strangled laugh and moved inside her. "I won't last."

"Now," she said for a third time.

He obeyed, pulling himself almost out of her and then surging forward to fill her. He did it again, growling as he did. Again and again, stretching her. The passion flared in her belly. The same inexorable climb to bliss.

He thrust deeply now, savagely, out of control. She joined him in his hunger, reality slipping away until she was left with nothing but him—his breath in her hair, his back under her palms, his manhood inside her. She reached the precipice again and flew over, taking him with her. He shuddered in her arms, cried out in his release, and collapsed on top of her.

She stroked his hair, raising the perfume of saar to her nostrils, and sighed.

After a moment, he rolled onto his side and slipped his arm around her waist, pulling her to him—her back to his front—and cradling her head in the crook of his elbow. "Ah, Kareth," he murmured into her ear. "You are a sorceress. I haven't felt like that since I was a lad whose breeches filled with lust at the mere thought of a woman."

Not any woman, though—Kareth knew that. Only his lady Eria. She of the copper hair, the sapphire eyes, and the alabaster skin.

"No," he said, as though contradicting her very thoughts. "I've never felt like that. Even with Eria."

"Then why did you continue to sneak into her bedroom after

she was married?" Dendra, forgive her for asking that question, loaded with envy as it was. Already she was slipping from her faith. Lovemaking was one thing—the hideous emotion jealousy another. Still, she lay holding her breath for his answer.

"I didn't sneak into her bedroom."

"But you said yesterday that Lord Rabal stabbed you as you were climbing out of her bedroom window."

"He stabbed me not because I was in her room, but because I was escaping from it."

"I don't understand."

He pulled her closer and kissed her shoulder. "I was still welcome in my lady's bed. I was even expected to keep her occupied while Rabal toured the countryside inspecting his holdings and finding his own amusements. What I wasn't allowed to do was drug Eria and run away."

"You did that?" she asked. "Even though you'd been happy with her?"

"Content, not happy. Until she married that stupid oaf. The two of them deserved each other, so I decided to leave them alone together." He smoothed a hand up her ribs and cupped her breast. "And I ended up here."

His fingers played over her bosom, making nonsensical patterns on her skin. Now on one breast, now on the other, now in the valley between. What would have set her on fire only moments before now comforted—so quiet, so tender, so intimate. She sighed again and snuggled back against him.

"How did you end up here?" he asked.

"I came of my own choice," she answered, lying. The order had given her a choice between the desert, a mountaintop, and the forest. But the decision to use solitude to search out her heart and soul had not been a voluntary one. Jahn had been allowed to seek his own solution to what had happened between them, and he had chosen to stay with the people who loved him. No—adored him, worshipped him. All that had been left for her was to leave.

"Who was he?" Thiele asked, reading her mind again. How

did he do that?

"Who?"

He nuzzled her ear. "The man. You've been with a man before."

"A priestess of Dendra isn't required to be a virgin."

"Who was he?" he repeated.

"My teacher," she admitted. "We became involved."

"And for that you had to be banished to the wilderness?"

"I wasn't banished."

"That's what this looks like."

She stroked the back of his hand in silence for a moment. In the hearth a log split, sending out a hiss and shooting sparks up into the chimney. "I was very privileged to study with Jahn. He took only the best, most promising students. I took advantage of our closeness. I tempted him."

"You tempt me," he said, hugging her ribs. "Where's the sin in that?"

"It's not supposed to be that way between teacher and student." She closed her eyes, trying to block out the memories. Being with Jahn in his study—rapture on his face, twining her arms around his neck, their lips meeting. Then their bodies falling back together onto the thick carpets in front of the fire. "It's supposed to be a spiritual bond, the most important one of the student's life."

"And who do you suppose is responsible for keeping the bond spiritual? The student or the teacher?"

"You don't understand," she whispered.

"Then explain it to me."

"Jahn didn't normally take women as students. I had to beg him even to consider me. I felt that I could learn more from him than the others, and I so wanted to serve."

"You served him well enough, I'm sure."

She rolled over to face Thiele. "He wasn't like that. He was a great teacher. If I hadn't given in to my urges, if I hadn't pressed him so hard to love me, I could have found enlightenment through his teaching."

Thiele stroked his thumb over her cheek. "He used you."

"No."

"Believe me, I know. I've been used my entire life. At least with churls and their masters, the using is done honestly."

"Jahn loved me," she said, not looking Thiele in the eye but staring at his chest. "He told me so."

Thiele slipped a finger under her chin and raised her face to his. "Then why didn't he marry you?"

"He had a wife," she whispered. "And children."

"The bastard," he cursed softly.

"You don't understand."

"I understand this. He took your innocence, didn't he?"

"I gave it freely."

"He didn't push you away when he realized what was happening between you, did he? Send you to another teacher?"

She lowered her gaze again.

"I thought not," he muttered. "I'll wager he wasn't even much of a lover. Was he?"

She looked back up at him. "How could you know that?" she gasped.

"Oh, Kareth." He kissed her gently. "Men who don't care about women don't learn how to pleasure them."

Dendra, yes, that made sense. The pain she had felt the first time with Jahn. How quickly he had finished each time after that. It hadn't been anything like what she'd shared this night with Thiele.

"And so you were sent away where you couldn't do any harm to his reputation or his marriage," he continued. "And so he won't take any more female students. At least not until some young, earnest innocent begs him to. Then he'll do it—oh so reluctantly. He'll have his pleasure with her, and she'll end up here or somewhere worse."

She rolled over, presenting him with her back. She couldn't contradict him, so she turned away from him. But he wouldn't let her get far. His arm snaked around her again, tugging her across the coverlet until she snuggled against him whether she wanted to or not.

"It's not your fault, little one," he murmured into her ear. "The men in charge—the Rabals and the Jahns—they get what they want, and there's precious little you and I can do about it."

"That sounds so hard."

"It's true. All we can do is protect ourselves as best as we can." His fingers moved again to her breast, and her breath caught as he toyed with the nipple. "And comfort each other."

His hand dipped lower, over her ribs to her belly, pulling her firmly against him, against the hardness that pressed into her backside. Dendra, he was ready again, and she caught fire inside— wanting him instantly. He lifted her leg up and over him and entered her from behind. Then his fingers parted the petals of her sex and dipped between them to stroke her. She gasped and rocked against him and forgot all about the universe outside.

***

Cammite had two properties that made it of value. First, it took on the hues of other elements, combining them with its own particular luminescence to produce an astonishing range of colors. Second, despite cammite's porosity, or perhaps because of it, its alloys were possessed of a hardness such that only special cutters studded with ground-up gems could scratch the surface. Perfect material for gaudy jewelry and for churl's collars.

Kareth had no special cutter and so had only her faith to remove Thiele's collar. Unfortunately, she didn't have his cooperation, and the afternoon had turned into a battle of wills. One that was rapidly getting out of her control.

She glanced at him now where he stood by the window, tapping his foot against the floor boards. "Come sit back down," she said. "We'll try again."

He looked over at her, and an eyebrow shot up. "That same gibberish? I'd rather not, thank you."

"They're prayers," she corrected.

"Gibberish," he muttered.

"Gibberish or prayers, they won't do you any good standing over there," she snapped.

He huffed and stood where he was for a moment. Then he crossed the room and sat back on the bed.

She took his hands and curled her fingers around his, interweaving them over his collar. "Now, concentrate," she ordered for at least the fifth time.

He glared up at her, his eyes gone bright emerald with impatience. "This won't work."

"Thiele..."

"You don't want this to work."

"Don't be ridiculous."

"If you get the collar off me, I can escape over the border. And you don't want me to leave."

She took a deep breath and stared at him. Dendra forgive her, as much as she wanted to give him his freedom, she couldn't deny that she didn't want him to leave. In the past few days that he had spent with her, she'd had more touching from him, more tenderness, than she'd had in the whole rest of her life. She might have mistaken what went on between them for true love, if she hadn't known that such was his profession, what he'd been trained to do.

"I'm doing my best," she answered, still holding tightly on to his fingers. "You might try to help me."

"Help with what?" he grumbled. "I'm no magician."

"Neither am I."

"You said you knew magic," he said.

"I said I knew something of it. I can't recite some charm to remove your collar. I need your faith, too."

He pushed her from him and rose. Hands clenched in fists by his side, he strode away again—this time to the hearth—and then turned back to glower at her. "I have no faith."

"But you must have faith."

"In your Dendra?"

"Not mine. The goddess belongs to everyone."

He snorted at that. "And so I thought, too, when I was a babe. Dendra would make everything right. If only I had faith in her. And where did my faith get me? Whoredom."

"You're not a whore," she answered.

"What would you call it?" he demanded. He rested his arm against the mantle and stared into the fire. "And the irony of it all, the merciless, crushing cruelty is that I made out better than the others. The ones who worked the fields until their backs were permanently stooped. The ones in the mines, coughing out blood with their last breaths."

"Dendra has nothing to do with that."

He glared back at her. "Dendra has nothing to do with anything. She's a figment of your imagination."

"No."

"And a tool the masters use to keep their chattel under their control."

"You must believe in something greater than yourself," she said. "You have to, or you're not fully alive."

"I believe in magic," he answered. "I've seen that with my own eyes. I've seen Rabal's magician bend cammite rods with his bare hands, turn water into blood."

"Mere tricks," she countered. "Magic without faith is a perversion of Dendra and the power she's given to all of us."

He snorted again and turned away from her, back to the hearth. "She hasn't given me any power."

"But she has. If only you'll look inside yourself to find it."

He stood, staring into the fire, his fist clenching and unclenching over the mantel. "Get this collar off me," he said finally. "Please, Kareth."

"I can't. Not by myself."

He left the fireplace to come to stand beside her. He towered over her, enveloping her in his scent, his warmth. "I'll do whatever you want," he murmured into her ear. "I know how to satisfy you. In these days together I've learned how to make your body sing."

"Thiele, don't."

He touched her breast, not roughly but without his usual tenderness. "This is what you want, isn't it?" he whispered.

"No, it isn't," she answered.

He straightened and glared down at her. "Don't deny it, Kareth. I've been with you. I know what you want. You want a handsome-man of your own, someone you can keep enslaved to pleasure you."

"That's not true," she gasped. And it wasn't. Dendra help her, it wasn't.

"You're no better than Eria," he gritted. "Worse, maybe. At least she dealt with me honestly."

"Curse you, Thiele, I am dealing with you honestly. I want to help you. I want you to be free."

"No, you don't. This is what you want." He gripped her breast more tightly, rubbing his thumb over the cloth of her bodice until the nipple beneath grew hard to the point of pain.

"Stop that," she ordered.

"And this," he growled, moving his hand to the place where her legs met. He groped her roughly through her gown, pulling at her sex in a cruel parody of their usual intimacy.

She slapped him, hard. The sound of the blow rang out, echoing off the walls of the tiny cottage. He reeled under it, taking a few steps backwards. His eyes filled with emotion, first surprise and then rage and finally pain.

She brought her fingers to her mouth and stared back at him, pleading with her eyes for him to understand. She hadn't meant to hurt him. But she couldn't let him do that to her, touch her in anger that way.

His stared back, and his jaw clenched, as if holding words inside him that he didn't dare let out. After a moment he turned and strode toward the door.

"Don't go," she cried. "We can get your collar off—together— if only you'll believe we can."

"I believe nothing," he snarled. He yanked the door open, slamming it against the wall. Then he stepped outside and walked down the path until he disappeared among the trees and ferns.

Chapter Four

He came back a few hours later, looking subdued and thoroughly ashamed of himself. He stood on the threshold, his hand still on the doorknob, and gazed at her out of little-boy eyes. As though he didn't know whether she'd welcome him in or slap him again.

She ought to slap him, of course. She ought to let him know beyond any doubt how boorishly he had acted. But the look of him took her breath away, as usual. And he actually had managed a blush of contrition. How could she stay angry with him?

"I'm sorry," he said finally. "You'll forgive me?"

"I already have."

"I have to trust you, after all you've done for me. I do trust you."

She smiled and nodded.

"It's just so hard sometimes..." He gripped his collar in his fist. "This thing..."

"I know."

"Perhaps you do. You care so much, perhaps you do." He cleared his throat and shifted his weight from one foot to the other. "I've made you a present."

"In the short time you've been gone?"

He smiled shyly. "Actually, I've been working on them for days now. They're not much." He reached inside his shirt and pulled out two tiny figurines—wood carvings. Of birds.

"The curo-curas," she exclaimed.

He closed the door, walked to her, and put the little figures in her hand. "I know how you love that loud pair."

Almost as much as I love you. No, please, no. She couldn't love him. He had to leave her, and she didn't dare love him. "Thank you, Thiele," she whispered.

"They're crude, I'm afraid. And I couldn't capture the colors at all."

She stared at the figures in her hand. He'd done an wonderful job—smoothing the wood to a fine texture and depicting the curo-curas in a life-like pose. He even had the crests right, the male's more prominent than the female's. "They're beautiful. But I don't have a gift for you."

"No matter." His smile grew into a grin, and the light of mischief she adored entered his eyes. "Now that I'm forgiven, maybe you'll sit with me for a while."

"Of course."

He took her hand and led her to the chair. Once there, he dropped into it and pulled her down into his lap. She half expected to feel the familiar hardness against her hip. She usually did when she sat with him this way. But it wasn't there this afternoon. Instead he nuzzled his face into her hair and hugged her close, seemingly content simply to hold her.

"I will have to leave, little one," he murmured. "Whether we get this collar off me or not."

And he would, she knew that. Thiele would never be safe anywhere near Rabal's domain, no matter where he hid. And she would have to go back to her contemplative life. But a tiny voice inside her cried out to know why. Why couldn't he just stay? Why couldn't they live together, sharing kisses and heartbeats, until they died in each other's arms?

"If the catchers find me with you, they'll take you, too," he said. "They're not much easier on people who help escaped churls than they are on the churls themselves."

She set the bird carvings in her lap and slipped her arms around Thiele's neck. "I don't care about that."

"But I do. I didn't when I arrived here, much to my shame. But I do now." He sighed against her skin. "Kareth, Kareth, you make me feel things...want things. Impossible things."

She pulled back and stroked his face. "Like what?"

He gazed at her, the green of his eyes so deep she could drown in it. "Like taking you with me."

"I couldn't go." She couldn't. She hadn't even begun to explore her inner life, the hungers and the failings that had brought her here. If she didn't know herself, how could she give herself to anyone else? Even to Thiele?

"And I couldn't take you to the outside," he said. "It's a wild place. People live in mud huts and slit each other's throats for no reason at all."

"So I've heard. Do you suppose the stories are true?"

"That doesn't matter. With no wealth, I couldn't offer you anything, not even protection."

She trailed her fingers along his jaw. "And if you were wealthy?"

"But I'm not."

"Pretend," she murmured. "Pretend you had taken all of Lady Eria's jewels with you when you ran away."

"Ah, pretend is it?"

She shrugged. "You know, a game."

"Well, then..." He tipped back his head and studied the ceiling. "If I had all of Lady Eria's jewels...let me see...I'd give them to you."

"No," she said, nudging him in the ribs. "That isn't very creative."

"I'll try again." He squeezed his eyes tightly closed, as though the effort taxed his brain. "I know. I'd use the jewels to start up a smuggling operation—liquors from the outside into Rabal's domain and churls from the inside out." He opened his eyes and grinned at her. "Very profitable business, smuggling."

"And very daring," she said. "Very like you."

"Then I'd set myself up as a border lord. I'd build the most fantastical castle for you, with huge banners flying from the turrets and with sharp-toothed rudwurms."

"And what would I do while you were accomplishing all this?"

"Nothing but satisfy my lust," he answered, his eyes sparkling.

"I wouldn't have anyone in the castle with us—not even servants—until I'd ravished you in every one of its rooms."

"Dendra," she exclaimed. "How may rooms would it have?"

"Dozens," he answered. "Hundreds."

"And you'd have your way with me in each of them? Even the
kitchen?"

"Especially the kitchen. I'd bend you over the work table and
take you with the smell of baking bread in my nostrils."

She shoved his shoulder. "And who'd bake that bread, I'd like
to know? And feed the livestock and wash the floors? And all the
other chores?"

"I hadn't thought of that."

She harumphed. "Just like a man. You work your women near
to death all the while insisting you keep us in the lap of luxury."

His slipped his fingers around her waist and rocked her gently.
"We'd have servants, then. But they'd have to stay out of sight.
And I couldn't let them see you."

"Why in Dendra's name not?"

His grin broadened and a gleam entered his eyes that was
absolutely evil. "Because I'd keep you half-naked all the time.
That's why. So I could always look at you."

Her cheeks flamed, and she squirmed in his lap. "Thiele..."

"No more than ribbons and scraps of shalisse." He slid his hand
over her shoulder. "Hanging from here, over your breasts, your
beautiful breasts." His fingers trailed down the valley between her
breasts to her belly. "Covering your hips but loosely so that the
smallest draft would lift the material and expose you to me."

"You'd like that, would you?" she said.

He smiled and parted his lips. She kissed them, using the moves
he had taught her in their days together. Breathing into his mouth
in exactly the way she knew would arouse him. It worked. He
rubbed himself against her, and his swelling manhood pressed into
her hip.

"You'd like to have me naked?" she murmured against his
mouth. "Even if I got cold?"

"I'd keep you hot," he answered, his voice husky with desire. "Always and forever hot."

"Then I do have a present for you, after all." She picked up the carved birds in her lap and rose. "Close your eyes, and don't open them until I tell you to."

He squeezed his eyes shut, and Kareth walked to the wardrobe. She placed his presents carefully on top, opened the door, and leaned inside to rummage around in the bottom. After a moment her fingers found the parcel where she had hidden it on her first day in the forest. She'd bought the thing in a dark little shop, meaning to wear it for Jahn. But in the end, she hadn't had the chance. She'd never thought to put it on for anyone else, hadn't really understood why she kept it. But now she had a reason, and Jahn no longer mattered. Only Thiele mattered.

She set the parcel on the floor while she stripped out of her gown and shift, letting them fall wherever they cared to. Then she bent, untied the string that held the plain brown sacking together, and removed the flimsy under-gown from inside.

"What are you doing over there?" Thiele demanded.

"You'll see soon," she answered. "Keep your eyes closed."

He crossed his arms over his chest and smiled.

She shook out the immodest garment and studied it. With its filmy, transparent material and its ribbons and bows, it fit Thiele's description perfectly. No doubt he'd seen such things—they weren't truly forbidden, only naughty. Except between a teacher and novice. For her and Thiele, it was perfect. She slipped it over her head, leaving her amulet underneath, and arranged the ribbons so that they highlighted her nipples and the curls between her legs, not hiding them at all.

Then she turned to face him full on. "You can open your eyes now."

He did, and he shot out of his chair, toppling it behind him. "Mercy, woman," he gasped. "Where did you get that?"

"Does it matter?"

"No." He swallowed. "I only...I've never seen...it shows everything."

"Isn't that what you wanted?"

He crossed the room in two strides and took her into his arms. He lifted her right off her feet as he pressed her to him everywhere. He bent his head and took her mouth in a bruising kiss.

She dug her fingers into his shoulders and answered him, opening her lips under his and sliding her tongue into his mouth. He growled in the back of his throat and pulled her hard against him. Her breasts crushed into the muscles of his chest, setting up a delicious friction that coursed through her veins to heat her sex. She extended her toes down to the tops of his feet to gain them some purchase so that she could move against his hardness. He lowered his face into the crook of her neck and whimpered, kneading her back in his fists.

She pushed her hand between their bodies and stroked him, and his whimpers swelled to cries as his hips began to rock. Back and forth, back and forth, bringing the thick ridge of flesh against her hand in a rhythm older than the forest. She squeezed him and felt him shudder.

Suddenly he pushed himself away from her, holding her by her shoulders, his chest heaving as he worked for breath. "I can't," he gasped. "Dendra, I can't."

She touched his chest, and he jumped nearly out of his skin. "It's too much, Kareth," he cried.

"But our castle, you said you'd take me in all the rooms. In the kitchen with the bread baking."

"That was fantasy. We'll never have that."

"Thiele..."

"Understand, little one. It's too much," he said, gazing down into her face. "Every time I love you, you get further inside me. I'm afraid the next time I'll lose myself completely."

"You're supposed to lose yourself," she answered. "My soul comes undone every time we make love."

"That's right for you. You can trust." He clenched his teeth and sucked in a breath between them. "For me...I can't...it's total surrender."

"Then surrender."

"No," he said.

She took his face in her hands and gazed into his eyes. "Do it. Give yourself to me. All of you."

"No."

"Trust me. Trust Dendra. Lose yourself. We'll bring you back."

"I can't."

She rose to her full height, calling up the goddess from deep inside her. Summoning everything she had—the wisdom of the trees, the tenacity of the fog, the power of her love. She opened her eyes wide and stared at him, straight on, eye to eye, mastering him. "You will surrender to me, Thiele. You will do exactly as I say, and we will merge until nothing separates us—not flesh, not blood, not breath. We will give each other life."

He looked back at her, unblinking, silent. Another moment and she'd own him. Just the right combination of words, the right entreaty.

"This is why you came here," she went on, chanting to him. "This is why you were born. For me—here and now. Do you understand?"

He nodded slowly. "Take me, school me," he whispered, reciting the ancient prayer. "I am yours."

She took his hand and led him to the bed. He sat on it, never taking his eyes off her, as though under her spell. She pulled off his shirt and threw it to the floor. Then she guided him backward, down until he rested on his back, still staring at her.

She climbed on top of him and captured his mouth, darting her tongue in and out, tasting him. She slid her body over his and teased his chest with the ribbons of her under-gown. Then she lowered herself, took one of his nipples into her mouth, and sucked.

He cried out at that, his voice rupturing the air around them. "Ah, woman, you'll kill me."

She lifted her head and found his eyes closed, his jaw clenched. Fighting for control, no doubt. And losing, losing badly. "You'll be reborn," she answered.

Then she pressed her lips to the other nipple and claimed it, too. Beneath her, his hips began to move, and she shifted so that she could press her palm to his manhood. He gasped, and she squeezed him, running her fingers along the entire length of him.

Slowly, slowly she slid herself even lower, until her head rested against his belly and she was face to face with the bulge in his breeches. She unfastened one button and then another, taking her time with him, drawing out the agony of waiting. Finally, she had them open, and his sex came free. She caught the shaft in her fingers and guided the head into her mouth.

He nearly floated off the bed then, and a roar tore out of a place deep in his chest. "Woman, stop," he shouted. "You don't know what you're doing to me."

But she did know. She knew exactly what she did as she sucked on the tip of him and stroked the length of his shaft, dipping her fingers into his breeches and between his legs to caress the soft sac there. His member throbbed in her hand, a thing with its own life. And she knew that he would come soon, no matter how hard he tried to fight it. He'd spill his seed, and when he did, she would take it deep inside her.

She rose and swung her leg over him, still holding his sex and positioning herself over it. She guided herself onto him and surrendered her own sanity to the pleasure. He filled her so completely, so perfectly. She howled with the joy as she pressed her hands into his ribs and moved herself. Up and down, bringing herself to him, over and over, stroking his length.

He matched her movements. He circled her waist with his fingers and held her while he pounded into her, pumping wildly and sending her to the edge. She closed her eyes and let the madness have her. The universe shifted, sensation crashing over her. Impossible, but real. Scents from childhood, music, blinding lights, and distant thunder. One loud clap nearby—Thiele's cry of release—and she dissolved with him into bliss. She slumped onto his chest and basked in the shuddering of her womanhood where she was still joined to him.

Slowly the world settled back into place. Her fingertips registered the smoothness of his skin underneath them, her palms measured his warmth. She pressed her lips into the furrow that ran down the center of his chest and sighed. His fingers slipped into her hair.

Thiele, beloved Thiele. He had surrendered to her, but so had she to him. The priestess' spell had turned itself back on her, and she would never be the same.

She ran her hands up his body, touching him everywhere, memorizing his arms, his shoulders, his throat. She found her beloved everywhere, and something more. No, not something more—rather something less. No metal. She opened her eyes and looked up at him.

His collar was gone. "Thiele," she whispered.

His hand pushed her head back against his chest, his fingers still making slow circles in her hair. "Not now, little one. Let me rest."

She sat up and searched again. Not a sign of cammite anywhere. Not even broken pieces lying beside him. The atrocity had disappeared completely. "Thiele," she said more loudly. "Open your eyes. Your collar's off. You're free."

He came alert at that, his eyes flying open. He sat up so suddenly he threw Kareth off him, and he ran his hands along his neck. A sobbing shout escaped him, and he twisted to search the bed, running his palms over it as though the hated collar had merely become invisible but still might lie somewhere on the coverlet. After a moment, he stopped and turned to her, his eyes wide with wonder.

"You did it," he whispered.

"We did it," she corrected.

The next morning Kareth lay in bed, eyes closed, listening to Thiele move about the cottage. The sounds he made weren't random, rather they cried out with purpose—the cabinet opening and closing, then the wardrobe. And always coming back to the table. She heard him move away, toward the door, and she cracked an eye open. Just as she had suspected—a bundle lay on the table top, and he was fully dressed, complete with cape and boots. He was packing, getting ready to leave.

She sat up, pulling the coverlet over her. "What are you doing?"

He turned and looked at her, surprise registering in his eyes. "Awake so early? I thought after last night you'd be exhausted."

As well she should have been. Freedom from his collar had released them both in so many ways. They'd spent the hours before dawn exploring that freedom and each other. Wonderful and intimate. But she'd known, too, that this was the last. That in the morning he would leave.

"What are you doing?" she repeated.

He walked back to the table, a water flask in his hand. "I think that's obvious."

"Weren't you even going to say good-bye?" she demanded.

He didn't answer, but raised an eyebrow and stared at her for a moment. Then he went back to packing, slipping the flask into the bundle and bringing the ends of the rough material up into a knot.

Curse him, he hadn't intended to say good-bye. He had meant to pack up her things and slip away while she slept. She climbed out of bed, walked to the wardrobe, and found her shift and gown where they still lay on the floor. She slipped them over her head and turned on him. "Let me help you," she snapped. "I wouldn't want you to forget anything."

"Kareth..."

"No, truly," she said, charging to the cabinet. "Let's see. You'll need meal." She opened the door and peered inside. "But it appears you've already taken it."

"Of course."

She crossed her arms over her chest and glared at him, fuming. "And knives. Have you taken them, too?"

"Only the big one," he answered.

How could he? After all they'd shared, he was simply going to steal what he wanted from her and disappear without a word. "Take the bird carvings, too. If you're not here, I don't want them."

She walked to the wardrobe again. She looked on top and found nothing there. "No," she cried, spinning back to face him. "You were taking them, without even asking. Give them back."

"You just said you don't want them."

"Give them back," she repeated. Breath of the Beast, those birds were hers. She crossed to the table, grabbed his bundle, and tore the knots open.

"Is this the priestess who taught me about trust yesterday?" he demanded. "I let you touch my core, and today you won't trust me with some possessions."

She got the cloth open and searched through the contents— foodstuffs, tools, but no carvings. "Where are they?" she shouted, tears threatening to choke her voice. "What have you done with them?"

He put his hands on his hips and glared at her. "I put them in your pack."

"My pack?" she echoed.

"Over there." He nodded toward the hearth. "If you'd asked, I would have told you."

She glanced over and found another bundle just where he had indicated. A smaller one, made out of her shawl. "You packed for me?"

"Just a few things," he answered. "Some clothes, the carvings, that under-gown."

"You planned to take me with you."

He put his hands on her shoulders and turned her to him. "You disappoint me, little one. Do you really think that I'd steal everything you have and leave without even saying good-bye?"

"But we agreed," she said. "I couldn't go over the border with you."

"I wanted to do the noble thing, leave you where you'd be safe, despite how much I loved you. You took that choice away from me yesterday."

She rested against his chest and sighed. "You love me?"

"Can you doubt it?" he rumbled from his chest.

She ran her arms around him and hugged him. He slipped a finger under her chin and lifted her face to his. "I planned to leave you, but you became part of me yesterday. If I lost that part, I'd bleed inside until I died."

"Truly?" she asked, her voice suddenly tiny.

"Truly," he answered.

"But I can't go," she said. "I haven't completed my work here. I haven't yet discovered Dendra's design for me."

"Can't you find that on the outside?"

"No." She pushed away from his chest and looked around her at her haven. "I belong here. This is where I've been sent to find the truth in me."

"Then I'll have to stay here with you," he said. "Unpack and stay and hope the catchers don't find us."

She twisted her hands together and tried to think. "That won't work, either."

"You'll have to decide. Here or the outside. But either way together, both of us."

"Dendra, I don't know."

He spread his arms wide. "Which will it be, priestess? Stay or cross the border?"

She studied him, the gleam of mischief, of triumph in his eyes. The sandy hair that fell into his face. His broad shoulders, muscled legs. Her haven lay in him, inside the circle of his embrace. That decided, the rest was easy, after all. "The border," she said.

His smile broadened as he walked to the threshold and opened the door. "Get your pack."

She flew to the hearth and picked up the bundle he'd prepared for her. Then she headed back to his outstretched hand. A few feet away she stopped, suddenly remembering. She walked to the far wall, took down the ax, and slid the handle through the knots of her pack.

His eyes widened. "For you, priestess?" he said. "A weapon?"

She walked back to him, gazing up into his face. "To chop firewood. To keep us warm."

He laughed heartily at that, still holding out his hand to her. She took it, and they crossed the threshold together.

About the author:

Alice Gaines has a Ph.D. in personality psychology from a large west coast university. She lives in the hills of Oakland, California with her husband of 16 years, 50 or 60 orchids, and one neurotic cat.

Alice recently sold a historical romance to Leisure Books. Currently titled **Waitangi Nights**, the story is set in 19th century New Zealand and features spirits from Maori folklore

The Gift

Jeanie LeGendre

To my reader:

    The Gift tells the tale of a woman who dared everything to find love and the man who challenged the boundaries of culture to cherish her. While the characters and their romance are very much fictional, their world is drawn from historical fact. With that in mind... Alessandra and Solimon's love story really might have happened.

The Ottoman Empire

"Behave, my lady," the Kislar Agha ordered, "or the Sultan will be greatly insulted. Calm yourself."

Alessandra de Got tugged the edges of the guimlik over her bare breasts, aghast at the command. Calm herself? When the very idea of bondage as the Sultan's concubine nearly made her faint!

The chief eunuch glared at her, black eyes peering from his face. "You are the Gift, and the Sultan has called you to him this eve. He wants to see how Ibrahim Pasha honors him. This is a chance to distinguish yourself, to earn a place as his favorite." His thick-set fingers gripped her chin, tilting her face upward, preventing escape. "The Sultan is young. His energies have been devoted to fighting and strengthening the boundaries of our beloved land. His haremlik is virtually empty. He has taken no wife. Do you understand what this means?"

Alessandra didn't care. But the words stuck in the back of her throat, and no sound passed her lips.

His mouth thinned into a tight smile. "His mother, the Sultan Valide, is dead. The women are his father's slaves with no one to rule them. The Sultan has called you to him this eve, my lady, and you alone have a chance to catch his eye."

"I am no concubine. I am a French woman—"

"You are the Gift!" He released her chin abruptly. "Your fate lies within the haremlik of the Sultan's Palace. You can live life as a lowly slave, or you can attract the Sultan and claim a position of honor in his household."

Alessandra's mind raced. A lifetime as a concubine! Sheer panic swept through her. She could not live her life imprisoned within the walls of the haremlik, her every action dictated by the lustful whim of a man. Slaves had no freedom. Every tale she had ever heard of the haremlik—and she had heard many—described a place rife with debauchery, mystery, and intrigue. She must persuade the Sultan to free her. Once he discovered she was the French Ambassador's niece, surely he would return her. He wouldn't risk diplomatic problems with France, would he?

Taking a deep, steadying breath, Alessandra straightened her shoulders, preparing herself for what was to come. She glanced up at the Kislar Agha and nodded.

He sighed in obvious relief. "All will be well. Just smile and remember what I've taught you." The sleeve of his emerald satin robe swept against her neck, and she trembled as he brushed strands of hair from her face. "There, there, you are exquisite. Your silver-gilt hair is as fine as spun silk, and your skin glows like a pearl. The Sultan will be enchanted." He reached for the corded bell pull. Instantly, the doors to the chamber opened, and she followed him past the gilded columns of the entrance into the Royal Salon.

Braziers glowed from all corners, and the melodious strains of the lyre filled the air. The Kislar Agha led her past silent rows of black eunuchs prostrated along the path to the throne. His words echoed in her memory instructing, "Never utter a sound and always keep your eyes lowered."

She focused on the silver rosettes of her slippers, willing herself not to stumble, to walk gracefully. Her heart pounded wildly in her breast, and she was keenly aware of her nakedness through the gauze garments that swirled with her every step. She fought the urge to cover herself, feeling shockingly vulnerable in the presence of so many.

In one fluid motion that belied his size, the Kislar Agha fell to his knees, stretching his wide chest flat to the carpet and pressing his turbaned brow to the Sultan's feet. "Grand Seigneur, I beg permission to humbly present the Gift."

He moved aside, and Alessandra slipped to the floor, conscious of appearing awkward in the wake of the Kislar Agha's more experienced bow.

"Rise, fair one. Let me view you," the Sultan demanded in a rich, smooth voice that sent a wave of trepidation through her.

Alessandra rose before him. The silk-bordered edges of the guimlik slid from her grasp with the movement, and she hastily drew the garment closed. At the intensity of his gaze, she bit her lip until it throbbed in time with her pulse.

"You hide your loveliness from me." The words were more a statement than a question. His long fingers brushed against hers, but Alessandra clutched the blouse over her breasts even tighter. "Clear the chamber," he commanded, the imperious tone of his voice slicing through her.

Sweet Mother in Heaven, she had offended him. The Sultan's power was absolute. With the mere snap of his fingers, he could have her killed, and no one would utter a syllable in her defense. A spark of resentment leapt to life deep inside. He commanded her to attend him garbed like a whore, then wanted, nay expected, her to acquiesce to his touch. But no matter what the punishment, she would not submit. She stiffened, only no reprimand came—just the shuffling sounds of the departing assemblage, and after what seemed to be an eternity, even those sounds faded away.

"Why do you resist?" he asked.

Although he had not spoken harshly, his question shattered the last vestiges of her composure. She had never been so frightened . . . so outraged in all her life. No matter how she willed it otherwise, hot angry tears slid from her eyes.

"Look at me."

With the greatest effort, Alessandra lifted her gaze. He stood before his throne, darkly beautiful and strong, just as she would have envisioned a proud Ottoman king. His expression was carved in stone, yet the fury she anticipated was not evident in the bold lines of his face. He was not angry, but curious. Her turbulent emotions eased slightly while the force of his unwavering gaze surged through her.

He was a tall man. A diamond-studded dagger flashed from the jewelled girdle around his waist. The scarlet robes flowing from his broad shoulders emphasized the sheer power of his frame. A white egret feather was fastened to his turban by a starburst of diamonds and rubies, but the exotic beauty of his dark face took her breath away. His features were so perfect, so full of strength, he appeared cast in gold.

The powerful Solimon.

As his eyes met hers, a foreboding shiver ran the full length of her spine. His hand shot out, catching hers in an iron grip, forcing her to relinquish hold of the silken blouse. The guimlik fell open to her waist, exposing her breasts to the warm, scented air.

His gaze raked boldly over her, the heat of his touch searing her flesh. She fought the desire to break away, to run from him. With unnaturally heightened awareness, she heard the thin warbling of the finches in the aviary, the soft patter of droplets from the fountain. The slightest trace of moisture hung in the air. She could see its sheen on the diamond-paned windows and the ornately-carved columns lining the walls, feel its misty shimmer on her skin.

"You are magnificent." He stepped toward her, so close, she smelled the spicy citrus scent of him. "Your eyes are the color of the richest amethyst. Not cold like the stone, but vibrant, alive, like the dew-kissed petals of a violet."

His deep-velvet voice poured over her, sending the blood rushing through her veins. She stared at him, pinned beneath his relentless gaze.

"Ibrahim Pasha honors me with your loveliness, fair one."

"My name is Alessandra," she said in a ragged whisper.

His expression did not change. But when his brow lifted ever so slightly, her courage faltered. The silence between them grew heavy, tense, and she could barely catch her breath, knowing he awaited some word of explanation to pass her suddenly dry lips. "I am not a slave."

"I agree, fair one. You are not a slave, but my slave, and there is a vast difference."

At his words, her hopes plummeted, but Alessandra was determined to make him understand. She shook her head. "I was taken . . . abducted from the Pasha's palace. I am a member of the diplomatic delegation. My uncle is the French Ambassador." She paused, waiting for his surprise, some sign of outrage at her cruel treatment, but the Sultan just stood there, seemingly unaffected by her news.

"And," he prompted her to continue as if they discussed nothing more important than the latest bloom in the garden.

"And I was abducted from the bedchamber where I slept, bound, gagged, thrown over some miscreant's shoulder, and brought to the Palace."

So the fair beauty had spirit. Solimon admired the flush of color that raced like a shadow from her rounded breasts to her heart-shaped face. The willowy outline of her legs through the diaphanous folds of the trousers caught his attention, and the thought of her pale buttocks poised over anyone's shoulder captivated him.

Abductions were fairly common, although an emotional and precarious way to fill one's harem. Even though he had never pursued that particular course, he knew of many who had, but couldn't imagine Ibrahim Pasha making a gift of an unwilling slave. There was more to this girl's abduction than she knew. He would send men to delve into the matter immediately.

"What is it you would have me do, fair one?"

"I want to go home!"

"You do not wish to serve me?" He could see by the expression flitting across her delicate features that the idea terrified her. She shook her head, sending silken tresses of pale-blonde hair tumbling around her shoulders. Her hair shimmered like shifting moonbeams, and the urge to feel the cool strands brushing against his bare flesh suddenly seized him.

The women he cared for in the Palace, the women who had never caught his father's eye, all ran toward his sire's tastes, golden-skinned and lush-bodied. Solimon could not recall one who rivaled the fair beauty of the exquisite creature before him. Perhaps the Kislar Agha was right—he had neglected his own harem too long.

He could not deny the spark of excitement that flared inside him. To introduce her to passion, to tempt her with his touch until all inhibitions melted away, praise Allah!—the very idea fired his imagination. "What do you think I would have you do as my slave?"

Her flush deepened like the lingering hues of sunrise on sand, but she remained silent.

He waited.

She lowered her gaze, the dark smudge of her lashes shadowing her fair skin. "Satisfy your . . . desires."

"And you find that thought distasteful?"

Her teeth tugged at the flesh of her bottom lip. Fascinated, his gaze travelled from the inviting fullness of her mouth, down the slender column of her neck, to the creamy white skin that peeked from beneath the loose edges of the sapphire guimlik. The blood pounded hotly in his veins.

Solimon reached out, his fingers enveloping the velvet curve of her breast. She inhaled sharply, startled, and her hand lashed out to strike his away. He caught her wrist with his free hand and held it firmly within his grasp.

"Do not fight me."

The jewel-like eyes, shocked and angry, clashed with his. He ran his thumb across her nipple, feeling it harden like marble in response to his touch. A gasp slipped from her lips, and a tremor visibly rippled through her lithe frame, revealing the passion that simmered beneath her reluctant surface. Was this fair beauty worth the time and energy it would take to coax away her resistance? As he gazed upon the sweetness of her body, he knew the answer.

He withdrew his hand, the warmth of her flesh lingering on his fingertips. She immediately folded her arms over her breasts, shielding herself from his view.

"I risk war if I insult Ibrahim Pasha by refusing his gift. Why would I do this?"

"I do not belong here. I'll die in captivity, Grand Seigneur." Her words came in breathless bursts. "I am an educated woman, respected for my intelligence, an asset to my uncle in business." Her plea grew more impassioned, her voice stronger and clearer, making him desire her all the more for such a spirited plea. "I must be free to learn, to think, to speak my mind."

"I hold my slaves in the highest regard. They have the freedom to think and to speak their minds."

Her hands clenched into fists at her sides, and her chin rose a notch. "A slave has no freedom."

"A slave has no freedom but what her master allows." Solimon stifled a grin. "Ah, fair one, you simply do not understand our ways. I respect my women above all else! They are Allah's most precious gifts, the life-givers, the pleasure-givers."

"You do not speak of wisdom or honor. I am more than a . . . a pleasure-giver."

"Is there anything more important than bearing life?"

"But there is so much more a woman can do."

Solimon took a step back and sat on his throne, regarding her curiously. The delicate angle of her jaw bespoke defiance, the seriousness of her argument. Should he be intrigued or offended? Women who dwelled in the seraglio could be manipulative and greedy, like those he had grown up with in his father's haremlik. He had neither the time nor the patience right now for those tricks.

She was a rare beauty, though. Slender and graceful, she had firm, uptilted breasts and skin like ivory satin. Her straight hair shimmered like sunlight on the Marmara, falling in a silver-white wave to her waist. Despite her defiant stance, she tensed at his continued silence. The need to tame her, to harness that gentle spirit for his own, overcame him. "For your disobedience, I could banish you to the farthest corner of the haremlik, where neither life-giving nor pleasure-giving would occupy your thoughts, but only how to fill your lonely days."

"I will perish in such a place," she said simply.

"You've no choice but to submit."

"I fear death less than losing my soul."

His admiration for her grew when she didn't back down at his threat. "Then, fair one, we are at an impasse. I have no desire for war or an unwilling slave."

She stamped her slipper-clad foot on the thick carpet. "There must be some other way. I simply cannot be a slave. If you knew anything about me, you would understand." Her voice quavered, rising like the chiming of bells. "Please. Give me a chance to prove how unsuited I am to such a life."

"You challenge me?" he asked, not sure whether to be annoyed or amused. But she would have to share his bed to prove herself unsuitable, and as he was struck by the possibilities, all thoughts of annoyance fled.

Surprise flitted across her finely-drawn features. "Yes. Yes, I do," she whispered in a rush of breath. "Give me three nights, Grand Seigneur, three nights to convince you how unsuited I am for a life of slavery. If I fail, I'll enter your haremlik willingly. But if I succeed, you'll send me back to my uncle."

He watched her for a long moment. Perhaps he had misjudged her. Such a challenge bespoke more boldness than intelligence, for insolence could earn her a trip to the bottom of the Bosphorus in a weighted sack. But then, she had said she would prefer death—and a quick death would be preferable to languishing in some remote corner of his haremlik.

The tremor that visibly rocked her willowy frame revealed the tremendous effort it took her to oppose him. So, this was no display of hysterical emotions. Was she like the majestic bird of the summer wind, unable to be tamed? He wanted to know. He respected strength and honor—even in a woman. "How do you plan to prove yourself?"

She hesitated only a moment, long enough for him to recognize that she had no clear idea of what she intended, but like the summer bird trapped in a net, grasped for any chance at freedom.

"I am schooled in diplomacy. I could help you better relations with any of the European countries, most certainly with France."

He could just imagine her sitting in the reception room, un-
veiled, chatting with the many rulers and diplomats he entertained.
One glimpse of those lush rose-colored lips and amethyst eyes
would likely incite a riot right within the Palace walls. But her
challenge presented some intriguing possibilities. He could easily
envision long, moonlit nights spent bettering relations with her,
melting the barriers of her innocence and stoking the fire he sensed
within. Solimon decided to play the game and smiled. "Each
morning I will send you a scholarly present, a book or some such
treasure, for discussion that eve. You'll have from sunset to sunrise
to prove why you're a poor choice to be my slave."

"And you'll allow me the freedom to speak my thoughts and
make my points?"

He nodded, growing more charmed with the game as each
moment passed. "And you vow not to resist my touch?"

That took her off guard, and her eyes widened. She obviously
wanted to refuse, evidence of her struggle sweeping across her
exquisite features. She finally shrugged in resignation.

"Then so be it," he said. "The boundaries are drawn. Is there
anything else you wish to add?"

"No, Grand Seigneur, you have been most generous." She
slipped to her knees, pressing her brow to his slippers.

Pleased with her show of manners, he tugged the bell pull, and a
page arrived to escort her from the Salon. "Prepare yourself well,
fair one. You will attend me tomorrow evening at nightfall."

She flew down the carpeted walkway, and Solimon eyed her
retreat in appreciation. The light of the sconces revealed her gently-
curved silhouette through the silk gauze of her garments. So fair of
form and feature, she should pique his ardor rather than his patience.

One person in particular would be delighted by this twist of fate.
The Kislar Agha paraded harem slaves before him like ripe fruits
in a quest to ensure the succession. Solimon could only imagine the
chief eunuch's delight that he had committed to this bedchamber
game.

"Three nights, Grand Seigneur?" the Kislar Agha squealed on an inrushing breath after hearing an explanation of the challenge. "Praise Allah."

"I am pleased my actions meet with your approval."

The florid rise of color that crept up the chief eunuch's neck revealed his embarrassment over such a vulgar display of emotion. "Forgive me such rudeness." He prostrated himself at Solimon's feet, kissing the hem of his master's robe in a grandiose plea for clemency.

Solimon resisted the urge to roll his eyes. "Never fear, my loyal servant. I did not doubt your response for an instant. You have been quite free with your complaints about how I neglect my haremlik."

The Kislar Agha stood, smoothing the folds of his embroidered robes and drawing his round frame up with impressive hauteur. "Forgive me for mentioning this, Grand Seigneur, but you have no haremlik. The women who inhabit the Seraglio passed to you through your father. All of them."

"I have had much to accomplish in the six years since I became Sultan. Even you must realize that establishing my strength as ruler takes precedence above all else. And that task has left me precious little time for anything more."

The Kislar Agha's plump features sharpened with determination. "And you have achieved your goal a thousandfold, mighty one. Now you need a wife. Yet every woman I bring you is cast into obscurity after only one night in your bed." He threw his hands up in despair. "You had me marry off the last three who claimed your attention."

"They were troublemakers." He waved his hand impatiently. "You cannot deny that. They caused dissension in the household."

"Any change will cause dissension. The women lived together before you brought them from your father's palace. They are too comfortable, too complacent. You need a wife to establish your household, to create order."

Solimon suppressed a sigh. Quite simply, he had yet to encounter a woman who came close to the standard he had set long ago. A wife should be more than a slave. She should be a partner, a lover, a friend. Was he foolishly searching for the perfect woman—a woman who didn't exist? Perhaps. But some unfamiliar emotion gathered inside when he thought of the violet-eyed beauty, his latest gift. He could not fathom why, but she intrigued him.

In all fairness, Solimon could not resent the Kislar Agha his opinion. His job was to manage the haremlik, to keep peace among the women—no mean feat. Yet despite his skill and competence, he would never understand Solimon's wish for a wife who would be his mate in all ways.

"I will send the fair one a book of romance for the first night." He came to his feet, standing before the throne in a gesture of dismissal. "Wrap it in a lavender silk handkerchief, bordered with amethysts."

"Lavender silk . . . amethysts? You do her great honor." The strained expression left the chief eunuch's face. He beamed, his full lips curving into a smile. In a rustle of satin robes, he bowed low, prostrating himself easily. "It will be as you wish, Grand Seigneur."

❧⟨♥⟩❧

The Sultan's present arrived with the dawn, and Alessandra unwrapped the rich packaging to reveal the first of her scholarly tools—a book. She had learned enough during her short stay in the Palace to know that the Sultan honored her with such a costly handkerchief. The women who had witnessed the arrival of his present whispered excitedly among themselves while inspecting the quality of the jewels.

She opened the book. The blood pounded hotly in her temples as she studied the pages, finding the tales between the gilded leather bindings so erotic she could not help but blush. The women chided her for such a maidenly display, reminding her that she was a concubine, subject to the whim and will of her master.

Alessandra fought down the hurt, well aware of their surprise at the Sultan's interest . . . and their envy.

However would she win the challenge if he turned her own game to his advantage? Yet she admired his cleverness and vowed not to underestimate him again. He had maneuvered her into a corner. She could not bemoan the nature of his gift without protesting the boundaries of their challenge, the very boundaries she had agreed upon.

Through the long hours while eunuchs plunged her into hot baths, massaged her with fragrant oils, then garbed her in delicate silks, Alessandra searched for some way to make the Sultan view her as a person and not simply a pleasure-giver. By sunset, she had formulated a simple plan—he must come to know her, know her history, her desires, her dreams—only then would he realize how unsuited she was to a life of slavery.

As the sun went down, she clutched the book against her breasts and followed the Kislar Agha down the beautifully-tiled corridor connecting the haremlik to the Royal Apartments. Alessandra thought she had reconciled herself to the upcoming confrontation, but the memory of the Sultan's bold eyes raking over her undermined her courage. As the carved doors to the Royal Chamber loomed ahead, her chest grew tight and panic mounted with every step. The Kislar Agha guided her into the room, whispering, "Make him burn to possess you. Allah will guide your path." He departed, the heavy doors echoing shut behind him.

The Sultan's private quarters were richly furnished. The paneled walls were inlaid with ivory and intricate pieces of coral, and patterned rugs decorated the floor. The Sultan lounged upon a reclining chair with a brocaded mattress, silken pillows scattered beneath him.

Alessandra barely recognized his long, powerful form without the adornment of royal robes. His gaze captured hers, then travelled slowly over her scantily-clad body while she sank to her knees in a bow. Conscious of his eyes upon her, she resisted the urge to snatch the embroidered coverlet from the back of his chair and cover herself with it.

"Come, fair one. Be seated." He motioned to the thick pillows around him.

Alessandra took a deep breath and rose to her feet, holding the book like a shield before her. His strength and will were legend throughout Europe. How in Heaven's name could she persuade him to release her? He would never convince her of the merit of carnal bondage, and she clung to that thought while positioning herself on the floor by his feet.

Sprawled across the chair, he wore only white silk trousers which contrasted sharply against his deep golden skin. Candles flickered lazily in ornate holders, casting a burnished glow along the lines of his muscular frame, and she was again struck by his incredible beauty.

"Pour us fruit nectar," he said.

Forced to set aside the book, her bare breasts were revealed to his perusal while she performed the task. Alessandra quickly realized the nature of his game. He knew she was embarrassed to the core of her soul at having to run around in various degrees of undress, and he planned to use that fact to disarm her. Somehow she had to conquer her modesty. Although how she would over-come a lifetime of propriety, she had no idea. Taking a deep breath, Alessandra handed him an etched-crystal cup, trembling slightly as his long, straight fingers brushed hers.

"Were you pleased with my present, fair one?"

He smiled, a slow, knowing smile that gleamed brightly against his handsome face. A ripple of awareness fluttered through her. What could she say? She would not let him see how his gift un-settled her—she would turn his own present to her advantage. After all, there was more to intelligence than simply knowing how to read. Crossing her arms over her breasts, she forced her voice to remain casual. "Your gift is most generous, Grand Seigneur."

He propped himself on an elbow to drink, motioning to the cup which still sat on the table. "Enjoy."

She eyed the drink with suspicion, wondering if he'd resort to aphrodisiacs in an attempt to win the day. He drained the contents of his own. "I drink with you, fair one. I have no need of potions to increase my ardor. Or yours."

Alessandra did not doubt his words. His presence was so confident, so male that the very air seemed charged and alive. After sipping the fruity liquid, she returned the cup to the table and opened the book before her. "Am I to believe these stories are scholarly treasures?"

"They are tales of romance, valued as treasures by my people, little jewels of an ancient art honoring the glory of sensual pleasure." Amusement twitched at the corners of his full mouth. "I can see by the color creeping into your cheeks this writing is new to you, so I shall read the first tale." He took the book from her, turning the pages until he found the one he sought. "'When young Ciclazade first lay eyes upon the fair Safiye, it was most surely an accident destined by Allah himself. He would never have been near the women's bath house had it not been for the Pasha's lust of sweetmeats and the cat-sized rat who fled with a pouch of Turkish delights between his sharp little teeth.

"'Mourning the loss of the Pasha's attention since he had grown so fat, Safiye languished around the pool, her thick hair tumbling in ebon waves to the floor, the soft lines of her naked body sparkling beneath the spray of the fountain. Water droplets rolled over her heavy breasts, their sable tips gleaming, taunting him with their dusky beauty. With slender fingers she traced a path down her stomach, over the gentle swell of her abdomen, to the place of her most secret desire. As Ciclazade gazed upon her loveliness and realized her need, honor demanded he save the alluring Safiye from the ravishings of the sugar-crazed rat . . . .'"

The Sultan's deep-velvet voice flowed through her like warm honey, conjuring up images of entwined limbs gliding over cool marble benches, of steamy caresses beneath the moisture-laden air. Her body grew heavy, as though she was drifting on a cloud, and a strange anticipation built inside her to hear what happened next to the beautiful heroine and her bold lover. The Sultan slid from his seat, taking a place beside her. He rested back against the lounging chair, the warmth of his flesh softly branding her own. Remembering her promise not to resist his touch, she forced herself not to pull away.

His voice never wavered as he lifted a strand of her hair, stroking it between thumb and forefinger. But he did nothing more threatening than touch her hair, his fingers twining in the tresses almost absent-mindedly. She gazed up at him, his profile outlined against the golden glow of the candle light. Her heart fluttered softly within her breast. His rich voice, low and melodic, penetrated her senses, the steady motion of his full lips mesmerizing her. Her limbs prickled in pleasant awareness of his touch, warm and liquid, his words summoning a curious sensation in the pit of her stomach.

Was this seduction?

His voice trailed off at the end of Ciclazade and Safiye's adventure in the bath. "What do you think of Turkish romance, fair one?" He turned the book around and placed it across her lap, his hand lingering along her silk-clad thigh.

Her flesh tingled where he touched her, and she tried to push aside the feeling, intent upon responding to his question with intelligence. "Written with the Turkish flair for drama, but humorous as well. Delightful. Sensual."

He propped an elbow on the chair and leaned toward her. "Definitely sensual. Do you enjoy this kind of literature in your country?"

"Oh, yes," Alessandra responded. "The French are great romantics. But I've never read any. Erotic literature is considered quite inappropriate for someone of my youth and status."

"Your status?"

"I . . . I'm a maiden."

His dark brow rose. "So I guessed."

Heat rushed to her cheeks. He brought his hand to her face, traced her lower lip with his thumb, then trailed a path to her jaw. Fire raced along her flesh to the places he touched. "In France," she said in a rush of breath, "in most of Europe in fact, it is considered improper for a woman to be anything but a maiden when she weds."

"Do you think it fair for a woman to go into marriage unschooled in lovemaking?"

"It is a husband's job to teach his wife of desire. And European women have many other duties. Like managing entire chateaus—"

"Duties." The Sultan cringed in mock horror. "Lovemaking is no duty. Lovemaking is a gift of pleasure; the ultimate intimacy between a man and woman. There are slaves to market and prepare food, slaves to launder garments and polish floors."

Alessandra rested her arm on the chair and faced him, intent upon making her point. "But as wives, European women share much more than lovemaking with their husbands. They become partners and friends." She peered at him intently, adding, "And they most certainly do not share their place with other women."

The Sultan chuckled. His fingertips caressed the arch of her brow, then ran softly over her ear. "Ah, your Christian ways. Where is the dishonor in sharing?"

She met his laughing gaze straight on, ignoring the tiny starbursts of heat that prickled her skin where he touched her. "I see where sharing affords you wondrous variety, but what is the benefit to your women?"

He hesitated momentarily, his dark eyes growing wide, and she experienced a small surge of triumph. He obviously had not considered that question before.

"Companionship . . . and luxury," he began. "Sharing the responsibilities of raising children and making a comfortable and inviting home for me. Those are clear benefits."

"But you don't live in the haremlik. You only visit your women when the mood strikes. They do not in truth create a home for you."

"But they do." He squared his jaw for battle. "They live there with my children, caring for each other in my absence. With whom does a lady of the chateau share her responsibilities?"

"Her ladies-in-waiting."

He raked a hand through his dark hair, sending a glossy black wave tumbling over his brow. He looked boyish. No, he looked roguish, she decided, then forced her concentration back to his words.

"They are not her equals. She cannot reveal herself as she would with another noblewoman, a friend of similar rank."

Now it was Alessandra's turn to consider his words. France was a hodgepodge of connecting baronies and duchies with many miles between one city and the next. Noblewomen commonly moved away from sisters and friends of similar station with marriage and did not see them again except during infrequent gatherings and celebrations. Did a noble lady of the chateau find herself alone on a lofty perch?

"What of your own mother, fair one?"

A wave of sadness washed through her. She squelched the familiar sorrow and let out an audible sigh. "My parents died when I was a young child. I barely remember them."

"Who is this uncle you would return to?"

"He raised me. He's my mother's oldest brother, the French Ambassador. I have travelled with him since my parents' deaths."

The Sultan's gaze swept over her gently. "I have made you relive your anguish, fair one, and that was not my intent." He uncrossed his legs and gathered her into the strong circle of his arms. "Do not be frightened. Relax against me. Let us lighten our hearts with Ciclazade and Safiye's adventures in the Chamber of Robes."

Something in his manner soothed her, and Alessandra did as he bade, resting against the iron-thewed wall of his chest, enveloped in the heady warmth of him. His nearness made her senses spin. With the greatest effort, she focused on the page before her. His hand caressed the curve of her shoulder, and she tried to steady her racing pulse.

At first, Alessandra's nervousness caused her to stumble over the words. Wedged between the Sultan's hard thighs, she heard the steady beat of his heart where her head rested against his chest. That she could not see his face helped ease her tension, and soon her voice settled into a rhythmic cadence.

The Chamber of Robes was one of the few rooms in the Pasha's palace that could be accessed by both the selamlik, where the men resided, and the haremlik, where the women were quartered. This, of course, lured the lovers to conduct their second tryst within its veiled walls.

Alessandra kept her voice steady while relating the beautiful Safiye's emergence from the racks of fabric. "'Safiye twirled and swayed in a silent dance, whispers of silk against satin skin the only sounds to announce their presence behind the rows of brilliantly-hued garments. With filmy gauze ties, she bound Ciclazade's arms to a rack, then moved seductively, just out of reach, while revealing tantalizing glimpses of rounded thighs and full breasts as she peeled away one veil after another.'"

As she described Ciclazade's growing anticipation, the desire that flared through his veins, her voice grew raspy, breathless. To her amazement and shock, an indolent warmth permeated her senses. The Sultan did nothing more than trail a fingertip along the inside of her arm, but his touch ignited flames along her skin.

While Safiye teased her lover's senses to life, whipping her heavy midnight tresses across his cheek and brushing a curved hip against his bare shoulder, the Sultan's strong hands enveloped Alessandra's waist, his fingers dipping into the waistline of her trousers then travelling upward to encircle her breasts. She inhaled sharply, but the Sultan urged, "Do not stop."

He did nothing more than cup her breasts within his palms. She focused her gaze on the tale, but as the sensual words rolled from her tongue, she grew preoccupied with his skillful hands upon her. Her blood pulsed defiantly, distracting her, agitating her. She longed for . . . sweet God in Heaven, she wanted him to touch her. Arching against him ever so slightly, Alessandra pressed her breasts more fully into his hands, a silent plea for something she had no name for.

His thumbs flicked lightly across the rosy nubs, sending a bolt of fire straight through her. She pressed her eyes tightly shut, losing her place on the page, the yearning so deep, so unlike anything she'd ever imagined. What magic did the Sultan cast upon her with his fiery touch?

His hands roamed from her breasts to her shoulders, and a sigh almost escaped her at the loss of that breathtaking sensation. But rallying her scattered thoughts, she opened her eyes and located her place on the page spread before her. Slightly embarrassed at having responded so strongly, so noticeably to his touch, she resumed the tale, trying to keep her voice as level as possible. If he noticed her struggle, he made no comment, only continued to stroke that sensitive place between her shoulder and the curve of her neck.

Safiye's seduction diverted Alessandra's wayward feelings for a time. "'The sultry heroine roused both her own passions and her lover's as she bared her lovely flesh in a tantalizing dance. But someone heard Ciclazade's heavy breathing. The soft patter of silken slippers on the tiled floor alerted them to the Mistress of the Robe's approach, and Safiye dove on top of her lover, pulling a mountain of fabric over their heads to conceal them.

"'The danger of discovery inflamed their already raging desires. Ciclazade strained against his bonds while Safiye unleashed his sword of arousal, stroking the rigid flesh with experienced fingers. Barely able to draw air through the diaphanous pile of silk that enveloped them, their breathing grew heated, their bodies slick with passion. Safiye refused to free her lover, instead she traced light kisses along his muscled chest and over his taut stomach, then down toward his pulsing—'" Alessandra sputtered, the breath catching in her throat.

The Sultan's gentle laughter rippled through the air. "Do not be embarrassed, fair one. You did quite well . . . for a maiden." Sliding his arms around her to grasp the book, he tilted it toward him. He rested his chin on her shoulder and read from the place she left off, relating the tale of Safiye's seduction with enthusiasm.

Alessandra had accomplished her goals of giving the Sultan

cause to reflect upon her questions and of learning something about her life and work. But as his deep voice sent swirls of newly-discovered pleasure through her, she wondered how many of his own goals he had met this night.

Solimon stepped from the terrace and strode the path across the tulip gardens with an eagerness he had not experienced since youth. The fair beauty intrigued him like no other. A tantalizing enigma, her mystery drifted just out of his reach, promising untold pleasures when he learned her secrets. Yet with the thought came another, one that sobered him instantly: her uncle had sold her to Ibrahim Pasha.

Even if Solimon was inclined to grant her request for freedom, he could not in good conscience return her to someone who cared so little for her best interests. The man would probably sell her again, and who knew if another master would see her gentle spirit and care for her with love. He would not take that chance.

The entire situation made him unaccountably angry. How dare a family member, entrusted to care for such a beautiful, tender creature, betray that trust for profit? Feelings of fierce protective-ness awoke in him, feelings he was unfamiliar and uncomfortable with.

A sultry breeze floated up from the Marmara, tugging at the loose fabric of his trousers and filling the air with the moist tang of the sea. He did not know yet how best to handle the situation, but he could not reveal her uncle's perfidy. Knowledge of such be-trayal would surely squelch her proud spirit, and that he would not do.

He entered the Moonlight Kiosk through silver-filigreed doors and quickly toured the palace, pleased to see the chamber awaited him in all readiness. Adorned with no furnishings save several low tables, the round room boasted an array of fat silk pillows in all shapes and sizes. Through windows which ran from the carpeted floor to the domed ceiling, the view of moon-bathed waters beneath a star-filled sky never failed to take his breath away.

Untying the robe, he slid the garment from his shoulders then kicked the slippers from his feet. The shifting flames of cinnamon-scented candles twinkled in the edges of his view. He gazed out over the silver water, wondering what his fair one thought of his second present. At the knock on the door, he contained his impatience. He'd find out what she thought of the latest "scholarly device" soon enough.

The Kislar Agha entered. "Grand Seigneur, I humbly present the Gift," he announced, waving his charge forward.

Solimon could not help but stare. The light of the tapers played along the amethysts and diamonds sparkling in her hair, and the blood rushed to his loins at the sight of her, so ethereal and delicate. The Kislar Agha slipped silently back into the vestibule, closing the door behind him. The fair one simply stood there, uncertain, then bowed low. Solimon admired the gentle curves of her body outlined by the sheer violet silk of her garments. Her shimmering hair fanned out around her, and he yearned to catch soft fistfuls in his hands, to pull her into his arms and feel her warm against him. "Good evening, fair one. Come. Share this magnificent view with me."

Clutching the latest present to her chest, she hid her glorious breasts from sight, and Solimon vowed not to send her another book. Yet despite her modesty, she came to stand beside him, appearing much more at ease in his presence than the previous eve. He was satisfied. "Do you like my gift?"

Her bright eyes rested upon him, and a soft smile played at the corners of her mouth. "Many thanks, Grand Seigneur. If at all possible, it is even more beautiful than the first. But this one does not contain Turkish romance. What do you call this—Turkish art, perhaps?"

Solimon nodded. "Each painting shows how the heavens govern different forms of pleasure." He took the book from her, enjoying a quick glimpse of her breasts, before opening to the first tissue-covered page. "This constellation suggests an embrace." Running his finger along the replication of stars, he then traced the silhouette of the naked young couple entwined below the night sky.

"Like finding imaginary animals in the clouds," she said, excitement evident in her clear voice. "What a wondrous book, for all its sensual intent."

Despite the gentle reprimand that edged her words, he was pleased by her graciousness. His choice of presents was rather calculated, clearly not what she intended, yet not forbidden either. He admired how she accepted each gift in stride then tried to turn it to her advantage. "Let's try this one," he said, flipping back to a page where the lovers stood embracing each other. Uncertainty flitted across her heart-shaped face. "Do not be frightened."

She inclined her head demurely in consent. Wrapping an arm around her slim waist, he pulled her against him. The edges of her guimlik fell open with the motion, and her breasts pressed full against his chest. She caught her breath sharply and stiffened. Loosening his hold slightly, he whispered against her ear, "I will release you if that is your desire, but I would much rather hold you. There is much pleasure to be had in a simple embrace."

His whole being filled with waiting. Would she pull away or melt against him? She leaned toward him slightly, so slightly he thought he'd imagined it until her straight hair cascaded across his arm in a cool wave.

Pulling her closer, he rested his cheek atop her head, inhaling deeply of her sweet lavender scent. He dared not move lest he break the spell and reveled in her pliant curves molding the contours of his body. She tilted her head back and studied him. "You are surprised," he said, watching her.

"You are so gentle. You are renowned throughout Christendom as the mightiest of warriors, yet you coax me like a frightened bird to your hand. Yes, I am surprised. By you. By your tenderness and understanding."

"A tender warrior." He chuckled. "Be careful where you tread, fair one. I may never let you leave the seraglio lest you spread tales that damage my fiercely-won reputation."

Her eyes widened for an instant, then she shrugged. "I only hope you learn as much of me as I am learning of you."

Hearing the seriousness in her tone, he drew her down to the floor. "Come, lay beside me." He stretched out full length, positioning the book before him. She unfolded her slender form over the pillows, careful not to touch him, and propped up on her elbows, chin in hand.

"As a child in summertime, I watched the ships sail over the Marmara," he told her. "Look, there's one now. Only just visible beneath the light of the moon." He pointed to a pearly streak gliding over the silver-black water. Lifting himself up on one elbow, he studied the elegant curves and angles of her face, watching her expression soften in thoughtful interest. "Tell me, fair one, what would you have me learn of you."

"I would have you see the woman who is respected enough to be asked for advice in business. The woman who is an asset to the French consulate."

Solimon rolled on his side to face her, sliding his legs against hers. His hand explored the hollows of her back, and to his delight, she did not shy away. "You speak much of business, but what of love? Was your uncle a loving guardian? Was there someone you had in mind for a husband?"

She cringed. "My uncle . . . provided for me. He is not a rich man," she said in way of explanation. "He devoted his life to serving the crown, and my parents' estate dwindled during my upbringing. I have no dowry, nor any lands to offer a husband, so I work as my uncle's aide." She fixed her gaze on the sea, her pink tongue darting out to moisten her lips.

Solimon realized the admission embarrassed her. That newly-discovered feeling of protectiveness flared inside him again. He grew infuriated at her uncle, a man he had never met, while envisioning the jewel-eyed child who never knew the love of her parents. Or the love of her guardian, it would seem. And along with these feelings came the realization that his fair one wanted to fill this gap in her life, that she searched unknowingly for love.

"The Moonlight Kiosk," she whispered. "It is aptly named."

Sliding his fingertips beneath the silk blouse, he trailed a path up the slim line of her waist to the contour of her ribs. Her skin was so pale against his own, like orchids in the moonlight. She shivered, and the blood tingled in his veins. "I could call this tiny palace nothing else," he said. Sliding the sheer garment from her shoulders, he revealed her bare flesh to his gaze.

She sat up instantly, burying her luscious breasts in a red silk pillow. "You twist the rules," she accused, violet eyes flashing fire.

"You did not expect me to try to turn your challenge to my advantage?" He sat up and faced her.

Her brilliant eyes deepened like the sky on a stormy night. She sat straight-backed and defiant, staring at him with ill-concealed fury. She was so close, so delectable, a bolt of desire shot straight through him. He could not tear his gaze from the lush moistness of her lips—so ripe they beckoned to be kissed.

Before another moment was spent, the red silk pillow sailed across the chamber and she was coiled within his arms. In a swift movement, he dragged her back into the cushions with him, breasts rasping his chest as he fitted one hand in the small of her back while burying the other in the sleek tangle of her silvery hair. Capturing her mouth with his own, he kissed her.

A silken sigh slipped from her lips, and the warmth of her sweet breath made him burn. As he explored every inch of that tantalizing mouth, delighting in the way she trembled against him, his ardor flared. He devoured her softness, demanding a response, and she raised herself to meet his kiss, the full length of her body nestling into his. The gentle caress of her hands on his shoulders sent his senses soaring. She was passion. He had known it from the first moment he laid eyes upon her. As her hips arched upward, enveloping the very core of his desire in her yielding flesh, an urgent need rushed through him.

He yearned to possess her, to pleasure her, to love her. His own excitement had never before leapt to life so quickly, so fiercely.

Her hesitant touch was intoxicating. A tender ache tightened his loins, an ache so great he grew breathless, and he was forced to abandon his exploration of her lest he lose the last shreds of his control and make love to her where they lay. But he desired more than her impassioned surrender. He wanted her to come to him willingly, to hunger for him like he hungered for her. Dragging his lips from hers, Solimon cradled her against him, listening to the sounds of their ragged breathing, the thundering of their hearts, stunned by their passion as she appeared to be.

His arousal cooled by slow degrees. The magic of the moment passed, and he could feel the subtle change in her body as she slowly drew away. Once again in control of his all-too-easily inflamed lust, he decided to guide her further down the path of ecstasy. "There is a constellation called Capricorn. Let us try to find it," he said, his voice sounding unaccustomedly hoarse to his ears.

Sliding the book toward her, Solimon exhaled sharply when she rolled onto her stomach, leaving him bereft of her velvety warmth. He reached out to bring her back, but realized the moment was gone. Tucking an oblong blue pillow beneath his chest, he propped himself up on his elbows, and turned his attention to the sky. He easily spotted the pattern of stars he sought, while the pages she turned rustled gently in the moonlit silence.

"Here it is." She kept her gaze shyly averted.

His humor returned with her modesty, and he again cautioned himself to tread carefully. "Can you identify that constellation among the stars?"

She gazed into the night for a long moment while he admired the finely-drawn outline of her profile. A strand of hair tumbled over her shoulder, and she swept it behind a perfectly-formed ear, leaving him fighting the urge to weave his fingers through the silken tresses.

"There." She pointed toward the heavens. "A bit north of the Eagle."

"You are familiar with astronomy?" Solimon asked, more than mildly surprised.

She faced him, a grin tipping the corners of her rosy mouth. "You didn't believe me when I claimed to be educated?"

"No . . . yes. I didn't doubt your claim, but I wouldn't have thought astronomy of much interest to a woman."

The lights in her deep violet eyes twinkled. "Aside from enjoying the beauty of the night sky, a lady uses her knowledge of constellations to determine the planting and harvesting schedules."

"Well defended, fair one." He chuckled. "I concede the point. Now, let me show you another way we use the constellations."

He guided her into his arms, her bare back full against his chest, rounded buttocks cradling the very heart of his desire. She relaxed in his embrace, and he rested his hand upon the gentle slope of her hip, inhaling deeply of her sweet fragrance while staring out into the black-velvet sky.

This delicious woman he held in his arms intrigued him as had no other. She denied her suitability as a love slave, yet responded to his touch with a vibrancy that promised extraordinary passion. Gentle-natured and innocent, she was unlike the women of his haremlik who were skilled in the art of pleasure. Her every thought was not to satisfy or manipulate him. Instead, she challenged him to coax her undiscovered desires to life. Was she the woman he had yet to meet, the woman who would be not only lover, but friend—his soulmate?

He played upon her responses like a musician. His hands trailed along the arc of her waist, and her shuddering intake of breath rippled through the tranquil air. He found her breast. Weighing their velvet heaviness in his hands, his fingers teased the rosy peaks of those pale mounds, and a silken moan escaped her. He pressed light kisses against the line of her cheek, the curve of her neck, the slope of her shoulder until she gasped in shallow draughts. Caressing her breasts with his hands, he gently tugged at their tight tips until her hips arched upward, seeking fulfillment.

He cradled her against him, flesh against flesh, sinking deep into the pillows. But before too much time had passed, the fluid lines of her body grew taut. "You choose now," he whispered as distraction. He was not willing to give up the newfound intimacy they shared and was eager to see if she would match his choice with courage or retreat with a faint heart.

She obviously understood the underlying challenge of his request. The tissue of the turning pages crinkled softly as she slowly scrutinized each and every position before finally settling on one—the Swan.

He met her gaze. Uncertainty was written clearly across her face, her pink mouth deepening in a frown. Solimon smiled, encouraging her choice while excitement seared his blood. Did she understand what glorious part of her anatomy she was offering him? "Shall I find it in the stars for you, fair one?"

She nodded, rolling onto her stomach and out of his arms. Solimon breathed a sigh of relief for this brief reprieve, a chance to check his own passion. His unbridled responses amazed him, and there was no doubt he would need every ounce of his usually-formidable control to survive this next position without the promise of easing his own desire. But he would not make love to her this night. They did not yet share the most precious of intimacies, and he would not risk their progress by behaving like an untried youth when he was a man of thirty and learned in the ways of pleasure. He would restrain himself no matter how he longed to do otherwise.

Gazing up at the tiny pinpricks of silver that flickered and glowed against the obsidian sky, he said, "There it is, nestled between the Dragon and the Dolphin. Do you see it?"

She tilted her head back and looked into the night. Her gilt hair, studded with jewels, shimmered as it fell in a heavy wave over her bare shoulders and back. "I see it," she said breathlessly.

Solimon bade her roll over and pressed her into the pillows. She lifted her arms as though to shield her breasts, but managed to resist the urge. Her slender white fingers curled into fists, revealing her struggle, and her whole being seemed to tense with expectation.

Did she think he would bite her? Stifling a grin at the thought, he rolled over, wedging his hips between her thighs and bracing himself above her. Her eyes flew open in astonishment. He held her gaze while sliding down, his chest raking across her nipples, his hips forcing her legs to part as she drew her knees upward to accommodate him.

"Oooh," she gasped aloud when he buried his face in her lush breasts.

He could not help but smile as her whole body tightened in response to his touch. "Do you like this?" He gently tugged at the rosy tips with his teeth.

She arched against him, her black lashes flying upward as she stared at him wide-eyed. He chuckled, resting his weight on one elbow and freeing his hand to join in the sensual game. "You look so surprised," he murmured against her gleaming flesh. "You were made for love, my fair one, made to share these pleasures." His tongue swirled lazily around first one nipple, then the other. He blew softly against the moist flesh, delighting when they hardened in response.

Her lips parted and a sigh escaped. She lifted her hands to stroke his shoulders, and a surge of desire shot through him at the mere touch of her cool hands. He traced the curve of her waist, then his fingers plucked apart the silken knot that held her trousers together.

"Grand Seigneur!"

He did not need to see her face to know of her shocked resistance. As she tried to pull away, her hips rocked within the limited confines of his body's embrace. "Do not be frightened, fair one. I would never harm you." He brushed the silk-gauze trousers from her hips and eased them down the length of her, revealing pale, shapely limbs to his appreciative gaze. "You have the power. Simply tell me to stop and I shall." His mouth trailed over her breast and down the soft skin of her stomach. "Would you like me to stop?" Her violet eyes glowed with a sultry inner light. He pressed languid kisses along the rounded line of her hip. "And now?"

"No."

His mouth found the place where her thighs met, his lips moving over the mound of her arousal. Her low moan echoed through his entire body. She was so sweet. His tongue traced her honeyed warmth, passion making her unfold like the dew-kissed petals of a blossom. His own need rose to frenzied heights as he found the center of her woman's desire and nipped at the turgid little bud. "Should I stop yet, fair one?"

Her thighs trembled, the soft flesh caressing his cheeks. He could feel her desire mounting, cresting as he drew on the tiny jewel. Her fingers twined into his hair, urging him on, and she gasped. "Don't stop."

With a surge of triumph, he abandoned himself fully to his tender ministrations, feeling every ripple, every shimmer that pulsed through her. He caressed her moist cleft with his thumb, drawing her to the edge and back, guiding her to even greater heights until she melted against him in ecstasy, crying out her rapture. A bolt of unleashed passion rocked him. He rested his face against her thigh until he found some relief from the turbulence of his own raging emotions.

He finally rolled onto his side and pulled her into his embrace, marveling at how quickly she scaled the heights of pleasure and at the intensity of his own response. She had risen valiantly to his challenge, but he would retreat to the safety of a position named Libra, giving the blood a chance to cool in his veins.

※)(ᴄᴏ)(※

Solimon stood unseen behind the stone-worked wall of the harem bath. Below him, several of the women strolled through the bathing chamber, pausing at wall fountains or grooming themselves, while others frolicked in the pool. His fair one appeared in the doorway, draped in a flowing caftan. The sapphire blue fabric swirled and shimmered around her slender frame like a waterfall. He could not drive the memory of the past night from his mind. Visions of her, soft and yielding, distracted him so he could think of nothing else.

At her appearance, the women's chattering quieted before resuming in an agitated fervor. The fair one straightened her back and entered the chamber, but as she passed by the edge of the pool, the women made unkind comments, laughing and splashing water at her. With her head held high, she ignored them and walked past, sitting on a low stone bench to comb the tangles from her glorious hair.

"It has been thus since her first night with you," the Kislar Agha explained. His voice betrayed no hint of emotion, but his obsidian eyes glowed accusingly.

Solimon ignored the pointed glare, unwilling to debate the topic again. The chief eunuch had warned him repeatedly about neglecting the haremlik. But that choice had been made long ago and he could only look to the future now. He had a favorite, and the women would adjust.

Yet he could not contain his disappointment as the scene unfolded below. The women could be kind and gracious. He had brought only the best behaved from his father's palace, and any troublemakers were quickly sent to plague some other man's household. Their jealous behavior was unforgivable, especially since his fair one already struggled to understand their way of life that was so different from her own. Even more unsettling was the possessiveness he felt toward her. He wanted to protect her from this hurt, wanted her to find acceptance and companionship in the haremlik.

"Her uncle sold her to Ibrahim Pasha," Solimon said. The blast of rage that seared him was a physical explosion, like the fury that overtook him in battle. Stunned by the intensity of the emotion, he could no longer deny the truth to himself. The fair one was more than a favorite—he had lost his heart to the violet-eyed beauty.

The Kislar Agha watched with a knowing expression. "I've heard, Grand Seigneur."

"Is there a breath of air I draw without your knowledge?"

"No, Grand Seigneur."

Solimon could not help but laugh, and his spirits lightened considerably. He gazed down again at the fair beauty whose fate he held so precariously within his grasp. Allah had brought her to him for a reason. They were fated to be together. No matter that their backgrounds and expectations differed, they could learn from each other. Above all she wanted love, and he had that in abundance for her.

She stood, sweeping the glimmering-gilt tresses behind her shoulders while unfastening the ties of the caftan. As the garment slipped from her shoulders, falling into a silken puddle at her feet, the blood surged through his veins. She was ravishing. The graceful lines of her body were still love-flushed from their night of passion.

"Bring her to me at sunset," he told the Kislar Agha, then strode from the room, suddenly certain of what he must do.

Alessandra's emotions were in a wild swirl. Was she frightened or excited to spend another night with the Sultan? He was not at all what she had expected, and after the past night, she realized just how badly she was losing the battle—and just how much she didn't mind. For the first time in her memory, she felt special. The Sultan would bind her to him as slave for a lifetime, yet he made her feel so...cherished, desired, as if being his slave was more than she had ever aspired to be. He was a legend throughout Christendom, a mighty warrior and lusty ruler with an insatiable appetite for women. But when he encircled her in his powerful arms, he was a gentle teacher, a tender lover, a man honorbound by his word.

Her emotions swung like a pendulum between excitement for the unknown future and fear of the very same. The Sultan wielded her own innocence as a weapon against her, but instead of resenting him, she found herself yearning for the glorious sensations his touch evoked. He had discovered some wild, impulsive fire smoldering inside her and had expertly stoked it until every inch of her flesh burned for him. Even the passing hours of daylight had not doused the flames.

And Alessandra faced yet another night of his ardor. Pleasure, hunger, desire suffused her. But most disturbing was that all fears paled in the swirling memories of his lips upon hers and his strong hands caressing her bare flesh. She wanted him, wanted him to make love to her. To love her. Did she love the Sultan?

The idea jolted her from her thoughts. No matter how thoughtful and considerate he had been, he still considered her no more than a pleasure-giver. She only had one more night. One night to convince him she was much more than a slave. Retrieving the amethyst-encrusted bottle, which had arrived that morning, Alessandra told the Kislar Agha, "I am ready."

She was led through the corridor to the Sultan's private bathing chamber. The chief eunuch prodded her into the disrobing room. "Your arrival needs no introduction this eve. Go to him, my lady, and may Allah be with you." He slipped out the door, and the clink of a key turning the lock sent a shudder through her. The final night of the challenge—there would be no turning back.

Passing through the finely-wrought gilt door, Alessandra stopped short in the entry, stunned by the luxuriance of the chamber. The entire room was paved in white marble, from the endless expanse of floor to the smooth dome of the ceiling and every narrow column in between. A beautiful cascade fountain bubbled and splashed like a waterfall on an opposite wall. The square pool in the center of the room caught her attention, for it was there the Sultan sat, in the midst of all this bright opulence, evidently so deep in thought he had not heard her enter.

He ran a hand through his hair, tousling the glossy black waves into dishevelment. Alessandra was suddenly struck by how solitary, how alone he seemed in the vast chamber. She remembered their conversation during the first night when he pointed out how isolated a lady could be with no one to share her responsibilities. Was he lonely sometimes? Even with a palace full of servants and a harem full of slaves, he was a man. And not just any man, but one with the weight of an empire upon his shoulders. With that realization, a wave of tenderness flowed through her. "You would have me believe the contents of this bottle somehow resemble a scholarly device?"

Her softly-spoken words disturbed the bubbling quiet of the room, and the Sultan's head snapped up, recognition softening his features. He approached her so suddenly that she did not have time to pay him homage with a bow. But he did not seem to notice as he grasped her hand firmly and seated her on the wide ledge of the pool. He took the bottle. "I can only plead for tolerance, fair one." The warmth of his smile echoed in his voice. "I wanted to tempt you with something truly special on our third night together."

His long fingers worked the amethyst-topped stopper from the bottle. Kneeling beside her, he poured its contents into the steady stream of water propelled into the pool by some hidden pump. The scent of lavender filled the air, and to her surprise, a froth of white bubbles spread along the surface in an ever-widening circle. She could not hold back the squeal of delight that slipped from her lips, and he watched her, clearly amused. "It's beautiful. What is it?" she asked.

He skimmed a handful from the pool and blew it at her. "Bubbles."

"Mmm. Smells wonderful." She wiped the foam from her nose and blew it back at him.

He brushed his own face clean, bowing his head deeply. "Lavender. In your honor."

Alessandra smiled, captivated by the boyishness of his gesture. "Another ancient form of Turkish art?"

"No. But only a person of true intelligence can appreciate relaxation and enjoyment."

"Like Ciclazade and Safiye perhaps?"

"No . . . well, yes." The Sultan laughed, a rich, deep sound that sent tingles through her. He came to his feet, strode to the disrobing chamber, and disappeared. "Since you so graciously indulge me, fair one, I will allow you to choose our topic of debate this eve," he called from the other room. "What would you like to discuss?"

She ran her fingers through the frothy confection swirling along the pool's surface, then blew the bubbles from her fingertips. "You. Tell me about yourself and your upbringing."

He reappeared in the entry, and the breath solidified in her throat. He was naked. Like a Greek statue of a god come to life, he strode toward her, muscles shifting with each step, bronzed skin in sharp relief against the stark whiteness of the chamber. She could not tear her eyes away and admired the set of his powerful shoulders and the smattering of black fur across the stony ridges of his chest. His flat stomach and trim hips brought memories of his flesh beneath her hands, the feel of his rigid arousal nudging her. Her gaze riveted to the very spot where his manhood nestled against the dark thatch of hair between his legs.

"Sweet Mother in Heaven," Alessandra choked, pressing her hand to her temple and closing her eyes.

"Of all the worldly subjects, you would discuss me?" he asked.

She could hear the ill-concealed laughter in his voice and did not chance a peek until the telltale splash of water resounded through the chamber. He leaned against the wall of the pool, only his face visible above the bubbles. "Join me, fair one, and I shall tell you all my secrets."

A passionate fluttering began deep in her stomach. She tried to push aside her shocked impropriety over his request, but failed miserably. His voice was a silken lure, urging her to the water, but a flicker of pride held her rooted to the spot. This was her heart, her entire life at stake. She must earn his respect before yielding the game. "I . . . I cannot."

"Why ever not? Can't you swim?" He stood to show her the water reached to only the middle of his broad chest. "It's not deep. I won't let you drown."

The scoundrel! She cast a quick glance at the locked door, the only exit to the chamber. Her gaze darted to his, her cheeks warming at the thought of swimming with him. She shook her head.

"Oh," he said. "I forgot. You're a maiden. What if I move over there, where I can't touch you?" He swam the length of the pool with swift powerful strokes. The water splashed against the gleam-

ing tiles, bubbles separating in his wake. "Not good enough yet?"
He turned his back to her. "What if I promise not to look while you
disrobe?"

Alessandra simply sat there, frozen.

"If you don't come in willingly, I shall come get you, and then,
fair one, I vow to touch every luscious inch of your delicious self."

Sheer panic swept through her. She stood then sat down
abruptly, uncertain of what to do. She could not swim with a naked
man!

"If you still don't trust me, I'll go under water. But please be
quick. I can only hold my breath for so long."

To Alessandra's horror, his dark head disappeared below the
surface. She glanced around frantically, seeing no escape. Leaping
to her feet, she kicked off her slippers and fumbled with the corded
sash that held the pink-spangled trousers at her waist. The garment
fell to the floor in a silken heap, and she kicked it away, dropping
the guimlik as well. Feeling every inch of her bare flesh, she slid
into the luxuriant water and sank down to her chin.

Several long moments passed, and yet he still did not appear.
She couldn't see beneath the bubbles. Had he drowned? Just as she
grew truly concerned, he erupted from the water in a forceful burst,
his wet flesh gliding full against her. She screamed, startled,
instinctively pulling away. His strong arms caught her, saving her
from going under. "I'm sorry." He flashed a wet grin. "I didn't
mean to frighten you."

Alessandra just stared at him, stunned by the feel of his sleek,
hard body.

"What would you know of me?" He swept the damp strands of
hair from her cheeks then traced the curve of her jaw. "Do you know I
find you delectable, that I yearn to feast on your sumptuous flesh?"

His mouth slowly descended to meet hers. He rained tender
kisses around her parted lips, nibbling her flesh, sending waves of
pleasure spiralling through her. Alessandra wanted to respond with
some semblance of reason, but turning their conversation into an
intellectual debate was far beyond her ability at the moment. She

had promised herself not to surrender, yet here she stood in his arms, quivering and naked, the smooth shaft of his desire pressed boldly against her.

"Do you want to know that I was raised in my father's palace, beloved by my mother and adored by my father's women, not one of whom ever came close to matching your exquisite beauty."

The heat of his body seared the entire length of her, and his breath came sweet and warm on her lips. Drowning in a tide of desire, she wanted to abandon herself to him, but was firmly caught in a trap of her own making. She could not yield, nor could she push him away. Her mind swirled with doubt. She wanted his respect. She wanted his love. And in that moment, Alessandra knew if she could not have both, she might have to choose only one.

"Do you want to know that even among the flowers in my haremlik, I have yet to know a woman who awakens such a powerful longing in me. Share this passion, fair one. Let us explore it together."

If she gave in to him, she gave him everything, her virtue, her life. And in return he would cherish her. Not as a wife, but as one of his women. A lifetime of slavery. The words echoed in her memory. Yet could she possibly live without this tantalizing love he offered?

As though he understood her struggle, he forged ahead with increasing vigor, determined to coax her over the precipice of her control. His hands stroked her every curve, the scented water enhancing the sleek feel of his fingers on her flesh.

"Discover this pleasure with me." His teeth tugged on the fullness of her lower lip. He found her breasts, his hands curling around them gently, teasing each nipple between his thumb and forefinger until she grew breathless and pliant beneath his caresses.

Perhaps she could survive without being loved, but living without this man who made her heart dance with excitement wasn't much of a future. Her head spun with his kisses, and she couldn't think of any way to win both his love and his respect.

As his tongue ravaged the soft recesses of her mouth, Alessandra slid her arms around his waist, abandoning all pretense of resistance. What was his magic that her will dissolved at his slightest touch?

She gave in to the urge to caress him, to explore the hard planes of his body. Her hands roamed freely over his tight buttocks and narrow hips. A savage groan escaped him when she found his hard shaft and stroked its throbbing length, gently, then more daring as he moved against her. She experienced an unfamiliar feeling of power as she recognized his need, his tightly-bridled restraint, knowing instinctively that only she could slake his thirst.

A tremor rocked his sinewy frame. Uncertain, she brought her hands to rest lightly around his waist and searched his darkly-beautiful face. He opened his eyes and peered intently at her, his breathing ragged, his black eyes smoldering with unfulfilled passion. Her heart fluttered wildly in her chest. Did she really want freedom when it meant giving up his love?

His mouth covered hers hungrily, and he brought her hard against him. Caressing her body in bold strokes, he shattered her composure with the fierceness of his touch. He aroused such exquisite feelings in her, feelings she couldn't resist. He slid his hot, pulsing length between her thighs. The throaty groan that tumbled from his lips sent the last of her will scattering like the tiny bubbles that converged and popped along the surface of the pool. She moved her hands over the sleek, plated lines of his chest, up the corded muscles of his neck, and finally cradled his square jaw in her palms, returning his kisses with abandon.

She flexed the muscles of her thighs around his rigid flesh. He grasped her buttocks and pulled her close, the water flowing between them, creating a slick tunnel where his pulsing desire glided silkily against her. The breath caught in her throat at the intensity of these awakening sensations and she held his face firmly in her hands, tasting his sweet tongue, knowing she would give herself to him if he would ease this ache in the very core of her being.

"Let us love, my fair one," he whispered hoarsely against her lips.

Her life for his love. Her freedom for his passion. She would have to choose. He willingly offered all that he had to give, and she would have to accept or deny him.

"Share this love with me."

His simple request eroded the very last of her control, draining the strength from her limbs, forcing surrender. She loved him. The realization flowed through her mind and body with such strength that she would have fallen had he not held her so tightly. If she had to choose between his respect and his love, Alessandra chose love. If she had to give up her world to be with him, then so be it. She loved. The word slid from her parted lips, an emphatic whisper. "Yes."

The Sultan's black eyes flashed in victory. Before another moment spent itself, he spun her around in the warm water, his mouth never relinquishing its hold upon hers. A heated languor spread through her, her legs heavy as they drifted through the water. He pulled her toward him and leaned back against the pool's edge.

"You are mine, fair one." Lifting her into his arms, he helped her wrap her legs around his hips, leaving the core of her woman's desire revealed to his probing hardness.

Suddenly he was filling her, stretching her open in a slow, silken thrust. "Seigneur," she gasped, arching against him when he met the resistance of her maidenhead.

"I am Solimon. Say it," he commanded, impaling her with his depthless gaze.

She could not suppress a shiver at the rough tone of his voice. And as his name slid from her lips, he drove into her. A bolt of pleasure-pain pierced her, and she cried out, only to find his mouth back upon hers, drawing the very sound from her. He swelled inside, and her flesh yielded to accommodate his thickness. She clung to him, only half aware of his tenseness, the passion he held barely in check.

Gripping her buttocks in strong hands, he drew her slowly

upward, withdrawing almost completely, then plunging into her in one controlled stroke. She gasped aloud, a tide of liquid fire flooding her tender loins. Trailing her fingers down the shifting muscles of his back, she filled her senses with him. His tongue demanded a response, and his surging maleness awakened an unimagined need deep within. She crushed her breasts to his ridged chest, rasping her nipples across the springy curls, even as he thrust back into her again, and yet again.

His husky moan rose over the lapping water and the gentle bubbling of the fountains. His mouth slid from hers, leaving behind only the spicy warm taste of his rough-velvet tongue. Wrapping his arms around her waist and hips, he locked her against him, embedded deep inside, then slowly moved away from the wall. She clung to him, lips pressed into his glossy black hair, gasping as each long stride pushed his hot flesh into her and sent waves of sheer rapture pounding through her.

When they reached the stair, he was forced to relinquish his possession of her and withdraw. A sound passed his lips as they parted, half-groan and half-gasp, and he swung her into his arms. They emerged from the pool, the coolness of the air sending a shiver through her body. With one broad sweep of his arm, he sent the neatly-folded piles of linens toppling off a marble bench. His eyes were heavy-lidded with passion as he pressed her back into the soft white mountain of fabric.

The spray of the fountain veiled them in its shimmering mist. His dark skin gleamed like molten gold, and Alessandra could not ever remember seeing such a magnificent sight. Bringing her hand to his face, she caressed the square line of his jaw in wonder. "Solimon, love me," she murmured, experiencing a rush of excitement at the look of raw desire on his face. She was his, and there was no where else in the world she would rather be.

"Ah, fairest one, you are perfection." He lowered himself into her tender embrace.

He thrust into her. He filled her body, her very senses. He was rapture and love. She molded to his hard form, overwhelmed by the fullness inside her, by the completeness she felt. His mouth found hers, and she yielded to his demanding mastery, swaying against him and meeting each thrust with a longing of her own.

"Love me," she gasped, the intensity of her need draining every thought from her mind. Their bodies met in exquisite harmony— surging, receding, plunging into awesome depths she had never before imagined. She was drowning in a golden wave of pleasure, diving into an eddy of sensation. A mighty shudder rocked his frame, and he took her with him, riding on the crest of ecstasy until breaker after breaker crashed along the fine-spun shore of their emotions.

Slowly Alessandra became aware of her heart hammering against her ribs and the feeling of their slick limbs entwined. The Sultan shifted his weight, carrying her onto her side, so they faced each other. He held her tightly, brushing damp tendrils from her cheeks, and rocked her back and forth, burying his face in her hair. "You are precious to me, fair one."

At the tenderness in his voice, a wave of sadness poured through her. Mingled with the awe of the moment was the under-standing that she had not only given this man her virtue, but her heart, and with those gifts, her consent to enter his haremlik. She loved him, would give her life to him. But no matter how much he wanted her, no matter how gentle he was, the Sultan still viewed her as a slave. Alessandra could not suppress a sob—she had found love, but lost the game.

"What troubles you, fair one?" He pressed a light kiss on her brow. "Have I hurt you?"

Swallowing hard, she met his gaze. "I have gambled and lost."

"No one has lost. We have both won. We are bound together." His arms tightened around her, and she could not suppress the slight shudder, the ripple of confusion that ran through her.

His dark gaze searched her face. "Is what I offer you so distaste-ful?" he asked, his expression serious, without a trace of humor.

"What exactly do you offer me, Grand Seigneur?"

The Sultan watched her for a long moment. He loosened his

hold on her and swept his arm around in a half circle. "All that I am. A place of honor in my haremlik."

Her tumultuous emotions rose to the surface. No matter how she willed it otherwise, tears welled in her eyes and spilled over.

He frowned, the flickering muscle at his jaw betraying deep frustration. "Is a lifetime spent laboring at your uncle's side truly more desirable than what I offer you here?"

She wanted to say something to magically erase the troubled edge to his voice, but could do no more than wipe the tears from her cheeks. He stared at her, and when she didn't respond, his face transformed into an inscrutable, kingly mask. In that instant, Alessandra no longer recognized her handsome lover.

"Once again we are at an impasse," he said. "The three nights have passed—whom shall we call victor?"

※≈(☉)≈※

"You may approach," the Sultan said from his seat upon the throne.

Alessandra thought him an imposing figure in his royal finery. Unlike her tender lover of the three nights past, he barely resembled the man who had captured her heart. A wave of apprehension coursed through her. He had triumphed. Forcing herself to leave the Kislar Agha's side, she crossed the Royal Salon, past the rows of silent eunuchs, then bowed low before the Sultan.

"It is sunset of the fourth night, fair one, and before we call an end to our game, I would ask you a question. Rise and face me."

Alessandra stood, pulse racing. She met his solemn gaze, hardly recognizing the man she had come to know so intimately, the man who had unlocked her heart and soul.

"I have learned there is strife within my haremlik, that my women have welcomed you in a manner that brings shame upon me. Is this true?"

She cast an accusing glance at the Kislar Agha, who scowled at her for such rudeness. What could she say? Upon her arrival at the

Palace, the women had welcomed her graciously, helped ease her fear of an unfamiliar world. But they had turned just as quickly when the Sultan committed to spending three nights with her. They had been both kind and unkind. Finding no words to adequately explain the situation, she fixed her gaze on the far corner of the room, where finches bobbed from perch to perch in a wrought iron aviary, and shrugged.

"I have witnessed their cruelty, fair one, and now must deal with it."

Alessandra cringed. Did the very walls of this Palace have eyes? She was more than mildly embarrassed that he, a man who bore the responsibilities of an empire, felt the need to concern himself with troubles so trivial in comparison. If she was going to spend her life in his haremlik, she would have to make a place for herself. "Grand Seigneur, I appreciate your concern—"

"I would ask your counsel on the matter." He leaned back on the high-backed throne and steepled his fingers before him. "How would you deal with this jealousy?"

He wanted her counsel? Alessandra stared at him, unsure if she had heard correctly. Despite a momentary flash of panic, she could do no less than tell the truth—whether it pleased him or not. "The women simply follow your lead. You do not spend time with them, so they lose all desire to make the haremlik an inviting place. With nothing more constructive to do with their days, they aspire to tasks loftier than those they now possess and scheme for your meager attentions. When you committed to spending so much time with me, I became a threat."

Some unrecognizable emotion glimmered in the depths of his eyes, and she swallowed hard before continuing. "If you would have them behave differently, you must treat them differently—like you have me."

He did not respond, and the silence grew heavy between them. Barely daring to breath, Alessandra forced herself to hold his gaze, back straight and head high, knowing full well the next moments would decide the rest of her life.

His voice shattered the tense quiet. "Clear the chamber."

She flinched, but resisted the urge to look away. Studying him intently while the occupants of the room departed, she wondered at his thoughts, wanted so badly to erase that distant expression from his face and see him smile. The realization led to another—he was right when he said there was no loser in this game, no winner either. If she left the haremlik, they would be apart; if he did not respect her, she would lose respect for herself.

As though he read his thoughts, he said, "You are wise as well as beautiful. You understand that neither of us can claim victory?"

She had been holding her breath without realizing it and slowly exhaled at his words. "I know."

He extended his hand, and without hesitation she placed her own within it. He looked down, silent, his dark fingers tracing her pale ones. "You have given me a gift beyond price, fair one. The gift of yourself." His gaze lifted to hers again. "I would give you a gift as precious in return."

She listened, bewildered. What could possibly compare to entering his haremlik? Her chest grew tight, and time seemed to hang on the edge of his words. Her fingers tingled where they twined within his.

His expression never wavered, but his grip tightened ever so slightly, so slightly, she might have imagined it. "I have learned there is a part of you which I cannot command or take, a part you must offer freely. I would have that part of you as well."

He rose from his throne. Still holding her hand firmly in his, he took a step toward her, the ceremonial robe swirling from the powerful set of his shoulders. "I will free you if you wish, but I ask that you stay."

He would disregard their bargain to make her happy. The knowledge filled her with tenderness. But Alessandra no longer wanted freedom. She wanted him—all of him. And that he asked her to stay willingly proved he could respect her as more than a slave.

The white turban covered his head, hiding all but his dark

features from her view. His expression softened, the cold mask melting away to reveal his heart's desire. "Stay with me, Alessandra. You already have my heart, I would give you my loyalty as well." He peered down at her, his sparkling gaze reaching into her very soul. "Be my wife in the eyes of Allah and your Christian God. Be the mother of my children, if we are so blessed. I don't offer you a lifetime of slavery, but a lifetime of love."

He spoke of love . . . and marriage. A haze of surprised emotions assailed her, and she could do no more than gape at him.

"I love you." Bringing her hand to his lips, he pressed a gentle kiss into her palm. "I will marry you in your Christian way and devote my life to your happiness. Will it be enough?"

Marriage! It was more than she dared hope. The shadows fled her heart. She felt fully alive, blissfully complete. Tears of joy prickled at the backs of her lids, and a sound, half-sigh and half-laugh, bubbled from her lips. "You offer me everything you are, and it is more than I ever imagined."

His dark eyes caressed her, promising to fulfill her dreams. She stepped into the strong circle of his arms and raised her face to him.

He smiled, a smile that brightened the strong lines of his face, a smile filled with love. "Come with me, my beloved. We have the entire night before us." His mouth slowly descended on hers. "And our entire lives."

About the author:

Jeanie LeGendre lives in Florida with her romance-hero husband, her two darling little girls, a feisty five-pound Maltese, and two stray tabby cats who adopted the family as their own. Born into a big Italian brood, she simply adores family — her mom and sister live close by, her various aunties, uncles and cousins are all near and dear to her heart, and she considers herself blessed with the most precious friends on the planet.

She has had a head full of romance for as long as anyone can remember — no one was surprised when she named her daughters after her favorite heroines — and believes the stories in **Secrets** really can happen. After all, she and her husband are living proof.

The Proposal

by Ivy Landon

To my reader:
    Sex of an unconventional kind for those who seek the hard to find.

"I have an important proposal I need to run by you tonight."
Craig's husky voice came through Tracey Vennet's speaker phone,
and the anticipation of seeing him sent a thrill down her spine.

Tracey made a note to have her secretary cancel her dinner
engagement with the Japanese trade group and reschedule for next
week. It was uncharacteristic of Craig not to give her more warning
of his sudden arrival in town. Usually their meetings were set
weeks in advance.

She kept her tone smooth and business like. "Is anything wrong?"

As president of Acton Industries, she was responsible to Craig
Logan, CEO and owner of Acton, and his demands on her time
took top priority. She tapped her pencil on her desk. In her mind,
Craig Logan would always be first.

She'd fallen in love with him the first time they'd met during
the Tinker Truck advertising campaign. While the other executives
sat around the enormous conference table, Craig had taken off his
jacket, rolled up his sleeves, and kneeled on the floor. With childish pleasure and intuitive genius, he'd pushed the Tinker Trucks
across the carpet, scooping up imaginary piles of sand. Afterward,
he'd quickly sketched his suggested design changes and diverted
the necessary funding to the appropriate department.

His maverick design and her hard work on the ad campaign led
to the most successful new toy on the market. When she convinced
a major film company to use Tinker Trucks in their movie, sales
skyrocketed, and Craig promoted Tracey to the presidency. Oddly,
he left her alone to run Acton as she wished, only rarely flying in
to check on his company.

Tracey looked forward to the intimate dinners in the private
company dining room where she had Craig to herself. On several
occasions he'd taken her to his penthouse apartment, and they'd

made love on his bed overlooking the city's skyline. Their sex life might not set her ablaze with passion, but she'd always believed torrid lust a romance writer's invention. For months now, she'd hoped for a proposal that would make their arrangement more permanent.

"Nothing's wrong," Craig's voice reassured her. She could almost see the corners of his lips twitching into a teasing smile. "At least nothing we can't fix over the weekend. Are you free?"

For him, she would always be free. "I'll give my theater tickets to my mom. Unless you'd like to go?"

"Let's keep this weekend private. I don't want to see anyone but you." At his sensual tone, her heart beat accelerated a notch. She imagined him looking lazily across his desk though half-closed lids that disguised the most brilliant intellect she'd ever matched wits with. Many a businessman had been taken in by his enigmatic expression, unsuspecting of a mind that was equally comfortable reading Homer's *Iliad* in Greek, sketching pigeons in Central Park, or calculating the mathematical equations for high-tech computer chips.

Tracey worked through the afternoon, a special lurch of excitement urging her to clear her desk of the most pressing items. Making a short trip to the private restroom off her office three hours later, she took time to pat a few stray hairs back into her smooth jet chignon. She freshened her makeup, giving just a hint of eye shadow to blue eyes glowing with anticipation. After using her pinkie to dab on fresh lip gloss, Tracey straightened her white silk blouse and navy skirt. Not the ideal clothes for a romantic dinner, but then Craig knew she'd worked all day, and he usually seemed much more interested in what she had to say than the clothes she wore.

One of Craig's better qualities was his ability to look beneath the surface, to see more with just a glance than others saw with a telescope. And he had an uncanny knack for anticipating what might go wrong, delving straight to the heart of a problem, and fixing it before others recognized a difficulty existed. She'd trusted Craig's judgment implicitly and hoped he hadn't spotted any problems at Acton.

Craig's lighthearted hint that they could fix whatever he'd noticed cast a slight shadow of unease on Tracey's anticipation. As she walked down the staircase to the private dining room, her blood coursed through her veins in expectation.

She opened the heavy wooden doors and walked across the plush oriental carpet. She'd been in this room many times, but never before had the scent of fresh cut flowers wafted to her nostrils. Never before had the crystal chandelier been dimmed and replaced by candles on the dining table. Craig waited with a velvet jeweler's box next to gleaming silver, delicate china, and a crisp lace table cloth. A silver bucket holding a magnum of Dom Perignon on ice sat in the center of the table with two crystal flutes.

When she entered the room, Craig's face broke into a grin and he rose to his feet, his dark suit fitting his lean and tanned body to perfection. "Come in. You're early, darling. I've only been waiting fifteen minutes."

He held out his hand, and by the teasing glimmer in his dark eyes, she knew he wasn't angry. She gave his fingers a gentle squeeze and lightly brushed his cheek with her lips. "Sorry, I took a last minute phone call from our Paris office."

His eyes boldly raked her silk blouse and plain skirt. "You didn't have time to change into something more suitable for our date?"

"I was working. As it was I had to cancel the meeting with—"

He interrupted with light teasing. "Another woman would have gone shopping, ordered something delivered."

"Is it me you want?" Her eyes narrowed. "Or me in designer clothes."

His eyes twinkled. "I want you naked."

"Craig!"

He waved a hand dismissing her outrage and the sudden heat in her cheeks. "Forget it. We have more important things to discuss."

Pulling out a chair for her, he pushed the velvet box in her direction before taking a seat. When she started to open the box, his hand gently pressed down on hers, stopping her. Raising her gaze to meet his, she arched her brow in a questioning gesture.

"I'm going to ask you something important."

Her mouth went cottony dry. Were her dreams going to come true? Was Craig going to ask her to become his wife?

"Yes?" She'd never known him to be so hesitant before and thought it rather sweet.

"First, you must promise not to answer my question for at least twenty-four hours."

"But why?"

"Because the answer you give me in twenty-four hours may be different from the one you give me now."

"If this is a riddle, I don't understand."

Craig paused, then leaned forward placing both elbows on the table and resting his chin in his palms. "Do you trust me?"

At his hungry stare, her heart thumped against her ribs. "Of course, I do."

"Will you do anything I ask of you for the next twenty-four hours?"

She had absolutely no idea what he was asking her. And it was unlike him to be so vague. "Could you be more specific?"

"Will you marry me, Tracey?" As soon as the words popped out of his mouth, he pressed one finger to her lips. "Don't answer that. Not until tomorrow. Instead I'd like an answer to my first question, will you do anything I ask?"

A swell of confusion engulfed her. "Why?"

"Because our sex life is not all it should be. Because if we're going to spend the rest of our lives together, I want to do certain things for you. Please you in ways you have never imagined."

She stiffened, all her fears crashing on her in a stormy convergence of black clouds. Her hands turned to ice. He'd found her inadequate in bed. Swallowing the sudden lump in her throat, she forced the words past her lips. "You weren't satisfied when we made love?"

His eyes blazed. "That's part of it. How could I be satisfied when you didn't enjoy it?"

"But I did—"

"You enjoyed the holding, the cuddling, the talking." His tone hardened in a voice he used in the board room when he dared anyone to contradict him. "But as for the sex—you tolerated me." His hands reached across the table and gripped her shoulders. "I want to shatter your inhibitions and release your passion."

If his hands hadn't gripped her tightly, she would have slumped in her seat. At the moment she wished she could say, "Beam me up, Scotty," and a transporter would whisk her away so she didn't have to face him. She should have known he would realize she didn't enjoy sex. Not that she hated the act. Tracey just thought it was a whole lot of fuss over very little. Still she'd always felt deficient in the bedroom, and she'd been so sure love would solve her problems. Only it hadn't. She loved Craig with all her heart, but she hadn't seen stars, and if she was honest with herself, she hadn't felt much desire.

And now he wanted her to give him a blind promise—so he could crash through her inhibitions. She forced a breath of air into her starved lungs, barely realizing she'd stopped breathing. Suppose he discovered she had no passion? Suppose something was missing from her? No doubt he wanted to find out before he saddled himself to a wife.

"Think it over carefully. Once you give me your word, I'll expect total cooperation."

"You mean obedience," she snapped.

He inclined his head slightly but didn't deign to give a reply.

The pads of her fingers worried back and forth over the velvet nap of the jewelry box, too large for a ring. She wondered what it held, then realized her thoughts fluttered in indecision, preferring to dwell on anything but Craig's proposal. To allow him to order her about, to give him the power over her like a master over a slave terrified her. The thought of losing her freedom to anyone, even a man she trusted might be asking more than she could give.

Yet as she looked across the table and discerned his excitement, his exhilaration sparked her sense of adventure. If she could experience the pleasure of orgasm with this man, it would be worth any freedom she gave up. And submitting to him would only be temporary.

Taking another deep breath, she nodded. "I'll do anything you ask for twenty-four hours."

She expected a smile of triumph. Instead his eyes glittered with excitement, and his face softened, aiming a quiver of fear at her heart. Somehow she knew that after today their relationship would never again be the same. After today he might never want to see her again, and yet, she'd never forgive herself if she didn't try with everything she had to keep this man.

"This calls for a toast." Craig popped the cork of the champagne and poured her a glass.

Looking deeply into her eyes over the rim of the bubbling wine, he clinked her glass with his. "To passion."

"To love."

The fizzy drink quenched her parched throat. Uneasily she set down her glass, waiting for what he'd do next.

Craig nodded toward the velvet box. "Open it."

She lifted the lid and sucked in her breath. A golden choker at least two inches wide and set with sparkling diamonds and sapphires rested elegantly in the velvet box. "It's gorgeous."

"The blue stones reminded me of the dark cobalt in your eyes," he admitted. "Come here and I'll latch it for you."

She did as he asked, turning her back. The gold choker settled about her neck, and she raised her chin to prevent the diamonds from scratching her. The clasp snapped shut with a click, the necklace fitting her as if custom made.

"How does it look?" She turned around for him to admire.

"It's perfect. The necklace will remind you of your promise. There's only one problem."

She swallowed hard, realizing the beautiful necklace suddenly seemed too tight about her neck. And somehow she knew he'd make her wear the necklace for the next twenty-four hours as a constant reminder of their bargain. "What's the problem?"

"Your blouse is blocking my view. Would you remove it, please?"

Her pulse raced. Although the elegant dining room was private, anyone could enter at any time. "But the waiter—"

"Has been told to knock."

"He could forget."

Craig didn't say another word. He strode across the room and slid the bolt home with a loud metallic clunk, locking them in privacy. Then he folded his arms across his broad chest and waited in silence, the light of anticipation in his eyes.

She inwardly quailed at the idea of submitting to his request. Craig had never even seen her in a swim suit, and although they'd made love several times, the room had been pitch black; she'd insisted on it, and he'd gone along with her wishes.

Until now.

As her hand went to the first button, her fingers trembled. The gold collar forced her chin up, and as she undid one button after another then slipped off her blouse, she watched Craig's lips break into a grin of delight. The cool air on the bare flesh of her shoulders and midriff gave her goose bumps, or was it due to his hot look?

Standing before him clad only in her bra and skirt made her stomach clench. But when she realized how much he enjoyed looking at her, she forced herself not to squirm.

"In the candlelight, your skin has a pearly luminescence. Please remove your bra next."

Next? Her heart slammed into her ribs with the force of a freight train. Next, implied he might ask her to remove every stitch of clothing. Her knees felt like they might buckle at any moment and despite her promise she didn't know if she could continue.

If Craig sensed her hesitation, he gave no indication of it. He returned to his seat and poured them another glass of champagne. However the moment her hands went to undo the clasp his gaze pierced her with a fierce brilliance, and she had to remind herself she'd agreed to this. The air-conditioning cycled on, and the cool air from the overhead vent tingled on her bared breasts. She had the urge to raise her hands and cover herself to stop his bold gaze from raking her. But she refrained from such a childish gesture.

Nor did she dwell on how she wished her bosom was bigger. Watching Craig's face, she reminded herself this was the man she loved, the man she intended to marry. There was nothing wrong with him staring at her bare breasts. So why did her insides feel so tight?

"You're lovely. Later I'm going to explore every inch of you. I'm going to caress you, and nibble."

At his words, heat rose from her breasts, up her neck, over her shoulders.

"Place your clothes, there." He gestured to a basket. "And then come have dinner before it gets cold.

Relief washed over her when he didn't ask her to remove her skirt. Still, she'd never done anything more difficult than fulfilling his request of sitting across the table from him while she remained exposed.

His hands removed silver platter covers and the mouth-watering scents of conch-and-shrimp fritters, a West Indian soup, and stuffed Cornish game hen wafted to her nostrils. She snapped open her linen napkin and placed it over her lap while Craig filled her plate.

If he'd ignored her lack of attire, eating might have been easier. But his gaze slid from her eyes to her shoulders to her breasts repeatedly. Her stomach tightened, and she couldn't eat a bite.

Apparently the view whetted his appetite. And while she sipped her wine, he ate and ate. Finally he stopped his fork half-way to his mouth. "Short of returning your clothes, is there anything I can do to make you more comfortable?"

"You could remove your shirt," she suggested. At least maybe then she wouldn't feel so underdressed.

Lowering his fork, he grinned. "Ah, perhaps my plan is already working if you're so anxious for me to undress."

He unknotted his tie and unfastened the buttons of his shirt in a prolonged strip tease. Suddenly her hunger returned, and she placed a forkful of delicious shrimp into her mouth, chewed, and swallowed.

"Don't think I'm anxious to see your bare chest, Craig Logan. I merely thought that what's good for the goose is good for the gander."

Craig grinned nonchalantly. "Uh-huh. Do you feel less vulnerable now?"

She raised her gaze from her plate and took in the sight of his muscular torso. Like his face and hands, his torso sported a golden tan. Light swirls of hair decorated his chest in a v-shape, spreading from nipple to nipple, then tapering to his flat stomach. Tracey gave up all pretense at eating.

Instead she watched him, watched his shoulders flex as he cut his food, watched the muscles ripple, and remembered the feel of him in bed. His body was very different from hers. He'd been right in thinking she liked the cuddling and caressing, she'd thought she might have felt something when he held her, but it disappeared when they'd made love.

He wiped his mouth with his napkin, then dropped it into his lap. "I thought after we marry you would live with me. Give up your job."

"But I like it here."

"Acton Industries is only one part of the empire. You can travel from company to company with me. There's more than enough work for both of us."

"Your people would think I earned the position in bed."

He shot her a devilish grin. "That remains to be seen. Come here." He patted his lap.

She stood and took a step in his direction, suddenly very aware of her swaying breasts.

"It's time for dessert. You can remove the rest of your clothes."

Knowing he'd intended to ask it of her didn't make the doing any easier. "Why?"

"Because I asked it of you. Need I remind you of your promise or that we are totally alone? No one can enter. The door's locked."

She placed her hands on her hips. "What makes you think this is going to work?"

"Have you ever known one of my plans to fail?" A mocking glimmer of satisfaction crossed his arrogant expression.

"But—"

"Relax. There's no bed in this room. I'm hardly going to rape you. In fact, we aren't going to make love."

"We aren't?" Surprise and relief mingled with her confusion, the tension inside her easing a bit.

"Am I shocking you?" his husky voice rasped.

She nodded.

"Good. Then my plan is working. Take those off."

As she complied, the zipper's noise seemed unusually loud. Her heart thudded in her chest.

"The panties and hose too."

She hooked her fingers under the elastic and lowered the panties and hose over her hips. Tracey turned to sit and finish the job but a mischievous smile on his lips told her he wouldn't let her off so easily.

He pointed to a spot four feet from the table and well within the candlelight's glimmer. "Stand there."

His crisp order shot a sizzle of electricity through her. No one had ever spoken to her in that demanding tone, expecting complete obedience, and she suddenly wondered what he would do if she changed her mind.

One look at his face, and she didn't dare ask. He appeared more determined than she could ever recall, and a tiny spurt of fear mixed with a sudden agitation.

Slowly, she walked to the spot he'd indicated. He moved his chair back from the table slightly to have a better look. When she began to slip the garment past her hips, he helped himself to some coffee.

"Turn around."

Her face burned. "Excuse me?"

"I want to watch your bottom when you bend over."

"I don't think—"

"Do it."

She spun around, almost losing her balance and blinking back a tear. This wasn't her idea of a good time. For one thing, heat flushed over her face, and she thought she'd choke on the embarrassment. As she bent over to roll the hose down her legs, she imagined his stare, and her bottom felt hot.

"Come here," he repeated his voice soft now and sympathetic. She longed to run across the four feet separating them, fling herself against his chest, so he would stop staring.

As she neared, his nostrils flared, and beads of perspiration dotted his brow. She saw how her body aroused him, and the heady thought washed away her embarrassment, leaving a feeling of power in its wake. She might be the one standing without clothes, but obviously he was the one having difficulty mastering his desire.

She slipped onto his lap and wound her arms around his neck.

His hand reached for a fresh strawberry, dipped it in melted chocolate and a dab of whipped cream before bringing it to her lips.

She opened her mouth and lapped off the cream, licked at the chocolate, then sank her teeth into the fresh berry. "Delicious."

"And you don't even have a smidgeon of sexual desire, do you?"

"No," she told him, ignoring the bevy of butterflies in her stomach. "Why do you think that is?"

"Perhaps you need an extra stimulus to get you started, to get you thinking in the right direction." He flipped her until she lay belly down across his lap. With the tips of his fingers, he traced light, circling motions across her elevated bottom.

She twisted back to look at him. "What are you doing?"

One powerful hand pushed the small of her back until her hands touched the floor. Blood rushed to her head, but suddenly all she could think of was her bottom, high in the air, and she wriggled in an attempt to get free.

In the struggle, her legs parted, and his hand slipped between her thighs. She gasped as his hand cupped her. Although he'd tried many times, saying he could please her, he'd only touched her there once before, and she'd been so miserable she'd begged him not to.

"You're dry," he commented as if she could be otherwise. "Haven't I been patient with you?"

"Yes."

"And it got us nowhere, don't you agree?"

"Yes."

"So now it's time to try something different." His hand slipped from between her legs and made tiny caressing circles with his palm over the crease of her bottom.

Fright made her voice rise. "What are you going to do?"

"Smack your bottom. Make the skin hot."

She squirmed in earnest, her buttocks clenched tight. "No, Craig. I'm not into pain."

"This won't hurt. Not a lot. Just lots of little slaps to stimulate you."

Her feet kicked, and she tried to twist off his lap. "Don't do this. I won't like it."

"Do you have any idea how the sight of your pert bottom turned up and struggling is making me feel?"

She didn't need him to answer. His arousal against her lower belly spoke volumes. "This won't work."

He smacked her. Her back arched in surprise more than pain. She'd been so sure she could talk him out of it.

His open hand smacked her in seven or eight lightly stinging blows. He hit her high across the crests, along her hips, down low on the curve of her buttocks.

She kicked wildly and then realized he'd stopped.

"Did I hurt you?" he asked. "Your skin is this delicate shade of pink."

"Of course you hurt me."

"What about now? Does it still hurt?"

She shoved on the floor with her hands, trying to get up, but he held her firm, forcing her to answer his question. She hated to admit it, but, probably because she had so much padding on her bottom, the area no longer stung.

"I feel hot," she admitted.

"Where?"

"Where you hit me," she snapped irritably.

Despite her efforts to clamp her thighs tight, his hand slipped between them. "And what about where I didn't hit you?"

Tracey couldn't believe it, couldn't deny the wetness his hand discovered between her legs. "Noooo!" she cried out, unwilling to believe she was so peculiar that pain could produce pleasure.

"Yes. Stand up," he ordered, giving her an extra smack on the bottom when she didn't scramble up fast enough to suit him. One light whack ignited her oh-so-sensitive nerve endings, sending molten lava coursing through her veins.

She stood as he'd asked of her, more stunned with her own reaction than by the fact he'd actually spanked her. He remained in his chair and pulled her onto his lap, settling her legs apart and dangling on either side of his hips. "Put your arms around my neck."

As soon as she placed her hands, he resettled her so her smarting bottom hung in the air between his spread thighs. Never in her life had she felt so open, vulnerable, hot. A mist of perspiration broke out on her brow. The air conditioner failed to keep up with the heat Craig aroused in her. She had no idea what he intended to do next, and the anticipation made her jumpy.

"Look at me."

She forced her gaze up to his face, afraid she might see disgust, but his warm eyes sparkled with amusement. His mouth twitched up at one corner. "Tell me how you feel right now."

"Ashamed. Embarrassed that you did this to me and are laughing at me."

"Wrong. First, there is nothing to be ashamed of. Any private behavior that is mutually pleasing by two consenting adults is acceptable behavior in my book. Second, there is nothing odd, peculiar, or strange about you. Pain didn't arouse you."

"Then what did?"

"A combination of two things." He reached up with his finger and tapped her head. "Your brain is the most sensitive sexual organ. And you love me."

He might be trying to make her feel better by explaining her odd reaction away with theories that were mere conjecture, but she knew differently. She'd loved Craig for a long time, and her body had never responded like this. Even now his hands traced tiny circles along the insides of her thighs, and she ached to rub her breasts against his chest. "But—"

"Heat from my slaps aroused you. The light smacks brought blood rushing to the area. And now that you're so sensitive, one or two whacks will bring the warmth back."

Craig leaned forward slightly, his arm reaching between her thighs to her exposed bottom. "And I now have your complete attention." He hit each cheek lightly.

Her lips parted in a gasp. She could think of nothing but what he was doing to her, what he would do next. The sting dissolved into waves of heat carried on a tide of excitement, swelling her breasts. Tracey wriggled, attempting to press her nipples against Craig.

His hands rested lightly on her hips, preventing her from attaining her goal of hugging him. "We aren't finished talking yet."

Her eyes widened in surprise and alarm. Her nipples tightened into hard, aching little points. "You want to talk?"

He moved his fingers in ever-smaller circles up the insides of her thighs. "I am merely pleased by your excitement."

She would have dropped her head but the collar prevented that. Instead, somewhere past the vicinity of his left ear, she picked a spot on the wall to stare at.

"Don't look away. I want to see your eyes when I put my finger inside you."

His black stare bored into hers. And she waited for his finger to invade her body. And waited. Tensing. When she felt nothing, she began to drop her gaze to see where he'd put his hands.

With surprise, she discovered exactly where he'd put one hand. He gave her bottom four short whacks. "Look at me. Don't look away again."

Her bottom ached, searing hotter than before. And the heat spread, and suddenly she released a flow of wet, slick, heat between her thighs. She recognized the reaction for what it was—desire.

Arching her back, she thrust her breasts toward his mouth. Her hips gyrated seemingly on their own volition.

"Don't move. Tell me what you want."

"Please, Craig. I've never felt like this before. Make love to me before I lose this delicious feeling."

"You aren't ready."

Tracey choked back a sob of frustration. Delicious tingling sensations prickled her skin. Craig had kindled a fire in her belly and the sparks blew and caught, firing her imagination at new possibilities. He'd made her feel wanting, yearning, raw need.

Was there nothing this man couldn't do? A surge of love for him rose up in her throat so she wasn't expecting his tender gaze to turned decisive. The waiting was over. The tip of his finger slipped inside her, and her muscles clenched around him, silently asking for more.

"Kiss me, please," she whispered, knowing if he complied, she could press herself against his chest.

He didn't insert his fingertip farther, but his thumb parted her folds. "Not until you whimper. And don't think of faking it. I'll know the difference."

She opened her legs wider in encouragement. Why did he have to take so damn long? When his thumb flicked over her most sensitive spot, she almost leapt off his lap.

"Be still. Close your eyes now."

His fingers continued their magic, creating a hollowness inside her. She discovered the sensations seemed more intense without visual distractions. Without conscious thought, her hips gyrated in an attempt to take his finger deeper inside her.

Whack! Smack! She received two hard slaps on her bottom for her futile effort to hurry him. Either this time he'd hit her harder than previously, or her already stinging skin was becoming more sensitive.

She expected him to continue the fiery caresses between her legs but he didn't. With her eyes closed, she tensed, waiting to see what he would do. Longing to open them, she didn't dare, wanting to avoid any more spankings. Her bottom already felt hot enough to set her panties on fire—that is if Craig ever let her wear panties again. After the way she reacted to him, she wouldn't be surprised if he wanted ready access to her bottom at all times. One thing about Craig, when he found a method that worked, he—

"Oh my, God!" she gasped when his mouth found her breast.

"It's much too late for prayers." He chuckled, his breath teasing her erect nipple. His tongue circled her other breast, shooting quivers of liquid heat to her loins. "Do you like this?"

"Yes. No. I don't know."

He leaned back then, and pushed her thighs wider apart. "Would you care to explain your last three sentences." The amusement in his voice had ceased to make her blush. Her reactions had gone far beyond blushing, far beyond embarrassment, to discover a sweet, aching fire that needed to be doused.

"Every time you touch me, I want more. But no matter what you do, it isn't enough."

"Good."

Startled by the concept that he thought her frustration was good, her eyelids flew open. When she spied his cocked brow, she remembered she'd just forgotten the spanks she would pay for not following his orders.

"Remember I owe you several pats on your bottom. I'll claim them at my leisure." And he always collected on debts. Clearly Craig didn't intend to discipline her now. He preferred to keep her guessing, off balance, aching for him to touch her.

"Please, stand up."

Her legs shook underneath her, but she did what he asked. When he stood and took her hand, leading her across the room, she breathed a sigh of relief. With the door locked, they could make love on the plush leather couch. She was positive it wasn't the first time the cozy room had been used for such purposes, although she doubted anyone else scented the room with fresh cut flowers and flooded it with candlelight.

Her heart skipped three beats when he led her to one end of the couch. Several boxes stood stacked by one side, and she turned to look up at him with some confusion. Didn't he know that right now she wanted him, not presents? Didn't he know she was doing everything in her power not tackle him onto that couch and tear off his clothes?

"I'd like you to put on everything you find in those boxes while I'm gone."

"You're leaving me!"

"I'm glad you'll miss me, but I'll only leave you for a few minutes. The last packages didn't arrive but a messenger promised to deliver them to the front desk." Craig scooped up her shoes and clothes. "You won't be needing these."

She sprinted across the room to him in a panic. "Wait! You can't leave me here without any clothes."

"Are you going back on your promise?" he asked softly, his eyes focused on her heaving breasts. "I'll lock you in. No one else has a key."

"But suppose there's a fire?" she wailed, unable to keep her unhappiness from her voice at the sudden turn of events. She'd expected to be on that couch with her legs wrapped around him, feelings sensations she'd never experienced. Instead he intended to lock her in the private dining room without a stitch to wear.

Craig shrugged into his shirt and fastened the buttons, then slung his jacket over his shoulder, refusing to even leave her that. "There's only going to be one fire. The one building inside you. While I'm gone, I'll expect certain things. One. Don't think of relieving your sexual frustration by your own hand. Two, I expect you to be wearing every item in those boxes, and Tracey—"

She swallowed hard. "Yes?"

He grinned, and his gaze boldly raked over her still-hard nipples. "When the lock clicks and the door opens, I expect you to be posing seductively."

"But aren't we going to make love?"

"I already told you, we wouldn't. Not here. Not now. Remember, when this door opens, you'd better—"

"I know, be posing seductively," she replied petulantly.

His hand smacked her bottom lightly. "Don't disappoint me."

Damn. Damn. Damn! As he locked her in the room, she swore silently, calling him every foul name she remembered. Why had he spoiled her mood? The precious feeling of arousal he'd worked so carefully to create vanished in smoke.

How dare he build up her expectations, then dash her hopes? Why was he even making her go through all this if he didn't intend to make love to her?

She kicked at the boxes in fury, toppling them over. One of the boxes opened and a pair of black stiletto-heeled shoes fell out. A rush of excitement filled her, replacing the anger. Perhaps he'd left her clothes after all. Unable to sit on her sore bottom without wincing, she knelt and opened the other packages. One-by-one, she withdrew luxurious, sensual garments, lace silk thigh-highs from France, a butter-soft black leather bustier, and thong leather panties.

Knowing she'd delayed too long, and Craig could return at any moment, she quickly rolled the silk hose over her calves, past her knees until they hugged her thighs. The thong-backed panties felt strange with the tiny piece of material clinging to the crease of her rear. As soon as she shrugged into the bustier, she realized what she hadn't seen in the dim light. The strapless cups didn't cover her nipples, but served to lift her breasts to beg for a man's attention. When she slipped into the elegant heels, her breasts lifted higher to compensate. The clothes Craig had picked out enhanced her nudity, and she understood that bare flesh was more modest than what he'd asked her to wear for him.

Tracey had delayed thinking about the inevitable but could put if off no longer. If Craig unlocked that door right now, she wouldn't be able to assume the seductive pose he'd asked for quickly enough to fool him that she'd been waiting. He wanted her seductively dressed, posed, and ready for him when he walked through that door.

Sitting on the couch or chair was out of the question. That left, kneeling—out of the question—standing, or draping herself upon the couch. If she chose the couch, she'd have to settle on her side or stomach. She considered the possibilities for a moment and wondered if he'd consider them sexy. She'd hate him looking down at her and decided to remain on her feet, facing the door.

Perhaps if she enticed him, she could even change his mind about making love. Tracey bent one knee, turned her hips, slightly and lifted her chin, wanting to see Craig's expression when he walked through the door. Odd how she didn't consider disobeying him, realizing she was having too much fun.

As she stood waiting in anticipation, her discovery that her feelings of arousal hadn't disappeared after all sent another flood of excitement washing over her. Since she hadn't been satisfied, the sensations surged back with surprising strength, and she wondered if she should have chosen the couch.

Too late to move. The soft tread of footsteps outside the door alerted her to Craig's presence. The lock clicked, and she stood straighter, tilting her chin to avoid the diamonds on the necklace.

The dancing light in Craig's eyes when he spotted her more than

made up for her hesitancy, and a toasty thrill of exhilaration rico-
cheted from her breasts to her core. As he crossed the room toward
her, his voice turned husky. "Don't move. You're gorgeous."

She trembled at his compliment, taking pleasure in his enjoyment of her newfound bravery. While wearing such exotic under
garments, she couldn't help but think of where he'd touched her
and how. Her exposed bottom, tilted high due to the heels,
throbbed with a pleasurable tingle. As Craig walked around her
slowly, her breasts ached for his caress.

His gaze stroked every inch of her, and her stomach tightened in
expectation. What would he do next?

"Hold still," he ordered, at the same time taking her hand. From
his pocket, he removed another velvet box, snapped open the lid
and removed a bracelet to match the diamond and gold collar
around her neck. This time when he clicked the clasp tight, she
welcomed another symbol of his love.

"It's beautiful," she murmured.

"Not half as lovely as you. I'd like to sketch you like that. Then
I'll never forget this moment."

Heat rose to her cheeks. Tracey didn't need a visual reminder to
remember. She'd never forget the dark, dilated glimmer in Craig's
eyes. Or the way the candlelight glinted off his high cheekbones, a
tiny muscle twitching in his jaw. His jacket emphasized his squared
shoulders, his proud carriage, his determination to sketch her.

Yet it was one thing to pose for his gaze alone but entirely
another for him to commit what he saw to paper. And with the heat
boiling inside her, she didn't know if she could remain still while
he sent sizzling glances her way.

"I don't think—"

Opening his briefcase, he removed pad and pencil. "Don't
argue. I have to sketch you. It'll just take a few minutes."

Pages rustled. He pulled up a chair in front of her, and she
stiffened, suddenly uncomfortable with his nearness. He was close,
so close she could feel the heat of his breath, hear him suck the
pencil's eraser in deep concentration. Then she imagined his lips

on her breasts and relaxed.

"That's better. Relax. Think of something besides sex," he teased.

If only she could. She watched his hands sketching in circles and recalled his fingers caressing the insides of her thighs. She'd wanted more. For the first time in her life, need, like grains of sand piled one atop another built a fragile castle of desire. Waves surged inside her, washing up more sand until she thought she would topple from the pressure. She shifted a bit, squirming at the realization that only Craig could satisfy her—and he had no intention of doing so.

From his position on the chair, Craig leaned forward and gripped the elastic panty band at her hips. He tugged her panties higher so the band no longer was horizonal but formed a deep V. As her flesh tingled, her lips parted in surprise. She could barely stand still with the exquisite sensations racing through her. Her breasts swelled. She wanted him—wanted him now.

"Yes. That expression is delightful. Don't move or I'll have to start over."

"Please Craig. Hurry."

"I'm almost done."

She no longer cared what he would do with his drawing. Her flesh had become so sensitive, his every glance darting a ripple of need through her until she almost writhed where she stood.

"All done." Craig's pleased smile drew her like a magnet, and she hurried to his side, pretending to want to look at her picture when she wanted him to touch her, take her. Every nerve ending screamed for release.

He turned the picture so she could see, stopping her forward progress before she reached him. "What do you think?"

It took a moment to recognize the sensual creature staring back at her. Craig drew only her face, with her eyes wide, her lips slightly parted. A raw sensuality dominated the drawing, making her more beautiful than any mirror. "Is that how you see me?"

"That's how you look."

He led her over to a mirror. She walked across the room and the panties slipped back and forth over sensitive areas. While she stared at the strange woman in the mirror, Craig came up behind her, and his hands cupped her breasts, flicking her nipples.

She squirmed, trying to face him. If she could have clawed off his clothes she would have done so. But when she attempted to turn, he tugged lightly on her nipples, effectively holding her in place.

"Look at your face, the full bloom of sexual excitement. I find your passion, your sexiness exciting."

She leaned her back to his chest and his arousal nestled against the crease of her rear. His face wore the expression of a hunter about to sight prey. And all the while his thumbs flicked her nipples, shooting tiny shocks inside her.

She had to have him. Knowing he found her so desirable set her hips wriggling against him. She received two light smacks on her bottom for her efforts. The sting brought back hot aching need.

"Please Craig, enough. Don't make me beg."

He took pity on her then, only not the way she wished for, gesturing to a chair by the door. "Put that on, and we'll go."

While he carefully put the sketch in his briefcase, she hurried to the chair, hoping the clothes would be decent. As she pulled the exquisite Chanel lace-over-silk cocktail dress from the tissue paper in the box, she sucked in her breath in appreciation, sorry she'd doubted him for a moment.

Like the other garments, the dress fit as if custom made. And although the strapless black left her shoulders bare, it would have been perfect for a night at the opera.

After she slipped the dress over her scandalous under garments, Craig picked up his coat and held out an arm to her. "That's how I want to think of you. Cool and discreet, a lady on the outside. And your insides are a bubbling cauldron with needs and fantasies only I can fulfill."

They walked through the lobby of the building, past the door-man, and no one suspected she was on fire for Craig's touch. Her jutting breasts, her stinging bottom, the tight panties wouldn't let her forget her newly awakened sensuality—not for one moment.

Craig opened the car door for her, and she gingerly settled into the seat. When he flipped the back of her skirt up, she gasped in surprise. The bare skin of her bottom rested on the cool leather, soothing her stinging flesh, yet another reminder of the evening ahead.

He drove to his apartment in silence, one hand on her knee, drawing indolent circles, a maddening hint of what might come next. He placed his hand on her waist as they walked the steps into his apartment building, and her blood simmered at the contact.

She couldn't wait to reach the privacy of his apartment and remove her clothes. With every step, her skirt swished against her bare bottom, her panties teased flesh aching for Craig's special brand of attention, and the tips of her breasts grew taut.

She had never been so aware of her body. She could think only of Craig, wanting him, needing him, hoping he would soon satisfy her need.

After a swift elevator ride to the penthouse, Craig unlocked the door and held it open wide. She grinned in delight at his new decor. Hundreds of bright neon helium balloons nestled against cantilevered ceilings. He'd strung a banner of glittering silver coins across the room. Gold kruggerands spelled the words, "Marry Me, Tracey."

Stained glass lamps emitted a soft glowing ambience, and the scent of jasmine wafted to her through the twelve-foot glass doors that framed the city's skyline and led to the balcony. Candles lit the hallway, and her gaze followed a path of rose petals to the bedroom.

He'd gone to so much trouble to make this night special and warm feelings of love made a lump rise in her throat. "Oh Craig, how romantic."

"There's a present for you on the sofa," he murmured huskily.

"But you've already given me the necklace and the bracelet."

"I intend to spoil you. Let me enjoy it."

She hurried into the living room, threading her way between the strings dangling from the balloons. Another jewelry box. She opened it, half expecting a pin or matching earrings to the exquisite pieces he'd already given her. But two delicate chains of diamonds were inside, each with a gold key, one set with rubies, the other emeralds.

Puzzled she turned to face him for an explanation. He'd strode across the thick carpet in silence and dropped to his knees at her feet. Taking the chain of diamonds, he snapped one onto each of her ankles. "These are the keys to my heart."

The collar around her neck, the bracelet on her wrist, and now the diamonds with the tiny dangling keys from her ankles marked her as his. She reveled in the special moment, knowing meeting him was the best thing that had ever happened to her.

If she lost him, it would be like losing a part of her soul. And as much as she wanted to make love with him, she feared she might disappoint him. Her stomach clenched. This time would be different. Craig would see to it. All she had to do was follow his directions and trust him.

Craig rose to his feet with the grace of a cat, and turned on his CD. Upbeat music flooded the room. "Would you like to dance?"

"Yes."

Craig grinned hot enough to ignite a brush fire. "You're overdressed."

She gave him a flirtatious wink and turned around so he could help with her zipper. His fingers grazed her neck, throwing a switch that jolted flutters of excitement through her. After the dress pooled around her feet, she began to step out of it.

"Don't move," he ordered.

She remained standing with her back to him, and he planted tiny kisses on her neck and shoulders. His fingers unfastened the leather bustier. Her breasts sprang free, aching and swollen for his touch. Craig's hands went to her hair, pulling out the pins holding her neat chignon in place.

"While we sit across the board room table, I imagine taking

your hair down as you stand pliant and ready to do my bidding."

At his words, reminding her she'd agreed to obey his every wish, a shiver of fear made her quiver. As lock after lock fell against her shoulders, teasing the peaks of her breasts, her legs trembled.

"What is it you wish me to do?" she asked hesitantly.

"Answer me truthfully. Is your bottom still hot?"

"Warm." She suddenly recalled how he always collected on his debts, and she tensed her bare bottom that was conveniently turned toward him.

He pulled off her panties. "Not hot?"

"Warm," she repeated, refusing to let him intimidate her.

Craig patted her rear. "Bend over and pick up your clothes. Do it slowly."

The undercurrent of tension was strong enough to drown an Olympic swimmer. She stood in the middle of his living room for all intent and purposes naked, while he remained fully dressed. From his words, she expected his hand to strike her. As she bent over, she offered him a prime target. But she no longer required a slap to stimulate her arousal. Just the thought of what he might do combined with the memories of what he'd done and what he still might do to her brought waves of desire surging up from the deepest pool of her emotions.

She retrieved her clothes without Craig so much as touching her, and yet every yearning cell in her body acted as if it craved his touch. She wanted his hands caressing her breasts, her sensitive rear, assuaging the ache between her thighs. She longed to turn around and throw herself into his arms. Instead she placed her clothes on the back of the couch.

His hands spun her, and before she caught her breath, his lips claimed hers; at the same time he danced her around the room. As he hungrily kissed her, her head spun. She clung to him for support, closed her eyes, and floated on the savory sensations.

She tried to press her breasts to his chest, but he prevented this with an unyielding hand on her waist, allowing only their mouths to touch. He tasted of mint, and wine, and pure maleness. His steps became faster, bolder, and she opened her eyes to find herself dancing down the hallway of rose petals into his bedroom.

Soft indirect lighting cast his king-sized bed in shadows. Champagne rested in a silver ice bucket on the night table. Black silk sheets with matching pillows and an Italian lacquered headboard dominated the room.

"Take off your shoes," he instructed, and she gladly kicked off her high heels, leaving herself clad in the stockings with his jewelry around her throat, wrists, and ankles.

"Climb into bed," he invited.

She scrambled onto the cool, crisp sheets. Finally, he would stop teasing her and give her what she wanted. But then she turned around to find him at the foot of the bed staring at her, and she wasn't sure of anything.

She had to remind herself this was the same man who had strewn rose petals across the room. He seemed taller and sexier, more domineering, more sure of himself than she'd ever seen him before. When he didn't undress, a shiver of anticipation made her both eager and hesitant.

She lowered her gaze in confusion. "What about you?"

"Lie back and bring your knees to your chest," he ordered.

She shimmied onto her back, and brought her knees to her chest, keenly aware of his scrutiny. Keeping her features deceptively composed, she glanced at his mocking smile and saw she hadn't fooled him for a moment. He was well aware of her unease but would accept nothing but her total obeyance.

"Now point your feet at the ceiling and support the backs of your calves with your hands."

"But—"

"Do it," he snapped. "Open your legs wider."

From between her parted legs, she watched him standing at the foot of her bed while she held herself open and ready for him. The position he demanded lifted her bottom off the sheets, exposed everything to his gaze, left her open, vulnerable, wanton.

He'd made her feel both decadent and like a lowly beggar. She was comfortable but miserable, alternately flushing hot with embarrassment and anger, then alternately eager for him to do something, anything to end this prolonged waiting. Within a few minutes she'd ceased thinking of anything except the burning ache between her thighs.

Craig removed his clothes slowly, walking around the room, yet always returning to stare at her. Each time he neared, she tensed. Finally the mattress at the foot of the bed sagged, and he kneeled between her widespread feet.

She'd never thought a man could look so beautiful. Craig's wide chest tapered to a rock-hard stomach. But his erection held her attention. He was large, thick, and more than ready. She wanted to touch him, to taste him, to urge him to take her.

He ignored her spread thighs and caressed her breasts. She groaned in disappointment. Damn him for never giving her what she wanted. He made her present herself to him then refused to take what she offered. His calculated teasing would soon drive her mad.

"Is there something you'd like?" he murmured, his tongue tracing a path between her breast and naval.

"Make love to me."

"You aren't ready yet."

"I am," she insisted, wiggling to brush against him.

"You're not even close. We're going to do this my way. You have no say when we begin. No say in what we do. No say in when we stop. You have to remember only one thing."

She could barely think, barely speak. "And what is that?"

"To remember the promise you made me."

His fingers parted the sensitive folds of skin between her thighs. If only he would ease the pressure building inside her. She gasped in disappointment when only cold air touched her there. "I didn't give you permission to torture me."

"Ah, but you did."

Craig sat back on his heels. "I'm going to hold you on the brink between pain and pleasure."

She shook her head, her hair twisting wildly on the pillow. "No."

"Yes. Now close your eyes."

The sheets rustled and the mattress sprang back then sagged once more under his weight. An ice cold droplet landed on her breast, and she jerked. He must have taken an ice cube from the bucket. As his warm tongue lapped away the cold, she sighed in pleasure and lost track of her thoughts.

Another drop fell on her bottom lip, and he sucked it away, ignoring her attempt to get him to kiss her mouth once more. The constant waiting and reminders they would do this his way or not at all strung her tight with tension. Cold drops fell on the inside of her thigh, and dripped toward her center, but he lapped them away without satisfying the aching need there.

He found her toes, her eyelids, her earlobe, and he spent several minutes on the hollow of her neck until she wanted to scream. Her breath came in shallow pants, and tiny animal whimpers came from the back of her throat.

"Craig, Please, I can't take any more."

"You don't have a choice. You are mine tonight to do with as I please."

An icy droplet trickled across her bottom, and his mouth teased and taunted, never landing where she wished. Her nipples hardened into points. Her blood hammered in her ears.

His fingers opened her wider, and he slipped a sliver of ice inside her. Despite her determination to obey his every command, her thighs attempted to squeeze closed, but his hands on her knees prevented her from squirming away. Then his breath found her, and his tongue stoked a heat hot enough to melt a polar icecap.

As he kept his promise, keeping her on the verge of pleasure, every muscle clenched, relentlessly building, hammering away at the last of her inhibitions. At any moment she would shatter. Every nerve ending would fire.

Her fingers dug into her thighs. Her skin prickled. She was

about to explode.

But he pulled back. Damn him! How could he do this to her? She barely controlled a sob of frustration.

"Turn over."

She opened her eyes, thinking the world would spin as crazily as her thrumming thoughts. He'd piled the pillows high on the bed, one atop the other. "On your hands and knees, woman."

He guided her shaking limbs until she lay belly down over the mound of pillows, her bottom raised high. He didn't demand she close her eyes, but she still couldn't see him.

"Grab the posts of the head board and don't let go."

Raising her arms up, she clenched the cool, lacquered head-board, wondering if he intended to take her from behind. They'd never tried this position, and she wasn't sure she—

Whack. Smack. His hand struck her bottom several times in quick succession. The unexpectedness of his spanking after his tender teasing brought a violent clenching in her belly. Desire whirled over her like a tornado, the heat from his stinging slaps raising her temperature to a fever pitch.

She lost control of her thoughts—to a place of instinctive feeling. Her hips bucked, and he held the small of her back firm with his hand while his knees kept her thighs from clamping shut to try and ease her savage yearning.

His fingers slipped into the warm, wet, folds of her flesh and teased until only his firm hold on her prevented her from writhing onto the floor. Without warming, her body clutched tight, releasing the pent up tension in a magical flow of pleasure.

For a moment, she relaxed thinking she'd stolen the pleasure he'd denied her. But his fingers never stopped, and her muscles went taut again. The feeling was akin to climbing a mountain, and though she'd slipped back a pace or two, his fingers urged her relentlessly onward, barely giving her time to breathe.

A fine film of perspiration broke out on her flesh, and she tried to turn, grab him. She received a slap on her bottom, and he pressed her relentlessly back down onto the pillows.

"What are you doing?" she screamed. "I can't—"

"You can and you will."

Her hips moved up and down of their own accord. He knelt between her legs and rubbed his erection along her sensitive flesh. She screamed and bucked. A tiny orgasm gave her a momentary release. Not enough.

"Don't stop. More," she gasped.

"No more." He pulled away. "Are you thirsty? Would you like a drink?"

She barely heard his words through her dazed frenzy. He couldn't stop. Not now. Not when she needed him more than her next breath.

But he seemed immune to what he'd done to her. He helped her off the pillows and placed her on the edge of the mattress with her knees folded beneath her. Then he handed her a glass of champagne. Her eyes widened at the ring in the bottom of the glass. She plucked it out, and he placed it on her left hand, her only remaining limb that wasn't marked by a piece of jewelry.

"Your engagement ring."

She barely looked at the diamond. She wanted him badly enough to attempt raping him—not that he'd let her. He'd made it more than clear who was in charge. She would be the one submitting, and she didn't know whether or not she could take any more.

And yet Tracey had never felt so sensual in her life. His refusal to give her a choice had freed her from all responsibility for her actions. She could simply react, without guilt, without worry, without humiliation. How had he known she would respond so passionately? As she sipped the champagne, she trembled at the pent up sensations coursing through her.

She needed to walk, shake it off.

As if reading her mind, Craig smoothed the hair off her forehead, then cupped her chin, forcing her to look up at him. His dark eyes turned smokey. "Part your knees wide."

While she did what she asked, he made her look him straight in the eyes. Her stomach knotted. Her bottom burned. He had her sitting on his bed, her knees spread wide before him, dazed and longing for sexual release.

He took away her glass of champagne. "Place your hands on your thighs. Sit up straighter."

She'd never sat so straight in her life. As his hand wandered over her face, her shoulders, and breasts, every muscle tensed.

His handsome face broke into a pleased grin. "We need to talk about our marriage."

She groaned. "I can't think."

His hand dropped between her thighs, teased and tormented. She sucked in a breath, trying hard to remain still.

"Can you think now?"

His implication was clear. She would discuss whatever he wanted when he asked her to or he would make her suffer sweet torment until she did. She bit on her lower lip. "What is it . . . you wish to discuss?"

When she acquiesced to his demand, she thought he would remove his hand. He didn't. His fingers continued to dance inside her until she held back a scream.

"If you agree to marry me, I want you just as willing as you are right now—one day a week."

"Oh my, God!"

When she failed to get out another word in reply, his fingers worked harder. Her hips gyrated, seeking more.

He pulled his hand back, leaving her hanging. "One day a week," he demanded.

"Yes. Craig." She'd say anything. Do anything. If he would just end the unattainable pleasure-pain.

His palms touched her cheeks. "You understand what I'm saying?"

She nodded. One day of every week could be like these last few hours. He'd have her permission to do with her what he wished. An icy shiver slid down her spine. Giving him such control scared her and yet excited her to the very marrow of her bones.

Even now as she longed for him to give her release, in another way she wanted to prolong the exquisite pleasure of waiting. The fact that the choice was not hers lent an added degree of excitement.

And it hadn't escaped her befuddled brain that Craig hadn't yet allowed her to answer his marriage proposal. He'd merely set the terms. Only there was no merely about it. He wanted unquestionable submission—one day a week. Could she do that? Did she want that? She didn't know.

But she'd never felt such intense sexual longing in her life. And without even being satisfied fully, she knew she couldn't bear not to feel this way again. With her bottom stinging, with her sitting naked, her knees open and waiting for him to give her pleasure, she'd never felt so sexy in her life.

He scooped her into his arms and carried her into his glass and marble shower, setting her under a warm spray. The water cleared the fog from her mind, making the moment sharp and clear. He lathered his hands with a jasmine scented soap and then slowly washed her shoulders, breasts, and belly working his way down her front with the slippery soap before giving her back and bottom the same treatment.

When she didn't think she could stand his sensuous fondling for another second, he handed her the soap. Finally she got her chance to touch him. She caressed the muscles of his shoulders and his broad chest, and flat, tight stomach, barely teasing his jutting erection. Two could play this game.

She ran her hands down his thick thighs and hard calves, asking him to turn around. The feel of his warm flesh under her hands made her quiver with longing, and she washed his back and lean flanks quickly, her resolve to taunt him as he had done to her weakening. Her palms itched to caress the hard length of him until he lost control, threw her down and gave her what she wanted.

His mocking smile told her he knew what she'd tried to do. With just a small shake of his head, he turned away and she lost her chance.

Craig exited the shower first and wrapped a towel around his waist. He gestured for her to stand on the bath mat. Yesterday she would have cringed to stand naked before him under the bright lights. Today she wanted him to look at her. He took out a fluffy white towel, and she waited for him to wrap her in it. Instead, he insisted on drying her everywhere. Slowly.

As he patted the droplets from her flesh, the raging energies he'd created over the last several hours returned with hurricane force. Her knees threatened to buckle and sensing her weakness, Craig once again carried her across the room and settled her in bed.

He kissed her tenderly. She clutched him fiercely, pressing her breasts against his bare chest. While his tongue explored the recesses of her mouth, she clung to him, wriggling, trying to get him to fill the overpowering void inside her.

Once more he denied her. His lips traced a path over the hollow of her collar bone to the valley of her hips and lower until his mouth centered on her core.

Her fingers wound her way into his thick hair, and she arched up to him. Inside the tension that had strung her taut for hours was building, higher, harder, hotter. When he pulled away she screamed in frustration.

"I want . . . I must . . . Craig!"

Finally he thrust into her welcoming flesh, and she met him half way. Her burning bottom slammed against the mattress. Her fingers clawed at him. She couldn't draw in enough air. Her legs tightened around his waist.

He moved inside her fast, claiming what he wanted in a movement as old as time. She bucked wildly, and her desire peaked. Her entire body shuddered, spurted, climaxing in several electric jolts of passion.

She lost track of time. The pleasure went on and on and on. And when she could not stand one more second, his fingers slipped between the slick folds of sensitive flesh and sent her higher. The spasms wracked her again and again, acute, powerful, endlessly wondrous.

She screamed, and he swallowed it with a kiss. Hanging suspended between time and thought, she bucked her hips in wild abandon. Finally he pumped his seed into her, and she relished a tranquil moment in his arms. It took many minutes before her heart beat returned to normal, minutes before she regained her breath and her wits.

"I love you, Tracey."

"But would you have loved me if your experiment didn't work?"

"I knew it would work. I just wanted to prove that you could enjoy the physical side of love as much as I do."

Nestling against his chest, she snuggled closer. "I love you, too."

He smoothed the back of her head and drew her cheek against his shoulder. "Enough to marry me?"

"Yes." A tiny thrill shot through her. For the first time she looked forward to spending hour upon hour in his bed.

"And you agree to my conditions?"

"I have one of my own," she said lightly.

The muscles of his chest tensed. His eyes smoldered. "What?"

She tired to smother a chuckle and failed. "One day a week won't be enough. Let's make it two."

About the author:

Ivy Landon is a pseudonym for a multi-published author who hopes her story will in turn shock you, and titillate you. Writing for Secrets was an opportunity to let her freedom of expression soar beyond all boundaries. She hopes you enjoy the reading as much as she enjoyed the writing. May all your dreams be spicy.

Secrets

Volume 2

Snowbound

by Bonnie Hamre

To my reader:

I was so pleased that Secrets 1 hit a chord with lovers of erotic romance, and doubly pleased to have a second novella to offer you. Snuggle up, free your mind from distraction, and enjoy…

Chapter One

Justin Stowe, fifth Earl of Howden, splayed the invitations in his hand as he would a deck of cards. Intimate little suppers, a ball or two, three musicales, whist parties and the theater. Grimacing, he looked from them to the view beyond the tall windows of his library. The blizzard still raged, white whirling flakes that blotted out the landscape and threatened to keep him marooned for days.

Excellent. He tossed the invitations in the fire and watched the papers catch. The last to go was a card bearing his name in a flowery, female script. The flames teased at the writing, devouring his family name, but leaving his title. How appropriate. It wasn't he who was so desirable a mate, but his prospects.

It amazed him that, despite his reputation as a rake and hell-raiser, his title made him the catch of the season. Perhaps when he was more used to being the fifth Earl, after his cousin's untimely demise half a year past, he'd grow accustomed to the plots to leg-shackle him. Even here, in the wintry depths of Hertford, merciless matchmakers had descended on him from every quarter. He had begun to think of himself as the fox in a particularly single-minded hunt.

He grinned at the image and, with the toe of his polished Hessian, pushed the rest of the card into the flames. While the blaze consumed it, Justin raised a glass of brandy, saluted the fire and swallowed a generous mouthful. The storm would provide a few days respite before the hounds gave chase again.

A discreet knock at the mahogany door ushered in Ordway, the butler he'd inherited along with Howden House. "My lord? There is a female at the door."

"A female? Out in this?" Justin glanced through the windows at the snow-drifts piling high against the panes. Ice-crusted tree branches sagged under the weight. "Is there no end to their machinations?"

"I would not venture to say, my lord."

Justin sighed. "I suppose you had better show her in."

"Perhaps you could come out, my lord. The lady appears to be near expiration."

"Near exp — what the hell?" Justin's long strides had him across the library and down the black and white marbled hall to the entrance before Ordway could precede him. His steps slowed.

Crumpled in a misshapen huddle on an upholstered settee, the woman resembled a discarded collection of dirty, sodden rags. Water dripped on his floor and trickled across the tiles in muddy rivulets.

At his approach, she lifted her head. The hood of her cloak slipped back to reveal her hair, matted by snow and ice, hanging stiffly around her too pale face.

She had a small, straight nose and high cheekbones. Her lips, perhaps a shade too wide for her delicate countenance, were bloodless. Although she appeared exhausted, there was a certain strength in her expression.

"M?" she breathed.

"What is that?" Justin bent closer to hear.

"M…" She peeled off a misshapen leather glove and struggled to pull back a portion of her dripping cloak. She cradled a bundle, small and round, in her arm. Drawing away a pink shawl surrounding the parcel, she revealed a perfectly formed baby's face. "Emmy?"

"My God!" Justin reared back. "An infant! What in the name of all that is sacred are you doing? Have you lost your wits, madam?"

Ignoring him, she patted the child with fingers crabbed with cold and dangerously white at the tips. Even as he evaluated her condition, Justin noted how small and elegant her hands were, the nails a dainty oval. She wore no rings.

Justin registered the sweet arch of her eyebrows, the large golden-brown eyes preoccupied only with the infant. Irrelevantly, he thought that at another time, if she smiled at him, those eyes would tempt the devil himself. He repressed a smile. If the gossips were to be believed, he was already on a first name basis with Lucifer himself.

The woman unwrapped several additional woolen layers bundled around the infant. The child opened a tiny pink mouth and uttered an ear-piercing wail.

Justin recoiled. "At least we can be sure it lives."

At the baby's cry, the woman's shoulders relaxed and her lips formed a half-smile. Justin caught himself staring at a dimple in the making and frowned. "Who are you, madam? What possessed you to be out in this weather with your child?"

"Not mine."

"Not your child? Whose then? Have you stolen it?"

"No…niece."

"This is a pretty coil." Justin crossed his arms over his chest as he stared down at her. What was he to do with a half-frozen pair of females? Tempted as he was, he couldn't cast them back into the storm.

With a shake of his head, he touched the woman's shoulder. "You may practice your wiles once you have warmed yourself." He lifted the child from her arms and held the bundle out to Ordway. "Go on, get the baby warm. I suppose it wants feeding, too."

"Feeding?" Ordway's white eyebrows arched toward his receding hairline. "We have no females in the house, my lord, if I may remind you."

Justin waved the objection away. "Then send someone to fetch a wet nurse from the village." He paused. "Temporarily of course, until I find out who this infant is and see it properly home."

"Very good, sir." Ordway started down the passageway leading to the servant's wing.

"No —" The woman stretched a hand out to the baby.

Justin had the impression that, had she been able, the woman would run after his butler, retrieve the child and flee.

"He will look after the child. But what about you, madam? You are frozen clear through. Come to the fire."

He took her hands in his. She tried to pull back. Ignoring her efforts, he rubbed them between his, noting the delicacy of her bones beneath her icy skin. He drew her to her feet.

She stood, shaking, while he undid the clasps of her cloak and took it from her. "Good grief, madam, how did you manage in this?"

She staggered and nearly fell.

He dropped the cloak and quickly placed an arm around her waist to steady her. "Come now. Lean on me." Her soft weight against his as she relied on his strength made Justin stiffen.

He was no callow youth to be undone by the soft curve of a woman's bosom, yet something about this bedraggled specimen unaccountably appealed to him. With her pressed against his side, he forced himself to think of his last bout at Manton's, yet all he could picture were her breasts. Instinctively, he knew that she did not nurse the child. Her breasts were too small and firm. He inhaled sharply, imagining his palm cupped over the shapely globes, his finger stroking the nipples.

Would they be cherry-tipped? Or perhaps they resembled apricots, warm and luscious in his mouth. His breathing quickened. His loins tightened. Damned fool! To be hungering for a taste of her breasts when she was half dead. What kind of a unprincipled, lecherous cad did that make him?

Ignoring the little voice in his head that answered his question in precise terms, he guided her toward the library. "Have you no sense?" he scolded with each slow step. "What can be so urgent that you would travel now? Why not wait until the weather clears?"

"Could not." Her teeth chattered. "Have to save Emmy."

"Save? From what?"

Her bottom lip trembled. "...to my aunt. She...expects us...worried."

Diverted by the fullness of that lip, and wondering how it would feel against his when warm and moist, he stumbled over her sopping hem. He righted himself and jerked his mind back to her distressed state. "Why are you afoot?"

"Coach...ice...too...fast..." Her voice trailed off. Justin glanced down in time to see her eyes roll back. She crumpled in a boneless heap.

"Good God, woman!" He caught her before she hit the floor, awkwardly holding her as though he didn't know what to do with a pliable female.

Her skin radiated the cold even through her woolen gown. With her eyes closed, her head hanging over his arm, and the color gone from her face, Justin feared the worst. He touched her throat and found a weak, thready pulse.

She lived, but not for much longer if he didn't get her warm and dry. Had she come from the main road, two miles away? If so, he marveled that she'd managed to get herself and the baby to shelter. She'd missed the village. If she'd missed his estate as well, they would have perished. Many men wouldn't have done as well. Cursing himself for interrogating her when she needed care, he scooped her up and crossed the hall with her in his arms.

"Ordway," he shouted as he climbed the broad staircase, taking the steps two at a time. Her woolen skirts dragged about his knees, tangling with his boots and curtailing his footsteps. Momentarily freeing the hand under her knees, he grabbed her heavy skirt and, holding the material away from him, he strode down the gallery to the nearest bedroom wing. In summer, the gallery was a delightful place, with huge windows spilling warm sunlight into the long, stately hall, but now with icy gusts slamming against the panes, the gallery was drafty and cold. With each long step resounding on the marble floor, Justin damned his forefathers for building and remodeling the house on such a grandiose scale. Why did they require so many bedrooms and each a day's march away?

"Ordway!" He kicked open his chamber door and placed her on his massive bed. She moaned, then pulled fretfully at her clothing. Justin recognized the quality of her black merino traveling dress and matching pelisse as she touched her ribcage, her waist and then searched her torso.

"Be still, woman." Justin moved his hands over hers, to arrest their frantic movement, he told himself, but the way she fingered her bosom made his fingertips itch. He eyed the plump mounds as they moved under her questing hands and yearned to assist her in her exploration. He moved her hands aside and pressed his ear to her generous chest. He listened for her heartbeat, trying but failing to ignore the soft, sweet woman's flesh under her garments.

He forced himself to withdraw before he did the unthinkable and caressed a helpless woman. A faint fragrance of roses followed him. He closed his eyes for a moment, inhaling deeply, before releasing her hands. "The child is quite safe."

She stilled. One hand fell to her side. The fingers were smooth, the palm uncallused. She did no hard labor. Ashen, she was insensible to her state, yet he had to try.

"Madam. Remove your clothing."

He bit back a grin. Usually, when he wanted a woman unclothed, he did it himself. Sometimes impatiently, other times taking his time to savor the moment. Now, he shook her limp arm. "Madam, you must remove your clothing before you take a chill." He heard his voice edge into desperation. If she didn't rouse enough to undress, he would have to do it for her.

And if he did, would she suddenly open her eyes and scream for help? Was this all a ruse to force him into a compromising scene? One designed to compel him to the altar?

Wincing at the thought, Justin realized even if she were after his title, he couldn't leave her in those clothes. He may not wish to be caught in parson's mousetrap, but neither could he cause a lady's demise. Damnation.

He bit his lips. There was no help for it. Briskly, he removed her boots and black woolen stockings to reveal long, slender legs blanched with cold. Justin swallowed as he unbuttoned her gown. Try as he might, he couldn't avoid brushing against the swell of her generous breasts. He drew off the heavy dress and the woolen crinoline despite the way the spongy wool clung to the curves of her body. Her simple chemise, almost transparent with the damp, revealed more than it hid.

He stared at pale ivory flesh, the veins a delicate tracery just under her skin. He touched the tip of his finger to one breast and followed the curve, relishing the softness and then, cursing himself and the situation, he removed her underclothing. He'd done this countless times with women willing and ablaze with passion, but now he found it difficult. Her body was dead weight in his hands, her limbs flaccid and uncooperative.

He wished he could say the same for himself. Her skin remained chilled, but drops of perspiration dotted his forehead. His yard reminded him of his usual activity with an unclothed woman.

Quickly, he tucked her into one of his own never-used linen nightshirts. In doing so, he disturbed the remaining pins in her coiffure.

Her hair, a deep honey blonde, fell in wild, tangled locks around her head and shoulders. He retrieved the loose pins, allowing that as his excuse to comb his hand through the damp, silky skeins. He felt her head, looking for bumps or cuts and found none. She was luckier than many. He scowled anew at her foolhardiness and dropped the pins on a nearby table.

Justin lifted her and with one hand, drew down the covers. Divested of her heavy clothing, she was no heavier than thistledown. He frowned at the image and placed her on the linen sheets and jerked the blankets up to her chin.

The woman didn't move. She lay oblivious in the wide bed, her slender body no more than a bump under the covers. About to brush back a curl at her temple, Justin paused. He clenched his fist, then relaxed his grip and tucked the covers tightly around her. She was still cold, too cold.

Where the devil was Ordway? Justin yanked the bell pull and kept at it until he heard running footsteps in the hall. Ordway arrived, followed by two footmen and Justin's valet.

"Yes, my lord?" Ordway panted.

Four sets of eyes widened as they studied the woman ensconced in Justin's nightshirt. "Oh, no," the valet wailed. "A female."

Ordway approached the bed. "Has she expired?"

"No, but she will damn quick if we don't help her. Make up the fire," Justin ordered one of the footmen. "I want it blazing in here."

Justin watched the footman tend the fire. "Good. Once you're done here, send the stable lads to search for the lady's conveyance. See if there are any others stumbling about in the storm. We shall have the care of them as well."

"Very good, my lord." The footman cast an inquiring glance at the woman in the bed, and then catching Justin's scowl, retreated.

Justin turned his attention to his valet. "Pruitt. Do something with those wet things."

Pruitt retreated a pace. He put up his hands, palm out. "My lord, I am a gentleman's gentleman."

"Oh for God's sake, Pruitt. She'll need dry clothing when she wakes. Tend to it."

Pruitt eyed the clothing distastefully but picked up the dripping mass. "May I remind you, sir, that you said we were to be a bachelor establishment? That we would do nothing but rusticate and perfect your technique with the épée?"

Justin spared a glance for his valet. "Circumstances have changed."

Pruitt sniffed. "Very well, my lord. Cook will want to know if he should prepare a meal for the lady. Something for an invalid?"

"Tell him to do as he thinks best. Oh, and Pruitt," Justin added as the man stepped through the door. "Have a tray brought to me here. Let me know how the child does."

Alone, with the woman seen to, Justin noted his own damp clothing. He pulled off his jacket and loosened his shirt at the waistband. Heat from the fire enveloped him and licked at his exposed skin. With the fire this hot, he'd dry out soon enough. He sank back into an armchair and studied the mystery woman.

He scowled. No doubt she had her reasons for going to this length to wring a marriage proposal out of him, but why would she bring a babe along?

It was all for naught. He'd never cared much for damsels in distress, and didn't intend to be caught by one now. No doubt she'd envisioned a different ending to her scheme. How insidious a plan, just like a female, to devise something so sly. No doubt she had accomplices at the ready, prepared to burst in and find them in a compromising act.

By rights, he should leave her alone to stew in the knowledge that she'd failed miserably. Someone else could look after her. When she woke, refreshed and rested, he would see that she put on her dry clothing, took the child and left. He'd lend her his own carriage, if necessary. It'd take more than a clever ploy to capture him.

Why, then, did his cock ache? Why could he think of nothing but keeping her, warm and wanton, in his bed?

Chapter Two

Even as he damned the rutting portion of his nature urging him to seduce her and be damned with it, Justin couldn't stay away from the woman in his bed.

He brought an easy chair to the bedside, lowered himself into it and studied her. Her chest barely disturbed the cocoon of blankets, but her breathing grew more harsh with every inhalation. He leaned forward to hear better.

With his forehead almost touching hers, each exhalation skimmed his cheek, a moist, warm reminder that she was ill, helpless, and now dependent on him.

It was also uncomfortably sensual. As her body heat returned, her fragrance rose, more opulent than before, to tempt his senses. How could someone so recently near freezing still remind him of a garden in springtime? Any moment now he'd swear he smelled lavender and lilacs along with the roses. Her hair lay in a luxuriant tangle, the glorious hue echoed in the thick, dark lashes resting on her cheeks.

He studied the curve of the cheek nearest him, then unable to resist, stroked it with the tip of his finger. Her skin, cool still but beginning to flush with fever, was velvety and delicate, fresher than a newly opened bud.

She stirred under his touch. He jerked back his hand and waited to see if she'd rouse, but she subsided once more, turning onto her side and curling up with one hand under her cheek.

Justin couldn't help himself. He stroked her face, barely touching her, from temple to chin. When she murmured, he took his hand away. He waited until he was sure she slept, then sat back and made himself comfortable. Cook sent up a dinner tray with a bowl of chicken broth for her, but she wouldn't awaken.

When the footman came to retrieve the tray, Justin inquired, "What news?"

"None, my lord. The stable lads aren't back."

"The child?"

"Sleeps now, sir, but she's hungry."

"Try some warm milk."

"Cook did, sir. The baby wouldn't take a drop, sir, not a drop."

Justin cursed. A baby was bad enough. A starving baby went beyond the pale. How was he to care for it if she wouldn't eat?

Shortly before midnight, the woman stretched, moaned and uttered several unintelligible words. On his feet in an instant, Justin bent over her.

"Yes, I promise..." she muttered. "You may count on me."

Justin's eyebrows rose. Whom did she reassure in her sleep? What promise had she made that so worried her? Did it have to do with him? The woman moved restlessly, disturbing the bedcovers, as if even in sleep she braved the storm still seething outside.

When Justin reached out to straighten the blankets, his hand brushed her breast. He froze, his fingers instinctively cupping the warm weight. He was right. She fit his hand perfectly. The nipple was an enticing presence in his palm. What would it take to fondle the nipple into a hard kernel?

Without volition, his hand enclosed the tender globe and squeezed gently. The woman murmured and arched into his touch, as if asking more from him. Justin caught his breath at the unspoken request and complied. One stroke, then two. Just as he had imagined, her nipple expanded in his palm.

My God, much more of this and he'd play right into her hands.

Cursing his impulses, he again seated himself to continue the vigil. While she slept, he dozed. Her mumbles brought him awake.

Once more he approached the bedside, leaning down so that his ear almost rested on her lips. She said nothing more but her body stiffened. Drawing back, he studied her. Her eyelids fluttered but didn't open. Nevertheless, he thought she was aware of his presence. "Are you awake?"

A small pink tongue edged along the seam of her lips. "Yes," she said in little more than a croak.

"Are you hungry?"

She managed a brief shake of her head.

"Thirsty, then?"

"Yes."

He eased his hand to the nape of her neck to lift her head. Her skin under the heavy mass of her hair was warm and soft. He imagined his lips on the silky skin, his tongue tickling her, drinking in the taste of her. When she glanced at the glass in his hand, he remembered what he was about. Holding the glass to her mouth, he let her drink. "Not too much at once," he cautioned when she guzzled greedily.

She sank back against the pillows. Reluctantly, Justin withdrew his hand.

He replaced the glass and watched as she struggled to stay awake. "Can you tell me who you are?"

"Sarah. Sarah Wilder."

"Well, Mrs. Wilder."

"Miss."

Justin sat back in his chair. A miss looking to be a countess. Just as he'd expected, he thought with a curious sense of disappointment.

"Miss Wilder, where is your home? We could try to get a message through..." Justin's voice trailed off as she slipped back into sleep. Her mouth was partly open, her lips beckoning him to sample them. He ran his tongue over his own lips as if he could already taste hers.

Something about her drew him. Whatever her reasons, and he had no doubt they were as pressing as the next husband-hunting woman's, she had survived the blizzard and kept the baby safe. That took courage and fortitude, and a steely determination, all qualities he admired in a man. To find them in a woman unsettled him.

Her teeth chattered. She rolled into a little ball, as if seeking greater warmth. Justin felt her head, then searched for another blanket. Finding none, he rooted through the *armoire* in his dressing room until he found his warm, cashmere robe. He placed that over her, but still she shivered.

He bit his lip, then, tight-lipped, he stripped off his boots and clothes and slid naked under the covers with her. The cold spread in icy waves from her body. Shivering, he hesitated. Until now, everything he'd done could be explained as caring for a lost wayfarer. Climbing naked under the sheets was another thing altogether. Climbing naked into bed with a beautiful woman was begging for whatever the fates decreed.

He slid back to the side of the bed and placed one foot on the floor. She shuddered and wrapped her arms tighter around herself.

This is for her own good, damn it. He drew her slender body into his arms. She stiffened, then bucked as an untamed filly, rejecting his hold on her, thrusting him away and once even striking him on the chest.

Her frenzied movement shifted the tails of the nightshirt above her thighs. He reacted immediately to the feel of her bare skin against his abdomen.

Cursing his errant rod and her, he wrapped his arms around her and pulled her into his arms, back to belly. Her heels drummed against his shins. He threw one leg over hers to keep her still. She continued to thrash about until, little by little, his body heat warmed her. Her restless movements eased until she lay motionless in his arms. She slept deeply.

Wide awake, Justin ground his teeth.

Her buttocks, soft fleshy provocation, lay nestled against his cock. His yard, uncaring that he wished to be anywhere but here suffering Lucifer's revenge, reacted predictably to the supple female flesh. He counted to ten, then twenty, then from thirty in reverse. Nothing helped.

In her sleep, she burrowed closer to him. Her thighs parted as if to allow his rigid cock entrance to her body. His shaft, that unscrupulous fellow, ardently accepted the invitation. He stiffened, gritted his teeth and pulled back as a tiny drop of moisture fell from his cock to her thigh. He would not fall victim to her cunning, no matter how he ached and longed to plunge inside her.

She turned to her back. Justin exhaled, his breath heavy. Better. At least that temptation had abated. She rolled to her side, facing him, and cuddled close. One of her hands rested against his torso, the fingers curling into his chest hair.

God. Justin went still. His back straightened into a rigid parade-yard pose, his thighs immobile. His breathing slowed. If holding her bottom to his belly had been torment, this was torture of the worst kind. With her breasts pressed against his chest, her nipples teased his. Every breath she took increased his fever. Each exhalation taunted his control. His cock swelled and grew harder. His blood boiled.

She curved her body into his. Her hips pressed into his. Her mound teased him. His cock probed the juncture of her thighs. He held his breath as the tip of his rod sought and found the warm, moist entrance. For a moment, he did nothing but relish the sensation. It would be so easy to take her. All he had to do was push himself in, take his pleasure and be done.

She'd never know.

He penetrated her, just enough to make him grit his teeth. She was tight yet her tiny muscles gripped him even tighter. The sweat beaded on his brow as he held himself motionless. All it would take was one thrust and he'd be deeply seated. His cock quivered as he pressed in. He groaned at the pleasure. And stopped short.

Rakehell that he was, he still couldn't take an unconscious woman.

He could have bellowed his frustration. Instead, he eased away from her. She followed, as if seeking his warmth, or was it to keep him with her? Bolting, breathing hard, he found himself at the edge of the wide bed.

The woman turned away, rolling back to the center of the bed. She pushed at the woolen robe, muttering and thrashing, until Justin leaned over and felt her forehead. She burned with fever. He pulled back his warm garment, but left her under the blankets. The quicker her fever broke, the sooner she'd be well enough to continue her journey.

He rose and dressed quickly. The feel of his shirt over skin sensitized by her nipples made him throb. He pulled the bell cord until Pruitt appeared.

"My lord?"

Justin gestured to the bed. "Stay with her. Waken me if her condition changes."

"Where shall I find you, sir?"

Justin paused. "The library," he said, his voice short. "How does the child?"

"She is fretful, sir. The wet nurse has not arrived."

"Damn. Do what you can for the child." After Pruitt left, Justin studied the unconscious woman for a few moments more, then made his way down the drafty halls to the library, his favorite room. He built up the fire, poured himself a large brandy and made himself comfortable in an armchair.

His smiled tinged on the ironic. He'd been here, only hours ago, reflecting on his safety, and look at him now.

He wanted to vent his outrage on the mysterious Miss Wilder, but all he could think of was joining her again in his large, comfortable bed. He wrenched his thoughts away from the vivid image of their sprawled bodies, intertwined, his buried so deep in hers she'd never feel the cold again.

The little bit of her that he'd already experienced made him hungry for more. Her soft bite had teased him and pleased him. Now he wanted it all.

He'd plunge again and again, sating himself in her soft satiny depths, pleasuring her until she cried out with the force of her orgasm, until his sperm shot forth and filled her every crevice.

God. He'd never been so hot.

$\mathcal{C}hapter\ \mathcal{T}hree$

Justin set his napkin down on the lace cloth spread before him and stared at the wintry morning beyond the dining room windows.

Ordway entered, wearing his most put-upon expression, and cleared his throat. "My lord, that child is at last asleep. It cried half the night. The staff did not sleep well."

"Have you found a wet nurse?"

"A stable lad fetched one from the village. She disliked the storm and the horse, but the lad promised your lordship would reward her well."

Has she fed the infant?"

"That is why it now sleeps."

Justin nodded impatiently. "Is there more news?"

"The grooms have brought in a badly damaged carriage, my lord. One of the horses had to be put down. John Coachman is dead."

"Pity." Justin drummed his fingers on the table. "I shall ask our guest if he is a family servant. If not, it will be up to us to see to the proprieties." He looked sharply at his butler. "Did they find any others?"

"No, my lord. We shall continue the search, but unless someone took refuge in the village…" The butler's tone said it all. "The trunks and valises have been brought in to dry."

"No doubt Miss Wilder will be glad of her own things."

"*Miss* Wilder, sir?" Justin caught sight of his butler's mouth hanging open. He nodded.

"Will the lady and the child be staying long?"

"Until the storm abates and Miss Wilder is well enough to travel. Is she awake yet?"

"She is, sir. Cook sent up a tray. It came back untouched."

Justin shot to his feet. None of this. He wanted her out of his house. In moments, he was pounding up the staircase, three steps at a time. At the door to his room, he managed to restrain himself enough to knock.

He heard a muffled "Come in," and pushed open the door.

His guest sat up in bed, propped against the pillows. Where last night he had left a sick woman, this morning he found a delicious creature radiating health. Her hand stilled as it stroked his silver-backed brush through the glorious hair streaming sunlit gold over his linen pillow cases. Her face no longer wore that cold, pinched look, but bloomed softly in shades of pink and cream that had his palms sweating.

The severe lines of his nightshirt made him look twice. Frothy lace, furbelows, silks that revealed more than they temptingly concealed, those he could
handle. His plain, white linen nightshirt covered everything but the pulse
beating at her throat. He stared like a schoolboy at the sleeves rolled up over
her narrow wrists and the collar too loose to button securely at her neck,

Her breasts pushed against the nightshirt. He could feel again the soft
weight of them against him, in his palm. Why hadn't he tasted them when he
had the chance?

"Good morning," he managed at last. "I see you are feeling better. I feared
you would be ill."

She turned her head to him. Oh, God. Those eyes. He'd been right about
them. Large, lustrous, their softly shining cinnamon color drew him closer, and
closer still, until he stood at the foot of the bed. He'd been right the first time.
They'd tempt the devil himself, and God knew he was no angel.

"Much better, as you can see." She dropped the brush in her lap and leaned
forward. "How is Emmy? Where is she?" she asked quickly, eagerly. "I wish to
see her."

Justin's gaze followed the brush, then traveled down her covered legs to her
feet and back again. He remembered the delicate arches, the slender ankles and
the perfect curves of her calves and had to restrain himself from fitting his palms
to them and caressing her through the blankets. He again eyed her breasts,
covered with maidenly modesty by the sheet she belatedly tucked up under her
chin.

He repressed the urge to whisk it back, to see for himself if her body was as
marvelous by day as it had been by candlelight. He swallowed hard at the
thought of exploring every curve and dip of her body, testing the hidden petals
to discover if they were still as heated and liquid. Maybe he shouldn't be in
such a hurry to see her gone.

"Is there something wrong with Emmy?" Sarah's voice rose as she put a
hand to her throat. "Oh, God, tell me she is not —"

"No, no." Justin forced his thoughts away from the delights of her body.
"Forgive me for not telling you immediately. There is nothing wrong. A wet
nurse from the village has seen to her. Your niece is sleeping."

Sarah fell back against the pillow, her hand dropping to her breast.

"Oh, thank you," she whispered. "I asked the servant who brought my tray,
but he could tell me nothing. I have been quite out of my mind with worry."

"Understandable. You must now rest and see to your own mending."

"Oh, I am quite recovered." She sat up and tucked the sheet about her
breasts again. "I enjoy perfect health."

"So I see." He edged nearer to the ornately carved footboard which hid him
to mid-chest. Garbed as he was in his usual buckskin breeches and superfine
jacket, there wasn't much chance of concealing his erection.

"I must thank you for giving us shelter from the storm. Emmy and I shall
continue on our way today, as soon as —"

"I'm afraid that will not be possible, Miss Wilder," Justin cut in smoothly. He expected to see a triumphant smile, some indication that she was pleased to see her plan succeeding.

Her nose wrinkled in a most delightful way. Justin watched it for a moment until he forced himself to think with his brain and not his cock. "I have bad news. Your carriage is severely in need of repair. Your coachman did not survive the accident."

"Oh, no." She looked down at her lap, then up at him. "Poor man."

Oh, well done! That hint of moisture in her eyes was an artful touch. Would she be as artful with passion? He dragged his mind back. "Was he a family servant?"

"No," she shook her head, making her hair ripple in golden waves. "I procured the carriage and the use of his services."

"I see. Give me the particulars and I shall notify his employers."

"Thank you. This leaves me in an awkward position, Mr. —"

Smoothly done. "Justin Stowe," he said with a bow, omitting his title.

"Mr. Stowe." She repeated his family name so easily he wondered if she had not heard the servants address him properly. "I must get Emmy to my aunt."

"So you have indicated, Miss Wilder, but —" He held up a hand to stop her protests. "You must remain here until your carriage is repaired." When her shoulders slumped, he added, testing her, "Unless, of course, you would accept the use of one of mine?"

Her face brightened immediately. "How kind of you, Mr. Stowe. I should not deprive you of it's use for very long."

Justin's gut twisted. She offered him just what he had thought he wanted. She desired to depart immediately, to leave him in peace, and he didn't want her to go. Damnation. How had she managed to turn the tables on *him*?

He checked his annoyance. "If you go so soon, you open the door to other claimants. Your scheme will fail."

Her brow furrowed. "Claimants? What scheme?"

"It was dangerous and foolish to risk the child in your intrigue. You are lucky neither of you came to harm —"

"I had no choice, sir!" she cried. "I had to do what I did."

"You had to arrive in the middle of a storm? Wouldn't spring have served as well? Soft breezes are far more comfortable for seductions than winter gales."

"Seduct..." her breath faltered. Her cheeks went red. "Sir! You convince me I must leave at once."

She should tread the boards. Confusion, modesty, maidenly blushes, her act was perfection. Was it possible she told the truth? It was conceivable, he supposed, yet in his experience, veracity and women didn't go hand in hand. Justin studied her. "Do you deny you are here to trap me?"

"Trap you," she echoed. "What on earth would I want with you?"

Her question stung. *Pricked by his own arrogance.* Could he be wrong? He hesitated, reluctant to let go of his suspicions, lest this be clever move to disarm him, yet her expression left him in no doubt. Whatever her plots and machinations, they had nothing to do with him. His spirit felt lighter, happier that he didn't have be on guard with her.

However, her reason for traveling in this weather remained to be explained. "You cannot leave until you regain your strength."

"I am quite well, thank you."

"You cannot travel without sustenance. Cook said you returned your tray untouched."

A slight smile touched her lips, making the lower one fuller, more luscious. Justin stared at the tiny dimple by her mouth.

"I am not in the habit of taking salt in my tea," she said, her voice mild.

"Salt?" His brow furrowed, then cleared. "Hellfire. Your pardon, Miss Wilder. Your next tray will be properly prepared." He strode to the wall and pulled the bell cord. When a servant came to the door, he directed, "Tell Cook to send up a fresh tray for Miss Wilder. I shall inspect the tray myself."

The servant paled and fled.

She thanked him with a dignified nod of her head. "Once I have my breakfast, I shall leave."

"No." The wind gusting around the corners of the great house gave Justin his excuse. He strode to the window and yanked the velvet drapes open. "Do you see?"

Obediently, she leaned forward. He noted the gap at her neckline and stared. His cock swelled in response to the downy cleft between her breasts. He forced himself to look away and gestured at the window.

Snow fell heavily and steadily as though it would never stop. Ice-encrusted panes obscured the view to the snow-covered gardens. The cold swept off the window in waves. His breath condensed on the pane, damp mist screening the colder air outside. He shivered and drew the curtains together.

"The storm is worse." He returned to warm his hands at the fire. "It is foolhardy to take the child out again in this weather. You were fortunate last night, but you might not be again. Depend on it — you may be here for days, yet."

"Oh, no! I must leave. Emmy — we are not safe…"

Chapter Four

"Safe from what? From me?" he demanded harshly. He didn't like the way she raised her hand to her mouth, or the way her eyes widened as she stared at him over her fist.

"You?" She dropped her hand. "Should I fear you?"

If she knew what he was thinking, she'd run. Justin recalled how her hand had rested on his bare chest and tugged at his hair last night. Heat rose in him as if she stroked him again. She would do that before she left his house, he vowed. This time, she would be awake and aroused.

"Give me your aunt's direction," he ordered after a moment. "I shall send word that you and the child are well."

"You do not understand." She toyed with the embroidered edging of his fine linen sheets.

He tore his gaze away from her long, slender fingers plucking at a loose thread. His body tightened at the thought of those cool fingers on his heated body. Would she welcome him, or curl up in maidenly fear and cower before his advances?

Or would she perhaps be passionate, adept at pleasing a man? Would she keep him hard for hours, controlling his erection until he was wild for her? Would she take his sac between her fingers and caress his balls even as she took his rigid cock into her mouth? Painfully engorged, he visualized her shapely mouth on him and swallowed hard.

What had she been saying? Oh, yes, something she claimed he wouldn't understand. "Explain it then. What frightens you?"

She stared at him for a long time, as if deciding what she could tell him. At last, she ventured, "My older sister was married to Colonel Sir — a soldier in Wellesley's army—"

"Why do you not call Wellesley by his title?" Justin interrupted. "Surely you know he was elevated to the peerage? He is the first Duke of Wellington."

She shrugged that off as unimportant. "My sister died several months ago. It was her last wish that I take Emmy to our aunt, to be raised and protected by her."

"My condolences," he said automatically. "But why your aunt? Surely she is elderly?" When she nodded, Justin continued, raising the question that most concerned him. "I do not understand your role in this. Why do you not undertake the care of your niece yourself?"

"I shall have the lion's share. As you noted, my aunt is in the autumn years."

"Why should the child's father not raise her? After all, if he is a knight, a member of Society —"

She shuddered. "I see I must explain more fully. The tale is not pleasant."

She looked up at him, then down at her hands. The fingers gripped the sheet so tightly that the knuckles shone white. Tempted to go to her, to offer comfort, he forced himself to stay where he was.

"My sister's husband, my brother-in-law, is fully occupied with the army. He would have to leave Emmy in the care of his household staff."

Justin saw nothing wrong in that. "Most children are raised by nannies and tutors. I was," he added when she made a deprecating face. "I don't believe I turned out so badly."

Justin forced himself to stand still under her inspection. She studied his face, her gaze lingering on his eyes, his mouth, then dropped to his torso. He watched her take his measure, her gaze dropping to his legs, to his booted feet. When she looked up, he caught her gaze, searching her face for her reaction to him.

What he saw pleased him.

A faint blush stained her cheeks before she dropped her gaze. She twiddled with the coverlet. She moistened her lips. "Be that as it may, my sister did not wish Emmy to be raised by servants. In addition, she wanted her to be in a more...loving home."

Justin's gut tightened. "You are telling me that your brother-in-law abused your sister? You are afraid he will do the same to you?" Unexpected rage spilled through him at the prospect of anyone inflicting harm on Sarah.

Her gaze shot upward. "I did not say so!"

"Your actions speak for you. Why else would you risk a journey in this weather?" When she refused to answer, he bent to her. "Was the storm a more acceptable hazard than facing your brother-in-law — that nameless colonel?"

"I cannot answer that."

"You do not have to. Do not protect that man."

"I protect only Emmy," she cried. "You must understand that. I will not allow him to take her from me. From my aunt."

Justin heard her impassioned tone. He did not stop to consider his abrupt about-face. Admiration for her determination and bravery pulsed through him. "You set yourself quite a task. Your niece is how old?"

"Four months."

"Just so. Four months and you propose to shield her from her father for how many years?"

Her mouth firmed. "Until Emmy reaches her majority, if need be. That man shall have no chance to mistreat her."

Justin smiled, the one he used before issuing a challenge. The one stalwart men backed away from. "You will give me his name." His voice was even, as icy as the climate. "I shall see that he does not harm anyone again."

"That is very kind of you, Mr. Stowe, but Emmy and I cannot allow you to do any more than you already have."

"Not kindness."

Her gaze flicked to his, questioning him. "As soon as the weather clears,

Emmy and I must be on our way."

"And where exactly is it that you go?"

She hesitated. "St. Albans, or close by."

So she didn't want him to know her exact destination. Very curious. The mystery she presented him was almost as compelling as the alluring sight of her slim, supple body in his wide, comfortable bed. Or as relentless as his desire, made more urgent by her interest in him.

Justin rose and paced before the fire. "Does your brother-in-law, this 'soldier' you refuse to name," he asked with contempt, "know where you are?"

"How could he?" she answered reasonably. "Even I do not know where I am."

He smiled at that. "Is he in the country?"

She inclined her head. "I believe so. He requested compassionate leave from the Peninsula."

"H'mm." Justin thought. "So he's with the army in Spain. He will be returning there?"

Sarah lifted a shoulder. "I do not believe he would want to resign his commission, not after he distinguished himself at Ciudad Rodrigo."

"Even a bully must have his moments." Justin narrowed his eyes as a plan unfurled in his mind. "Does he know by which route you travel?"

"He must. There cannot be very many roads from his house to my aunt's residence."

"We are a sufficient distance away." He pulled up a chair and sat. Leaning forward, elbows on his knees, he held her gaze with his. It pleased him that she returned it with a steady intelligence. "The soldier does not know that you and your niece were in an accident. All he can find out is that you have not yet arrived at your aunt's home. Do you agree?"

"Well, yes, that certainly appears to be logical."

"Then, since you have no prior connection with me, with this house, how could he know to look for you here?"

Her eyes widened. "You suggest that Emmy and I remain here?" She dropped her gaze under his satisfied look. "He could make inquiries along the way. Maybe someone in the village could tell him about the wet nurse."

"I should be delighted if he did appear on my doorstep."

She blinked at his harsh tone. "But you just said —"

"Whatever happens, Miss Wilder, you will be safe here." He paused, distracted again, this time by the sight of her small, pink tongue as she moistened her bottom lip. He could imagine any number of better uses for it. He closed his eyes, shutting out the vision of that tongue on his bare flesh. Heat raced through his veins; his groin tightened. He glanced down at his trouser buttons, certain they'd pop from the strain.

After a moment, he managed to continue. "I shall notify your aunt that you and the child are well and enjoin her to secrecy."

"But if you can send a message to my aunt, why can Emmy and I not depart?"

Because I want you here. "Miss Wilder. A man on horseback can ride through places a carriage cannot. Even to St. Albans, or close by." He watched the color stain her cheeks as he stressed her inexact destination. "A man can slog through snow drifts that would stop a woman and child. Think of your niece, Miss Wilder," he coaxed. "Think of Emmy."

Her mouth pursed. "That is the first time you have called her by name, Mr. Stowe."

"Is it?" He reflected. "Perhaps it is because I have now assumed protection of you and her that —"

"A moment, sir! I have not agreed to this plan of yours."

"Why the hell not?" He stopped abruptly at her shocked expression. "Your pardon, but why not?"

"You are unaccustomed to having your wishes questioned, Mr. Stowe, but you have forgotten my sister's husband. When he does not find Emmy there, he will search for her." She worried at her bottom lip. "My aunt may not be able to withstand his methods of questioning."

Justin frowned at the implication. "Your aunt has no male servants?"

"None younger than she."

"Very well. I shall send some of my more robust footmen. They will safeguard your aunt as necessary."

She swallowed. "Why are you doing this, sir?"

"You may consider it part of the hospitality of my home."

"You are too modest, sir. I see that my gratitude discomfits you."

Her small, knowing smile singed his backbone. "Say no more, I pray you."

"There is still one more thing. Are you married, Mr. Stowe?"

He recoiled and forced down the knot in his windpipe. "No." His tone was adamant, a warning to her. "I am a bachelor, Miss Wilder. Content to stay that way."

"Oh, dear." She chewed on her lip. "Then I cannot remain in your house."

Justin tore his attention away from the lip he wished to nibble. "Why the devil not?"

Chapter Five

She flashed him a puzzled look. "Surely you comprehend the reasons."

"We face a quandary." Justin cleared his throat. "My household at the moment is entirely male. Oh," he exclaimed with some relief. "I forgot the wet nurse. There is another female in the house. You see, the proprieties are satisfied."

"It is not as I would wish." Her soft, pensive voice almost brought him to his knees. He studied the tilt of her head, the considering look in her eyes, the way she nibbled at her bottom lip. The neckline of his nightshirt had slipped, revealing the delicate curve of her collar bone. He stared. Under his gaze, her nipples pushed against the fabric. He clenched his fingers together.

"Still..." Blushing faintly, she looked away. "Perhaps, just this once, we could allow the realities of the situation to overcome the niceties. For Emmy's sake, of course," she added hastily.

Justin swallowed hard. "For Emmy's sake," he managed. His heart thumped in his chest.

A knock at the door interrupted his gratification. A footman entered with a tray, placed it over Sarah's knees and hastily departed as Justin glared at him.

Sarah looked at the closing door. "You should not remain here, Mr. Stowe."

"Are you frightened of me, after all?"

She held his gaze with her own. He noted the pulse beating at her throat, the way her breathing quickened. Her eyes darkened. She swallowed. For a moment, there was nothing but the connection between them. Justin's chest expanded as he fought for air.

She moistened her lips. "No."

Justin almost smiled as he examined the contents of her breakfast tray and poured chocolate into the single cup. "It appears to be edible."

Her hands shook as she took a small sip, then licked a drop from the corner of her mouth. "Delectable."

Justin longed to taste her, to explore the warm, sweet recesses, to curl his tongue around hers. He imagined the slick, soft texture, her unique flavor and felt heat race through his veins. Would she lick and suck his yard the same way, eagerly, avid for every last drop, every last sensation?

He took a roll from her tray, buttered it and added a spoonful of blackberry preserves. He popped it in his mouth. She watched, that tiny dimple forming in her cheek, as he chewed and swallowed. The bread stuck in his throat when she tilted her head in question.

He swallowed quickly. "Your pardon, Miss Wilder. I am hungry."

"Then you had better go see to your own breakfast."

He winced at the asperity in her tone. He gestured to her breakfast. "There is enough for two."

He settled on the bed beside her and took another roll.

His hip rested against her thigh. Her eyes widened. She edged away, but caught by the tray over her knees, could not move far. "Really, sir. I insist you leave."

He studied her. Anyone looking on would not take her for a woman intent on his title. Seeing her en dishabille, still in bed, an onlooker would take them for lovers. They would be, he vowed. Soon.

She touched her throat. "This is most improper, sir."

"No doubt, but I suspect none of the gorgons at Almacks are hiding behind the curtains to peep out at us."

Sarah looked disconcerted for only a moment. "I pay no attention to that sort of thing. It is enough that I know you are here."

"But no one else does." Justin gave her his most engaging smile, expecting her to soften and smile back.

She did neither. She handed him the tray and pointed at the door. "You are obviously more in need of this than I."

He laughed and replaced it over her knees. His knuckles brushed her thighs. He felt her tense at his touch, her muscles stiffening and yet he swore he felt a tremor, the slightest fluttering of muscles held too long in check.

He read her hesitancy, her unease, and yet, simmering in the depths of her eyes, he read curiosity. Her innocence lit her face with a delicate warmth.

Cautioning himself to go slow, to do nothing to make her retreat, he deliberately slowed his motion, easing his fingers across the satin comforter covering her. The rasp of his fingers over the glossy fabric sounded loud in the sudden, tense silence between them. He heard her catch her breath.

He lifted his gaze from the tray, moving slowly, indolently up her bosom, lingering on the sight of her nipples peaking under his study, then past the pulse at her neck, and her slightly parted lips to her eyes, wide open and fixed on his.

This close, he saw the golden flecks in her brown eyes. Hints of spice hid in the warmth, as if waiting for the right man to find and reap their treasure. He responded immediately to the challenge.

Her breathing quickened, tiny gasps that echoed the way her heartbeat made the nightshirt pulsate over her breasts. He flicked a glance at the small vee of ivory and pink skin exposed in the neckline of his nightshirt. At this distance, he noted the shadow between her breasts and saw the way the globes trembled as she breathed. He inhaled, drawing in her soft fragrance, then let his gaze rest on her lips.

Rosy, luscious, the bottom lip slightly fuller than the top and quivering as she moistened it with the tip of her small pink tongue.

He bent over the breakfast tray and finished the job for her. He touched her lip with the tip of his tongue, then eased it across her bottom lip. She gasped, stiffened, and shivered, but she didn't move her head away. Her pressed his lips to hers.

Her lips were soft, more tender than a budding rose, and moist, as though dew-kissed. Under his, they grew warmer and tremulous.

He withdrew only an instant, just long enough to slant his head the better to savor her mouth, but she whimpered at the loss. Immediately, he took her lips again, harder and more possessively this time. He rubbed his lips against hers, testing both her willingness and the texture of her lips.

Both pleased him. He touched her lips with his tongue again, teasing and questing, until her mouth shyly parted and he felt for the first time the intimacy of her tongue. She tasted of heat, of sweet chocolate and the summer taste of blackberries.

He all but groaned.

Lifting the tray, he set it down on the floor beside the bed. He sat on the edge and took her face in both hands. "Sarah?" he murmured, just before he captured her mouth and cut off all speech.

Her response delighted him. Provoked him. Tantalized, tempted and teased him. He wanted more. He pulled her down to the bed beside him and kissed her. Once this way, as a young man tests his first maiden, then that way, as a lover caresses a virgin, and then again, like that, as a man arouses the woman he intends to bed.

She gasped and quivered and made little noises in her throat. He swallowed them along with the taste of her, hot and sweet and passionate. His hand went to the mother of pearl buttons at her neck and opened the first two. Her hand came up to stop his, even as she murmured deep in her throat and arched against him.

Her small hand enclosing his was torment. His was the greater strength; he could overpower her and take what he sought, what she unconsciously offered, but those slight, delicate fingers on his stopped him more effectively than raw power would have done.

He drew in a deep, cleansing breath and pulled himself up to a sitting position. She lay sprawled, half beneath the bedcovers, her hair tumbling around her shoulders, her cheeks flushed and her mouth swollen and red from his kisses. Her chest heaved as did his.

Her fingers still enclosed his hand. He lifted them away from him, marveling at their delicacy, at their shaking, and lifted her hand to his mouth. He kissed each trembling finger in turn, and when done, he folded her hand and laid it against her breast.

She inhaled, a small, jerky sound that told him she was as affected as he. "No more. Please."

"I am sorry if I have offended you."

"I did not say you offend me, sir." She bit her lip, then whispered, "When I look at you, I am quite pleased with what I see."

He pressed a kiss to her throat. "Elaborate, if you would, Miss Wilder."

"H'mm. You are suitably tall. You do not slouch, nor does your stomach protrude."

Justin chuckled as his stomach muscles contracted as though she'd touched him. So she approved of the hours he spent in physical exercise, did she? "What else?"

"You are pleasing to the eye and the ear. Except that is," she hastened to add, "When you are issuing orders and expecting to be obeyed."

He kissed her. When he let her go, he murmured into her mouth, "Shall I perhaps suggest that others do my bidding?"

"That would be a beginning, sir."

He chuckled. "And what other facets of my character need improving?"

She studied him. His skin warmed under her gaze. "I shall have to think on that. For now, I can tell you that I do not care for your hair in this style. I do not think Lord Byron an admirable character."

Justin winced. "I shall tell, no suggest" he amended when he caught her eye, "to Pruitt that he change it."

"Very good. Do you wish to hear more?"

"Oh, indeed I do. This is most enlightening. Just look at the improving effect you have on me."

She cast a glance down his body. His erection bulged.

Her eyes widened as she gasped, "You are shameless, sir." She averted her eyes. "Stop that!"

He smiled at her stunned expression. "It is merely my body's reaction to yours. I have no control over that part of myself."

She wrapped her arms around herself. "You must not be here, not like this, sir. You must leave."

He studied her defensive, protective posture. To come this far and then frighten her into retreat. Anger at his lack of self control made his voice harsh. "Have I frightened you so badly, then?"

She flinched. "This is not right. It is most unsuitable."

Justin blew out a breath. By rights he should thank her for keeping her presence of mind. "You are correct," he said heavily, forcing himself to think with his head and not his engorged shaft. He moved away from her. "I apologize for forcing myself upon you."

"That is not necessary, sir. I am equally to blame."

Her remark halted his abrupt retreat. He paused to study her face. "Do you attach fault to kissing me, Sarah?"

She looked away to the far reaches of his chamber, anywhere but at him. Her distress cut him deeply. He should be whipped for tormenting her, but he could not allow her to think ill of herself.

He reached down to take her chin in his hand, forcing her eyes back to his. "Do you, Sarah?"

Her chin trembled under his touch. "I should —"

"But you do not?" Hope made his voice tender.

"I cannot." She blew out a shaky breath. "I find it…difficult to keep my mind when you are near me."

He felt his mouth drop. "You do?"

"You know you are most attractive."

"I am?"

"Sir, you look like a fish, yet you bleat like a lamb."

Justin stifled a chuckle at her tart comment. "I pray you, do not repeat that in company. I am reputed to be something of a wit."

"It is your reputation that I wish to preserve. And mine."

He turned to face her more directly. "Your reputation shall come to no harm at my hands, but why do you concern yourself with mine?" Justin was flattered, half amused, that she'd worry about his standing in Society, he whom half the *haute ton* buzzed about.

"You must be aware that your appearance commands the attention of women. I am quite convinced that you have them swarming like bees."

His stomach tightened. "Why do you say that?"

She tilted her head. "Surely you have heard this before? You know you are handsome sight, sir. You must take pity on my lack of experience. I do not have your worldly wisdom."

"I like you just the way you are, Sarah."

She hid her gaze from him, but not before he saw her contented look. "I like you too, sir." She spoke softly, her words barely audible, but he heard them all the way to the innermost man.

Curiously pleased, he wondered at the intriguing turnabout to their dialogue. Most women demanded to be complimented and he used honeyed words and soft comments to caress and seduce. How strange to be on the receiving end. How delightful a change. "And what is it about me that most pleases you?"

She gave him a tiny, secret smile. "I think it is your eyes, and these hollows to your cheeks that add to the fascination." She demonstrated by touching the corner of his eye and the line of his jaw. "You look quite forbidding, very romantic, with your brooding black eyes and that mysterious cast to your visage. I am sure you must have females swooning at your feet trying to make you smile at them."

The women chased and dropped at his feet, but not for his face, he thought bitterly. The title was far more attractive than he.

What a wondrous balm for his soul that Sarah liked him, Justin Stowe, the man, not Justin, Earl of Howden.

Chapter Six

"Pay attention," Pruitt snapped his foil under Justin's chin. "Begging your pardon, your lordship, but I could have ripped your heart out."

Justin lowered his fencing sword and wiped his brow. "Never."

"You're going through the motions, sir. I thought you wanted to practice. Your lunges are off. Your parries are clumsy." Pruitt snorted in disgust. "A child could have gotten through that quinte."

Justin forced his mind away from Sarah. Frustration made him grind his teeth. "Anything I'm doing right?" he asked dryly.

"The flèche wasn't too bad. Shall we try again, my lord?"

Justin dropped into on-guard stance, executed a feint and immediately scored a touch. "There, Pruitt! See if you can stop me now."

His valet leaped into the fray. Their footfalls thudded on the parquet floor of the ballroom turned fencing salon. The clash of foil against foil rang in the air. No sooner did Justin gain the advantage with a riposte than Pruitt created a counterattack.

Justin's breath came hard and fast. He ignored the sweat dripping from his forehead and beading on his chest under his half-opened shirt. This was what he needed. Hard exercise to work his body and empty his mind of all but the next move. He'd been lax of late. He panted and forced himself on.

He had Pruitt on the defensive now, parrying his thrusts with a lightning fast seconde when Justin spotted Ordway enter the room.

Justin slowed enough to allow Pruitt to even the score.

"Attention!" Pruitt rapped out. "You cannot take your eye from your opponent, not even for a moment!"

Ordway inclined his head. "My lord, Miss Wilder is departing."

Justin dropped his foil and ran for the door. "Why didn't you stop her?" he shouted over his shoulder.

"It is not my place to hinder a lady, my lord."

Cursing Ordway, cursing himself for leaving her alone and above all cursing Sarah, Justin raced down the hall until he spotted her on the wide staircase.

"Where the hell do you think you're going?" he roared.

Wearing her heavy cloak, Sarah halted, one foot extended to descend to the next step. Guilt flashed across her face.

Justin pounded up the steps until he faced her. Standing on the riser above him, she still barely came to his shoulder, yet she looked him unflinchingly straight in the eye.

"To the village, Mr. Stowe."

He planted his fists on his hips. "Why?"

Her gaze drifted to his chest. In his hurry, he'd neglected to button his shirt. The sweat cooled on his torso but didn't calm his temper. Or his desire, as he noted the quick way she licked her lips. Instead, it grew more sharp as it fueled his anger. She wasn't going to sneak out of his house like some demimondaine.

At last, she lifted her gaze to his. "I intend to hire a conveyance."

"Why?" he repeated, not bothering to hide his emotions.

Her eyes had a soft, languid look to them. A blush stained her cheeks as her mouth parted, her breathing erratic. His pulse raced.

She drew her cloak closer about her throat. "I cannot stay. Not after..."

Justin moved closer to her. Good intentions be damned. He wasn't going to let her go. "You forget the storm."

"I forget nothing!"

"You cannot go out in the blizzard."

Her chin rose. It couldn't have been easy, but she managed to look down her nose at him. "Accompany me to the door, sir, and you shall see that I can."

No one questioned his authority. Narrowing his eyes, Justin leaned forward until his face was inches from hers. She didn't retreat. He lowered his voice. "I will not allow it."

"You cannot stop me!" She moved to walk around him.

He put out a hand to restrain her.

She feinted to the right, then to the left. He parried easily, amused now, until she executed a compound attack, darting to the left again and raising her hand to ward him off. When he hesitated, she slipped his guard. In moments, she was running down the stairs.

Admiration for her spirit and quick thinking delayed him for only an instant. He turned and gave chase. He jumped two and three steps at a time and caught her arm.

She spun around in his grasp, her cloak billowing about his knees. Her mouth fell open in surprise.

Before he could think, he'd stopped her protest with his lips. He plunged his tongue into her mouth, capturing and possessing all in the same moment. Her quickened breathing inflamed him. He felt his rod swell and harden as the heat from his body rose up to envelop them both.

She broke loose. "Sir!" she panted. The cloak fell open to reveal her breasts rising and falling in her agitation. Her gown seemed to have shrunk, for it clung indecently to her curves. He saw the nipples pushing against the fine black wool and immediately hardened even further.

"Your clothing is still damp. Is catching your death in the storm preferable to being with me?" He pulled her close to him and plundered her mouth again.

She tasted sweet and dark, like the finest chocolate. She was hot and fiery, more potent than brandy. He couldn't get enough. Again and again, he kissed her mouth until she whimpered.

He relaxed his grip on her, just enough to let go of her arm and slide his around her back. With one hand gripping her hip, he kept her immobile in his grasp. He caught her chin and forced her to look at him.

"You are not leaving. Do you understand?"

She tried to shake her head. "I must."

Justin eased his hold on her face. "Without Emmy?"

She swallowed. He felt the movement of her throat against his palm and was almost undone. "I shall return for her once I have a carriage."

"Why didn't you ask for one of mine?"

Sarah jerked her head out of his grasp. "I want nothing more from you, sir. Please unhand me."

He turned her by the hip until her back was pressed to the wall. "And if I choose not to?" He kept his voice low and seductive.

She stiffened. "A gentleman does not keep a lady against her will."

He didn't bother to hide his smile. "You take me for a gentleman, then?"

She glanced over his shoulder. He saw her gaze roam the hall, no doubt taking inventory of the contents. "You must be. This house—"

"Others would say I am no gentleman. They would swear I care little for rules."

"I know you better," she averred, sounding desperate to convince him of his better nature. "You saved us from the storm. You even offered to help Emmy and me."

"Perhaps I have a payment in mind."

Her eyed widened as she took his meaning. It had to be difficult not to, when he let his cock push into her soft belly. She gasped.

"Mr. Stowe!"

"Miss Wilder," he murmured as he lowered his head to taste her again. He flicked little kisses along the tight seam of her lips, laughing when she refused him entry. Next he dropped kisses on her jaw, her cheek, her temple as she stood stiff and unmoving in his arms.

He chuckled as he let some of his weight rest against her and he felt her knees buckle. Immediately, he pressed his advantage and used his body to anchor her to the wall.

When she opened her mouth to object, he kissed it. When she raised a hand to slap him, he stopped it with a love bite to her palm. When she moaned, he swallowed it with his mouth.

"Stay with me," he commanded against her closed eyes.

Her eyelids fluttered under his lips. "No."

He arched his pelvis into her. "Yes."

She caught her breath, then exhaled it in a long shuddering sigh. "I can't think."

"I shall think for you." He moved slowly toward the staircase, propelling her against the wall by touch and kiss. Her warm breath against his neck seared him. Desire rode him hard and fast.

"I must go," she cried. "I cannot do this!"

He murmured against her mouth as he lifted her to the first step. "It is snowing."

"I shall manage."

"You will take cold." He propelled her up another riser, then the next.

"I am too warm already," she whispered.

On the seventh step, he kissed her until she moaned. "I will warm you even more."

She broke away and held on to the railing as she all but slid down several steps. Her breath came fast and shallow.

He lifted her in his arms. "I did this last night," he reminded her. "I put you in my bed then, too."

Halfway up the staircase, he lowered her down his body until she stood once more on the riser above him. His kiss this time was slow and provocative, deliberately seductive and compelling.

She sagged against him, then slowly, her arms lifted and embraced him. Justin felt the change in her and tempered his kiss, teasing her, tempting her to kiss him back. When the tip of her tongue touched his, delicately, shyly, he exulted.

On the landing, he stripped her cloak from her. "You will not need this."

She clutched at it as he sent it sailing over the balcony. "What are you doing?"

He swallowed a laugh. "I thought it would be very clear by now, Miss Wilder. I am going to make love to you."

"But, sir, I..." Her words were lost as he picked her up and strode down the long hall. Last night he had cursed every step of the way, today he used the time to kiss and fondle her until she all but purred under his touch.

Her eyes were half-closed, dreamy and slumberous. Satisfied, he dropped another kiss on lips already red and swollen. If she looked this way now, how much more satisfied she'd be later.

Much later.

Chapter Seven

Justin kicked his bedroom door shut behind him. He put Sarah on her feet long enough to turn the key in the lock but he didn't free her.

She turned her head, looking at him with wide eyes. Deliberately holding her gaze with his, he unbuttoned her buttons, slowly, one by one. Her breathing quickened.

The gown parted, revealing the pale skin of her back. He slid a hand in, caressing first the line of her spine, then slid it around to press her to him by her midriff.

Justin put his mouth on her neck and shoved the gown to her waist. She shivered. Ignoring her soft cry, he loosened the ties to her chemise and pushed it off her shoulders. It caught on her breasts. He flicked it free, then cupped one breast.

Oh God. She felt so good in his hand, warm and soft and blooming. He rubbed her nipple between the tip of his finger and thumb, exulting when her nipple kerneled at his touch. Her head fell back onto his shoulder.

He kissed her temple, then her shoulder. She shuddered and pulled out of his embrace.

"Are you frightened of me, Sarah?" Deliberately, he used her Christian name for the first time.

"No." Her golden brown lashes hid her expression from him, but the telltale flush visible at her throat gave her away. Sweet Jesus, did she know what that did to him?

Color rose to her cheeks as she whispered, "I should be."

Justin wondered whether she tried to convince him, or herself. Either way, he determined to slow down, to handle her as cautiously as a maiden. "Because we are going to make love?"

She swallowed convulsively. "Because of the way you make me feel," she whispered. "It is wrong."

He touched a loose tendril of hair at her temple. "You are concerned for yourself, or because Society says you must reject my advances?"

She looked puzzled, then her brow cleared. "I do not give a fig for Society."

"I shall be gentle with you, Sarah." Justin reined in his passion. If she needed time and seduction, he'd give her those, even if his body paid the price for it. "You will come to no harm at my hands."

She looked down at one of the hands in question. It pulled hers away and lowered the fabric to reveal her breasts once more. Her breath came faster.

He cupped her anew. "You fit my hand perfectly, see?"

With a tiny moan, she allowed his caress.

"You like that, Sarah? Do you like this as well?" he asked against her lips as he pulled slightly on her nipple, elongating it.

She expelled her breath into his mouth. "Oh, I must be very wanton..."

"You are perfect." He cradled her breast in his hand. With his thumb, he caressed her nipple. "You do like my hand on you, do you not, Sarah?"

"Is it improper of me to like this?"

Heat pierced him. He cleared his throat. "Not if it gives you pleasure."

Her lashes flickered as she stole a glance at him. "Truly?"

"Between a man and a woman who want to —" He paused, searching for the right word. Finding it, he smiled down at her. "— to delight each other, nothing is wrong."

She pushed him back so that she could stare into his eyes. He felt them searching his expression as vividly as if she touched him with her hands. "You are persuasive, sir, but I am aware of the consequences of our actions."

For a moment, he felt cornered, like the fox as the hounds bayed their triumph. He shook it off. Surely Sarah referred to more personal, intimate issues. He thought of the French letters in his dressing room and smiled. "Do not worry. I shall protect you." He kissed her, slow and sweet and hot. She trembled in his arms. "Let us enjoy each other and forget everything but us now."

"I must think!"

"Do not think, Sarah," he urged. "Feel. Feel how much I want you. Allow yourself to admit how much you want me." He pressed closer, making sure she knew how hard, how aroused he was. "I shall make it sweet for you, Sarah. Put yourself in my hands."

She gasped. Her eyes widened, then darkened. "You are too near, sir."

"Let me come nearer. Let me come inside you."

Her eyes turned darker, her body softened. He felt her knees tremble. Tightening his hold on her, he watched as her own rising desire warred with her sense of propriety. Encouraging her, he kissed her tenderly, persuasively. He knew the moment she surrendered to her passion.

His kiss turned possessive as he worked at the remaining fastenings of her dress. She seemed not to notice as it pooled to the carpet. "You will not be sorry," he promised.

He felt her breasts move with each breath she took. Each tiny upheaval was a caress against his chest. He pulled his shirt off and tossed it over his shoulder. Taking her hand, he placed her slender fingers against his heart. "I feel your heart beating. Now feel mine. It almost bursts for want of you."

She left her fingers there. He couldn't believe it, but yes, she was actually caressing him, tweaking at his nipples in a gentle imitation of what he had done to hers, pulling at his chest hair.

She seemed fascinated by it. He glanced down to see her fingers buried in it. The contrast between her soft, pale hand and his dark furred chest made him catch his breath.

It appeared she noticed, too. "All this dark hair. It makes me feel quite weak in the knees."

"I am strong. I shall take care of you." He whirled her to the bed, where he dropped her and followed her down to the enveloping softness.

"Justin!" she gasped as she landed on her back. "What are you doing?"

"No more talk, Miss Wilder." He lifted himself on an elbow to smile down at her. "Now I am going to make love to you."

"I cannot sway you from this?"

He looked deep into her eyes. Warm, spicy with arousal, they looked back into his. He read excitement, daring, fascination, a hint of fear, and above all, what excited him most, acceptance, even eagerness.

He smiled. "Never."

She smiled back, scorching his brains. "Then, would you mind very much kissing me again?"

He complied, again and again as her breast swelled in his hand and her kisses grew fiery against his mouth. He ached to thrust himself into her, again and again, until he found the release he craved.

Justin felt his rod harden to aching proportions and settled himself against her.

"You must get off me, sir." She pushed at his chest, but he refused to move. The feel of her soft little hands against him, even through his clothing, was enough to sear his lungs.

"You are heavy, sir." When he lifted himself slightly, resting his weight on his elbows, she inhaled and ran her hands over her chest. "Your shoulders, see how much broader they are than mine? You could engulf me easily."

"I could. Would you allow me?"

"Allow you?" She traced a muscle in his corded arm. "How could I stop you?"

He looked into her face, into the disquiet posed as a question. "You have nothing to worry about, Sarah. I promise you."

"Men promise very easily. They also break those promises as easily."

He framed her face with both hands. "We are talking about more than you and I, are we not?"

Chapter Eight

The light went out of her eyes. Justin cradled her head and pressed a tender kiss to her brow. "Who has hurt you, Sarah?"

"It must be obvious that a promise made to me was broken." She surprised him with the steadiness of her voice, by her cool tone.

"Who made the promise, Sarah? A man?"

She exhaled, a long shuddering breath that broke his heart. "I was engaged to be married to a subaltern in my brother-in-law's command. My sister's husband promised me he would keep Robby safe, but he sent him into combat."

"Sarah, sweet Sarah. Many men die in battle."

He meant to console her, but she turned furious eyes on him. "Do not preach of manly heroics to me, sir! Robby was killed deliberately because I..."

"Because you what, Sarah?" Justin asked, his eyes narrowing as a suspicion formed.

"Because I would not allow my sister's husband to force his attentions on me!" Sarah finished in a rush.

Justin closed his eyes to hide the pain of his supposition confirmed.

"See? Even you admit I am guilty."

His eyes flew open. "No, never." He pressed kisses to her brow, her cheek-bones, the tip of her nose. "I am proud of you, Sarah, for refusing what he had no right to ask." He kissed her tenderly, a butterfly-light touch of his lips to hers. "I am only sorry that you had to suffer for it."

"Oh, Justin," she murmured against his lips. "You make me feel worthy. So happy. I had forgotten how it is to feel joy."

He nuzzled her throat at the hollow where her pulse beat. The fragrance of spring flowers rose up and surrounded his senses. "I am thankful that I can do that for you. Will you allow me to give you more?"

"What more can there be?"

He hid his smile in the beguiling hollow between her breasts. "Allow me to show you. I shall do my best to make you happy."

"You still wish to make love to me?" she whispered.

"I do." He kissed her hard and deep and pressed his rigid erection against her belly. "Does that tell you what I want?"

She smiled, a slow seductive smile that cast warmth and delight into his deeper reaches. "I believe that will do."

For a moment, he was startled by the change in her. On reflection, though, it made sense. When Sarah determined to do something, she did it with her whole heart and being. She had rescued her niece and made it through the storm to his doorstep. He admired that single-mindedness of purpose, that devotion, so he should not be surprised when she turned her attention to him.

Now that she had made up her mind, she was beguiling, sensual and all woman. He'd never bedded a woman with this much spirited conversation before, but he liked it. He liked her quick wit, her acceptance of the passion between them, her lack of artifice. He liked her. "For a start, at any rate."

"You will show me more?"

"You must put your trust in me." When she smiled up at him, giving him that assurance, he all but shook. "A moment, Sarah." He went into his dressing room and returned with a French letter.

He dropped it on the bedside table, then sat to pull off his boots. He cast them aside in blatant disregard for their shine. He stood again to undo the buttons of his breeches and pushed them off his hips, all the while conscious of her eager gaze on him. *God.* He'd never had a woman look at him with such demure delight, such admiration.

Fully naked before her, he felt himself grow larger and more powerful. Did she know what she did to him just by looking at him that way? His cock stood at full mast, straining to find its home within her soft, delectable body. He'd dreamed of this. Now that the moment was here, could he last?

"I am naked before you, Sarah. Will you permit me to remove the rest of your clothing?"

She blushed, but allowed him to disrobe her.

Her arms dropped to cover her mound. Justin gently peeled her hands away. "Do not hide yourself from me, Sarah." He learned the shape of her, the gentle curves, the softest rose of her nipples. "You are a delight to me, so smooth, so beautiful."

She met his gaze. "Am I really?"

He gave a passing thought to the dozens of women he had paid meaningless compliments to, and, tracing the puckered flesh of her aureole, he knew without a doubt that he would never think of Sarah in the same terms. "You are the most precious thing I know."

"Ah," she murmured and surged into his arms. The feel of her breasts against his chest made Justin inhale sharply. Pleasure surged through him at her courage, at her desire for him.

"Sarah, Sarah." He placed her against the pillows and devoted himself to kissing her. Long moments later, he lifted his head and gazed with satisfaction at her swollen lips, at her glazed eyes. "You are a wonder."

She traced the lines of his jaw, his mouth, then down his throat to his chest. She followed the shape of his muscled arms, then lifted her head to kiss his shoulder.

"You are very large, sir. And velvety soft to the touch. I thought your skin here would be as hard as your hands."

His breath hissed out.

"Does it distress you that I touch you?" she asked when his cock quivered against her belly.

"Distress?" he echoed though his brain threatened to explode. "No. Quite the contrary."

"Ah. In that case..." She placed a string of tiny kisses across his collarbone to the center of his chest. "You do not mind?"

"You must please yourself," Justin replied, though he nearly strangled.

"How kind of you." Sarah lightly pulled the hairs that covered his flat nipples, then burrowed with her tongue to lick one, then the other, in imitation of his mouth on her breasts. "You do not mind that I...play with you?"

"Please...play." *Sweet Jesus!* He gritted his teeth and vowed he'd withstand her inquisitive, investigating touch. He'd endure anything to make certain that Sarah should suffer no shame, no pain.

When he went to lower himself beside her, she stopped him. "Stay just so a moment longer, sir." She rose to her knees. Sinking back onto her heels, she studied his body. "You are a beautiful man, Justin."

"Not beautiful," he chuffed. His stomach contracted as she touched it with the tip of her finger, then smoothed her palm across his flat belly. "God!"

"May I touch you...there?"

He couldn't trust himself to speak. Closing his eyes, he nodded. The anticipation of her small hand on his engorged shaft had him breathing in harsh gulps.

When it came, it was more than he'd imagined. It was heavenly. It was torture. It lasted only a moment, as he quivered and jumped under her fingertip.

He opened his eyes to see her draw her hand back, her eyes wide and her mouth a small O. He wanted to fill her mouth, to fill her every crevice, to teach her all the delight a man and a woman could share together.

Instead, he made himself be still.

Cautiously, she touched him again. "You are so hot. So smooth, like satin."

She ran her finger down the length of him, while Justin braced his legs and forced himself to endure the most agonizing arousal he'd ever had. He threw back his head and closing his eyes, he gritted his teeth. For an untutored maiden, she managed to reduce him to a state of mindless desire. He groaned.

She took her hand away. "Is that displeasing to you?"

"Ah, no," he managed.

"May I touch you again?"

The thought of what else she could do to him had his blood boiling. "Yes."

She placed her hands on his hips and ran them down his flanks, his thighs then back up the insides of his thighs until she could go no further. He sensed her hesitation. Silently, he willed her to experiment, to touch him as she pleased.

As if she heard his silent acquiescence, she delicately touched his sac. When his balls rolled, she gasped, then lightly played with him until he felt ready to burst.

"You have a magnificent body, sir."

"Justin," he reminded her.

"Justin," she repeated obediently as her small hand burrowed between his legs.

He shuddered. He'd never felt this way before, impaled by his desire, capti-vated, his blood so hot he could hardly bear it. All he wanted to do was come into her, to thrust himself into her, to bring her the pleasure she brought him.

She lifted her head to gaze at him. "Do I shock you?"

"Yes." His breathing sounded harsh in the quiet room. "No. More."

Emboldened by his request, she applied herself to learning more about his body. She touched, she stroked, prodded and patted. Smiling, she curled her fingers and slid her hand down his cock. Finding a rhythm, she did that repeat-edly, experimenting with pressure, with the way the cockhead bulged and the veins flared.

Justin gasped for breath. "Enough!" he all but shouted when a drop appeared on the tip of his rod. "I shall embarrass myself before I have pleasured you."

She opened her hand, but did not release him. His yard pulsed on her palm. "You shall pleasure me, Justin. You are pleasuring me now."

"Stop, Sarah. Allow me to attend to you."

"Not yet, Justin, please. Tell me what else I can do."

Her pleading tone did him in. "Are you sure?"

She touched the tip of his penis with her finger, then brought the whitish drop to her mouth. Her tongue flicked out, tasting him. Sweet Jesus!

His breath came harsh and loud. "Sarah, do you mean it?"

She nodded, her gaze fixed on his throbbing cock.

"Touch me with your tongue. Lick me."

She raised wide eyes and stared up at him. "Lick you? Here?" When he nodded, too far gone to speak, she moistened her lips.

The touch of her tongue, hesitant, wet and warm, undid him. He groaned and fell back on the bed.

"Justin?"

He heard the doubt in her voice and forced himself to speak. "You are a delight, Sarah."

He felt her smiling as she bent to him and licked him again. Growing bolder, she stroked his yard and kissed his quivering flesh.

An unselfish woman. Oh, Lord, what had he done to be so rewarded? Justin grasped the sides of her head, burying his hands in the soft strands of her honey hair and held on as his body bucked and throbbed under her hands. He came, a great wrenching orgasm that arched his back and neck. He cried out as he spewed forth.

"Did I do something wrong?" she asked in a small voice.

When he could speak, he touched her hair. "Far from it. I am the one at fault. I have not satisfied you."

"You haven't?"

"Not the way I shall," he promised. "If you will be patient with me for just a short time."

"Why?"

He slid her hand through his chest hair, down his belly until it came to rest around his now flaccid cock. "That is why."

She gripped him, gently, but possessively. His cock, hardening again, rose in an erection he would never have thought possible. He turned his gaze on Sarah. "You are a witch. How did you do that to me?"

Her eyes, shining and warm with passion, flickered over his rod, and then met his gaze. "I think you have underestimated yourself, Justin."

"Not I. This resurgence is all your doing."

"Mine? It appears to me that it is your...appendage which stands between us." He chuckled. "Nonetheless, you have a magic touch."

She stroked the sensitive skin between his legs with her finger tip. "I am glad you think so."

"Shall I tell you what else I think?"

Her smile was pure enchantment. "Please do."

"I think I shall play the sorcerer." He sat up and brought her to his side. When she rested comfortably, he lowered and took her mouth with his. She tasted of him, of the most masculine part of him. He might once have been put off by such a thing, but now he reveled in it, sharing with her his joy that she had taken — and kept — him in her mouth while he convulsed.

His tongue penetrated, probed and touched each slick curve and moist crevice of her mouth. With one hand, he smoothed his way down her throat to her breasts, and took one into his palm.

He lifted his head and stared down at her. "Now it is my turn."

She sighed, languid and yet her eyes were filled with deviltry. "One must be fair, I suppose."

Chapter Nine

"You have been so ingenious in your attentions, Sarah, that I shall have to be extra careful in return."

She stretched beneath him. The feel of her breasts rubbing against his nipples set him afire. His belly contracted as she ran her hands down his flanks.

He reached behind him and grabbed a hand. "No. That's enough experimenting. Let me return the favor."

Holding her hand in his, he bent to her breasts once more, devoting himself to pleasuring her the way she had attended to him.

When her nipples peaked in raspberry kernels, he let her hand go to place his palms over her globes, then taking a nipple between two fingers on each hand, he pulled, elongating them even further. He licked his lips at the way she arched her back to press her breasts into his hands. She sighed, a long drawn exhalation of pleasure, of pain.

"Do you like this, Sarah? Did I hurt you? Are you frightened?"

It took her a moment to answer, and when did, she responded with a smile of exquisite satisfaction. "I am not frightened by you, Justin."

"By something else?"

She wriggled against the sheet. "Not with you."

"Shall I continue?"

With all the gravity of a monarch holding court, she tilted her head. "Please do."

Grinning, he slid down her body, relishing the way her softly curved abdomen quivered under his touch, the way her breath came soft and quick. He tongued his way down her ribcage, to her navel, buried it in her belly button, making her squirm and laugh, then lifted his face to look into hers.

He grinned. "Have I found a ticklish spot?"

"Do not tease me," she begged.

"I have just begun," he contradicted her. "Before I am done, you shall be laughing and crying with the pleasure I give you."

"I hardly recognize myself," she whispered and arched her pelvis at him. "Look how wanton I am with you."

"You are marvelous, Sarah." He returned his attention to her body. Her skin tasted of lavender, of roses, of springtime. He licked her belly, skimming his tongue over the pale honey curls on her mound, then darted unerringly to find her clitoris. He licked her bud, once, twice, experimentally, testing her, tasting her.

"Justin," she cried. "No, no, you must not do that!"

"Yes, I must." He spoke firmly, gently. "Did I not allow you to play with me?"

"It is not the same thing!"

"It is. Did you not say you would be fair?"

"You are a devil, to turn my words against me."

"You are an angel, to allow me this heavenly delight." He put his mouth to her again, lightly flicking his tongue against her warm flesh.

She tensed, then relaxed as he found her most sensitive spot and settled down to pleasure her. He fluttered his tongue against her until her bud stood up in arousal, then suckled her, at first gently, until she pushed her hips against him.

With her hands on his head, pressing him closer to her, he swirled his tongue against her swollen flesh, pressing into her until he entered her heated passage. She cried out.

He redoubled his efforts, licking and sucking on her bite, sticking his tongue in her again and again while she moved restlessly on the bed. Her knees clenched against his body, making him yearn to be enclosed within hers.

Ruthlessly, he controlled the urge to sink into her.

"Oh, no more, please...please."

He ignored her pleas as he moved his head just enough to sink a finger into her. Her muscles immediately clamped down on it, making his balls sweat. She bucked against him as he inserted another finger, then another. He spread them within her, massaging the hot confines of her inner passage.

Her breath came in labored gusts as she undulated under him. She grabbed his shoulders, trying to pull him away from her privities, but he ignored the sharp scoring of her fingernails. Using fingers and mouth he drove her higher and higher until her muscles clamped tightly around his fingers and she came in a great liquid gush. He buried his mouth in her, lapping, smiling, enjoying her pleasure.

When she calmed, flesh still quivering, he withdrew his fingers and licked them clean. "You taste of honey, of sweet woman."

She half-opened her eyes to look at him. She wore a sated, drowsy expression that satisfied him, and yet left him hungry for more. He touched his fingertip to her mouth.

Immediately, she drew it in and sucked it as she had his rod. He'd thought he was as hard as he could be, but he hardened, almost painfully. He felt the fever in his sac as his sperm boiled hot.

He grabbed a French letter and expertly tied it on while she watched, her eyes wide. He was by turns discomposed by her interest and yet fiercely proud that she exhibited no missish squeamishness.

He moved over her, reassuring her with soft words, with gentle caresses until she parted her legs and allowed him to find his place between her thighs. "Just so, Sarah. Do we not do well together?"

"Is this the way?" She welcomed him, pulling him closer with her arms about his shoulders.

"Just so, Sarah. You have the way of it." The heat rose from her, scented and humid, as he probed with the tip of his cock. Finding the soft, wet entrance to her body, he pushed in, just a little, then withdrew.

She moaned and clutched at his shoulders. "Justin!"

Justin swallowed. He hated the pain he must cause her, hated the discomfort she would face at his entry, but he had no choice. "Forgive me, my sweet."

He flexed his hips and plunged into her. Sensations swarmed over him. Wet. Hot. Tight. Muscles gripping him. Sinking, sinking, sinking. He heard her swiftly indrawn breath, felt her stiffen under him, noted her nails scoring his back, but it was nothing to the overwhelming joy of joining his body to hers.

Forcing himself to do nothing, to overcome the urge to slam into her again and again, he rested, motionless, barely breathing. "Sarah. One moment, I beg of you. It will be better in a moment."

Her breath leaked out. "Justin?" Her voice sounded tiny in his ear.

"Is it very bad?"

She swallowed. "I am not sure. It is different."

Indeed it was. He'd never felt this pleasure before, never known how right it was. Sarah was his. "I must move a little, Sarah. Tell me if it pains you."

He eased himself out of her tight channel, then slowly re-entered. She stiffened, as if bracing for an onslaught. "Sarah?"

"It is not so bad."

"You are extremely brave, my heart. It will be better, I promise."

"Is this all there is to it, Justin?"

"Oh, no," he whispered, keeping his expression gentle and reassuring when the inner man wanted to howl his possession. "There is much more. Shall I show you?"

Her sweetly murmured assent was all he needed. Gently at first, he withdrew and re-entered her, again and again, gradually increasing his pace and the force of his thrusts.

She arched beneath him, making small little sounds in her throat that inflamed him and spurred him on. She was small and tight around him, hot and moist, her body opening and welcoming his. Justin threw his head back as her sensuality overtook him. His balls slammed against her sweetly curved buttocks with every stroke. "Aa-aah!"

"Justin! I can't…it is too much!"

"Bear with me! Any moment now!"

He pushed himself to the limit. Harder, faster, deeper, he thrust himself into her, filling her, filling him with heat, with passion, with ecstasy. Her muscles gripped him, making it hard to pull out, clasping him, greedily welcoming him in again.

He withdrew and pulled her legs up over his shoulders. Fully exposed to him, she lay beneath him, flushed, perspiring, pupils dilated, breasts pointing at him, her body working with his every movement as he dipped into her once more.

"Justin!" She stiffened, then came in orgiastic fulfillment. Her juices gushed as he pulled out of her, then plunged back in, buried to the hilt in wet.

He barely recognized his voice as he shouted his own release. Hot semen spurted into her, poured out of him, as he gave himself up to exquisite pleasure.

At last, sated, exhausted, he slumped to her side, still in her, still throbbing, still half-hard. She let her legs down, to rest atop his, anchoring him to her. Justin raised his head and pressed a kiss on her neck.

"You are glorious," he murmured. "I regret I had to hurt you to give you pleasure."

"A moment only," she demurred. "Did I give you enjoyment?"

Chapter Ten

"Any more and I should have expired on the spot."

Her lips twitched. "I am glad, then. I thought my ignorance would hinder the…ah, the proceedings."

"Ah, yes, the proceedings." He rolled up on his elbow to kiss her mouth, soft and lax now with satiety. She tasted of him, of fragrant woman. He kissed her deeply, drinking in the sweetness. "You need have no concern on that score."

Satisfaction curved her lips into a sensuous smile. "Yes, I though I did quite well for an amateur."

"Amateur?" he spluttered, then began to chuckle. "You may consider yourself an apprentice, then. I shall be the master craftsman showing you the art of love-making." He laughed, anticipation filling him with warmth. "I shall be a very patient teacher. Over a period of time, you shall perfect your skills."

The contentment left her face. "We do not have time."

"Why not?"

She turned her head away. "You know I must leave."

"I thought we had settled that." He waited and when she did not face him he tipped her chin toward him. Her eyes, still sated, still half-aroused, looked misty. A tiny tear lodged in one corner. "After what we have just shared, you must not hide anything from me."

He touched her teardrop with his finger tip, then brought it to his lips. "Can you not tell me?" he whispered.

She sighed in surrender. "If I stay, even one more minute than absolutely necessary, I give my sister's husband more reason to bring charges against me."

"Charges for what?"

She straightened her spine. "When I refused my brother-in-law's attentions, he threatened to put it about that I had accepted him. He warned me that unless I chose to allow him certain favors, he would make sure everyone knew I was an immoral woman."

"The devil he did!" Justin's wrath exploded. "I shall attend to him at once!"

"No! He'd take Emmy from me. He would charge me with immorality, with being an unfit mother to Emmy."

"What is to stop him from doing that at any rate?"

"I…I don't know," she admitted. "Since he let Robby die, I thought he would have no reason to persist in his attentions to me, but he did not. After my sister died giving birth to Emmy, he suggested I should stay in his house. He was very clear what he wanted."

Justin could well understand why the man had been unable to let Sarah be. The beauty of face and form combined with her purity of spirit was enough to drive any man to possess her. That she was too innocent to understand made him doubly aware of her allure.

His heart opened to her. "I shall take care that he never troubles you again. You shall be under my protection."

She shook her head. "That is not possible."

"Why?" He sat up and pulled her with him into an upright position, face to face.

She curled her legs under her. Her gaze flickered, then she looked steadily at him. "I did not refuse my brother-in-law only to accept another in his place."

Wounded, insulted beyond words, Justin could only stare at her. His breath rasped. "You liken me to that bastard?"

"Oh, Justin," she placed her hand against his cheek. "You must not be offended. What we have shared here is very precious to me, but I do not fool myself into thinking it more than it was."

"Which was?" The muscle in his jaw pulsed against her soft hand.

"A fantasy. A dream. A perfect moment between a man and a woman. It cannot be repeated."

"Why not?"

"I must think of Emmy."

He blinked. "What has Emmy to do with this?"

"Emmy must have every care. She must grow up properly."

"She shall have the best there is, I promise."

"You do not understand." She shook her head, making the honey tresses cascade over her bare shoulders.

One curl fell to her breast. Justin traced it with his finger, pleased when her nipple bloomed under his touch.

She shuddered, then pushed his hand away. "I cannot think when you do that."

He touched her again, circling the aureole with his fingertip. "Tell me why you worry about your niece."

"Justin." She held his hand in both her own. "I am a woman with a child not my own. I have responsibilities to Emmy. I must take great care of my reputation that it does not soil hers."

"She is only an infant, Sarah. How could you tarnish her name?"

"An infant now, a young woman of marriageable age soon enough. I would not have her chance at happiness marred by any mistake of mine."

He raised their clasped hands to kiss her fingers. "That is certainly an honorable aspiration, but how could you do anything to blemish Emmy's character?"

"You know the answer to that yourself, sir. I am an unmarried woman, with a lover."

"Yes." He said with a great deal of pride. "I am your lover." He narrowed his eyes at her. "You consider me a mistake?"

"No." She inclined her head. "But others might do so. I cannot allow —"

"Stay with me." The words were out of his mouth before he knew it, but once said, he didn't want to retract them. He didn't know how it had happened, but somehow in the last few hours, he had lost all suspicions of her. He saw her now, not as a devious female after his title, but as a woman who honored her promise to her sister. An honorable woman. A loving, passionate, unselfish woman. Now that she had entered his life, he didn't intend to allow her to leave. He'd do what he must to keep her. "Stay, Sarah."

"Oh, Justin, do you not see?" She expelled her breath in a long, sad exhalation. "If I remain with you, we will be subject to the worst sort of gossip. I can bear it for myself, but Emmy must have every chance."

"She will. I promise."

"And how do you intend to manage that?"

"You shall be my wife."

Her eyes widened. "You jest."

"No, Sarah, I do not." He didn't know where the certainty came from. Just yesterday, he'd been seeking sanctuary, escaping the importunate females who wished to make him into a husband, and here he'd given himself up. Like a dog, rolling over and offering his tummy to be rubbed. He would have smiled if it hadn't been so important. "I wish you to marry me."

"No."

His mouth opened. He clamped it shut. "You reject me?"

"Do not look so surprised, sir. Surely you cannot be serious, proposing marriage to a woman you barely know."

"I would hardly say that." He ran a hand down her naked back to cup her warm buttock in his hand. "I would venture to say we are very well acquainted by now."

She pushed his hand away. "That is not what I meant, and you must not tease me."

"I am perfectly serious, Sarah. We shall marry and care for Emmy ourselves. Think of the benefits," he coaxed. "You gain a husband and an uncle for Emmy all at once. I shall protect you both from your sister's husband. Emmy will grow up with every advantage."

"Truly?" Her eyes studied him. He lost himself in their cinnamon-spice depths. Uncertainty gave way to hope, then anticipation, as her face brightened, her cheeks turned pink. "You would do this for me? For Emmy?"

"Do not forget that I expect to derive some measure of satisfaction from this arrangement."

Her lips quivered then broke into a wide smile. "Oh, you tease me, Justin." She threw her arms around his neck. "You really do wish to marry me?"

Her breasts snuggled into his chest. Through the heat racing in his veins and pooling in his groin, he managed, "I do."

He expected that if he ever voiced those words, the heavens would open and rain down hail and brimstone, but he heard nothing but the sound of Sarah's soft breathing and the crackle of the fire. He felt only her sweet, moist breath and the warmth of her generous breasts on his torso.

"Oh, Justin. How fortunate that we stumbled upon your doorstep!" Her voice bubbled on. "We shall be so happy!"

Justin added his share to the dream. "And one day Emmy will make an advantageous marriage."

"What do you mean, 'advantageous'?" Sarah lifted her head to peer at him. "I will not have her marrying some Society ninny, if that is what you infer." Her voice brooked no opposition.

Justin sat back, curiously stung. "Why are you so opposed to Society? It has been my experience that most people are eager to be considered part of the *haute ton*."

"Rubbish. All that my lording and my ladying and your grace this and your grace the other. It is a wonder people do not trip over their tongues."

He laughed. "It seems you have a problem, my heart, for you shall certainly be addressed as 'my lady'."

She looked at him through narrowed eyes. "You have a most peculiar sense of humor, Justin."

"Perhaps. I have a confession to make —"

A loud rap at the door brought Justin's words to an abrupt halt. "Who is it?"

"Pruitt, my lord. I have the infant for Miss Wilder."

Justin drew the sheet up to cover Sarah's nakedness before he rose to unlock the door. Pruitt and a footman bearing a child's cot entered and stood open-mouthed at the sight of him.

Justin threw them both an irritated look. "Get on with it."

While the footman set up the cot as Sarah directed him, Pruitt brought Emmy to a blushing Sarah. She took the baby and pressed a tender kiss on her brow. "Hello, my precious. Did you have a nice nap?"

The valet kept his eyes discreetly averted. "Will that be all, my lord?"

"My lord?" Sarah repeated, her eyes shooting golden brown sparks at Justin.

"Out." He glared at the two men. "And keep your mouths shut."

The footman bowed and scuttled for the door. Pruitt looked affronted. "Sir. I am a gentleman's gentleman." He bowed himself out.

Sarah stared at him through narrowed eyes. "My lord?"

Justin lifted a shoulder. "I was about to tell you myself. I neglected the title when I introduced myself."

"And just which lord are you?" Sarah's mouth compressed into a thin line as she enfolded her arms about Emmy in a protective manner.

Justin gave her his most conciliatory smile. "Actually, I'm Howden. Fifth earl."

Sarah's eyes grew wide and round, then narrowed in disdain. "You are *that* earl? I have heard of you. You are a rake of the worst sort."

Justin lifted his palms. "Once we are married, you may reform me and make me the best of husbands."

Her eyes glittered. "Do not for one instant believe that I shall marry you."

"But you agreed —"

"That was before I learned your title. Oh, for shame, Howden, to hide such a thing. It changes everything."

He could not believe his ears. After shunning the marriage mart, avoiding the over-zealous candidates for his title, here he was, proposing to someone who wanted no part of him! His tone stiff and aggrieved, he muttered, "I do not see how it changes a thing."

She waved his statement away. "I do not wish to marry a nobleman. You are not ready for marriage. I have heard how assiduously you protect your bachelorhood. Furthermore, we know nothing about each other. I cannot believe you would wish to be leg-shackled to a female you have just met."

He grabbed her hand in his. "All that might have been true at one time. Now I have met you and I am ready to marry." He kissed her fingers and tucked them into her palm. "I already know a great deal about you. You are brave, trustworthy, honorable and utterly desirable. If I searched for years, I could not find another with your qualities."

"You still remain a peer," she accused.

"You wish me to renounce my title?"

Chapter Eleven

His alarmed tones still rang as she considered his offer.

"No. You cannot help being who you are."

He felt humbled. "Help me reform."

"A challenging task, but quite impossible."

He took Emmy from her arms and settled her in the cot. "I shall have to persuade you, then."

"By what means?" She tilted her head, watching him suspiciously.

"Fair or foul, my heart. Just as I have assiduously avoided parson's mouse-trap, now I shall set the cheese myself."

She bit her lip, but he saw the laughter in her eyes. Encouraged by that, he kissed her. When her mouth softened under his, he deepened the kiss.

He felt her melt against him as he devoted himself to pleasuring her again. Where once her body was unfamiliar, a treasure to explore, now he felt the joy of familiarity, of knowing where she was most sensitive and responsive. He knew now how to touch, how hard, how gentle, how often, here a light, flickering touch, there with more insistent pressure.

As he dedicated himself to her, he was caught up in a surge of passion so strong it all but blinded him. His heart roared, his breath came hot and harsh. Eagerly, he gave of himself, offering her everything he was or could ever aspire to be. She moaned and arched under him, proffering herself, giving him more satisfaction than he'd ever had before.

He rose over her, spreading her legs, wrapping them around his hips. He positioned his rod at her entrance, rubbing himself against her heated flesh, until he could endure it no longer and plunged into her.

Their lovemaking was fast, furious and frantic. He cried out as his orgasm overtook him, as his seed spurted into her, as he gave her his life. She cried out herself, her voice high and thin, as she reached her own pleasure. Her inner muscles gripped him tightly, milking him, holding on to him, until at last, she relaxed, her body going lax.

He collapsed onto her, his breath still coming in grating gulps. When Justin could at last think straight, he was appalled that he had taken her so roughly. "Did I hurt you?" he whispered, almost afraid to look at her face and see the ravages of his assault.

She squirmed under him. "M'mm." She stiffened. "Emmy! I cannot believe I forgot about her."

Justin rolled off her and went to check on the baby. "She sleeps. She does not care what we do."

"Are you sure?" Sarah asked as she sat up. She gasped.

He returned to her immediately. He bent by the bedside and took her into his arms. "I am sorry, my heart. I forgot that you were unused to this."

"I will be all right."

Justin winced. How brave, how generous she was! What a greedy bastard he was, to inflict himself on her like that. "I can soothe the pain. Will you let me?"

She spared him a wary glance.

"Please, Sarah."

When she nodded shyly, he rose, and pouring water from an ewer into a basin, he knelt by the fire until the water warmed. He procured a soft cloth from his dressing room and went back to the wide bed. She lay sprawled, sated and drowsy, yet he saw the way she flinched when he moved her leg to sit by her.

He wet the cloth and wrung it out. Carefully, he parted her legs and eased the damp cloth against her tender flesh. She tried to close her legs against him, but he persevered, murmuring reassurances until she relaxed and let him tend her.

Gently, he cleansed the swollen petals, washing away the blood stains and his semen. His eyes widened as he took in the import of his actions. He cursed himself at the evidence of his rough treatment of her. When he had bathed and soothed her, he lowered his mouth and kissed every sweet, fragrant inch of her in atonement.

She murmured, she stretched, she accepted.

At last, he cuddled her in his arms. "I am sorry to be so importunate with you, Sarah. Can you forgive me?"

She hugged him. "The pain is nothing, nothing compared to what you have taught me. I did not know it would be so beautiful."

"It will only get better with us. Though I must abstain from making love to you for a day or so, I would not care if we were snowbound forever."

She sighed. "It cannot be. You know I must leave, Justin. Or should I say 'my lord'?"

He winced at the bitterness in her voice. "I thought we had settled this."

"Our discussion was…postponed."

"So it was." He grinned at her. "I warned you I would employ whatever means necessary."

"You are a cad, sir." She smiled, taking the sting from her words.

"Have I banished your reticence about marrying me?"

"Not at all."

"It must be, Sarah," he insisted. "We have made love twice now. We are married beyond redemption. It needs only the formalities to make it proper."

Her face blanched. "Beyond redemption? You make it sound like purgatory."

"Never so, my love. We shall be the happiest of couples. We shall make our own paradise." He hesitated. "I forgot to sheathe myself this last time, Sarah. We might have already created my heir. We must marry."

She made a sound, half laugh, half sob. "But why you, Justin? You, the Earl of Howden, notorious member of Society? I did not want a man like you."

"You already have me."

She shook her head. Her hair, honey soft and fragrant, teased his bare flesh. His groin tightened. His yard pressed against her soft belly.

"I do not want to marry as a result of..." she gestured to the bed.

"I proposed before we made love this last time, my heart," he reminded her. "I cannot deny that our marriage is more imperative now that I have given you my seed, but, listen to me," he urged when she tried to break free. "What we shared together was more than I could ever expect to find, and yet, I would want you even if our lovemaking gave us a fraction of the pleasure."

"I...is that true?"

"Stay, Sarah. Be my countess. Be my love."

"You speak so easily of love, Justin." She lifted confused eyes to his.

He swam in them, saw himself as he could be with her, happy and fulfilled. From being the skeptic peer no one wanted for himself, so determined to avoid being leg-shackled he'd hidden himself in the country, here he was begging her to free him from of his cynical doubts. From being inflexible in his resolution not to marry, he was now casting all reservations aside and flinging himself at Sarah.

Sarah, who didn't want him.

What a comeuppance for an arrogant, cynical bastard like himself. She humbled him by her bravery, her honor, her willingness to set aside her own future for Emmy's sake. What had he done to compare with her generosity?

"It is the hardest thing I have ever done, but it is also easy." He brushed a tendril of silken hair away from her temple and placed a kiss in its stead. "It comes from my heart. Sarah, if you will allow me, I will be a good husband to you. You and Emmy shall have the moon, I swear it."

"Hush, Justin. Do not make impossible promises."

"Sarah. Sarah. Take pity on me. Bring your warmth and bright spirit into my life. Make me see through your eyes. Help me, Sarah."

She shuddered in his arms. "You are a devil, Justin Stowe, to tempt me like this. How wicked you are."

"Change me," he suggested. "Make me into a good husband, a father."

"You would be a father to Emmy?"

Justin thought of the means by which he would make sure Emmy stayed with Sarah and with him. That nameless soldier would be lucky if he still had a regiment when he was through with him.

"Justin?"

He looked down into her worried face. "I shall be a very good father to Emmy, and to our own children." He paused, thinking of a number of honey-haired daughters with Sarah's cinnamon-spice eyes. They had best have brothers to protect them. Strong, arrogant pups like their sire. He grinned. "I can hardly wait."

She inhaled, then expelled a lingering sigh. "Perhaps I shall marry you in the spring."

He thought of flowers, of fresh green grass, of Sarah warm and fragrant and swallowed hard. "Spring is too far away. Next week, by special license."

"Next week?" she echoed. "I cannot — it is too soon."

"At the rate I intend to ensure that I am a father in my own right before the year is out, it will be too late."

"Ensure?" She laughed, a bubbling, frothing, frolic of a laugh that warmed his groin and made his already rigid cock strain to find its home. In a move that delighted him, she ran her hand down his chest and cupped his rod. "You are very determined. Must you always have your own way?"

"Always, Sarah." He pushed against her palm, all but moaning when she circled and stroked. "When it comes to satisfying you, I shall always have my way."

She lifted the covers to glance down at him. "I see." Her approbation made his blood boil. He pulsed in her hand as a tiny drop appeared at the tip of his member.

"I had never thought of myself as a countess, Justin. I do not know how to go about as a member of Society."

His knees trembled at her acceptance of her new role. "You need not concern yourself. The *ton* shall learn from you. All London shall envy me."

Sarah licked her lips and closed her hand around him. He gritted his teeth against the pleasure that threatened to overtake him from both the physical sensations and the knowledge that Sarah trusted her sensual feelings enough to explore.

She squeezed him lightly. "Could we not live a quiet life in the country and forget town?"

A thought occurred to him. "Perhaps later. I wish to present you to Society." He began to laugh. "I want to see the faces on all those matchmaking mamas who have been shoving their daughters my way. All their machinations for naught!"

"For shame, Justin." Sarah tried to frown, but her lips quivered and her enchanting laugh pealed over them. "You *are* a devil."

"But you love me anyway," he suggested.

"I must," she agreed. "Why else would I accept you?"

He hugged her, content at last. He would give her anything she wanted. "After our first visit to town, we shall stay to ourselves as long as you wish, my love. As for now, so long as we remain snowbound, we have nothing to do but care for Emmy and make love."

She fit herself against him, nipples peaking. "Then you must pray for snow, Justin."

About the author:

Born in Ecuador and raised in Chile, Bonnie Hamre was educated there and in the United States. She has also lived in Italy, England and Scotland, where she gained an appreciation for her Scots heritage. She now makes her home among the coastal redwoods south of San Francisco. Published also in book-length women's fiction, Bonnie finds there is nothing as satisfying as an emotionally gripping tale of two people making a commitment to each other. She writes with sensitivity, with passion and with the touch of humor that makes sensuality fun.

Savage Garden

❦

by Susan Paul

To my reader:

Savage Garden is a sizzling historical romance woven around one man, one woman, and a passion for revenge.

In the savage gardens of Mexico you'll meet beautiful Lady Raine LeFleur and ruggedly handsome revolutionary Miguel Chavez. In the middle of a war with France, the last thing Miguel Chavez needs is to be irresistibly drawn to the daughter of a French major! Nevertheless, braving impetuous desire, forbidden love and a revolution, Miguel and Raine at last unite in their fight to save the only thing that matters to them … their undying love.

I hope you enjoy Raine LeFleur and Miguel Chavez's adventures!

Chapter One

Sinforosa Canyon, Mexico
July 1865

The mountains to the west of the French army stronghold turned purple as the sun slipped down behind their massive shoulders. An owl hooted from the gnarled branch of a tree; crickets chirped. A warm breeze shivered softly through the white lace curtains of the glassless-window, promising little relief from the intense heat of the night.

In her room, Lady Raine LeFleur inhaled the sweet scent of the desert in bloom. The fragrant flowers of the feathery-leafed mesquite enveloped her senses. As her gaze scanned the savage garden beyond the fort, her hands shook and the delicate tea cup rattled on its china saucer. She steeled herself as she lifted the cup to her lips and swallowed the last of the tea-like concoction. The housekeeper had promised that the ancient remedy would bring on a blissful night's rest. She would believe it when it happened.

Raine made an abrupt turn and plunked the empty cup and saucer on the vanity. Her bare footsteps moved across the room making quick, angry strides. In only fourteen days, she would say good-bye to her father and return to France. The thought of her wedding set her teeth on edge.

Lately, she suffered from insomnia and seldom slept more than a few hours a night. Worried over her uncertain future, she shifted her gaze to the bed that brought her no rest. Discarding her silk robe, she stretched. The warm air was a pleasant and balmy caress on her naked skin. With a small smile on her lips, she headed for the bed.

When Raine caught sight of her fiancé's photograph on the bedside table, her eyes narrowed. *He* was the reason for her sleepless nights. Though she knew young women married men they didn't know every day, distress filled her being at the thought. Was it so unreasonable to want love to come before the marriage?

Apparently.

With a groan, she reached and flipped the ornate sterling silver frame face down with a thump. Arranged marriage or not—duty or not—she didn't want to marry this man. She hadn't seen him in three years. How could she love him?

The air felt thick and heavy as Raine put out the lamp. She stifled a yawn as the housekeeper's ancient remedy began to work its magic. She crawled into bed and slipped between the crisp white linen sheets. Her body settled into the softness of the feather mattress. Under the cover she laid defiantly nude. In Mexico's oppressive climate it was more comfortable, although she knew even to think of such an act was considered sinful. Her father and most of his troops were out on patrol. She was alone in the house. With a rebellious little smile, she flung the top sheet aside and fell into a deep sleep.

Half the night was gone when the dream began.

He was there, mysterious and magnetic, just as he looked twice before on her daily rides. Mounted on a dark stallion far in the distance, the golden rays of the setting sun silhouetted him on top of a ridge. The vision so vivid, her breath caught in her throat. His skin was a dark bronze. She couldn't see his face clearly beneath the wide brim of the hat. Still, she thought him handsome. With his regal posture... how could he be anything but?

From atop her horse she gazed at him, desire fueling her thoughts. His powerful presence seemed to engulf her; his rough masculinity aroused her mind and senses. The knowledge that this man was a revolutionary and, with the rest of Juarez's people, deep in battle with her countrymen to reclaim Mexico, heightened the danger. A jolt of sharp need, a fierce urge surged between her legs. She wanted to be filled by this stranger, feel the presence of his rigid sex; needed to hold and keep his manhood in her soft-walled tunnel.

Deep in the throes of her dream, the revolutionary returned her wanton look. Her mouth opened halfway in unconscious invitation. His soul reached out and spoke to her without saying a word. Come to me, it said—come to me fully and completely.

This man so tempted Raine that her heart hammered. The bursting bud, no longer sheltered by its hood, throbbed. When he spurred his horse forward, the fear of him and the unknown excited her. So much, she had no desire to turn and flee, but waited, seemingly fused to her gelding's back.

Was it because any type of intimate relationship, much less one with a Mexican revolutionary, an enemy, was forbidden—that made it so tempting?

Then, too fast, horse and rider appeared at her side. The dark territory of the revolutionary's eyes was intense beneath the wide rim of his hat. His face was chiseled, stark, masculine. He looked wild and undisciplined, in total contrast to the way she had been raised, so fascinating that her breath caught in her throat and a heady warmth invaded the deeper regions of her womb.

He pinned her with his seductive gaze and dismounted in a rush. Flashing an arrogant smile, he lifted his large, sun-browned hands and placed them around her waist to lift her from the sidesaddle. Helpless against the sensuous spell his black-gaze cast upon her, she leaned forward and allowed her body to slide down the long, hard length of his. Her thighs trembled as he pulled her closer still. She gasped when he placed his powerful hands on her breasts. They swelled; the sensitive nipples hardened as they begged for rough contact with his broad chest.

Breathless and weak with desire, she let him ease her down to the desert floor and pin her against the dusty earth with his body. She didn't attempt to escape as he undid the delicate pearl buttons of her blouse; or when he shoved her batiste camisole down to free her breasts into his callused hands, which was merely a prelude to his tongue's wicked ministrations. Overwhelmed by the foreign sensations that coursed through her untutored body, as he tossed up her skirts and wedged his knees between her thighs. They parted without protest.

He tore open his pants and she saw him. Tall and thick, his organ stood engorged and stiff. The veins pulsed and snapped with every beat of his heart. The lair of hair, black as night at its root, curled tight and was coarsely elegant; the dark pink ridged head shiny and swollen with raw need...

Raine's breath caught. Her vagina pulsed and sent a shock of moisture between her legs. Under his arrogant scrutiny her heavy breasts ached, the nipples tightened until they hurt, and her sex throbbed. Her heart raced; her stomach tied in knots. She swallowed, opened her mouth to speak, but shut it again not knowing what to say.

Then he was on his knees before her. His thick erection stood taut and proud, and she wanted him with an inexplicable desire. Unable to help herself, her tongue snaked out and lightly traced the smooth inner skin of her parted lips in breathless anticipation of the hot, distended head of his shaft invading her hungry depths. He stared at her for a very long time. His eyes looked as deep and dark as the sea.

He gave her a wicked smile and brought her hand to his erection. She gasped; her gaze flew to his. His hard member pulsated beneath her palm. She whimpered and moaned, attempted to pull away as if the shaft burned her. The look in his eyes said, no. Hold me. Hard.

She shook her head. The reaction automatic, had nothing to do with what she really wanted. He refused to surrender her hand and wrapped her fingers firmly around its solid girth, moved her hand down the warm length of him. At once his size surged, and the broad head expelled a single drop of clear fluid from its neat slit.

Lust flared through her body at the sight. Her empty vagina contracted with desire for him; her gaze inched its way down his full erection that strained to be inside her already drenched vulva. She wanted his domination in a desperate way. Without shame, she welcomed the hard evidence of his arousal with a broken cry that tore from her throat.

At that point, Raine threw her head back and her arms above her head as a river of desire ran through her body. To her, the visions that played in her slumbering mind seemed so real, so wonderful, so powerful—and oh so *erotic*—she never wanted to awaken. And though she knew, if she had been in a conscious state when this strong, handsome warrior took her with force, ravished her against her will, it would frighten her.

Yet, in this dream, the possibility fascinated and aroused her, allowed her to enjoy her long-dormant sensuality. She was free to imagine the feel of a hard-bodied, mysterious lover thrusting his rigid tool straight into her, without caution or preliminaries. The passionate stirring of her blood made her private parts throb so hotly, she expelled a tortured moan and dug her nails into the mattress.

The cry struck Miguel Chavez just as his men were about to cut and run.
He couldn't risk endangering the mission, it was too important to the
revolution. He sent the men ahead without him, then turned and moved toward
the sound. Just outside the commanding officer's quarters, he stopped short.
He saw her through the open window.

Miguel knew to go inside would mean disaster, but ignored the last hopeless
complaints of his common sense and reached for the window's sill. In one fluid
motion, he hoisted himself and swung his leg over the single barrier that
separated him from his revenge. The French major's daughter.

Silver moonlight streamed into the room. Though dark, the moon cast
enough light for him to see the woman he intended to rape. He arched a brow,
surprised to find she wore nothing to bed.

Miguel drew in the night air. He paused and listened for the deep even
breaths that signaled sleep. Raine LeFleur's beauty was undeniable with her
naked body laid out like a veritable buffet before him. He wanted her, and not
only because of his need for revenge against the man who was responsible for
the death of his family.

The air was sticky, and wet heat seemed to rise all over his skin. He studied
Raine's feminine undulations with the dedication of an experienced lover. He
could make out the small mouth, sensually sculpted, parted in sleep, and he had
the desire to kiss her. For her to kiss *him*. He could already taste her lips, damp
and salty…

With his need for vengeance enhanced, the task took on a whole new
meaning. He had the sudden urge to stay with her, in this room, for an endless
time. Heedless of circumstance, his body responded to headlong lust. Now, in
no great hurry, he slipped his body the rest of the way into the room. When his
booted feet touched the floor, he crossed the distance between them in three
swift strides on catfeet.

Miguel stopped next to the bed and removed his boots as he gazed down
the length of the slim, yet well-shaped body. He licked his parched lips. Having
seen her before, knowing who her father was, her uncommon beauty should not
have affected him. But it did. Raine LeFleur was even more beautiful than he
remembered.

He concentrated on her hair, the way the long, jet-black waves flowed in a
haphazard fashion across the pillow; how small tendrils lay moistly around the
edges of her heart-shaped face. A face with a flawless complexion, cameo white
in the moonlight, that must captivate men all over the world. He wondered how
something, so beautiful, could have a cold-hearted murderer for a father. He
wondered if she knew the truth.

Miguel let out a breath. He pressed his hand against her breast, moved to
fondle the nipple. She did not awaken. Instead, she made intoxicating small
sounds of pleasure that beckoned him as surely as a voice. Her nipples, the
flushed tips hardened with frank enjoyment of his touch.

In her slumber, Raine raised her hips off the mattress and murmured, in a
heated, suffocated sound, *"Please."*

A small shudder traveled down Miguel's spine, followed by the corresponding hardening of his sex. He gave a low groan with the torment of it. As he continued to focus on her plump breasts, he placed his snakelike whip around the bedpost above her head. He spread his thighs apart and pressed the heel of his hand down the growing length of his erection.

Miguel became wild with the need for her to caress his sturdy shaft, sensing that only *she* could bring him what he craved. His breathing quickened. He watched a long-fingered hand stray down her slender hip and slip over the bare thigh toward the very source of her need.

Soon, she groaned and parted her legs, wide. His gaze froze. She reached down to touch the dainty vee of tight curls, and with her other hand spread her labia apart with two fingers. It was as if she meant to drive him into a frenzy.

A hunger that demanded he penetrate her consumed him. He wanted to take her with the full length of his flesh, with no thought of her pleasure. Even so, he held his fierce lust in check. No, he thought, giving her pink lips, moist and flushed with readiness, an intent perusal. His revenge against her father would not be complete if he raped her. She had to want him to take her virginity, better yet, beg him. And she would, right under the noses of Major Armand LeFleur's soldiers. He would make certain of it.

Miguel opened his he pants and put his hand to the full evidence of his arousal. In one strong tug, he freed himself from all constraints. "Soon, my sweet," he murmured and he stripped the shirt from his back.

A lock of his long, undisciplined hair brushed across Raine's smooth brow as he bent his head lower, and brushed his lips across hers as if it were his right. "You like that, do you not?"

She smiled. "Mmm."

He licked her stomach. She moaned in a way that told him surfacing from her deep sleep was secondary to the carnal pleasure she was experiencing from his tongue. With the faintest pressure, his fingers slid over her swollen vulva and the French beauty quivered. She sighed a delicious small sound, and he smiled, gratified.

At some point he knew that he might have to restrain her. He bent to take a sweet nipple with languid strokes as his hand went straight for the bandanna around his neck, and placed it on the pillow next to her exquisite head. She whimpered when he released her nipple to shift his body above her.

Miguel kissed her neck, tasting the rich perfume of her scent, and she sighed. He pressed his stiff sex against her. The pressure on the pulsating tissue of her vagina drew a low groan of pleasure from deep in her throat. He waited, then his palm drifted down the soft curve of her breast. His mouth trailed a path of kisses down her jaw. He removed his pants and took his erection in his hand. Parting her with the swollen tip, he stroked his hardness over her wet flesh in a delicate message. She groaned and lifted her hips, pressed herself hard against his stroking member, as if her craving for him was uncontrollable.

Somewhere between wakefulness and sleep, Raine knew that his sturdy shaft entered her opening. She met it with relief, but he slipped it in only an inch or so, then rested. He moved again and she gave a desperate groan when he withdrew, aware of the emptiness. Her mouth opened to show her hunger, her body's willingness to take him, and he entered it.

It was then that Raine opened her eyes in an unconscious effort to see her lover. Uttering a faint cry, she realized…this was no fantasy! Her gaze flew wide and her breath caught in her throat. In an instant she was fully awake—pinned and spread beneath the very man who had been driving her to distraction in her dream.

Miguel stopped, his mouth half parted, only a breath away from hers. He pressed the pad of his index finger to his lips. "Shhh, shhh," he whispered.

At that moment Raine couldn't have spoken if she'd tried, because it took all of her efforts just to breathe. It seemed she couldn't do anything but stare into her revolutionary's seductive eyes. No. This was not happening; it was just another part of her elaborate fantasy. She blinked, twice, thinking he would disappear.

He didn't.

Stunned, it took Raine a moment to find her voice. "Y-you are not here."

His grin was wicked and enchanting, just as in the dream. With the raise of a black eyebrow, he ran the tips of his callused fingers across a distended nipple. Again, it hardened with pleasurable pain.

"Oh…but I am," he assured her, his voice hoarse with restraint, "and it pleases me to know that *I* am the one who has you *so hot* and withering in your bed."

Raine opened her mouth to scream, but she couldn't utter a sound.

Without hesitation, he took the bandanna from the pillow next to her head and brushed it across her mouth. He sighed. "You are a very beautiful woman. I would hate to cover even an inch of your tender skin…" He paused to trail a wet tongue in a slow gliding process across her lips. "Still, if you make too much noise I will have to quiet you. So you will accommodate me and remain silent, no?"

Raine's heart lurched. He spoke in English, but she understood him. She nodded in haste. Her eyes widened. She was confused and afraid, though some part of her thought there was something wicked and titillating about having the choice taken out of her hands.

"*Bueno.*" As he smoothed the hair away from her face, he gave her a smile that showed his straight white teeth. He cupped her chin, and said, "I will not hurt you, señorita. I am only going to give you what you need."

Raine shivered at the look in his smoky eyes. She should beg him not to do, but then he pressed his hand into the crease of her fluid sex. When his finger massaged her organ—nothing mattered but the sensations that bewitched her senses. Soon, she was ready to accept from him whatever else he was willing give.

By his expression she could tell he was beyond ready. Still, she gasped in loud surprise as he pressed his forefinger inside her body until he met with a slight resistance. He paused and smiled, as if he'd already expected to encounter the evidence of her virginity. Instinctively, her thick flesh cushioning his finger tightened and he moved it out a little, and in again. She groaned and began to move her hips, increasing the contact.

He leaned forward and kissed her softly on the lips. "You want these pleasures; do you not? And to discover further delights?" Raine nodded. He flicked his tongue across one taut nipple and a powerful shudder passed through her into him. "No, my lovely señorita, you must tell me."

"Mon Dieu! Oui!"

At once he gathered her breast in his hands and thrust it into his mouth. He sucked wildly, intent on easing the physical hurt of her first time by giving her other more pleasurable sensations. He adjusted the position of her body with the deftness of much experience, and moved into her warmth. She sucked in a breath. His gaze came up and met her blue one. "It will only hurt for a moment."

Raine nodded. Some locks of his long hair caressed her cheek as the solid strength of his honed body remained poised above hers for the moment. A sensual heat spread through her entire body. She wrapped her legs around his hips and gave him a groan of pleasurable want. Her fingers kneaded his thick muscled shoulders; he moved, kissed her eyelids and then her mouth. He eased his hardness deeper into her body, and she was flooded with a rush of divine pleasures so strong she thought she would surely die.

With his arousal hard against her maidenhood he thrust forward quickly, accurately. When his full sex tore through her barrier, she threw her arms around him and swallowed her small cry of pain as his hardness filled her. A tidal wave of passion engulfed her being immediately after, and when he withdrew a long moment later, she whimpered with the loss. In response, he slid his hands beneath her bottom and cupped it in his hands. He squeezed her cheeks and slid back into her hungry depths with infinite slowness and moved in and out, insinuating his enormous length into her tightness with unhurried strokes.

Enslaved by the delicious sensation of ravishment that heated her body, Raine yielded herself completely to this man. He was potent, more viral than in her dream. A flaming heat ignited deep inside her and she kissed him, shameless in her need.

"Please...more," she begged, her nails digging deeper into his back, her body so sensitive and flame-hot she could no longer distinguish pleasure from pain.

He held her firmly in place so she could not move, and forced himself into the throbbing center of her body. She clung to his shoulders, locked her legs around his hips. He drove deeper and deeper, as if he wanted to put his mark on her. With each hard thrusting stroke he pushed her further over the edge.

Raine began to peak when the hungry suction of his mouth drew on her breast. Then he pulled hard and pushed into her with all the strength of his powerful body. The muscles of her inner thighs trembled and the deep throb of orgasm splintered as it claimed her.

She met every one of his lunges with force. Her body gripped his as spasm after spasm racked her, and his grip tightened as the inevitable shudders coursed through his body.

In the dim gray light of dawn Miguel held Raine until her trembling subsided, lax and spent, and flew from release to a deep slumber.

Raine awoke several hours later, when the bright yellow sunlight played without mercy on her closed lids. She stretched and yawned. There was an unaccustomed ache between her thighs and the odd feeling that the world around her had somehow changed forever.

And then she remembered.

Oh God! She pressed a knuckle to her mouth. In half-panic, she jackknifed to a sitting position and snatched the sheet up to cover herself. Her gaze flew to the brilliant day beyond her open window.

Perhaps she didn't remember anything at all. It was a blur…her thoughts jumbled, as erratic as her heartbeat, heated memories of her dream lover coming to life, and taking her to the edge of ecstasy and beyond…

"It *was* a dream," she said aloud.

Raine forced herself to remain calm, to breathe in through her nose and out through her mouth. She had heard older and more experienced women speak about their erotic dreams, of young virile men experiencing orgasms while they slept. It only made sense that women could have them too.

Yes, what she remembered was no more than a seductive dream — an apparition — not something beyond all propriety and reason. After all, where was her nameless lover now? If a man had truly taken her virginity, he would still be there. Wouldn't he?

She'd experienced a night-loving, brought on by an unnatural sleep and her obsession with this mysterious and elusive revolutionary. It was only natural. She'd fantasized about the man ever since the first time she saw him far in the distance. Raine jumped out of bed and slipped on her robe. She walked straight over to the full length mirror and stared at her reflection. "No, dreams cannot become reality," she said aloud to her other self.

Suddenly, she felt a sticky wetness seep out from between her legs and onto her inner thigh. As she gazed down and saw the vermillion evidence of her lost virginity so undeniable, she almost fainted.

Chapter Two

At mid-afternoon, the only things moving inside the cramped stagecoach were the flies. Raine LeFleur never realized how bleak life could be, especially when you were on the way to your wedding.

The taste of dust rode on heated air, and she scowled at the desolate landscape as it rolled by the window. Her mind churned, tossing up the problems that plagued her. She was angry with everything, but in particular with her father. Just because he returned to the fort to find a few crates of rifles gone, that was no reason to make her leave for Paris on the next stage.

If only her father knew the whole story.

Her fiancé expected a virgin on their wedding night, and she wasn't one. *Anymore.* When he found out, she was certain he would toss her out on her noble ear. Of course, she didn't give a hoot about an annulment. She didn't want to marry him in the first place. However, she did care that all of Paris would know the reason.

Now, what was she going to do?

She drummed her nails across the leather seat. Well, her phantom lover could always appear on his dark stallion, brandishing his sword as if he were Prince Charming, and whisk her away to Paradise...

Raine groaned and folded her arms across her chest. All right, so that wasn't going to happen.

Outside, the hot sun beat down, while inside the air smelled stale and rancid. She had enough dust in her lungs to stuff a mattress. The fat man across from her, sitting next to his wife, snored like a freight train. If he didn't shut his mouth soon, she was going to stuff her lace hanky in it!

Weary from the arduous trip, she slumped against the hard seat and covered her nose with her hanky. She narrowed her eyes and scrunched up her face. That fat man had exactly one more minute to stop snoring!

Raine took a breath that should have calmed her. She looked over at her escort and found him swabbing his sunburned neck with a wrinkled white handkerchief. Afraid an armed patrol would draw unwanted attention her father had assigned only Philippe, his personal attaché, to escort her. Philippe's orders were simple. He was to put her aboard the ship to France and remain at the dock until the ship sailed.

The sound of gunshots in the distance jolted Raine back to the present. The stagecoach bounced and lurched, tossing the passengers around in their seats. Philippe's face turned red and he gasped for breath. Raine sighed inwardly. Some escort.

She heard the stage driver slap his reins and yell, "Getup!" When the horses surged forward, the force of it threw Raine into Philippe. She could see the tight strain of Philippe's jaw. She supposed he had good reason to be afraid. After all, her father would hold him responsible for her safety, and there was rapid gunfire exploding outside the coach.

The other woman was screaming herself hoarse, and, although her fat husband tried to calm her, she wouldn't stop. He had definitely stopped snoring though. She smoothed the front of her gown, she sat up, and leaned across Philippe to peer out of the window. Raine recoiled in horror at the sight of a man on horseback, riding so close to the coach. Averting her gaze, she tried to block out the thunder of hooves.

Being held up was a common occurrence in this war-torn country, but never in her wildest dreams had she imagined it would happen to her. She'd heard stories about what they did to women—.

Nothing to fear, she reminded herself, these bandits only wanted money. But if they wanted anything else, or tried to harm any of them, she would fight with everything she had at her disposal.

The stagecoach hit a pot hole and left the ground. The woman across from Raine screamed louder. When they came back to earth, Raine scrambled to her seat. Sliding her hand into the secret pocket sewn into the folds of her skirt, she touched the welcoming cold steel of the small bejeweled dagger. She curled her fingers around its handle.

With her other hand, she clutched her reticule closer to her, so that if she needed to, she could reach the derringer her father had insisted she carry. The gun made her feel safe. Though she would have preferred to have the six-shooter, a soldier at the fort had taught her to use on the sly. She could also use a rifle quite well, but since she had neither at her disposal, the derringer would have to do.

Finally the sound of gunshots slowed, but so did the stagecoach. Raine's escort turned to face her, and she saw that he was sweating profusely. Philippe would really have to calm down. They couldn't afford to let the bandoleros know they feared them. She hissed through her teeth in frustration and poked the Frenchman in his arm to get his attention.

"Look at you," she cried in French. "For the love of God, wipe your brow and at least try to act like you are in control."

Bug-eyed and breathless, Philippe managed to pull a handkerchief from his suit pocket. He attempted to dab his brow before stammering, "I am sorry, mademoiselle, but I am sure we are being held-up by bandits!"

Raine rolled her eyes. She was so exasperated with the man, she thought she would swear, but ladies never swore — not aloud, anyway — unless…they had a damn good reason.

"Oh, for heaven's sake, of course we are being held-up. Any fool would know that! Does that mean you have to act like a buffoon? Pull yourself together, monsieur."

Raine sighed. She liked the young man well enough, but she might as well have made the trip alone for all the good he was. When she got to

France, she would write her father and inform him of the poor choice he'd made for an escort.

To the south, three men rode their Spanish mustangs out of Sinforosa Canyon. A slight breeze played, but it brought no relief from the sweltering heat. Miguel Chavez's sun-darkened face and forearms glistened with a sweat in the late afternoon sun.

Miguel pulled back on his reins and knocked the dust from his hat. "Mother of God, this heat is going to kill me," he said in Spanish. He lifted his arm to wipe the sweat from his face, then with a practiced hand set the hat back on his head.

The oldest revolutionary shoved his hand through a head full of dark hair that curled like watch springs. "We have just delivered two dozen crates of stolen rifles to a group of revolutionaries — of questionable character," he said, "and you are worried about the heat killing you?"

Miguel almost laughed at the absurdity of it, but suddenly the earth rumbled beneath them, followed by a series of rapid gunfire. Out of the dust appeared a stagecoach surrounded by a group of bandoleros. Surging ahead of the coach, two bandoleros grabbed the horses' reins and forced the stagecoach to come to a blinding halt.

Automatically, Miguel checked the load of his Winchester and felt for the black whip around his saddle horn. He heard the high-pitched screams of women. His first instinct was to ride to their aid. Even at this distance, he could see the driver was dead, or would be soon. The women on board were at the bandoleros' mercy, and with those Mexicans, there would be none.

As much as he wanted to help, Miguel felt his sense of duty out-weighing his sense of instinct. More revolutionaries were waiting for rifles. He and his men needed to get back to Copper Canyon. They didn't need any more delays. If they failed to make the next gun run on time, many more lives could be at risk than the few on that stage.

"Time to take cover, *mis amigos*," he said. Miguel jerked sharply on the reins, turned his horse around, and spurred him into a gallop.

His men had already pulled the revolvers they kept strapped to their hips, and without hesitation they slapped their reins. As if by magic, horses and riders seemed to vanish in the smoky dust. Damn blood-sucking thieves! Miguel kept a close eye on the bandoleros.

The stagecoach rocked on its wheels, the woman across from Raine screamed *again*. Outside, a bandit fired three times in the air to get the passengers' attention.

As if they didn't already have it.

The stage door was jerked open and a bandit aimed his gun inside. He smiled, showing yellow teeth. A dirty serape covered his shoulders and a battered sombrero hung over his back. It occurred to Raine that this Mexican would not be seriously injured if he were held under a water pump for half an hour.

"*Su dinero, por favor*," he said to everyone as he waved his pistol. Then he reached over the woman across from Raine and snatched her husband's watch.

The wife gasped and nearly had an attack of the vapors.

Two seconds later, the bandit grabbed the arm of the fat man and pulled him out of the coach. The wife screamed, as usual, and he tugged on her arm until she too tumbled out. They disappeared.

"Your money, or your life," the bandit snapped in English, his gaze sweeping Raine and her escort.

Philippe looked like a rifle had just fired three inches from his ear.

Raine grimaced, but she got an idea. Although she knew the other bandits were still around, by stroke of luck, one door was now open and unguarded. Her lips turned up the slightest bit.

"*Ahora!*" the bandit yelled.

Raine stiffened. So, he was becoming impatient. Now, indeed! Very well, she'd give him what was in her purse, if he insisted. With a thin smile, she opened her reticule and reached inside. Her derringer might only have one shot, but it would do well enough at close range. The revolver was in her hand when she heard Philippe's deep sigh, but obviously he anticipated something other than what she meant to do.

Her fingers tightened around the derringer. While they still concealed her hand within the purse, she eased back the hammer with her thumb. Finally, she raised her eyes to those of the bandit and gave him her most endearing smile. One that any man would have thought was special, only for him.

"I am sorry to have kept you waiting," Raine apologized in Spanish, which appeared to have pleased the bandit, if his relaxed posture was any indication.

Raine quickly withdrew her hand and pointed the derringer at his chest. "Baja la pistola!"

She was quite pleased with herself when she saw the bandit's eyes widened in disbelief. However, her optimism dropped considerably when his initial shock wore off and instead of dropping the gun as she'd ordered, he threw back his head and laughed.

"*Mon Dieu, mademoiselle. Non!*" Philippe broke in. So much for hiding their nationality. At least one person took her seriously, although the wrong one.

"*Oui,*" she replied, not taking her eyes or the gun off the dark-skinned man in front of her.

Philippe fainted.

The bandit gave her an unpleasant grin, which she was sure was because he knew now that she was French. With an icy tone and in rapid Spanish he yelled at her. Raine understood about half of what he said, but that was enough. He meant to rape her — or beat her — or both, and he wanted her to put down the gun. Was he insane? Not on her life! Her back straightened as she spoke. "No!"

Her matter-of-fact tone threw the bandit into rage. Raine forced herself to smile and then moved the gun a little from side to side, showing she was serious.

"Put the gun down!"

Instead of doing as she had said, the bandit stayed right where he was.

Well, come ahead Raine thought, and we will see who gets hurt.

"You are crazy," he said, reaching for her gun.

That was what he thought, the devil's spawn! Raine squeezed the trigger and the derringer exploded.

All too aware that she had no time to reload her pistol for a second shot, Raine wasn't going to wait to see if she'd killed the bandit. When he clutched his chest and staggered backward, she did not need any more encouragement. She lifted her skirts and bolted through the open door of the stage.

She hit the ground running as hard as she could. Having been raised an only child of privilege, she wasn't exactly what one would describe as a good runner, especially on unfamiliar turf. She had gone about twenty-feet when she tripped and hit the hard, dusty ground with a loud *oomph*. "Oh, no!" She let out a muffled scream of frustration just as a series of rapid shots came too close.

Her mouth was as dry as the dust on which she lay, when she raised her aching head off a rock. After tossing her hair away from her face, she saw an ugly lizard with beady eyes staring her right in the face. More scared of her than she was of him, it darted away before she could scream. With a shiver, she crossed herself.

The rocky ground had torn her skirts and the skin off her palms, which were bleeding. Her entire body hurt like the devil. She'd have to worry about her aches and pains later; she knew she had to get out of there fast.

She was terrified of moving, but what else could she do? Being caught by these bandits was not a thought she wanted to entertain. Especially now, since she had just put a bullet in one of them. She refused to give in to her rising fear. If she didn't get moving while she still had a head start, she knew she would leave this savage country alive. She could only hope a moving target would be harder to hit.

She wished she had thought of all this *before* she decided to pull her derringer and jump from a stage in the middle of God-knew-where. Now she wasn't at all sure it was the wisest thing to do. Thankfully, her knife was still in the pocket of her skirt, and if her luck held, the bandits might not come after her until they'd seen about their friend.

Scanning the area, she saw a group of large boulders not far ahead. Some distance beyond that stood a small copse of trees. Maybe she could make it that far. At least, it was a possibility. Of course, the bandits could shoot her before she took another step.

She allowed herself to hope.

Chapter Three

Shielded by yucca and mesquite, Miguel gripped the rifle across his saddle with an iron grip. At first sight of the woman's face, he stiffened and swore under his breath.

"No." For the smallest moment he hesitated, not able to believe the woman who had jumped from the stage in a flurry of skirts was *Raine LeFleur*. He knew it was. He also knew that he should let those stinking bandits kill her; let her die as his mother and sister had died, fighting rape, while his father was forced to watch until the French had cut his throat.

He closed his eyes, but he couldn't stop the memories of Raine that surfaced in his mind. His sex swelled even now, and pushed against the confinement of his pants. For a moment, the desert faded and he was there again, climbing through the window of the fort, his hungry gaze fixed as her pale fingertips brushed against the tangle of dark curls that surrounded her sex and then concentrate on the one burning spot between her legs. Next time his tongue would exert that pressure over the spot of heat in her groin — darting back and forth across her erect bud.

Miguel wanted her. Not for revenge against her father and the soldiers that had come to the *hacienda* and massacred his family — taken what had been Chavez land for a hundred years. No. He just wanted her...always available.

Sudden shouts and curses erupted around the stage, the sound of pistol shots boomed and the crack of rifle fire vibrated through the air and seized Miguel back to reality. He saw Raine scramble to her feet.

She wouldn't get far.

Miguel turned to his men, and spoke in the sign language his Indian mother had taught him. He counted the number of bandits on his fingers and put the four fingers across one finger of the other hand, to indicate a man on horseback.

"Cover me."

Again, reckless gunfire erupted from around the stage. Miguel's gaze flew back to Raine. She ran, long masses of dark hair streaming behind her. In the next instant, a bandit spotted her and gave chase. Miguel's gut twisted. The bandit on horseback was gaining on Raine, fast. When he caught up with her, he would kill her, *or worse*. Unwelcome memories came flooding back as he watched her run for her life.

With an effort that caused him pain and made his muscles tense beneath the dark trail clothes, he closed his mind against the vivid images. As though driven by muses — or the devil — he spurred his Blaze to a full gallop.

Raine could hear the thunder of hoofbeats behind her, and panic rose like bile in her throat. She ran so hard that she was taking air in fast gulps. The muscles in her legs burned and she knew they would give out at any moment. Dear God, what could she do? As tears streamed down her cheeks; she looked back, sweeping the hair from her eyes.

Any second the horse and rider would catch up with her. Nausea twisted her stomach and she stumbled, but somehow managed to regain her footing. Tears blurred her vision. The rider's shouts and wild yells sounded so close; she imagined the horse's breath on the back of her neck.

In a twinkling, he scooped her off the ground and threw her into the saddle in front of him. Raine screamed, "Nooo!"

Unable to stop herself, Raine peered out from behind her screen of hair to see the cruel promise in the bandit's eyes. He horrified her with a wolfish smile that made her feel unclean.

Out of her mind with fear and desperate to free herself, she beat on her captor's chest and hacked at his face with her fingernails. The bandit howled and brought a broad, dirty hand to his bleeding face before raising it high. The blow fell with a resounding whack on Raine's face, causing her to let out a painful scream as her head jerked back from the force of the blow.

Then rocks stung Raine's legs and she heard a deep voice from behind say, "Do not move." It was her only warning before a strong arm encircled her waist and roughly swung her up into another saddle, in front of different man. She let out a strangled scream; she couldn't imagine how one bandit was any better than another.

Instead of being grateful for just having been rescued from the torments of hell, Raine wrestled like a lassoed wildcat. Then she jabbed him hard in the ribs with her elbow, and almost got away, very nearly taking them both to their deaths.

Raine heard a curse that burned her ears, then, "You will not do that again!" She squirmed to retrieve her knife from the pocket of her skirt.

The bandit swore in Spanish as he reached down to recover the rein he'd lost while tangling with her. When his hand locked on the back of Raine's jacket bodice, she yelped.

The sound was cut off when she was lifted off the saddle again and her stomach made hard contact with a pair of muscled thighs. She struggled to free herself, and when she caught her breath, she screamed in protest. The horse picked up speed. A good bounce took Raine's wind but that didn't stop her from twisting her head around.

When she shot him an angry look, he asked, "Who are you trying harder to kill — me, yourself, or both of us?"

Raine gaped at him and thought she must be seeing things. Her mysterious lover couldn't be rescuing her...but he was. The familiar black eyes glittered beneath the wide brim of his cowboy hat. "I-I thought — I thought you were kidnapping me."

He gazed down at her with a shuttered expression and she felt a sudden chill of apprehension. His eyes were grim and cold. "I am."

Raine's heart skipped a beat. If he'd said that to frighten her, it worked quite well. He could consider her subdued.

Miguel rode like the wind. He had gained a good distance on the bandit who had tried to kidnap her when he flattened one huge palm on the small of Raine's back.

"No matter what happens, do not move," he shouted.

Raine saw nothing as his body stiffened beneath hers. When he drew his six-gun, she could not help herself, she raised her head to try to see.

"Stay down!" The words registered on her when her head was shoved back down. Jerking his body to the side, he opened fire, and was rewarded with a bloodcurdling scream.

The bullets came so rapidly then that Raine closed her eyes and covered her ears with her hands. Just when she thought he'd emptied the gun and it was safe to open her eyes, he let go of her, causing Raine to have to hold onto the saddle for dear life. She heard him slam in the second loaded cylinder. Again the bullets flew over her head, but with longer intervals between them than the first time. This time he was taking careful aim. Finally, the six-gun fell silent, but the distant rifles didn't.

Miguel slowed the horse to a canter. Without warning, his powerful hand grasped the back of Raine's short jacket. Lifting her off her stomach, he placed her in a sitting position on the saddle in front of him. She heard him shuck the spent cases from his six-gun, then reload and shove his weapon into the holster.

Raine had not yet caught her breath when he clamped his arm around her waist and pulled her to him. She fought against the warmth of his body radiating through hers, then stiffened when he leaned down and put his mouth against her ear.

"Do not try to get away from me again. If you do...I swear, I will beat you severely."

Before she could determine what feelings he'd just stirred inside her, she looked over her shoulder and stared at his face. That one brief look told her it was the wrong time to tell him what she thought of his threat.

Miguel knew his men would meet him back in Copper Canyon, and retreated into the cover of the ravine. He was grateful he couldn't see Raine's startling blue eyes, because that meant she hadn't seen the hunger swelling in his. Her hair smelled of wild-flowers and her slender waist felt far too good to him. Her small hands clutched his arm, and the heat of her touch seemed to go all the way to his toes. He stiffened. Did he have no control over his feelings for the beautiful daughter of his enemy?

Heated anger consumed him, a reaction to the curtailment of his violent desire. Miguel cursed his unbridled response to this woman. Those who allowed themselves feelings, received only pain as a reward.

After the horrors his family had endured at the hands of the French, he'd headed back to the revolution — not as a surgeon, for which he was educated in Europe — but as a revolutionary. For the past year, he'd fought for Juarez, obsessed with winning Mexico back from the ruthless French invaders. When the war was over, he'd reclaim his father's land — the land Spain had granted his family long ago.

In Copper Canyon, the Tarahumara Indian medicine man would handle most of the healing. The old shaman was thought by his tribe to have supernatural powers and often used sleight-of-hand to perform tricks and impress his tribal members. Of course, the Indian was not always successful and Miguel would have to treat the more difficult medical problems himself. But medicine was almost impossible to come by now, and the old man had taught Miguel all he knew about herbs and their healing powers.

Miguel reined in his horse. "We will stop here," he said, his voice cold.

With unnerving swiftness, he removed his arm from around her and dismounted. When he reached up and grabbed her around the waist, Raine remained silent. Cheeks flushed, she lifted her heavy lidded eyes and stood gazing at him; her breasts heaved.

The fragrance of her womanhood and the gardenia-flowers' dust intoxicated Miguel. Evoked by the double ruby pout of her lips, the pulses in his temples beat the strong urge to thrust the tip of his stiff weapon of pleasure into her mouth. He wanted to drive his sex hard against the back of her throat until only the drawn up sack was left hanging outside, piercing yet another of Raine's virginal openings and filling it with his sweet violence.

Why was he so eager to make love — no that was the wrong word, bed Raine LeFleur? As he continued to gaze at her, a curious possessiveness came over him. Suddenly, he wanted to keep her captive *forever*, be alone with this gentle creature in this savage garden called Mexico, every night for the rest of his life. He thought for a moment that his imagination had gone mad, and that which transpired between them in her bedroom had been a fantasy.

He snatched Raine from the saddle and set her on the ground.

In his arms, she shivered. Then took a deep breath, and whispered, "I do not even know your name."

"I am Miguel Chavez."

Raine stared at him, repeated his name to herself. His sexual appeal showed in every line of his chiseled face, and he was handsome, maybe not like the men in the French court, but in a very rugged sort of way, with his gleaming black hair and his dark deep-set eyes. She couldn't fathom why he would feel the need to kidnap her. Surely, he knew he could have her again if he wished.

Miguel's gaze caught the spiky lashes framing her brilliant almond-shaped eyes and gently flaring brows, as black as her midnight hair, the tiny beads of sweat tracing her high cheekbones, and her small straight nose. He watched as her tongue eased out to wet her full lips and it made him groan. Her eyes widened at the sound, eyes such a dark blue that they were almost identical in color to a lapis stone. Then her sudden fear was evident in every taunt line of her delicate heart-shaped face.

"W-what will you do with me?" Raine whispered, her French accent distinct, shaking him to the very core of his being. It was as if the earth had just been jerked out from beneath his feet.

For a moment Miguel stood frozen, and so did she. Then like a cobra coiling for the strike his movements were slow and deliberate. He threaded his fingers deep into the mass of hair at the back of her hair in an inescapable grip. Raine grimaced.

"I am taking you to my home, where you will remain my guest."

"Y-you cannot be serious; you must take me back to the fort, my father —"

Miguel's grip tightened on her hair and cut her off, but when she whimpered he wanted to kick himself. "I *will* take you, and I *will* keep you for as long as I wish."

He released her and flags of color marked her cheeks. "Miguel, you do not have to —"

"I do not have to do anything," he said curling his lip.

Raine sucked in a breath and Miguel felt her body tense. When she gazed up at him, he tried to forget how beautiful she looked, remember that she was French. An enemy. But she looked so fragile, almost helpless with her dirty face and tattered clothing. He was compelled to bring his arms around her in reassurance. That was all. He was indifferent to women other than for the sexual pleasure they brought him. Unfortunately, he wasn't immune to this woman who had the face of an angel and a body that would make a bishop kick out a stained glass window. And although she was French, he could hardly be indifferent to the softness of her breasts crushed against his chest, or her captivating beauty, which he was sure Raine had seen in his expression, but just failed to understand.

Her scent was like a brand on Miguel. As if the arms holding her had a mind of their own, they tightened around her. He brought his face down to hers. His body reacted to the feel of hers pressed against him.

Warm breath fanned Raine's mouth, and the familiar sensations caused her to suck in a breath. She was scared and out of control, but the brawny strength of him around her was exciting. Why was she unable to ignore this hot, unpredictable passion that washed through her whenever he was near? Probably because he had awakened those sexual appetites, and they had not died when she awoke that morning to find him gone.

The strong arms pressed around her were unnerving but glorious, and Raine had to force herself to breathe. With hands that trembled, she clutched her skirts, and the hard blade of the dagger in her pocket brought her to her senses. No matter what feelings this wild revolutionary pulled from her, she couldn't allow him to keep her captive. It was her duty to escape and find a way back to her father. And…if needed, she'd use the knife to get away.

She began concentrating on a plan of escape, instead of the erotic urges, and wrenched free of Miguel's hold. She didn't get far. He gripped her wrist, and jerked her right back to him. "Ouch!"

"You are going to behave until we get out of here."

Raine's eyes narrowed. She still had no idea of where he was taking her, or why. More importantly, *what* he was going to do with her when he got her there.

Before she could concentrate on "what" for long, she forced herself to remember Miguel was a Mexican revolutionary and Mexico was in the middle of a war with France. Which wasn't a good thing where she was concerned, no matter how she looked at it. Even if she believed he was going to harm her, which she didn't. Well, she was almost sure that she didn't.

Again, she tried to escape his ironclad grip, but Miguel held fast to her wrist. Her eyes narrowed even more. She was getting damn tired of him jerking her in every direction!

Raine snapped up her head and railed at him, "Enough! I demand that you release me."

In an instant, the mood changed.

Miguel's smile was mirthless, a small showing of white teeth. She bit her lip to keep from crying out as he tightened his hold on her wrist, and stopped fighting. "You must allow me to return to my home."

This time, his smile was even colder than before, and his eyes much darker. "Come now, you must know it is too late for that."

"B-but I am only one woman," Raine protested. "I have done nothing to you. I was the one who was wronged by you." She took a step back. Well almost, anyway. She did go as far back as he would allow, then cursed his solid strength before taking a defiant stance.

For the moment, anger surpassed fear and Raine found her voice. "Enough!" she cried. "I demand to know what you plan to do with me!"

"You are not in a position to demand anything. And until I tire of your company, you will remain with me."

"W-what?"

"You heard me."

Raine still could not believe what she had heard. "Y-you plan to keep me against my will?"

"I have already made it clear that you will remain my guest."

She swallowed. "Guest? What you mean is your prisoner."

Miguel lifted his brows.

"You cannot!"

"I suggest that you do not doubt me."

Raine became furious, she'd had enough of this! "If you don't release me, my father will —" She stopped short, and lost what color she had left.

Miguel's spine went rigid and his jaw flexed. "Oh, do not stop now. Your father will do what?"

She squared her shoulders. "H-he will be beside himself with worry when he hears the stagecoach was attacked by bandits, and that I am missing. When he finds I have been kidnapped, he will come after me with all the means he has at his disposal."

He said nothing and the realization hit Raine. Miguel wanted her father to come after her; he meant to use her as a hostage, at great cost to her father, and France.

"Do not worry," he said. "No harm will come to you."

Raine refused to meet his gaze. He'd said it so automatically, she couldn't doubt the truth of the statement, but she wasn't so naive as to think it was the whole truth either. Oh, he'd probably see that she got home to her father all right — but after her father would have to trade, God-only-knew-what for her. Maybe even himself.

Never.

The bastard.

Championed by the dagger still unknown to Miguel, Raine gave way to whatever complicated emotions were driving her. Like a cat, she sprang close to him and dug in her heels, surprising him. She raised her hand and took a swipe at him.

Miguel easily evaded the blow, then laughed at her continued, and very real, efforts to land a solid whack on his face. Finally he immobilized her, enfolding her in his arms. Raine writhed to no avail and gave up. There was no way that she'd escape his hold. Filled with fury, she stared at him with contempt.

His smile was cold and dangerous.

Raine stood paralyzed. Dear God, what if he never let her go? He might even kill her. No — no, she was just panicking. He'd never kill her. She gazed into his eyes. "Why are you doing this?"

The corners of Miguel's mouth lifted. An attractive mouth, that hinted of aggression, and satisfaction, and triumph. "Because I want you."

"For how long?" she challenged.

Miguel laughed. "I will let you know. Now, just behave and do as I say. When the time is right, I will consider negotiating an exchange with the French."

Raine retained a gasp. "You mean, give them a price," she spat.

"Finally, I am liking the way you think, although I'm tired of arguing with you." Miguel paused to run a finger down her pale cheek. "You have enjoyed being under my control before, and you will again. So I do not wish to hear another word."

Raine froze so stiff that a good wind might have caused her to crack. She could only stand there and stare at Miguel. The impression of his face was that it belonged to a very handsome, but dangerous and lawless man. She studied his black shirt, the vest of chamois leather and an American cowboy hat. His eyes held a predatory look. He gazed at her in a way that made her very nervous. If she could have found her voice, she would have screamed. Instead, she jumped back and pulled the dagger from her skirt pocket, and pointed it at him.

Unaffected by her threat, Miguel pushed the brim of his Stetson off his forehead. Raine had no time to react before she heard the clear sound of a revolver being cocked. She looked down to see his Colt forty-five pointed at her chest.

Giving her a slow strange glance, Miguel pried the fancy jewel-encrusted dagger loose from her fingers with his free hand. "Properly raised young ladies should not be playing with knives; they might get hurt."

Tears burned behind Raine's eyes and her resolve weakened. So much for using the dagger to escape, she thought. Oh, my! She shouldn't have been so impulsive.

Raine never looked away from the gun as she crossed her arms defiantly over her chest. She might have lost the battle, but she hadn't lost the war. She would just have to wait for another opportunity to present itself. Giving up wasn't in her nature.

After slipping the knife in his belt, Miguel returned his Colt to the holster. He moved closer, and demanded, "Why did you do that?"

Raine amazed herself when she stood her ground in the face of his anger. "And what was I supposed to do, *monsieur*? Stand here and not try to escape from a man who is kidnapping me?"

Miguel leaned forward and pulled her to him. She took a deep breath to steady herself and straightened to her full five-feet three inches. "Let go of me!"

Chapter Four

Miguel's jaw bunched in suppressed anger. For several seconds Raine thought he might slap the black right out of her hair. "Make no mistake about it," he said, "you are going to be with me for quite some time. So I suggest you do not give me any further trouble, and I warn you that I have no tolerance for troublesome women."

A chill traveled down Raine's spine, for she sensed Miguel meant what he said. The deep voice had sent sensations through her that caused her to back away from him, when fear hadn't. She couldn't seem to keep her gaze from him. He was so tall, and so very handsome, even though the sun had begun to draw lines from the corners of his eyes. Those dark eyes seemed so oddly piercing against the sun-darkened skin. This man was any woman's dream — or in her case, nightmare.

Miguel frowned and his face looked like it was carved out of rock. "There will be no more attempts at escape. Do you understand me?"

Raine tensed and her mesmerized gaze turned to one of disbelief. "I certainly do not! You cannot really expect me to go along with my abduction?"

He kissed her forehead. "You are unable to do otherwise. I have your weapon now, remember?"

"I hate you," she hissed through clenched teeth.

Miguel's eyes seemed ablaze when they looked at her. "Oh, my lovely señorita, you do not know me nearly well enough to hate me, *yet*. But you will," he replied, then kissed her thoroughly.

Raine thought if she had a gun she would shoot him dead. The problem was she did not have a gun. She didn't have anything. And now she was feeling defeat, something she'd never experienced before. Her exhausted legs threatened to buckle beneath her, and she found herself wanting to cry. Obviously, she wasn't going to get back to her father without some cooperation on her part.

When released her, Raine pretended that she was unaffected. Lifting her skirts, she turned to walk away. Something caught her blouse and pulled her back to him — his hand. She came up hard against Miguel, which resulted in two emotions that didn't sit well together.

Lord help her.

He brushed her hair aside and kissed the back of her neck. Raine cried out in frustration and spun around to face him. He cupped her face in his hands, made her look at him. She sensed the fire in his soul, but it was the flame in his eyes that kept her silent.

Miguel's gaze moved over her face. "Believe me," he said, his voice low, "if you do not quit fighting and come with me willingly, I will tie and gag you. The choice is yours."

Raine stared at him.

He must have read the bafflement in her eyes, for his expression changed to one that clearly showed he was waiting for her answer. "Willing or not that was the question."

She swallowed hard and refused to cry. "You would truly have me ride a horse bound and gagged?"

Miguel arched an eyebrow, his look intent. "I will have you ride *me* bound and gagged if I feel the urge," he said, grabbing Raine's hands in a tight squeeze.

"*Mon Dieu.* You are mad."

The gaze that surveyed her was cold and predatory. Without saying a word Miguel let her know just how much he'd enjoy tying her up and having sex with her.

Terror seized Raine and she struggled to wrest her hands from his. "*Non!* You would not dare!"

Miguel's lips curled into an unpleasant smile. "You think not? Señorita, you doubt the wrong man." His tone was dangerous. "I will do just as I want with you — whenever and however I please."

Raine's anger blazed like the center of a red-hot flame and he had to know it because, he said, "If you're on fire, show me."

"Never!" she cried out in rage and flung herself at him, clawing for his eyes. Miguel snapped his head back but not before the vicious nails raked one cheek, leaving deep furrows that sprang red. New anger seemed to surge through him. With lightening speed he caught both of Raine's wrists and wrenched them behind her.

He began unbuttoning her torn, dirty blouse, and his dark eyes twinkled in the light of the late afternoon sun, and Raine wanted him to take her, right there where they stood. She pretended she didn't.

He spread the front of her blouse and laid his palms against the skin between her breasts, his fingers splayed. "I want you, Raine. I want you now."

She sucked in her breath and closed her eyes for a moment when he eased her blouse out from under the waistband of her skirt and unbuttoned it. Reaching for her camisole, he pulled the delicate fabric upwards and ripped it apart so that her breasts were completely bared.

Raine whimpered when he found her nipples and began stroking them lightly with the rough pads of his thumbs. As he laid the tip of his tongue to the taut buttons, he swore, "I will make you beg for my touch."

He came up and pressed his body against hers, his knee went between her legs. His was sex hard with aggressive male desire, and the hard wall of a boulder pressed its imprint onto Raine's back.

"Loose me," she demanded, pushing against his chest, just as afraid of her wakening desires as she was of being his virtual prisoner.

"No," he replied with his mouth a hairsbreadth from hers.

Tears of frustration and indignation sprang from Raine's eyes and ran unbidden down her cheeks as she continued to struggle.

Miguel kissed her. The smell of a woman always excited him; he loved the sweet rich perfume of Raine's scent. He was already wild with desire, and knowing she reveled in his touch but still intended to fight him, only served to make him want her with an intensity beyond his control. Finally she gave up, exhausted, panting beneath him, pinioned up against the huge boulder despite her struggles. He lowered his bloodstained face to hers and kissed her roughly. Raine jerked her head from side to side but her efforts were futile against such determination and strength. He continued to hold her immobile, caressing her breasts, then her bare white thighs beneath her skirts, forcing her to kiss him, filling her mouth with his thrusting tongue, ravishing her.

She moaned as his hands reached between her thighs and tore off her drawers and tossed them aside to expose her sex. Miguel held her body immobile as he parted the slick folds with ease. He dipped his finger into her wetness to moisten his finger, then caressed her until her inner muscles tensed and convulsed with the anticipation of the pounding thrust of his harsh erection.

It was shaking to Raine, being forced, strangely exciting. She shivered at the frission of sensation that ran through her, the deep throbbing desire that made her ache for him. But the resentments of being forced still consumed her, and she refused to grant him the satisfaction of responding. She remained inert beneath his touch, knowing that her passivity would anger him far more than anything.

"I will no longer fight you so get on with it," she commanded him in a whisper.

"As you wish," he said and wasted no more time. He dropped to his knees and forced her legs apart, exposing her secrets wide open, her sex gaping. He inserted his tongue causing her to draw a swift intake of air. Hot wet flesh against hot wet flesh of a similar yet different kind. The sweet friction his tongue generated as it probed and titillated the soft regions of her bliss grew more intense with each passing moment. Raine cried out with a pleasure that she didn't want to feel and arched in search of his lusty tongue.

As if to punish her, Miguel paused at the slick mouth of her pleasure. Raine quivered right before she caught his long raven locks and pulled them. He brought himself up and placing both hands on either side of the rock wall above her shoulders, gazed into her startled blue eyes, and whispered, "Tell me."

"No," she cried, attempting to cover her exposed throbbing flesh with her skirts.

She stopped when his hand went to her sensitive organ and stroked it. He drew his finger back through her wet folds, moved to leave a trail of moisture in his wake. The shivering tension of Raine's body told him she was beyond ready for him to take her, but he wouldn't. He made her wait. "I know what you want," Miguel said. "Will you still deny it, or will you ask me for it?"

"Please."

Miguel took off his gunbelt and opened his trousers. His sex was massive now as he removed first his boots and then his pants. When he shifted against her the thick heat of his erection pressed against her thigh, and her whole body trembled. He caressed her gently, large, powerful hands lingering over the column of her throat as he slipped his tongue down the length of her ear, sliding down to just graze the tops of her breasts.

When he lifted his head, Raine was breathless. "Do you wish to be?" he asked. She was dazed, confused. "What?"

"Filled with my flesh. "

Raine didn't answer, but her lips parted and her head fell back in invitation. Again, he tormented her by stroking her damp soft crevice, harder this time, almost hurting her with painful pleasure. She made herself wider for him and he moved between her legs. His penis surged against her soft pulsating flesh and her inner muscles rippled and contracted on the assuaging fullness. However, he allowed her only a small amount of himself, a brief tantalizing taste of the sweet hardness she craved before taking it away.

"Please," she begged.

"Do you want all of me inside of you?"

Raine caught her breath, faltered, then whispered in defeat, "I want you to be inside me."

Miguel slipped his hands under her arms, flattened his palms against the flat rock behind her shoulder blades to protect her back and plunged into her, catching her shocked welcome in her mouth. All the while he was kissing her, Raine's body arched in pleasure as Miguel's hips executed a rhythm against hers, his thick shaft prolonging the pulsating waves with the measured thrust of his body. Again and again he repeated the move. She was wild, begging him to stay within the depths a little longer. He brought her to a tumultuous climax before he allowed himself to reach fulfillment.

As the waves of pleasure died away, Raine was mortified by her body's traitorous desires for this man.

Raine opened her eyes, appalled that he'd just taken her against a boulder, in the middle of the desert, as if she were no more than a whore. "Now that you are quite finished taking what you wanted from your captive, would you please remove your person from my body?" she whispered brokenly.

"I did not *take* anything," Miguel said with measured control. He moved to touch her tear-stained cheek. "You wanted it as much as I did, and asked for it."

Raine cringed from his touch. He left her quickly and dressed. After she'd righted her skirts, he took a calming breath and tried again. He extended a hand to her.

"Just leave me alone!" she sobbed, turning away from him.

Miguel stared at her recumbent form, her unseeing, tear-filled eyes averted from his. It upset him to know that he was the cause of Raine's pain and humiliation, and this guilt was foreign to his nature and upsetting. His revenge had not been what he'd imagined, but the only emotion he could bring himself to identify was anger, which he turned on her.

"You have forgotten that I saved your life," he said, "but since I *am* keeping you…I can tell you that being held a prisoner by me is the least of your worries," Miguel finished, looking from her to the vast expanse beyond.

Raine faced him then and their glances met. Miguel appeared filled with anger and, some strange emotion. Was it regret?

She hesitated but only for a moment. "I understand perfectly, *monsieur*. You are not a kidnapper or rapist by trade. You merely hold me captive because you are opportunistic," she said in a clipped cool voice.

Miguel flinched. Nerve-racking silence followed while he struggled to regain control of his emotions, his anger was so great. He felt no reluctance at this point though. "I guess you could put it that way. Regardless of my reasons, the facts remain. If I allow you to leave my company, and my protection, you will be dead, or worse, before the first echo of your screams comes back from the mountains. If the bandits do not get you first, the wolves or coyotes will."

Raine turned white under her dirt smudged skin, but snapped, "You are just trying to frighten me into subservience!"

Miguel shrugged his big shoulders. "You can believe me or not. In truth, your presence will cause me considerable trouble, but so far I have been compensated for my troubles." Then he smiled. "As you were so quick to point out, I am not above making the best of a bad situation. Still, you've lived in this country. Sheltered or not, you should know that there are not many white women here that are not whores, or wives of French soldiers. I should think you would be quite a prize. Of course if you want to go out there alone then you're welcome to try."

Raine shivered. She said nothing; she simply stared at him.

Miguel realized that he might have gone too far in his anger. Suddenly, she looked so small and frail standing there. He wanted to take her in his arms and hold her. The instinct to protect her was so great. Did she know what she was capable of making him feel? Or was he just imagining things? He told himself that it was no more than he would feel for any woman in the same situation.

Their gazes locked. When he moved toward her, Raine stepped back. He didn't stop. In an instant, her breath was on Miguel's face, and his hands on her shoulders. "There is no need to fight this."

Raine looked up at him and his arms naturally slipped around her waist. She noticed the shirt he wore was wet with perspiration and it clung to his bulging muscles.

What was she doing, a member of the royal family, allowing a strange man — a revolutionary — an enemy of France — to possess her? She ought to be repelled by his touch, but she wasn't. All she wanted was to arch her back against him repeatedly.

Raine forced herself to think of her father; she couldn't let this man get to her. She had allowed things to go far enough. Then she decided that she had best remove herself from this situation with haste. She moved to leave Miguel's embrace but he would not allow it.

She raised her chin a notch. "I-I will not give in to your seductions again. If you force me to remain with you…you will have to force me every time."

Miguel's eyes changed and dark fury seemed to etch the lines of his face.

"Maybe, but I think not. All the women I choose give themselves to me willingly, just as you did," he said.

Raine blanched and shoved him away from her. She'd never been more insulted or embarrassed or confused in her whole life. He'd spoken with such disgust. It had never occurred to her that he hadn't been taken with her, as she was with him—that he might think her nothing more than another one of his many conquests.

That broke the dam, it seemed, and great racking sobs came from Raine and the tears flowed copiously. Miguel reached out to her then, but she would be damned if she'd let him comfort her now.

Raine quickly moved out of his reach. "Y-you can go to the devil!"

Before Miguel could respond she turned on her heels, lifted her skirts, and fled, as if she really meant to go out into the frontier alone.

Dammit!

"Raine!" Miguel called after her.

She kept running.

Fine!

Go, then!

Besides, if he kept her with him she'd only end up being more trouble than she was worth.

Chapter Five

Five minutes later Miguel, wishing he had a drink, started to go after her. In another second, he decided the hell with it, she wouldn't go far. Something would frighten her royal butt and she'd be back. He snatched the Stetson from his head and slapped it against his thigh. It was just as well she'd stalked off, because he needed time to cool his temper.

Feeling a good deal better about the whole thing, he went to feed and water his horse. Hell, he'd wager that before he was finished Raine would be crawling back with her tail between those shapely little legs of hers. He groaned, wondering how a simple gun-run had turned into something so difficult.

Not more than a hundred feet away, Raine swiped at her tears with the back of a dirty hand. Hot and discouraged, it hadn't taken long for her to realize that she had no idea of where she was going.

As a rule she despised whining women and never allowed herself to cry. But, considering what had happened to her today, she felt entitled to a few sniffles. Her predicament was inconceivable, but it had happened nonetheless.

Several times she had to stop and dump the sand out of her shoes. All this running was making her perspire and itch, and the hot sun overhead made her wish she still had her hat. Her luck had definitely run out.

Raine realized she was becoming desperate, but she knew that when darkness fell, she'd be even more frantic. Then what would she do?

As she plodded her way, it occurred to her that she hadn't been thinking clearly since she had the idea to jump from the stage. Then she'd compounded her problems by stomping off into the middle of nowhere. She didn't know why she'd done it, other than wanting to get away from that man.

However, now that she was out in the desert alone, with darkness only a short time away, Miguel Chavez's company wouldn't be nearly so offending.

Raine stopped and scanned the bleak landscape around her. There was nothing near to run to. Only wilderness. She had no idea where she was, or in what direction the fort lay, and she was thirsty and hungry. Her entire body ached and was covered with dirt.

Pápa, she thought with a sigh. He'd be searching for her just as soon as he received word that she was missing. Maybe, if she could manage to stay in the area, he would find her. The realization made her feel a little better.

She sniffled a couple of times and wiped her eyes dry with her shirtsleeve.

Yes, soon her father and his soldiers would come for her and this terrible nightmare would be over. Unfortunately, she also knew Miguel had been right. She needed to go back and stay with him. But, she told herself, only until her father came for her. She had not other choice — unless, she could use this opportunity to gain his trust. Why not? If he thought that she cared for him just a little, then maybe…Of course she didn't really have feelings for him. She knew that, but under the circumstances, she'd do just about anything!

A coyote howled, and Raine took off running.

Miguel stopped pacing and kicked the ground with the toe of his worn boot. Where the devil was she?

Raine hadn't meant to try to escape. No, of course not. She couldn't be that stupid. Still, he wouldn't be surprised if the stubborn woman had meant to escape, after all. From what he'd already witnessed, she had enough nerve to try it.

It occurred to him that Raine might very well be lost. What if she was hurt? What if she'd been found by a wolf? It was a distinct possibility that unnerved him even more. Although he had definite doubts that even a wolf would want to tangle with the likes of her, he was becoming more than a little concerned. Then he reasoned, he'd have heard her screaming if something had attempted to do her harm.

However, the idea she might be hurt continued to nag at him. Mother of God, he actually cared what happened to her. But he'd forgotten how to care. *Do not even think it! She is French.* Pretentious and privileged. And no doubt, scared to death. Damn that woman! Should he go looking for her or to stay right where he was?

His hands began to sweat. His brow, too, and not because of the heat, but because she had been gone such a long time.

Miguel shook his head. He thought he'd killed enough of the pursuing bandits to scare the remaining ones off for good, but he wasn't taking any chances. He never took chances. That was what insured his survival.

Then it occurred to him that if Raine had gotten herself lost in the desert, she'd never find her way back to him in the dark, not even if she wanted to. And night out here wasn't just as black as pitch, but also colder than a whore's heart!

With a low curse Miguel went looking for her. Though he was half Spanish, the skills of his Indian heritage ran deep in his blood, and he moved with a conscious effort at silence. It was simply a necessary way of life for him. Luckily, with his skills for tracking it didn't take him long to find her. He paused, going down on one knee, to watch her silently.

She was something to see, wringing her hands as she searched for whatever had sent her into a frenzy. Pale with fear, her eyes were large and dark as her gaze darted around. In truth, she looked frightened to death, and he cursed the sympathy he felt for her.

She'd shed her jacket and was breathing hard. Her dirty blouse, sweat-soaked and unbuttoned at the neck, clung to her, and revealed the swelling contours of her full breasts. The relief he'd felt at finding her was now mixed with a strange anger and excitement. He stifled a groan.

A moment later, from the corner of his eyes, Miguel caught sight of a large diamondback rattler silently slithering its way toward Raine along the dry, dusty earth. With the agility of a mountain lion, he shot forward. Raising a hand like a striking snake, he grabbed the back of Raine's blouse and jerked her to him. With a strangled cry, she turned on her attacker and wildly flailed her fists at his face.

Miguel grabbed her wrists and held them fast. "Stop, Raine," he said, keeping his eyes peeled on the snake. Any other time he'd have taken its life with his Colt, but right now he didn't want to risk drawing unwanted attention. He was relieved when the snake slithered off an in search of other prey.

Raine heart was beating so fast she thought it might never slow again. She had trouble catching her breath. This was the second time he'd come up behind her and snatched her to him without warning. She was going to kill him!

"Do all revolutionaries make it habit of sneaking up on people?" she cried.

Miguel's gaze swung back to her, and he shrugged his broad shoulders. "Sometimes there is just no way around it."

Raine shot him a hate-filled glare.

He smiled. "I didn't mean to frighten you, but that rattler was about to send you on the road to heaven." He cocked his head in the snake's direction, adding a great deal of credence to his statement.

Raine's gaze followed the direction he indicated and almost fainted when she saw the huge reptile. With a startled sound she clutched the first thing she could, which was Miguel.

"Do not worry, the snake is leaving," he said, holding Raine against his chest. "Are you all right?"

Raine was dumbstruck. When she lifted her head and returned her gaze to his, she could only nod. She remained against him motionless, her heart slamming hard against her chest.

"You should not have run off," Miguel thundered as he grabbed her shoulders and gave her a good shake. "I ought to beat you!"

Raine hadn't heard a word he said. She was so grateful he'd found her before the snake bit her, she flung her arms around his neck. "Oh, thank you for saving me! Please do not leave me, Miguel!" She clung to him as if for dear life. Surprisingly, he clung right back.

"Not on your life," he said in a low voice.

Raine sighed as an odd weakness uncurled her body. Some great escape, she thought. Miguel ran his hand over the back of her head, and pressed her even closer to him. She smiled at his at his attempts to comfort her while kidnapping her. Apparently, this revolutionary didn't do anything in a normal way.

Suddenly, Miguel tensed. "If you ever endanger your life like this again —" He stopped when she raised her head and stared up at him with frightened eyes.

Raine stiffened, filled with apprehension. She wanted to stay with him, and yet knew she would try to escape again. For her father's sake she must find a way. Beneath his smoldering gaze, she felt pure panic. She couldn't look at him any longer; if she did, he would see those emotions. Yet he must have sensed them because he brought one hand up to caress the back of her head as if he were trying to soothe her.

Miguel shook his head. "I will never hurt you, but I cannot allow you to leave me either," he whispered. Then in the heat of the moment, with an unconscious need to tell her what his heart said, his lips moved along her throat.

Raine sighed as his deep velvety voice washed over her like warm bath water on a cold night. Sensations shot through her that she'd never imagined existed. He tipped her face up so he could see her, but he didn't know her heart skipped a beat every time he looked at her like that.

The glimpse of her breasts rising and falling beneath the folds of fine lawn sent a jolt of heat through Miguel. Now, bathed in setting sunlight and with her skin shiny with a wet heat, he found her more desirable than ever. As his gaze moved over every inch of her there was a shortness in her breath, but she didn't try to get away.

She is just a woman, Miguel reminded himself, remembering the anger that crept up his spine when he'd seen her the first time and known she was Armand LeFleur's daughter.

Are you so sure it was only anger? intruded his conscience.

Trying to ignore it, and not think what could have happened had they met in another time, another place, he asked, "Where is your jacket?"

Raine looked around, then shrugged. "Somewhere between here and where I left you."

"Wait here!" With a curse that made her wince, Miguel abruptly released her and backtracked. It didn't take long to find the jacket, torn beyond repair, probably by coyotes, and not thirty feet away.

Knowing that the ripped garment could have just as easily been Raine's body put the finishing touches on his temper. He snatched what was left of the jacket from the ground and stalked back to her.

"See this," he said. He shoved what could no longer be considered a jacket toward her.

Raine nodded and took the shredded garment from him.

Miguel pinned her with a heated gaze. "Now do you see why you frightened the devil out of me?"

She blinked. "I frightened *you*?"

Miguel saw her trembling, and it softened his anger. Stepping forward, he said in a low voice, "Yes, you did." He shook his head in exasperation, then continued, "Now, I want you to stop this foolishness. If you don't, you will get yourself killed."

Raine nodded. The reality was that what he'd said was true. She had no other choice but to stay with him.

Then she noted that she wasn't as nearly as unhappy as she should have been. Dear God, she should regret her foolish actions on the stagecoach. Because of them, she might never see her father again. Because of them...she was with Miguel, and not on her way to France to marry a man she did not love.

When she took a shaky breath, Miguel slipped an arm around her and pulled her more fully against him.

Raine closed her eyes against his warm breath fanning her neck, his mouth leaving a cool wetness in its trail. She gasped as the most delicious shivers ran down her spine. Her nails dug into his skin, causing him to moan and press his face harder against her neck. Desire swirled around her. She'd never felt passion before Miguel, never imagined a man could make her feel this way.

She curled her fingers around his neck and held him. It was as if her body were making all the decisions on its own, as she touched swirls of chest hair, caught a whiff of his spicy scent. He felt so wonderful, she thought, with his stubbly chin rubbing up against her, his masculine arms tight around her. She snuggled closer.

Miguel raised his head to stare into her dazed eyes. They were filled with astonishment and burned with a need as hot as his own. Her soft breasts heaved against him and his breathing became erratic. He was expecting her to come to her senses and push him away, but she didn't. Not able to help himself, he slid his hand under her knees and carried her behind a small group of Yucca. Under the trees, on a rare patch of soft green grass, he laid her down and undressed her. All the while he murmured endearments, stilling her fears and timid protests with soft caresses, seducing her with a gentleness Miguel had never imagined he possessed.

Raine sighed. "I don't know what is happening to me, but I know I need to be with you. I want you inside me again."

Heat flooded Miguel. Her simple passion beguiled him. His glance swept over Raine's naked form, as if he were memorizing her. He watched her for a long time, and then, without thought, brought his face down to hers and tenderly tasted the softness of her lips.

As if her breasts ached, Raine pressed them harder against him. He kissed her again, opening her mouth under the pressure of his lips. Then he stroked and caressed her, slid his fingers over her bare thighs toward the very source of pleasure. She quivered and shuddered beneath his touch when he toyed with her moist folds. His kiss was hungry and invading. While his hands moved to the sides of her face and held it, he glided his tongue over her lips and then her cheeks and then returned to her lips again, to encircle them. She imitated his actions.

Miguel groaned. He drew back from her for a moment and looked at the delicate buds that topped her milky-white breasts. He took her left nipple between finger and thumb and rolled it, until it was hard and the areola was dimpled. Raine moaned and grasped her unattended breast with her hand and held it up like an offering to him. He lowered his head and took the nipple in his mouth, grazing it with his teeth before clamping his lips around the hard roundness of her breast. He sucked carefully to begin with but then increased his intensity.

Raine whimpered. She thrashed beneath him in a way that told him she was unable to control the desires of her own body. His fingers moved to squeeze her nipple hard and she screamed aloud.

"Did I hurt you?" Miguel whispered into her tangled hair.

Raine's eyelids fluttered. Her lips parted. She shook her head as she clung to him, her arms laced around his shoulders. Then her hands moved over his broad back, across his buttocks and his hips. Miguel flinched and groaned as her fingers fondled his testicles. She stopped, and whispered, "I want to use my mouth on you, as you have done to me."

Miguel's eyes shone with gut-deep pleasure and searing passion. He kissed her lips, and rolled off her and onto his back. "Are you certain?"

Raine stared at his the rigid length of his erection, standing proud, and her smile brought with it a sense of triumph. Her whole body was rocked with flood of white-hot sensations. A trickle of liquid escaped from between her thighs. Then she nodded and he moaned deep in his throat as she put her lips there. His body jerked as she slid her tongue up and down his swollen shaft. She sucked the tip and let her tongue swirl along the slit at the top, learning him with her tongue, her teeth, her lips.

He groaned, a suffocated sound of barely controlled restraint. His body grew tense and his chest heaved, his scrotum had become compact and wrinkled and had begun to ascend toward his body cavity. Her eyes already heavy-lidded with desire, Raine marveled at the hardness of him, so engorged with need that she wanted to suck him deep and hard — then all thought fled. Miguel's hands were on her waist, raising her, lifting her, positioning her on top of his hard shaft. She responded by sinking to her knees, supporting her weight evenly on both legs, clasping his hips and thighs with her calves. She used both hands for leverage, entwined over his chest, as she sought the hot organ already impressed on her hot wet mouth of passion.

Very gently and slowly he inserted his hard shaft into her, deeper, more utterly than ever before. In a flashing heartbeat, her breathing changed, intensified, she felt like he wasn't just filling her vagina but her entire body. On instinct, she began rotating her hips and gripped his hard flesh with her interior muscles. She moved up and down his length, then tried to ride him. But he thrust his splendid arousal to match her movements, and grasped her hips with his hands. It was he who began moving her body with his hands, his hips, back and forth, from side to side. With each thrust her swollen folds brushed against his dense, dark hair at the base of his shaft, bringing her closer and closer to paradise.

Raine's eyes were half-closed, as riotous sensation flooded her mind. Those feelings intensified when he allowed her control over his hard rigid length and began stimulating her sex and her breasts with his fingers, goading her climax. When the first faint contractions of pleasure came, he moved faster, and keeping himself inside her, Miguel rolled on top of her. Enveloped in her warm throbbing flesh, with her arms wrapped around his back, her legs locked around his hips, he continued his slow rhythm. He caressed her tenderly, and her lips parted with the rapture she was experiencing. She met each of his forceful, measured strokes. His breathing was harsh and rapid, his masculine scent touched her nostrils, his warm whispers brushed her neck, long tendrils of damp dark curls

touched her cheeks and forehead. She returned his kisses, crushed her mouth to
his, ran her hands over his magnificent, hard frame as it slammed against her
tender flesh.

She stiffened, keening a soft cry of rapture as she experienced ecstasy. With
a loud groan he matched her new rhythm, following her, until at the peaking last
he drove one final thrust, and held himself hard against her. With his mouth
pressed his mouth against hers, he filled her with his warmth.

At last he moved off her and lay beside her, propped up on one elbow. He
ran a light finger down her belly. "God, you are so beautiful," he breathed.

She sighed a small delicious sound and Miguel smiled against her mouth.
Wordlessly he lay back sated and pulled an exhausted and dazed Raine against
him, so that her cheek rested on his shoulder.

Raine gazed at his face, drinking in ever detail of his exquisite features. His
glance of tenderness made her realize how much power he had over her, and it
was a power that could destroy her. Because she knew, in that resplendent
moment that this was what she had wanted from the first time she'd seen his
strength, his wildness, his black gaze on hers. The thought stunned her. She
knew she was falling helplessly in love with him.

Raine turned her head to the side and looked away from him, not wanting
him to see her tears. Tears of fear, and shame. She knew nothing about this man
except that he was a revolutionary, an outlaw, and she had freely given herself
to him. Worse, when she was with him, she forgot everything but her all-
consuming desire. The shame surrounded her, seemed to encompass her soul.

"You can let go of me now," she bit out. She felt his muscles tense under her
fingers as he released her.

"As you wish, *mademoiselle*," he growled as if insulted, hurt, and moved
away from her. He said nothing as he dropped her clothes over her naked form.

Immediately, Raine realized he'd mistaken her show of emotions. He assumed
she'd come to her senses and wanted nothing more than to get away from him.
And that is exactly what she'd allow him to believe. She had to. She turned
away and dressed before he could see the pain in her expression.

Miguel shot to his feet and shoved his shirt in his trousers. He needed to
stay away from her! What kept pulling him back? Attraction? Definitely.
Loneliness? Maybe. Need? Hell, he didn't know! He couldn't believe he'd let
her get to him like that. Had he lost his mind? Apparently.

He quickly increased the distance between them by five paces. Although he
had his anger under control, for the moment, his restraint was not limited and
Raine seemed to have a special gift for inciting abuse. He needed that distance
when he looked at her. It was not that he did not want her anymore — he
wanted her all right, more than he had ever wanted any woman. That was the
damn problem!

The realization shocked him. Miguel stared at her, his mind fogging over.
He'd never thought such wanting of another human being was possible. What
the devil was the matter with him? Never mind that Raine was a woman, and not
remotely responsible for the death of his family. She was Armand LeFleur's

daughter, and he was responsible for the murder of his family. He hated her for it. He hated himself at that moment, hated the humiliation he felt over wanting her.

He eyed her, waiting for his temper to cool. She didn't say a word. Then he grabbed her hand and pulled her against him hard. She gasped.

"Try my patience like that again," he hissed, paused to raise an eyebrow, "and I will make you sorry you did."

"Please, release me," Raine moaned, tears streaming down her face.

Miguel pushed her hand away. At that moment, he disliked himself. Disliked the things this woman made him feel and do. Dammit, he wasn't a cruel man, and what he'd just done was cruel. His conscience burned with a great need for redemption. Christ, he had not even thought he had a conscience any longer! Damned if he didn't feel compelled to explain his hatred for the French, to tell her about his family. Pain burst like fire from his eyes as he said, "Your beloved French soldiers slaughtered my family."

Raine gasped, scooted back. "S-such terrible things happen in a war."

He shook his head as he moved forward and made up for the slight distance she had put between them. "No. This was not a result of the war, my sweet. My family died only because your countrymen view murder as some sick form of entertainment."

Raine inhaled sharply. Was it possible? Then she knew it was. The truth was written all over his face. Now, she knew why he fought as a revolutionary.

Shame came over her again, crushing her soul. No wonder he hated the French. He had every right. She couldn't comprehend it, couldn't accept it. Never. What kind of men would do such a thing?

Though she knew it wouldn't help, she needed to acknowledge her feelings with words. Turning solemn eyes to him, she said, "I'm s-so sorry."

Miguel had gotten used to the pain, as had others who'd lost loved ones in the war. He knew it would be more intense talking about it, but he wasn't prepared for it to be mirrored in someone else's eyes. He pretended the sympathy he saw there didn't exist.

"I am too." His tone was pure acid. "Unfortunately, they are gone now and I cannot do a damned thing to bring them back. But I will have my revenge, I promise you that."

Raine moved toward him. "I understand your anger, and I don't blame you for your hatred." She raised her hand to cup his face.

"Don't," he said sharply, as he grabbed her wrist. His gaze met hers. "I warned you once. I will not do it again."

Chapter Six

Miguel swore under his breath and mounted his horse. Raine hadn't noticed before but it was one of the finest horses she'd ever seen, quite large for its species, even larger than her father's large bay mustang. Rich black in color, it had a racy, powerful build, and a fine head with fiery eyes. At first she thought the horse to be mean, but she soon saw that he had just had spirit. Like his master, she thought with chagrin.

Settled now, Miguel extended a hand down to Raine. She took it and he swung her up into the saddle behind him. With a grumble, he kicked the horse into a run .

For two days they slept little and spoke even less. Without looking at her, Miguel had asked twice how she was doing. Raine had replied both times with an abrupt "Fine." Yet she wasn't fine. She was exhausted and dirty. Her hair was thick with sweat from Miguel's wide brim hat, which she wore at his insistence to protect her face. She longed for some shade to hide her from the sun, but the only sign of life was an occasional roadrunner. They crossed one river and refilled the canteens. After that, the land grew more dry and barren. The few shrubs and trees they had seen gave way and revealed a flatter land that was mostly rock, white sand, and fissures in the earth.

They ate in the saddle when they had the chance, something dry and hard, called "jerky," and drank water from canteens. Raine didn't want to know what this meat-like substance was; it was awful. But she was in no position to complain and they did stop her stomach from grumbling.

Just because Miguel was the handsomest man she'd ever seen was no reason to lose her common sense, Raine thought as they plunged into the gathering dust. Nevertheless, her senses had quite deserted her. Maybe it was because she, a supposedly well-bred lady, was becoming aware of her feelings for this revolutionary.

Raine reasoned that even if she wasn't in the middle of Mexico, and a captive being taken to a hideout, that this man wasn't for her. She was a countess of noble parentage. Louis Napoleon's cousin, for heaven's sake! The Emperor of Mexico's wife, Carlotta, was her friend. Miguel was what? An outlaw. A revolutionary. A renegade, hellbent on revenge. No, he was not for her.

Since she was a normal young woman, perhaps her attraction to this wild man only meant she was starved for a man's affection. Then she thought, after what she'd done, what man of her station would want her? If one would want her, would she want him after she'd had a man like Miguel?

Oh! She'd never been so confused in her life.

It didn't take her long to decide that ignoring her disturbing train of thought was better.

The trouble was, she was settled firmly on Miguel's lap with both her legs dangling over the mustang's left side. With his arms cinched around her stomach, she was hotly aware of the contact between her derriere and his strong thighs. She didn't feel well at all. In fact, Raine was certain she had a fever.

Miguel wasn't exactly comfortable either. As he rode hard over the arid land, heading toward Copper Canyon and the misty reaches the Sierra Madre held, he wished there was some way he could position Raine so that she wouldn't touch the ever-revealing part of his anatomy. Putting her behind him was out of the question, because she'd already dozed off once and almost killed herself when she fell off the horse. Luckily, he'd caught the waistband of her skirt before she'd hit the ground. When he'd hauled her back onto his lap, she'd hit him, as if it were his fault she'd fallen asleep.

He checked the Colt in his holster, making sure it lay ready to fire. The journey had been uneventful, but there was no guarantee it would remain so. Without thinking, he drew Raine closer to him.

Raine shifted and slipped comfortably into his crotch. It was the best position she had been in since they started riding. Then she realized that her hip rested against something hard. She twisted around and their gazes met and held. Her eyes widened with understanding, while his, wild and bright, searched through the silent, sweeping veils of dust. For long moments, she listened to the labored breathing that spoke of Miguel Chavez's unease.

Miguel cleared his throat. "I'm sorry," he said, and shifted her back to her original position. "It is not something I can control."

Raine's heart raced, and she felt hot all over. "Oh." The word came out on a breathless whisper.

Miguel narrowed his eyes against the sun's brilliant reflection off the sand. "We will be safe soon."

She smiled a little. "I'm glad, I don't feel well."

"I know. You're just exhausted."

Raine shook her head. "No, that's not it," she insisted. "I'm afraid I am becoming ill. I think I have a fever. My whole body burns from the inside out."

Miguel raised his hand and touched her forehead. She might very well be ill. Stress could bring on a myriad of physical and mental ailments, and Raine had been under a great deal of stress.

He sighed. "You don't have a fever. What do you mean, your body burns from the inside out?"

Raine fidgeted in his lap and wet her lips in an unconscious, sensuous way. "I don't know what I mean. I just do," she snapped and pursed her lips into a pout.

If she wet her lips that way again, Miguel knew he would kiss her. The thought of her running her tongue over his lips made him groan. Just then, she squirmed, and switched her bottom sideways.

"Will you sit still?" he growled.

"I don't feel well and I'm uncomfortable," she complained. "Do you think I am sick?"

Her question interrupted his thoughts, and he stared at her for a long moment. She blushed, and picked up the material of her skirt to wipe the sweat from her upper lip.

Miguel thought, she doesn't know what she feels is desire. "No, I don't think you're sick," he snapped, pulling himself back to reality. "You will be fine after some rest." He could only hope he would.

Pulling a hanky from her skirt pocket, Raine fanned herself. She'd give everything she owned to be able to take a bath. The sweat trickled down her sides and between her breasts, and she pressed the cloth against her throat to absorb the dampness.

That night he kept as much distance between them as possible.

Around noon the following day, Miguel finally reined them to a halt at the top of a cliff. "We're here," he said.

The big mustang shifted beneath them, and Raine gazed down at Copper Canyon for the first time. She saw a deep, wide canyon with green plateaus and a swiftly flowing river. "It's so beautiful," she breathed. "Where are we?"

Miguel's face broke into a broad grin. "The Tarahumara Indians call it Barraca de Cobre."

"They should have called it God's country," she replied, in awe of the beautiful land below them.

"You have heard of the Grand Canyon in the United States, no?" Miguel asked.

Raine nodded. "In the Colorado Territory."

"Well, this canyon system is five times larger than the Grand Canyon. It has an interesting history, too. Many Indian tribes have lived here over the years, and there's a hidden village, called Batopilas, just below the rapids cascading over those huge boulders.

A few minutes later, Miguel guided the horse down into the tropical bottom of the Canyon, past the rapids, to Batopilas. As far as Raine could see, it was a village of dusty roads and adobe huts with smoking chimneys. Just inside the village, they stopped to rest the horse. Miguel stroked the big animal, an action that Raine guessed was second nature to him. He crooned softly in Spanish to his mustang.

As they continued, Raine saw Indians, cowboys, a few Jesuit missionaries and lean prospectors with their heavily laden mules. She supposed they would soon be on their way in search of more silver.

"This is your home?" she asked Miguel.

"This is Batopilas," he clarified. "I live a short distance from here."

"Remarkable," Raine said, never having seen anything like it. "This place is *charmant*."

Miguel smiled. "*Sí*."

He didn't know why the French language, which had so annoyed him before, was suddenly adorable, but it was. Shaking his head, his gaze swept her.

Raine's filthy blouse was a few buttons shy of its original number and was plastered indecently to her, showing much of her well-shaped breasts. Positioned on his lap as she was, her skirt and petticoats were hiked up so high they showed a good amount of her slender calves and ankles. Her thick hair was in total disarray, knotted in back like a rope with the long ebony tail slung over her right shoulder.

Miguel thought she was very different from the highborn French lady he'd rescued from the bandits, three and a half days ago, but he'd also never seen a woman of greater beauty than she appeared to him right now.

Raine looked over her shoulder at him, and he smiled. He thought she would be pale and near tears by now. Instead, she sat across his lap with her shoulders back and her head held high even in her disheveled state. Miguel admired her. She wasn't all fluff like most of the ladies he'd known.

He not only had respect for Raine, he had desire. God yes, desire for her. He hadn't felt any of this in as long as he could remember. Shouldn't feel any of it. Couldn't afford to feel any of it. Eventually he'd use Raine for the revenge he needed so desperately. And he would be whole again.

Fifteen minutes later, having left the town of Batopilas behind, Miguel and Raine reached his hacienda. Raine pulled his hat farther down to shield her eyes as they passed through a gate in the massive adobe walls and emerged into the courtyard. As she looked around, she gasped in delight.

Sunlight painted the house in a golden glow. In the center of the yard, surrounded by large trees, stood an enormous fountain. As the house and its courtyard shared the skies with the giant mountains, so did the fountain's cascading waterfall.

"Mon Dieu! This is Paradise," she exclaimed, more to herself than to Miguel.

Miguel's expression suddenly became serious. "Paradise and Hell can both be earthly. Unfortunately, we carry them with us wherever we go."

His comment took Raine by surprise. How could anyone be so cynical in the midst of this incredible beauty?

"You are obviously a man of great wealth. Why do you continue to fight in the Revolution?" Raine hesitated. "Or is the Revolution why you are so wealthy?"

Miguel's smile was sardonic. "No, the Revolution is not why I have money. My family had money long before they came to Mexico. Most of it is still in Spain." He looked away from her. "Although the French soldiers took everything they could when they murdered my family."

Suddenly Raine wanted to cry for him. And for her. Not even for a moment, she knew, would he ever forgive her for something she had no part in. She gave him an understanding look, and said in the merest of whispers, "I am sorry about your family, you know that, but I don't understand why you have to punish me for their deaths."

Silence fell like lightening between them. Raine gripped her hands together, desperately trying to sort out the dilemma she was in.

Miguel was angry, but in a perverse way, the emotion pleased him. Being angry with her was safer. Already his blood boiled, and she had yet to stay with him one night in the hacienda. How could a French woman, beautiful or not, raise such long-dead emotions in him?

Not for the first time, he wondered if he could use her for revenge or exert the self-control needed to give her back her freedom.

Raine lifted her chin with indifference, although her eyes misted with unshed tears. "How long will you keep me here?"

He was becoming used to broken trains of thought. "Until I tire of your company, and make an exchange with the French."

She winced.

Welcoming the anger he felt, the look Miguel shot her was hard.

Raine's response was immediate. "I want to go home."

"No."

Tears filled her eyes. "I hate you! You are a...a pighearted man!"

Raine stared. Miguel stared back. His jaw clinched and his gaze became intense. "Pigheaded," he corrected.

She snatched Miguel's hat from her head and slapped it back on his. "I may not speak the slang of your country perfectly, but I am not so stupid as to believe the only reason you are keeping me is revenge!"

Miguel's eyes shot daggers. "Oh, it's revenge all right. I will extract it when I am ready."

Raine's head snapped back as if Miguel had slapped her. With a disgusted look, she jumped off his lap. The trouble was, her legs had so far to go, and were so weak from the days of riding, that when she hit the ground her ankle folded. She screamed, and tried to keep her balance, but ended up crumpling to the hard ground on her hands and knees.

Miguel vaulted off the horse and caught her head just before it hit the ground. His anger fled. Dammit! Had she made it through hell only to be overcome by exhaustion or heat stroke? He shook her gently. Guilt and fear overwhelmed him.

He laid her gently across his lap, and smoothed the hair away from her face. Raine moaned and her lashes fluttered.

"Are you all right?" he asked, not knowing why his heart was pounding so dammed hard. For a moment, Raine looked at him blankly, vaguely, then tears of pain welled up in her eyes.

"Where does it hurt?" he asked as he stroked her long tresses. She was still staring at him, and he remembered it was his fault she had jumped from the horse. Had she wanted to get away from him that badly?

"My ankle," she said with exasperation.

The doctor within him resurfaced with astonishing speed. "Let me see."

Pushing his hand aside, she glared back at him. "The foot, it is fine."

"Sit still," Miguel said as she tried to rise. "It could be broken."

Raine stopped struggling. He took her foot in his hand and removed her suede shoe. With gentle motions he examined her ankle.

She gasped from the pain, but refused to cry.

He was sorry to have to hurt her and admired her fortitude. Fortunately, he didn't think it was broken, but it was a bad sprain and had already started to swell.

"Does it hurt much?"

Gritting her teeth, she shrugged. "It only needs some ice on it."

Miguel shifted on the balls of his feet to face her, and for the briefest of moments, he had an image of Raine with her arms outstretched, a smile on her face, waiting for him on the steps of the hacienda.

"Sorry, mademoiselle, the icebox is back in the civilized world. Here we have no such luxuries. Elevation, a splint, and bedrest will have to do."

Before Miguel knew what she was doing, Raine tried to stand — only to slump to the ground again.

The muscle in his jaw twitched. "All right," he announced. "If you are trying to make me mad, you have."

Brushing her hair from her face, Raine pursed her lips but held her tongue.

Miguel continued, "If you persist in being so stubborn, you will break your ankle. Then it will have to be set."

He said nothing more, only reached down and lifted her into his arms.

Raine stiffened, every muscle tensed. Miguel cocked an eyebrow. "I'm warning you. You had better not give me another moment's grief!"

Her mouth opened to protest, but she thought better of it when she saw the taut lines around his mouth and the threatening look in his eye. She hugged herself instead as he strode purposefully for the house. Raine felt she could safely say that things couldn't possibly get any worse. Her filthy hair had long ago fallen down, her clothes torn and rumpled. She was in the middle of nowhere, in a hideout no less, with the most difficult man who had ever lived. Not to mention that she was hungry, in pain, in desperate need of a good scrubbing, and needed to go to the bathroom!

Miguel mounted the front steps two at a time. When they reached the door of the hacienda, he called out something in rapid Spanish. As he raised his knee and kicked the door open, an older man appeared.

"*Bienvenido, Señor.* Welcome home," he said.

"Carlos, I need some materials to make a splint. After you get them, would you please bring them up to the bedroom and then tend to my horse?"

"*Sí,*" the older man said, and headed toward the back of the house.

Miguel climbed the stairs to the second story of the house and proceeded down the hallway. He shoved the door to a room open, went in, and placed Raine on a large four poster bed.

Chapter Seven

A small breeze came through the windows and labored to stir the stifling heat. Miguel knocked the dust from his hat and tossed it onto the dresser. He propped Raine up on the feather pillows, then squatted beside the bed. "This will hurt, but I have to remove your stocking."

Raine lifted her chin in a stubborn movement. "I don't think a splint is necessary. My ankle is just sore. It doesn't even hurt much anymore."

His manner was deliberate, as he raised her skirts to her knees. When he lifted her foot and removed her stocking, she had to bite her lip to keep from crying out in pain.

Miguel cleared his throat. "Since you are in no shape to argue, why don't you leave the diagnosis and treatment of your injury to me?"

Carlos came into the room. He carried a tray filled with medicines and the materials Miguel had requested. Putting it on the bedside table, he asked in Spanish, "Is there anything else I can do?"

"Yes," Miguel said. "This is Señorita Raine. She will be staying with us for a while. Would you please prepare a bath for her?"

Carlos looked toward Raine and smiled. "Sí, señor."

When Miguel shifted his attention back to Raine, she was staring out of the window. Suddenly, he wanted to kiss her again, let her know that everything would be all right. Tightening his control, he said, "After your bath, I will splint your ankle. But I am going to give you something for pain first, so it won't be too bad."

Raine's emotions gave way, and she shot him an angry look. "No! I don't want anything. I want you to leave me alone." Her eyes brimmed with tears.

Miguel swore under his breath. Ignoring what she'd said, he straightened to pour a spoonful of something she assumed was for pain.

Not wanting to take anything, she shook her head stubbornly. "You will need it," he insisted and she believed him. Giving in, she opened her mouth, and when she swallowed, shivered in protest at the bitter taste.

She lowered her gaze and picked at the bedspread with a fingernail. "I-I need to use the bathroom, and not just to wash," she said, her voice as thin as thread.

Miguel raked his hand through his hair. "I'm sorry, but I don't have a bathroom," he said. "That, along with the ice, is back in the civilized world. We do things simply here in Copper Canyon. You will bathe in the kitchen and, since I have no toilet, a chamber pot will have to do."

Raine stiffened. She opened her mouth to protest again, and Miguel cut her off with a steely look. "I have some things I need to do downstairs. You had better stay put until I get back."

His tone invited no argument.

A few minutes later, Miguel bent down and slid one arm beneath her knees. With the other wrapped securely around her back, he lifted her easily into his arms.

He looked her straight in the eye, and warned, "Don't try my patience."

Raine gnawed on her lower lip. Miguel carried her straight to the kitchen at the back of the house, a large airy room that contained a table, four chairs and a cozy adobe fireplace. When she saw the big copper tub filled with steaming water, her arms tightened around his neck.

"I'll be right back," he said, as put her in a chair.

Miguel left the kitchen and went down the hall. He returned with a chamber pot and placed it in a small room off the kitchen. Needing to relieve herself, Raine stood and started to hop toward it.

Firm hands grabbed her shoulders and prevented any forward motion. "Stop being so stubborn and let me help you."

The pain medicine had taken effect and Raine was pleasantly drowsy. She smiled, as he lifted her into his strong arms again. Common sense told her that at this point, it really didn't matter how she got to the chamber pot as long as she got there. Besides, being in his arms again was delightful.

Miguel set her down carefully, just inside the doorway. "All right, in you go, and don't step on that foot. Hold onto the pantry shelf for support."

Raine was left with conflicting emotions waging war in her mind, a sweet confusion holding sway. She couldn't seem to drag her gaze from the strikingly attractive maleness he exuded.

He cocked a dark eyebrow. "I can see the pain medicine is working. Do you think you can manage?"

Raine's answer was an endearing smile and a slow nod.

Miguel gave her a sideways glance. "I don't trust this sudden calm, whether you are under the influence of laudanum or not." He released her, but not before saying, "I will wait right here."

Though she'd been hugging each enchanting memory of the times she had spent in his arms, his comment brought her back to the present. *Mon Dieu,* Raine thought, so mortified that he might overhear her relieving herself!

When she was done, Raine shyly opened the door, and Miguel carried her back to a chair by the tub. On another chair, close by, were two large towels, a washrag, a wide-tooth comb, and a bar of lavender soap. A woman's things, she thought with dismay. Although refusing to use the necessities would be foolish, she would rather scrub her body with lye and brush her hair with twigs than use his mistress's things.

She lifted her gaze to his. "That soap and comb can't be yours."

Miguel stoked his stubbled chin. "No, you're right. The soap and comb belong to Carlos' wife. I have also asked her to lend you some clean clothes until we can get you some new ones of your own."

"I'm so thrilled," Raine said. "I always enjoyed dressing up like a gypsy for the Masquerade."

Miguel shook his head as he rolled up his sleeves and then helped her to a standing position.

Without the slightest hesitation, his fingers went directly to the buttons that remained on her blouse. Raine's eyes grew wide, and she slapped at his hands.

"What do you think you are doing?" she cried, and clutched at her already torn bodice.

Miguel glared down at her and stubbornly refused to remove his hands. "I am undressing you."

She gritted her teeth. "I-I can manage on my own!"

"No, you can't." With a swift tug, he snatched her blouse open, sending the few remaining buttons across the room.

An ugly expression crossed her face. "You bastard."

She snarled as he grabbed her around the waist and hauled her up against him. Her legs bumped his hard, muscular thighs, but she hardly felt the stab of pain it caused in her ankle. He turned his dark gaze to her and she saw desire in it, along with anger and frustration.

"Stop swearing at me. It isn't becoming."

Miguel's eyes seemed to dance, just for a moment. "What are you so damn angry about? You were more than willing to lie beneath me outside in the middle of the desert."

The reminder of her weakness toward him made Raine even more angry. "I wish you would go to hell," she said in a shaky voice.

Miguel was tense. "If I believed such a place existed, I am quite sure I would get there without any help from you," he said bitterly. He undid the button at the back of her skirt and tugged it free. It fell to the ground about her feet.

Raine's eyes turned a darker shade of blue as the significant bulge in the crotch of his pants pressed hard against her stomach. He pulled her more fully against him and held her. "I'm sorry," he said. "I shouldn't have done that."

The tear that slid down her cheek tore at his heart, the heart Miguel no longer thought he had. He swore softly between his teeth and backed up, but still held onto her so that she wouldn't fall. Looking looked down at her ankle, he saw that it was more swollen than before, and it had turned an angry red and purple. He knew if it wasn't for the laudanum, she'd be in an extreme amount of pain. Even with the medicine, she must be feeling some pain.

Placing a finger beneath her delicate chin, he urged her to look at him. When she finally did, he could barely stand to see the way she felt about him, mirrored there. "Raine, your ankle is getting worse. I have to get you into bed as soon as possible. Will you please let me help you bathe?"

She gave a defeated sigh. With a lowering of her eyelids, shaky fingers undid the tiny pearl buttons at the front of her chemise, then untied the ribbon of her pantalettes. Not knowing what to say, Miguel helped her remove the underthings before lifting her into the tub.

As the water covered her body and his arms, she sucked in her breath. A heavy silence hung between them as he knelt close to the tub, and to Raine. When he caught her pained glance and held it, he saw she was woozy from the medication. "Don't worry. I'll be careful. I know your ankle hurts."

Again, he was shocked at his reaction to this woman. Why was he always so eager to make love to Raine LeFleur? he wondered. He had spent the last three years of his life hating everything French, determined to have revenge on her father, and her people. It couldn't be just because she was beautiful. There were lovely women all across Mexico. Still, he had some strange attraction to her, an attraction far removed from lust. Raine was his enemy's daughter, he reflected. Taking her virginity was certainly an act of revenge, but she had come willingly. Was that what gave him such driving desire, and the need for her to give herself to him again, and again?

Miguel shook his head. "Just relax. I will have you washed and back in bed in just a few minutes."

Raine took a deep breath, rested her head against the tub wall, and closed her eyes.

He found himself staring—just staring. His gaze devoured every inch of Raine's splendid beauty as she lay gleaming white in the tub before him. Her thick, dark mane swirled about the water and veiled her breasts, which were now revealed high and creamy, tipped by small taut amber-colored nipples. His gut tightened, his heart thundered, and blood rushed to thicken his shaft. It was almost his undoing.

He groaned and stiffly adjusted his position by the tub. A flood of crimson swept over Raine's face, but she didn't say a word. Nor did she open her eyes.

Annoyed with himself, and with her, for getting into this situation in the first place, Miguel swiped up the soap and washrag and leaned over the tub. The water, resting a few inches below her nipples, as her entire body was presented to him, so slender, so delicate, so…beautifully feminine.

Miguel slammed the washrag into the water, and her eyes shot open. He worked up enough lather to cover the entire top of the water with an opaque film. Then he pressed the washrag against her stomach and rubbed with a vengeance. He felt her shiver at his contact with her naked skin.

He eased the pressure. After all, he was the one who had so stupidly insisted on washing her. It was not her fault that he was so hard his shaft cramped beneath his pants, making it increasingly impossible for him to stand—or kneel. He was the reason she was lying there naked, like a wanton, her breasts bobbing about with every movement of the washrag, making him to want to slip an arm beneath her back and lift her until he could take those perfect nipples in his mouth and suckle them she screamed with wanting him. She hadn't wanted him to help her at all! Dammit! Why hadn't he listened to her?

Raine bit her lip as desire visibly climbed up her neck and into her cheeks.

"I'll be finished soon," Miguel said.

Finally, he stopped scrubbing and slid his hand under her long length of her hair, letting it fall over the edge of the tub to pool on the floor. When he placed a folded towel under her neck, Raine mumbled a shaky thank you.

A cold sweat broke-out on Miguel's forehead as he ran the thin, soapy cloth over her soft skin. Goosebumps appeared on her white flesh. He took a deep, unsteady breath. As he bathed her, it was as if nothing were between his hand and her slick skin.

Raine gasped when he touched a sensitive spot on her inner thigh. She grabbed the hand holding the washrag and snapped at him, "Could you just help me wash my hair so we can be done with this?"

She jerked the washrag away from him so fast, it went flying across the room and sloshed to the floor. Miguel's head jerked up just as fast to stare at her. The fire present in her eyes told him that she was feeling much the same sensations he was.

Raine sat up and raised her knees in an attempt to cover herself, but the movement must have succeeded in causing her a great amount of pain. She groaned as she fell back against the tub.

"Take it easy." Miguel stroked her hair, then stood. "I'll get a bucket of water, so I can wash your hair while it hangs outside the tub. I can finish faster that way."

Raine glared at him. "Oh, so now you are in a hurry, oui?"

"Oui!" he imitated gruffly. "And, I'm sure I do not need to explain why."

"Talk about well-laid plans," he muttered under his breath, walking away.

Ten minutes later, Miguel finished pouring the last of the clear water over Raine's hair. He threw down the empty bucket and stood over her. "When I bend down, you grab hold of my neck and I will lift you out of the tub."

When she wrapped her arms around his neck, he lifted her to a standing position. Quickly, he wrapped a large towel around her naked body. He looked up, eyes narrowed, at her sharp intake of breath. She lifted her chin in a stubborn movement as he hauled her into his arms and headed for the stairs.

In the bedroom, Miguel placed her on the turned-down bed and went to remove the towel. Raine tried to evade him, and he grabbed a fistful of the towel and snatched it from around her. Air swept over her naked skin, and he could smell her clean lavender-scented body.

"Hell! You can forget your modesty now, because there is not one part of your body that I have not already seen!"

Raine saw heat darken his bronze skin and heard him groan as he covered her with a quilt. Relief at no longer being naked in front of him spread through her and she felt heated color rush back into her face. The quilt was warm and soft, and carried his scent. She was surprised to find that inhaling his scent could give her such a wonderful sensation. Her gaze lingered on his face for a moment.

Miguel sat next to her on the side of the bed. With an audible sigh, he wiped his forehead with the back of his hand and retrieved the same dark bottle and a spoon as before from the bedside table. But this time when he uncorked the bottle, he measured a considerable amount into a large spoon, and held it out to her.

Raine made a childish face, and when she opened her mouth, he popped in the spoon.

"Swallow," he commanded with an imperious tone.

Holding his stare, she swallowed, but grimaced and shuddered as the medicine went down her throat.

"It's laudanum," Miguel snapped. "It will help with the pain when I splint your ankle, and it will also help you get some rest. It won't kill you."

"Imagine my relief," she returned.

Before putting the bottle back on the table, Miguel thought briefly about taking a slug or two of it himself. When he turned back to her, Raine's thick lashes swept up, and the blue gaze that fastened on him was not only lovely, but somber and searching.

He moved closer and touched her cheek. "I'll try very hard not to hurt you."

Raine's lips parted as if she were about to say something. Unable to stop himself, he gathered her warm body into his arms. When she sighed a delicious small sound of surrender, Miguel smiled against her mouth and lifted his hand to stroke her neck. He caressed her back, and his fingers slid over her bare shoulders toward her breasts. With deliberation he pushed the cover away from her skin and toyed with her nipples until she quivered. In response, Raine's arms laced around his neck and pulled him to her. She pressed her tongue to his. Her hands moved down his shoulders, closed around his back, as though she would press herself to him forever.

Miguel was relieved to hear footsteps on the stairs, for although he would have liked nothing better than to continue, now was not the time. "Someone is coming," he whispered into her tangled wet hair.

Raine's eyelids fluttered, her lips still parted with desire. He forced himself to release her and cover her nakedness with the quilt. When he gazed into her eyes, they were wide with unanswered desire and disappointment at his release, and more than a little glassy from the effects of the laudanum.

It was then that he knew he had to keep his distance from her while she was hurt. He didn't trust himself, and he could no longer ignore that he wanted her to stay with him. Something he knew could never be possible.

A swift knock on the door preceded Carlos' wife into the room. Her many silver bracelets shivered and sang with every movement. Halting at the end of the bed, she smiled at Raine and handed Miguel a stack of clothes just as colorful as the ones she was wearing.

Miguel put the clothes on the end of the bed. "Thank you, Anna Maria."

Again, the older woman smiled. "Carlos said that you would need help with the señorita."

Miguel nodded. "Yes, I do. Will you stay?"

Anna Maria nodded. "Sí, of course, señor."

Suddenly curious as to why Raine remained quiet, Miguel turned and saw that she was sleeping peacefully beneath the sunlight that poured through the window. The second dose of laudanum had produced the desired effect and he was relieved.

He worked swiftly, and carefully, but even with the extra dose of laudanum, Raine winced and groaned several times in her sleep as he and Anna Maria put a gown on her and wrapped her ankle. Miguel hissed a curse and released a thin breath every time he witnessed her pain.

When they were finished, he dismissed Anna Maria. "Thank you."

"*De nada*," she said and left, closing the bedroom door behind her.

Miguel was badly in need of a bath too, but when he left Raine's side it was only to move a chair close to the head of the big bed and sit beside her.

He frowned. She was pale again and her hair was a tangled mass about her head, since it had not been combed after the washing.

He leaned forward and checked her forehead and hands for fever. Thankfully, she had none. At least one thing was going in his favor today, he thought, and reached for the comb on the bedside table.

Miguel had never in his life combed a woman's hair, and he thought that he should probably have Anna Maria do it, but strangely, he wanted to do it himself. As he gently lifted Raine's head, he arranged her damp hair over the pillow. He could relax a little now that he'd splinted her ankle and she was sleeping peacefully.

When he gazed down at her, he was all too aware that her lips were pale. He knew he'd pushed her too hard during their long ride into of Copper Canyon, and more since she'd injured her ankle. She'd done amazingly well and he'd given her no credit at all. No preferential treatment for being a woman. He shook his head. With most women would have given him nothing but tears and sulking. But Raine, he thought grimly, had given as good as she'd received. And in return he'd let his temper get the best of him, just because he'd been hard, and hot, and frustrated.

Without thought, Miguel bent his head and kissed her lightly on the lips. Even in sleep they were full and soft against his. He had to force himself to close his heart against a passion he never knew existed. Before it consumed his very soul.

Miguel combed the tangles with great care, keeping the tugging as light as he could manage. He trailed his fingertips over the wet silkiness, noting how exquisite it was. How exquisite she was. The part of him that desperately wanted a closeness with this woman marveled again at her beauty. Though the practical part of him was furious with himself for wanting something that could only bring misery to them both. He decided to leave her alone to sleep. The laudanum would keep her in that unnatural state for several hours yet, and he needed as much time to convalesce as she did.

Chapter Eight

The next week was like sunshine after a storm and Raine's ankle healed rapidly. However, when word arrived that the war raging just outside the peacefulness of the hidden village was rapidly coming to a close, tensions returned.

Quite suddenly, twilight descended and bathed the hacienda in lavender moonlight. Miguel drew rein on his mustang and gazing up, toward the second floor, saw a faint light spilling from his bedroom window. The air carried the sweet desert scents of a midsummer night. For a moment, a half smile almost curved his lips. Then his thoughts changed direction. He stiffened and the horse jerked up his head and stomped on the hard packed dirt.

"Easy," Miguel murmured, and patted his mount's neck before dismounting.

As he climbed the front steps, he knew better than to pay any attention to the beguilements of summer because winter always followed. Of all people, he should know that, bitterly, he thought. Still, no matter how he tried to put a distance between himself and Raine, she still kept pace with him.

Miguel knew he should tell her the news, and right away. To wait any longer would only make things worse for him. Soon, he decided, to hell with it. All he could think of was Raine in his bed, and how he wanted long, slow, deep, wet kisses that lasted three days. But first, he went to the study and had two drinks, trying to avoid facing the fact that this all might end tonight.

Thirty-minutes later he walked into the bedroom. A small oil lamp burned a low flame; the room was cool now, night mixed with the dim light and created exotic shadows across the length of the room. He stood for a long time, listening to the muffled noises of his own breathing, and hers. She looked so peaceful in sleep, so fragile with her long dark lashes resting on her cameo cheeks.

Unbuttoning his shirt, his heart whispered, "Do you love me?"

Raine lay on her back with one arm thrown above her head, her ebony hair in enticing disarray on the white pillow case. She had an arresting profile, delicate, feminine, each beautiful feature well defined. He loved her full red mouth. Gazing at her lips, knowing how they tasted, how soft they were against his, made his member grow throbbing and thick, strain painfully against his tight pants.

He gave a low groan, as he watched with rapt fascination, the slow, even intakes of breath. His gaze moved over every inch of her. From the mahogany-streaked blackness of her hair that rippled over her shoulders, to the bare toes peeking out from the bottom of the cotton quilt.

Exhaling an expansive breath, Miguel removed his shirt and sat on the bed.

As he reached out to touch Raine in her sleep, kiss her neck softly, her breasts rose and fell above a narrow waist. They were round and firm beneath the cover, and filled his hands. He knew them by touch, smell, and taste. His sex was rigid and ready when her long-lashed eyes lifted, bright with startled vivacity.

Awakening, Raine encountered a hungry look in the soft glow of lamplight, and for a second, glimpsed the brief bewilderment of Miguel's emotions. Then, suddenly aware of the weight of his hand on her breast, her nipple tightened and she sucked in her breath. It seemed she'd lost the total knowledge of how to breathe, let alone speak.

His dark, muscled chest glistened with sweat. The moonlight drew dark contours along the defined lines of his stomach and shoulders. He lifted one eyebrow in silent question, and she waited for him to say something, remove his hand, anything. He didn't. His eyes boldly swept her figure, and she felt a flicker of tingling fire in her core.

He gave her a small smile, and the sight seemed to light up the room. Forgetting everything but him was so easy, heedless to all but desire. Uncertain, confused, and too aware of the dangers of succumbing to his seductive charm, she wondered how deeply her naive emotions were already entangled.

Miguel stood and stripped away the rest of his clothing, releasing the full length of his erection. Raine uttered a faint cry as she devoured him with her gaze. Her lips parted. Then the bed dipped under his weight. He moved closer, so close she felt his heated breath upon her neck. She gave a low groan of pleasure. He he caressed her with his hands, the movements skilled and sure, as ran his fingers down her soft curve of her of her breast. She shivered at the pulsating heat that raced deep inside her.

Angling his face, Miguel touched her lips, forcing her mouth open with his. He teased her senses with his tongue, as he continued to run his hands over her body, and lifted the soft cotton gown. She was breathless when he released her and took her face in his hands.

"I'm going to fill you with my flesh. If you want me to stop...you'd better tell me now."

The words alone sent blood rushing through Raine, her heart knocking against her chest. She wished he hadn't put it that way. It sounded much too ominous. But she didn't tell him to stop, she couldn't. She wanted him with all her heart and soul, if only for this one brief moment in time.

Raine's breath quickened. "Do you want me because I am French, and taking me is somehow revenge?"

He shook his head. "It has nothing to do with revenge. Not anymore," he whispered. "It has only to do with want and need."

Miguel removed her gown and settled the inside of his thighs on the outside of hers. A soft moan escaped her throat. The hardness of his stiff sex pressed against her, and was so demanding, it scattered the last of her wits. He took her hands and placed them around his waist. Slanting his lips over hers, he brushed them with a feather light touch.

She responded by running her hands up and down his warm muscular back, over his firm buttocks, between his legs, until her long fingers trailed across his taut sac and wrapped around his sturdy shaft.

With a low groan, he rested his face against the soft curve of her throat. "You have possessed me since the first moment I laid eyes on you. I'm no longer going to try to control it."

"I thought —" Raine stammered.

"You thought wrong."

At his words, tiny sparks burst within her. Something strange was happening, as strange as this part of the world and just as beautiful. She shoved against his chest, needing the room to breathe. Miguel allowed her space, but slid a hand up the back of her neck as his fingers closed around her silky mane of hair. His gaze raced down her body, and the intensity of it made her shiver.

Miguel hauled her close again, his hand trembled as he touched her cheek. "Before I ever touched you, I wondered if it were possible for your skin to feel as soft as it looks." He took her face in his hands, ran his thumbs over her jaw, pressed his lips to her forehead, her temple.

When he stopped and gazed at her, Raine saw every detail of emotion flicker in his eyes. First wanting, followed by resolve, then brief doubt, and finally just wanting. He rested his face against her breast and kissed it. His body quivered and his lids dropped shut as he twisted her face so that her head would rest in his hand as he took her mouth in his as if he'd been hungering for eternity.

This was no gentle lovemaking, it was hard and needy, and Raine could do nothing but open her mind and body to his. His mouth was hot, wet, and all consuming, his hands rough as they sought her breasts, and his touch burned a fiery path to her heart. Her nipples tightened deliciously. She cried out, moaned against his mouth, and the raw sound was one of pleasure not regret.

"You're so very beautiful," Miguel whispered.

Raine's body stiffened and shook. He kissed each part of her body, his tongue probed and titillated every soft region of bliss. She responded uncontrollably, shoving her fingers into the thickness of his raven locks and pulled them until he moved above her, gritted his teeth. Breathing as if he had run a hundred miles, he captured a taut nipple with his mouth and suckled needily. She arched her back moaning, entwined her fingers deeper still in the back of his hair, and pulled him desperately against her.

Her fingers tightened on his scalp the more he suckled. She wanted him to stop. She wanted him to fall on top of her and thrust his throbbing shaft deep inside her and pump out his lust between her legs. Sweet, hot need consumed her body. Wordlessly, she shifted her gaze to his as he straightened she saw his eyes were very wide and more black than she'd ever seen then before. His hands tightened around her waist and pulled back. He would not lose all control yet; she saw it in his gaze on her, heard it in the rasping of his breath.

A seething, hungry fire twisted in Raine's core. Air rushed out of her lips in a long sigh as they parted. She closed her eyes and waited. He touched the tip of his tongue to her eyelids and the unexpected caress stole her breath away. Softly, he stroked her thighs, touched the moistness of her sex, caressed her with his fingers. She raised her body up toward him as his fingers continued to explore her slick opening.

"I love every inch of you," Miguel breathed against her mouth.

Then he pressed the evidence of his arousal against her hips, his chest against her breasts, covering her with his love. He was heavy, full, hard, stirring with every beat of his heart. The telltale softening of Raine's body against his was unnerving and enthralling all at once. He needed her the way fire needed oxygen to burn. The thickening of his blood with passion made his voice low, almost rough, "Lay your head back and let me feel of all of you, your texture, taste of your essence."

Raine cried out as he moved down her body and ran his hands up the inside of her thighs, parting them. The touch of his mouth against the swollen wet folds startled her. Her breath caught when he took her sensitive organ gently between his teeth and flicked his tongue across it. The deep repeated sensuous penetrating and retreat of his tongue sent cascades of shimmering sensations through her. Any moment, she thought she would surely die from the pleasure.

Almost as quickly as the unexpected caress had begun, he retreated and came to her face, placing his thighs between hers, and pressing his hardness just inside the mouth of her sex. "Did I displease you?" he asked in a low voice.

"N-nothing could have pleased me more," she answered breathlessly, as the tip of her tongue traced the place where his teeth and tongue had touched her.

"Next time you will taste me."

"And, after I do…will you taste me again?" she asked seductively.

Miguel groaned. "Until you can no longer stand it."

The heated promise in his eyes caused a liquid fire to leap deep within her and escape her softness. A low sound tore from her throat. He moved his hand between their bodies and cupped her living heat with his palm. He watched with measured eyes, the fire created by his touch consumed her, drove her to near madness.

Miguel lowered his face and seduced her mouth with slow, sure strokes that echoed those of his hands. He made love to her with words, slid his wide, strong hands down the back of her thighs and with one swift motion he lifted her to his waist. She clutched his shoulders as he positioned her and wrapped her legs around him in a flurry of need. When he claimed her fully, he threw his head back with a fevered moan, but his taking of her was slow and tormenting and brought her even greater pleasure.

Raine was intoxicated as he moved inside her, withdrawing and gently filling her again. She made sounds like a woman in delirium. He gasped for air like a man near drowning. Her body heated by degrees and she moved around him, twisting, urging him on, her head tossing from side to side, her hands frantically clawing his thickly muscled back.

The pleasure, when it peaked this time, was so extreme that it sent her body racing far above the heavens on crazy streaks of bright light—so intense, she thought she couldn't stand it. Finally, her soul left her body and she fell back to earth sated and exhausted.

She was back just in time to see Miguel throw his head back and stiffen in her arms. After several deep, desperate thrusts, he gave a loud cry and convulsed within her before exhaustion claimed him and his knees gave way. They lay there together for a long time, breathless and trembling.

Sometime later, Miguel sat up on the edge of the bed and squeezed her hand. "There was a time when I couldn't imagine spending my life with anyone. Now, I can't seem to imagine spending my life without you. "

Raine couldn't believe her ears, and she was so much in love. But she had to know, "Do you love me?"

Miguel reached out and carressed her face. "I love you more than I ever imagined I could love another human being. Will you marry me?"

Raine put her arms around him and pulled him close, resting her head against his shoulder. "I love you, too," she said, "and I want to marry you...but what happens when the war is over. What about my father?

"There is something I must tell you," he said.

A shudder moved through Raine's body. His voice was calm, but there was something in it that raised fear in her heart. "W-what is it?"

Miguel took a deep breath. "When the Mexican soldiers came for me earlier today, it was to take me to General Juarez. The war is not officially over, but the last major battle has been fought."

"Are you certain?" Raine asked in soft voice. "They could be wrong."

"No, they're not wrong," he said, then hesitated. "I have seen it. Many men are dead on both sides; even more are injured."

Raine lifted her gaze to his. "Y-you went to a battlefield? Why?"

Miguel sighed, deeply. "Because I am a doctor, and men needed my help."

Again, Raine could not believe her ears. "B-but you are a revolutionary."

Teeth clenched against the pain, he nodded. "Only since this war began."

She gazed into the face she knew so well — and so little — listened to words that made no sense at all to her. Unwinding slowly from his embrace, she reached out to touch his arm with a trembling hand. "Do you know who led the French in this battle?"

Miguel lifted his hand and brushed a wayward tendril from her face. "Your father."

Raine gasped and her hand flew to her throat. Oh, God...Pápa! Tears streamed down her cheeks. "Tell me...is he alive?"

He took her in his arms and held her fast. "Yes, your father is fine. My men have him safely hidden, not too far from here."

Raine was unbelieving; she pulled away. But swiping at her tears, she couldn't help but feel a surge of hope. "H-he hasn't been taken to a prison?"

Miguel shook his head. "No, my sweet. It seems that General Juarez feels Mexico owes me a debt of gratitude. To repay this debt, he will overlook the escape of one French prisoner of war."

She touched his shoulder. "You did this for me...but why?"

Miguel smiled. "Because, I love you."

Raine moved to throw her arms around him, but he stopped her. "Now that you know your father is safe, and both of you are free to return to France, do you still want to marry me?"

For a moment Raine was at a loss for words. Then, she said, "You just try and rid yourself of me, Miguel Chavez."

The kiss he gave her was like lightning, striking her to the core. Then, without warning, Miguel jumped off the bed.

"Hurry and dress," he said. "I have a surprise for you. Something that I hope will prove to you how much I really do love you."

Raine scrambled to her knees. "Tell me what it is!"

"Like I said," replied Miguel, "It is a surprise."

She leaned forward and took a swipe at him, but missed. "You black-eyed devil! At least, give me a hint!"

Miguel wagged a finger and made a tsk-tsk sound. "If you want to know what it is, then hurry up."

They had barely reached the bottom of the long staircase when the front door swung open and Raine's heart caught in her throat.

She looked up and saw that a gray-haired man in a dusty uniform was standing just inside the doorway, staring at her as if he was stricken.

Raine's fingers flew to her mouth. "Pápa," she whispered.

About the author:

Susan Paul lives in south Georgia with her husband, two daughters and a cat named Gretzkitty. She models for Gayfers, holds a first degree black belt in Tae Kwon Do and took a gold medal at the 1995 National Championships in Atlanta. Some readers may remember her from Romantic Times Magazine's 1995 Booklovers Convention in Fort Worth, Texas where she posed in the Mr. Romance Cover Model Pageant with the winner, Rob Ashton.

She and her very own cover-model husband, James David Paul, are featured on Heather Cullman's bookmarks for her latest historical romance. Since she was a teenager, Susan has loved to curl up and read romance books — no one was surprised when she began to write them. If you are attending the 1996 Romantic Times' Booklovers Convention in Baton Rouge, you can see her in the Mr. Romance Cover Model Pageant, the costume competition, and autographing at the book fair.

Roarke's Prisoner

by Angela Knight

To my reader:
     Will there still be romance and passion in the future?
I hope so! Here's one vision of what may be in store for
future generations. Enjoy!

Chapter One

Captain Elise Morrell sat at her command center and wondered if she'd feel something beyond this numb defeat when the ship's engines exploded. She doubted it. Roarke's next blast would drown her star frigate in nuclear fire so fast none of them would even have time to feel the heat.

Around her, at the five horseshoe-shaped stations that surrounded her own, her bridge staff sat with bent heads and white faces, staring down at disastrous readouts as their hands darted over the controls. Vidscreens surrounded them with images of the chaos on the ship's lower decks as her people struggled to save the *Star Raker,* while on the primary screen ahead of them, the *Liberator* cruised through space, waiting for Roarke's order to destroy them.

Her private communications unit beeped, and Elise looked down at the vid inset in her station just as Henry Voronnin's face popped into view. Her second in command must have finally gotten a chance to report in. Elise had sent him down to lead the damage control teams, and she knew he had his hands full.

"How bad is it, Henry?" she asked.

He rubbed a big hand over his head, leaving a streak of soot on the hairless pink dome. Dark shapes raced around in the smoke behind him, training hand foamers at the tongues of flame licking up from equipment panels. "Well," Henry said, "we haven't blown up yet."

She winced. "I'd hoped the sensors were exaggerating."

"They weren't. That last shot turned the drive room into an inferno. We lost the entire engineering crew, not to mention the engines themselves."

Ignoring a stab of agony at the thought of those deaths, Elise set her jaw. "Which means no weapons and no defense screens."

He nodded, his broad, meaty face grim. "We're at that sonofabitch's mercy — and I haven't noticed that he's got any."

"Any hull breaches?"

"One, but the emergency systems sealed it. We've still got the battery backups, so we won't start sucking CO_2 for at least a couple of days."

Assuming Roarke doesn't blow us to plasma first. She didn't voice the thought.

Henry paused, staring into her face. "You did everything you could, Captain. The *Liberator's* four times the size of the *Raker,* and it's got six times the firepower. Once Roarke caught us, it was over."

There was no response she could — or would — make to that. "Get that fire out, Henry."

"Aye, aye." He paused. "Good luck, Captain."

The vid went black. Elise lifted her head and looked at the central screen and the armored shark that was the *Liberator*, cruising through space a hundred kilometers away. The Rebellion dreadnought bristled with sensor dishes, beamer projectors and D-screen generators — devices normally recessed into the hull to survive the stress of Superlight travel, now extended for battle. It was fully as lethal as it looked; the *Liberator* had already captured or destroyed every other Coalition ship assigned to this sector. Only the *Raker* had managed to elude its lethal pursuit, though she knew Roarke had been hunting them for the past year.

Now all they could do was wait for him to finish them off.

Unless she was willing to beg. Roarke would like that. He might even like it enough to spare the *Raker*.

As Elise considered that dubious hope, her communications officer spun his chair toward her. His young face was too pale, and his eyes were wide, though she could see how hard he was fighting his fear. "Captain, I'm getting a call from the *Liberator*."

God, this would be humiliating, but she was going to save her crew if she had to grovel to do it. "Put him on."

Michael Roarke filled the forward screen, the blue and gray uniform of the Rebellion Starforce stretching across his muscled torso. Even Elise had to admit he was a handsome bastard, with broad, angular cheekbones and an aggressive chin. The bridge of his nose was narrow, yet the nostrils flared, a combination that gave him a faintly wolfish appearance enhanced by the pelt-short cut of his hair. His eyes were black, intelligent and wary, deep-set under thick dark brows. In contrast to those cool lupine features, his mouth was blatantly erotic, with lips that were every bit as hot, soft and skilled as they looked.

Best not to think about that.

"I've been evaluating our options, Captain Morrell," Roarke told her, his voice rich and faintly British.

Elise leaned back and crossed her legs, lifting an inquiring eyebrow. Her heart was pounding. "That's kind of you, Captain Roarke," she said, too sweetly. "And what are your conclusions?"

He smiled like a courtly wolf. "You can surrender, or I can blow you to hell."

Oh, he was going to be a son of a bitch to deal with. But then, he always had been. "Providing you allow my people to…"

"No," Roarke interrupted, his tone flat, almost brutal. "The only thing I'm going to accept is your unconditional surrender."

She was willing to surrender, but not unconditionally. Not to a commander with his reputation. "You're not going to get it."

"Captain, you are not in a position to refuse." His grin was nothing short of feral.

Elise displayed her own teeth. "My engines may not be up to generating D-shields, but they'd make a very pretty fire ball."

Roarke's amusement vanished, wiped clean from his handsome face. Then he smiled and lifted a brow. "Nice try, Captain, but suicide isn't your style.

Particularly not when you'd be taking your crew along for the ride."

"At least engine implosion is quick and clean. I'm not so sure about whatever you've got in mind."

"Unlike the Coalition, the Rebellion doesn't abuse prisoners of war."

"So your propaganda says."

"I've sampled the Coalition's hospitality, Captain. Believe me, ours is preferable."

"And you'd know, wouldn't you?" She shot him a grin of pure malice. "Such a shame you escaped."

His fine upper lip curled into a snarl. "But you won't."

"You don't have me yet."

Roarke's grin was slow and malicious. "Don't I?" He stopped and stared into her face, as if reading her determination, gauging her strength of will. Caution flickered into his eyes. When he spoke again, his voice was as coolly businesslike as a banker's. "I swear to you on my honor as an officer that your people will not be harmed — unless they attempt escape."

"We wouldn't dream of it." Elise felt a knot of fear unwind in her belly. If Roarke promised her crew's safety, they were safe.

At her implied surrender, there was a faint but visible loosening in the set of his shoulders. "And I believe you," Roarke said, his tone silken. "After all, I've seen how very loyal and obedient the *Raker* crew is."

She inclined her head. "Thank you."

"Which is why you're going to serve as my hostage."

"I beg your pardon?"

Roarke leaned an elbow on the arm of his command seat. His biceps strained his sleeve. "You heard me. With you as a hostage, I won't have to deal with any heroics from your crew."

Elise stared at him, remembering the last time she'd been at his mercy.

His fingers brushing paths of fire across her bare, aching breasts.

He gave her a silky smile. "Do you accept?"

His skillful mouth sucking, biting gently, the thick ridge of his erection pressing into her belly.

If she became his personal captive, he'd plunge her back into that eager animal submission she'd known on Tyus. And she was damned if she'd let him turn her into his toy again.

But — there was the crew to think of. Henry, Amanda Yancey, Don Hart, Dr. Rodriguez, all the others who wouldn't be here if not for Elise Morrell and a Coalition admiral with a political agenda and an ugly grudge. She couldn't let them die, not even to save herself from Michael Roarke.

"I accept your terms." The words tasted like acid in her mouth.

"Very good. Prepare to be boarded. I'll expect to see you waiting for me at the *Raker*'s primary airlock." He didn't bother hiding the menace as he added, "Alone and unarmed."

She'd agreed.

Roarke felt the muscles in his neck unlock for the first time since he'd gotten the anonymous communiqué revealing where the *Star Raker* would emerge from Superlight.

It had been far too close.

Standing, he nodded to his second in command. Knowing Roarke's plan as well as he did, Hendricks moved to take the command station as he headed for the bridge hatchway and the docking bay where his troopship waited. As he passed, Yolanda Boniface fell in beside him, the top of her head barely reaching his shoulders.

The instant the bridge hatch closed, the little engineer flashed him a wicked grin. Her dark Asian eyes glittered with unholy amusement. "Scared the shit out of you, didn't she?"

Roarke turned his head to stare at her. Anyone but Yo would have backed up a pace. "I beg your pardon?"

"Save that look for someone who hasn't known you for seventeen years," she told him. "You handled the *Raker* like a glass eggshell trying to take Morrell alive, and then she threatened to blow it up herself. She really had you going."

"Of course not," Roarke lied. "I knew she wouldn't suicide."

"Uh huh. So tell me. Now that you've got her, what are you going to do with her?"

A deeply sensual memory flashed through his mind — the way Elise's sex had felt, tight and slick around his probing fingers. He forced the thought away. He wasn't going to lose control this time. "I have no idea."

Yolanda looked at him, one brow lifting. "Uh huh."

"You do realize somebody betrayed us," Henry told Elise as they stood waiting in front of the main hatch to the docking bay. Roarke's troopship would be arriving at any moment.

"It is pretty obvious." Behind her back, Elise's fists clenched. "Roarke should have had no idea where we'd emerge from Superlight, but he was there waiting for us. Somebody told him where we'd be."

"You think it was Price?"

Lieutenant Gloria Price was the *Raker*'s morale officer, but she was also a spy for Admiral Frank Scordillis, Elise's superior in the Coalition Stellar Service. And Scordillis was gunning for Elise. "I doubt it," she said finally. "I've been monitoring her communication traffic for some time. Can't read the communiqués themselves, but I know the destinations, and nothing went to Roarke."

Henry's lip curled. "If it wasn't Price, Scordillis did it himself."

"Probably."

He swore.

"My thoughts exactly." Elise grimaced. "You know, my father warned me months ago something like this might happen. I should have had the sense to resign before they sacrificed the *Raker* to get to me."

"It's not your fault." Henry swiped a big hand over the smooth dome of his head in a gesture of frustration. "Who'd have thought they'd throw us to the wolves just because your father's big in the Reform Party?"

"He's not just big, Henry," Elise said drily. "He just may be the next president of the Coalition."

"If the Reformists can get control away from the military. And that's a very big 'if.'"

"Which gets even bigger if Roarke kills me." Catching his questioning look, she explained, "Dad advocates letting the Rebellion Worlds have independence. If a rebel kills me, the military could use it to discredit him."

"I'm beginning to think the goddamned Rebels have a point."

"Commander, lower your voice," Elise snapped, then added more lightly, "My father would tell you the best way to change the system is from the inside. Why do you think I'm still in the CSS?"

"I don't know, Captain — why *are* you still in the CSS?" a female voice cut in.

Elise and Henry turned to watch as Gloria Price sauntered up the hall to join them. Her blonde hair foamed in gleaming curls around the shoulders of her stark black uniform, and her tall boots shone. There was an expression of malicious amusement on her elegantly boned face. But then, there usually was; as Scordillis' pet, she thought she was untouchable. "I understand you'll be playing hostage to Captain Roarke," Price said. "That should be interesting. Particularly considering he's not very fond of the Coalition Stellar Service."

"If he was, he wouldn't be a rebel, would he?" Elise growled. She'd put up with the blonde's games for the past few months because she knew Price was under Scordillis' protection, but that was before the admiral had betrayed them all. Now she was seriously considering throwing the little twit in the brig.

"True, but there's more to it than that." Price sent her a sly smile, completely oblivious to the danger. "You do know Roarke once spent two months in the CSS prison camp on Elba? I understand one of the intelligence agents there tortured him with a neurowhip until Roarke finally murdered him and escaped." Her full lips curved. "You know, they never did find that whip."

"You've got far more to worry about than the captain, Price." Henry taunted. "Everybody on this ship knows you're working for CSSIntel. You'd better pray nobody lets that little fact slip to our captor — or you just may find out if he's got that neurowhip the hard way."

Before he could add anything more, Elise cut him off. "That's enough, Commander. If I want the Lieutenant disciplined, I don't need Michael Roarke to do it for me." She glanced coolly at Price. "Dismissed."

Even Scordillis' spy knew better than to buck her when she used that tone. "Aye, aye, Captain." She pivoted on her heel with a military snap and retreated.

They watched her go. "Henry, I want you to do something for me," Elise said softly.

"Shoot Price?"

"Tempting, but no." Her brief grin disappeared. "Save my ship. If you see a chance to escape, do it. If you've got to leave me behind, do it. That's an order."

He swiveled to face her, thick brows flying toward his non-existent hairline. "You don't seriously expect me to abandon you?"

Elise let her gaze chill. "Expect you? By God, I'm ordering you to. The *Raker's* your first and only consideration."

"And what's Roarke going to do to you in the meantime? Remember Tyus? By the time you got away from him, he had you half-naked."

"He won't rape me, Henry, if that's what you're worried about." She gave him a reassuring smile, but it felt thin and tight. "Roarke's not the type to bother; he already thinks he's irresistible."

Henry just looked at her, his opinion of that statement clear in his eyes.

A soft warning chime interrupted before she could make another attempt to convince him — and herself. Turning, Elise looked over her shoulder at the airlock hatch. The vid screen set in the wall above it revealed an image of a blocky troop transport finishing its docking procedure. "I've got to go."

"Captain —" He broke off and sighed, giving the sailor's traditional blessing. "Fair winds, Elise."

"Thanks, Henry." She hit the key panel, waited barely long enough for the airlock to open, then ducked through. Before the hatch closed again, she looked back at him. "Get my people out alive, Commander. That's an order."

The airlock rolled closed with a hollow, lonely thud.

Walking out onto the cargo deck, Elise listened to the echoing thrum of the *Raker's* engines and the bang and clank of the troopship settling in. She picked a spot to wait and fell into parade rest, resisting an impulse to dry her damp palms on the fine fabric of her dress trousers.

She hadn't seen Roarke in a year.

Oh, there'd been plenty of encounters since then, but all of them had been over the bridge vidscreen during some military game of cat and mouse. Yet even then, with kilometers of space between them, she'd always been too aware of him, the memory of their first meeting vivid in her mind.

Looking back on it, Elise suspected that particular disaster had been another of Admiral Scordillis' attempts to set her up. A ship's captain had no business playing spy, yet Scordillis had sent her and Henry Voronnin to the planet Tyus with orders to pose as pirates with a captured cargo to sell. They were supposed to discover who was smuggling supplies to the rebels.

She'd met Roarke in a bar there, of all places. He'd been trying to buy ship's stores for the *Liberator*, and someone had directed him to her. At the time, they hadn't met in battle and Elise was new to the sector, so he had no idea who she was.

It had gone well at first. She'd even been attracted to him; Roarke was witty and intelligent, not to mention handsome enough to tempt a neophyte spy to forget her common sense. In fact, when he invited her for a walk on the beach, she'd almost accepted. But in the end, Elise decided not to take the risk, just as Roarke turned down her deliberately exorbitant price for a cargo she didn't even have.

Still, it had been that invitation that had given her the idea for a moonlight swim late that night. After calling Henry to tell him where she was headed, Elise put on a stringsuit and went down to the beach behind their hotel.

Battling ocean swells for a brisk hour burned away the last of her adrenalin; by the time she emerged from the water, she was nicely tired. Elise dried herself off and wrapped her body in the thick, warm robe she'd brought along. Savoring the glow of heated muscles and pleasant exhaustion, she bent, meaning to pick up the sheathed knife she'd left wrapped in a towel. She was, after all, still in enemy territory.

Elise pulled up short as the wet fabric of her stringsuit dug into her skin. The outfit was nothing more than a set of fine cords which looped around her neck, wove together at strategic points as they descended, and dipped between her thighs to come up behind and tie at the waist. And at the moment the suit seemed to be chafing each and every one of those strategic points. Reaching past the lapels of her robe, she adjusted it to lie where it was supposed to.

"Lisa Morrow?"

She turned, a smile forming at the sound of Roarke's voice — a smile that froze across her teeth as she came completely around.

He was holding a beamer pointed between her breasts, the red glow of its charge burning deep in the weapon's dark barrel.

"You told me you were Lisa Morrow," Roarke said, his deep voice sounding almost metallically chill. "But that's not really your name, is it?"

"What else would it be?" The knife still lay wrapped in the towel at her feet. If she could get to it...Casually, she started to bend over.

"Captain Elise Morrell of the CSS frigate *Star Raker*. And leave the blade where it is, Captain. I'd hate to shoot you."

"I'd hate to be shot," Elise said easily, though her stomach was twisting with the sick realization that everything had just gone straight to hell. "You think *I'm* CSS?" She shook her head in carefully feined astonishment. "Captain, I hate those bastards. No way would I work for them."

"So you said — just a bit too loudly." Roarke began to circle around her, keeping his weapon aimed between her breasts. "Oh, you're a good actress; you sounded damn convincing talking about the way they'd screwed you. And that's what made me wonder, because no real rebel would tell a stranger that much." He smiled mockingly. "I don't know if you've heard, but Tyus is crawling with spies."

She tried out an apologetic smile. "I suppose I should be more discreet, but is that really a reason to kill me?"

He snorted. "Give it up, Morrell. I got an anonymous tip half an hour ago telling me exactly who you are. I checked it out with Starforce, and they confirm." The black eyes chilled. "But even so, I don't intend to kill you unless you give me no choice. Lie down on the ground. Kick the knife away first."

Elise shrugged and started to obey, but just at that moment gust of wind grabbed at her robe, dragging it open to reveal her stringsuit clad body and its nearly naked curves. Roarke's eyes widened.

She knew an opening when she saw one.

Pivoting her body into a hard, tight kick, she struck his wrist so hard his beamer spun out of his hand. Elise reversed direction, meaning to plow her foot into his jaw on the return stroke, but Roarke wasn't caught napping twice. He grabbed her ankle and jerked, dumping her on her backside in the sand. Even as he pounced on her, she was launching another attack, punching her palm upward in a strike calculated to drive the bones of his nose into his brain. He jerked his head aside, turning what would have been a lethal blow into one that did nothing more than bloody his mouth. She pulled back for another shot, but he grabbed her hands in both fists and pinned them to the ground. "Surrender, Captain," he grunted. "You don't want to go one-on-one with me."

"I could say the same to you," Elise growled, fighting to brace a foot against his body and kick him away. As she surged against him, she breathed in his scent; a faint tang of male sweat, a hint of something woodsy that must have been his soap, the trace of scotch on his breath. She ignored it and tried even harder for the throw, but Roarke applied a counter pressure and kept her down, mashing her breasts into the hard wall of his chest, his powerful thighs imprisoning hers between them.

God, he was strong. Even worse, he had the combat skills to match. There was a host of techniques she knew to flip him clear or strike sensitive nerve groups; punches that could have incapacitated him, kicks that could cripple, but he countered every move she made. With a growl of rage, Elise realized that infuriating male body would prevail; she was just wasting strength she might be able to use to escape later. She had no choice but to submit and watch for her chance. Sooner or later his guard would drop.

Feeling her go limp, Roarke nodded in satisfaction. "That's better." He pulled back slightly. "You..." His eyes widened.

Following the path of his gaze, Elise gasped.

Her stringsuit had slipped aside in the struggle, revealing the thrust of one nipple. Something about the way the cords pressed against the hard little nub made her breast look more erotically naked than it would have if she'd been nude.

Instinctively, Elise looked up at her captor, who stared back at her with a sort of disgruntled arousal. He liked what he saw, she realized, but he didn't like liking what he saw.

"At least let me belt my robe closed," she snapped.

To her surprise, Roarke released her hands and sat back on his heels, still straddling her. Which was when she realized that he had a massive erection.

Without thinking twice, Elise plowed a punch right at that very prominent target.

With a roar of raw fury, Roarke caught her fist just before it struck. He fell on her like the wrath of God, crushing her into the sand, pinning her arms and legs in a wide spread eagle under his powerful body.

Looking up into the rage in his black eyes, Elise felt her mouth go dry. She forced herself to shrug. "I couldn't help myself."

A slow, very nasty grin spread across his mouth. "Neither can I."

Roarke's head dipped. She knew at once what he was going to do, but there was absolutely no way she could stop him. His biceps working against the side of her head as he controlled her struggles, he parted his lips and took her bare nipple into his mouth. Instantly the pink bud hardened. Pleasure zinged through her.

Looking up to gauge her reaction, Roarke smiled around the sensitive flesh. His tongue pressed it against his teeth, then began to swirl a hot, wet dance around it.

"You've made your point." Elise fought to ignore the tingling rush of delight roaring through her nerve endings. "Now get off me!"

"When you leave your toys out," he rumbled, "you shouldn't be surprised if somebody wants to play with them." He went back to teasing the captive nipple.

He had a very wicked tongue. She drew in a hard breath. "Arrest me if you're going to. Hell, kill me if you're going to. But *stop* that!"

"Not on your life."

"I could have you jailed for assault!"

"Oh, I know. I just don't care." Roarke drew the nipple deeply into his mouth as, with a single rough pull, he jerked that side of the string suit all the way off her right breast. She cursed him, then broke off when she realized her voice sounded like a croon.

Injecting some steel in her tone, she growled, "Let me go, Roarke. Now."

He looked up at her. Her nipple felt suddenly cold without his hot mouth around it. "I've wanted to get you in this position all evening, Captain. I'm not stopping until I'm finished." Still watching her, Roarke nipped the pouting pink tip. She strangled a moan. He whispered, "And that won't be for hours yet." Grabbing the other side of the stringsuit, he freed her left breast with a hard jerk.

Then, like the wolf he resembled, Roarke began a leisurely feast, biting, sucking, licking at her erect nipples, sending a barrage of delight roaring along her nerves that ripped every thought of protest out of her head. His free hand worked whichever breast his mouth did not, squeezing and stroking, knowing just the touch, just the rhythm, to waken her hunger and twist it tight.

Dimly she realized he'd transferred both her hands to one of his. She knew she should try to pull free, but she didn't even have the strength to try. It was as though he were suckling away her will to resist with each tug of that wicked mouth. Until nothing else mattered, not rank, not enmity, not fear. Nothing but her need to feel him touching her.

Elise threw back her head at the storm of sensation, pressing her face against the hard bulge of his biceps. Barely aware of what she did, she opened her mouth and bit into the firm muscle. He tasted of desire and male sweat. Roarke growled, squeezing her breast between his long fingers before releasing it to continue his seductive explorations.

His hips rocked against hers. He was massively hard in a long thick ridge that pressed against her belly, scalding her with the need to feel him naked and strong in the cradle of her body.

She had to stop this, Elise told herself, but the thought was vague, powerless against the desire Roarke was building so skillfully.

He shifted over her, and his clever fingers moved down the V of bare skin revealed by her stringsuit, then wormed their way under the tightly woven cords that concealed her sex.

"Roarke," she moaned.

"Shhh," he whispered. "Let me touch you. Let me make you burn." His fingers found her, stirred the fine down at the juncture of her sex. "So soft," he crooned.

He discovered her clit, brushed it with a feather touch. She caught her breath as rapture seared her.

Elise was still reeling when he slid a big finger deep inside her. "Wet and hot and tight," Roarke murmured, "You want me as much as I want you. And God, how I want you."

He plunged two stiffened fingers into her. She cried out.

"It's good, isn't it? And it's going to get even better." Slowly, seductively, he pumped, until she could almost feel them locked together, his body bucking against hers, plunging so very, very deep.

Abruptly Roarke pulled away, his expression nakedly feral. "We can't finish this here, it's not secure. I'm taking you back to my ship." As if unable to resist, he ground his hardness into the notch of her thighs. His eyes closing, he murmured, "Then, in a day or so, when we're finally done, you're going to tell me where you left the *Star Raker*."

Elise blinked, feeling stunned and stupid, still in the grip of his spell. But even dazed as she was, she knew there was danger here. Danger to her ship.

Grabbing both her wrists, Roarke hauled her up off the sand as he bent at the waist. She realized he was about to throw her over his shoulder.

He was going to make her tell him where the *Raker* was. And against that dreadnought of his, her people wouldn't have a prayer in hell.

A wave of adrenalin drowned the erotic fire he'd so carefully built, leaving Elise cold and aware. "No," she whispered. "No, goddamn you, you're not getting my ship!"

With every ounce of her strength, Elise smashed a knee into his groin. Caught off-guard, Roarke roared in pain and dropped her. She rolled across the sand, sprang to her feet, and ran like hell. The sea breeze felt cold on her naked breasts, still wet from Roarke's sensual feast.

"Dammit, come back here!" He lunged, grabbing for her. Half-crippled as he was, he missed.

Elise scrambled down the beach kicking up sprays of sand. She couldn't afford to let him put his hands on her again. She rounded a dune...

And ran right into Henry Voronnin on the other side.

"Captain!" Henry said, startled. His eyes fell on her naked chest. *"Captain!"* "Elise!"

Roarke, bulling his way around the dune after her, spotted Henry and drew back a fist. Before he could strike, Henry plowed a foot into the side of his knee. It buckled under him with an audible snap. He hit the sand swearing.

A snarl on his face, Voronnin reached for him.

"Come on, Henry!" Elise yelled.

"We can take him hostage!"

"The Rebellion gives their people radio implants! We'd never get off the planet with him. Besides, his knee is broken," she told him, taking in Roarke's bloodless face with practiced eyes. "He's not going anywhere but to a medic. Let's get out of here before somebody comes!"

Grumbling, Henry turned and followed as Elise broke into a run.

Behind her, she could hear Roarke's deep-throated bellow of fury, "We're not finished, Elise!"

They'd run like hell back to the hopper. Roarke hadn't stayed down long; they'd barely taken off when they picked up the *Liberator*'s sensor signature roaring in pursuit. It had taken them another three days of hiding and evasive maneuvers to make it back to the *Raker*, with Roarke hunting them the whole time.

But even as they made good their escape, Elise had known he was right: he wasn't through with her.

A year later, Roarke chased her down, defeated her in battle, and forced her to surrender to his overwhelming strength of arms.

Now he was on his way to take her hostage.

The exterior airlock opened, revealing ranks of mammoth armored shapes, beamer rifles held at ready: the boarding party. Watching them advance, Elise swallowed, wondering which jointed gray suit held her enemy.

And whether he intended to take up where he'd left off.

Chapter Two

When Roarke and his boarding party marched onto the frigate's cargo deck, he found Elise standing at parade rest, proud in her black dress uniform with its silver piping, tall dress boots emphasizing the delicious length of her legs. She wore her blonde hair arranged in a businesslike bun that would have looked ridiculously prim on any other woman, yet the regal tilt of her chin turned it into a crown. Still, queenly as she was, he was surprised by how small she looked. Almost defenseless.

Then again, he was used to seeing her on his bridge vid screen, larger than life, playing out one of her elaborate combat strategies. But not this time. This time he had her. At last.

Roarke stopped a pace away from her, flanked by his fifty armored troopers. Keying his suit face plate open, he said, "It's a genuine pleasure, Captain Morrell." He could feel his lips curving into a grin he knew revealed too much.

Elise looked at him with those slanting go-to-hell green eyes. "I'm afraid I can't say the same, Captain Roarke."

"I know." He paused to drag the grin into a more professional expression. "Have you prepared any interesting surprises for us, Captain?"

She lifted a brow. "Why don't you see for yourself?"

"I do believe I will." With a nod and a gesture, Roarke sent his troopers fanning out, their beamer rifles held at ready, to search the area for snipers. Snipers who would be damn sorry to be found, considering that the armor made each trooper not only virtually invulnerable, but ten times stronger than anything human.

Roarke unslung his own rifle, pointed it at her, and said mildly, "I certainly hope they don't find anyone."

Elise gave the weapon a contemptuous glance, then ignored it.

God, she was something. Even watching her over a rifle sight, he felt the effect of her body on his — the long, sleek legs and narrow waist, the curve of her hips, breasts swelling and lush even in a uniform designed to minimize them. His mouth went dry as he remembered what those gorgeous breasts looked like bare, the nipples stiff and wet from his mouth. God, he loved her breasts.

Roarke gritted his teeth and banished that treacherous memory. She had a way of sending his professionalism right out the airlock — and he could swear she did it deliberately. Elise Morrell was a deadly little mantrap baited with lush tits and long legs. And he, God help him, tumbled right in every time.

Her face made the whole deception work. Knowing what an indomitable warrior she was, Roarke would have expected sharp, classic features, beautiful but cold. Instead there was an elfin delicacy about her. Her cheekbones and chin were softly rounded, her nose pert, her eyes wide and leaf-green. And her mouth — God, her mouth. With those wide, seductive pink lips that threatened and taunted and curled into dangerous grins. He had a recurring fantasy of sliding his aching hard-on into that mouth.

It irritated him.

Here they were, aboard an enemy vessel crawling with cornered Coalition forces, and he was focusing on Elise Morrell and his own lust. He was a captain of a ship at war, dammit. He couldn't afford this kind of distraction. He knew the price of failure too well.

Besides, she was a Coalition officer, for God's sake. She should disgust him. He desperately wished she disgusted him.

Through the radio implant behind his left ear, he heard the boarding party begin to call in. "Clear, captain."

"Looks good here."

"Doesn't seem to be anybody around."

Roarke waited for the last of them to confirm it, but even when confirmation came, he didn't relax. Staging an ambush in the cargo bay was the obvious thing to do. Elise never did the obvious. The ambush would come from the direction he least expected.

"All right," he said at last, "Assume your assigned positions and stay alert."

Slinging the rifle back across his shoulder, Roarke removed his helmet, pulled off his bulky gauntlets and handed them to the yeoman who stood a discreet distance away. Finally he turned to Elise. "Lace your fingers on top of your head and spread your feet apart."

She looked up at him, green eyes narrow and hard. Just when he was wondering if he had to force her, she lifted her hands and obeyed. He stepped closer, acutely aware of how small she seemed against his armored body. The perception sent another unprofessional surge of lust through him.

Careful not to linger, Roarke searched her for weapons, skimming his hands along the fine muscles of her arms, the narrow waist, the sweet rounded curve of her rump. And down those long, long legs that seemed to make up most of her body.

Which was when he realized he should have ordered someone else to conduct the search. Yolanda Boniface, for one, wouldn't have gotten a hard-on.

Erection or no, it took him just less than sixty seconds to find the knife tucked in her dress boot. Raising a brow, Roarke stared up at her as he drew the six-inch stiletto from its sheath. Elise shrugged. "Just checking to see if you're awake."

"I'm awake," he said drily. Handing the knife to the yeoman, he reached into one of the belt pouches on his armor and drew out a pair of neurocuffs. Though they looked like thin silver bangles, each generated a neural field that locked the prisoner's muscles, immobilizing his arms in place. Because the captive's own strength held him, the delicate shackles were impossible to break.

Roarke should know. He'd once tried desperately to break a set just like them.

Elise paled, then hid her fear and curled her lip. "What's the matter, Captain? Afraid you can't handle me even with boarding armor and a hundred-pound advantage?"

"No, I'm making damn sure your crew grasps your situation," he snapped. "I didn't tell you to take your hands down, Captain. Lace them on top of your head."

Moving stiffly, Elise obeyed as he stepped behind her. Catching one slender wrist, he pulled it around to the small of her back and locked it in a neurocuff, then captured the other wrist and manacled it to the first. Instantly, her arms went rigid as the field kicked in, paralyzing them. Grimacing in distaste — he knew too well how it felt when the 'cuffs locked down — Roarke moved in front of her.

And was suddenly, intensely aware of the way her captive wrists arched her spine, trusting her breasts outward. An image popped into his mind: Elise, lying naked on his bed, her arms 'cuffed under her, her stiff pink nipples pointed at the ceiling. Inviting his hands, his mouth, the lust that had been scalding him for months.

Cut it out, you lecherous bastard.

Disgusted with himself, he keyed his radio implant with a flex of his jaw muscles. "People, please be aware that we're in a very hazardous situation here. Captain Morrell has probably instructed her crew to disregard her safety. I'm assuming they'll be reluctant to endanger her once we parade her by in neurocuffs, but I could be wrong. Stay alert."

He thought he heard her growl.

Taking Elise's arm, Roarke guided her toward the hatch, his eyes sternly directed away from her lushly jutting breasts.

The next three hours were some of the darkest in Elise's life as she marched through her own ship surrounded by armored invaders. She could only watch as Roarke deployed his troopers to herd her crew into their quarters and take control of the posts they were forced to leave. Despite her helpless rage, she focused on every move he made, every order he gave, hoping for a mistake, an overlooked opening she could use to free her ship.

Nothing. Elise wanted to howl in frustration.

But the worst moment was when Roarke strode onto the *Raker*'s bridge and ordered his remaining troops to systemically search the bridge crew. When he was satisfied that no one had managed to stash away any weapons, he sent her staff off under guard. Until finally he and Elise were the only ones left on the bridge.

She tensed, but Roarke ignored her, busy directing the boarding parties through the radio implant behind one ear. Elise had nothing to do but sit down in a bridge chair and hatch far-fetched escape plans.

She was beginning to wish she'd blown up the ship.

By the time Roarke stood up almost two hours later and reached for the seal of his boarding armor, she was actually relieved. Finally, a diversion from her own spiraling desperation, even if it meant fighting another losing battle with Roarke.

He caught the expression in her eyes and paused. A wry grin twisted his mouth. "No, I'm not getting ready to attack you, I've just got to get out of this suit. I'm drowning in my own sweat."

She shrugged. "Whatever you say."

Roarke eyed her, his grin going wicked. "Ah, if only you meant that." With a flourish, he hit a button. The armor's chest plate split open with a pneumatic hiss, and he quickly wrestled his way out of it. The thin, sleeveless skinsuit he wore underneath was wet with sweat, and his short black hair was slicked tightly to his elegant skull; apparently the coolant systems in Rebellion armor worked as poorly as that in the Coalition's version.

Unfortunately for Elise's peace of mind, the result of that poor design left the skinsuit practically transparent. The thin, damp fabric hugged Roarke's broad torso, displaying his body to her reluctantly enthralled gaze. Chest, arms, ribs, belly — it seemed every inch of him was covered with rippled plates of muscle. Roarke looked armored even when practically naked.

Throwing back his head, he sighed, the cords of his strong neck flaring. "God, that cool air feels good." Bending over, he went to work on the bottom half of his armor, his big hands brisk and competent on the catches. Hard muscle shifted in his tight, masculine rump, and his thighs bunched as he pulled his legs clear and turned toward her. Elise's eyes widened.

The skinsuit cupped his genitals as though presenting them for her approval. And there was a lot to approve of. Elise swallowed, remembering how he'd felt in full erection, rocking seductively between her legs.

She really had no business being intrigued.

It was going far more smoothly than Roarke had any right to expect. Evidently his ploy had worked; the knowledge that Elise was within his armored reach dampened her crew's interest in rebellion. At last report, they were all safely locked in their quarters and under guard.

Which left him entirely too much time to think about the captive sitting bound and helpless a few feet away. His lovely enemy, defeated at last, looking like the recurring erotic fantasy he'd been having since Tyus — and playing merry hell with his self-control. The situation was just too damn tempting: a beautiful CSS captain at his mercy, just as he'd been a prisoner of the Coalition. Though, of course, he had no intention of mistreating her, the possibilities inherent in holding her captive were so lush and dark they'd been haunting his dreams for months.

It didn't help that he'd had to work his ass off to capture her. In the two years since his escape from CSS custody, Roarke had defeated far more powerful ships than the *Star Raker*. When they'd begun this running war a year ago, he'd expected to make Elise Morrell his prisoner within the month.

Unfortunately for his frustration level, Elise turned out to be an elusive opponent, staying one jump ahead of him no matter what he did. He had to admit she was better than any CSS dreadnought captain he'd ever fought; if she'd had a ship equal to his, she would have been a major threat. But luckily all she'd had was the underpowered, under-armed *Star Raker*, and now Elise sat on her own bridge in neurocuffs.

And there wasn't a damn thing to stop Roarke from feeding the hunger that had tormented him for so long. The *Raker*'s crew was safely locked away, and damage control parties were hard at work making sure he had nothing else to worry about. And he was alone with Elise.

Elise, her slim body deliciously nude, stretched out and cuffed in his bunk.
This is damned unprofessional.
Elise on her hands and knees, ready to be mounted.
He was getting hard.

But a captain in the Rebellion Starforce did not sexually abuse his female prisoners, no matter how beautiful or how tempting. It was dishonorable.

Now, if he'd been a Coalition captain, and she a captured rebel…

He'd go to her, and he'd peel her out of that pretty dress uniform, and he'd force her to her knees. He'd make her open that soft, beautiful mouth. She'd use her tongue as he commanded, licking slowly at the erection he could feel swelling his skinsuit.

But he was a Rebellion captain, and he was supposed to treat his captives with mercy. Even Coalition captives.

Even when the Coalition had been merciless to him.

The memory of his captivity rose up in a dark, choking wave, as it so often did when he was tired or distracted. But this time, Roarke let himself remember it, knowing it would kill his arousal if anything could: Amin Nygaard's thick, wet smile as the little bastard used the neurowhip, creating agonizing sensory illusions with every touch of the device. Skin being flayed slowly away, bones shattering, muscle ripping, eyes torn from sockets; the injuries themselves may have been illusion, but the pain was real. As real as his screams.

As real as Nygaard's blood on his hands.

Roarke realized he was staring at Elise again. She sat quietly in her seat, her arms pulled behind her in the cuffs, her high, round breasts thrust outward in that hated black uniform of hers.

That Coalition uniform.

She hadn't been there, he told himself. She'd had nothing to do with what Nygaard did to him on Elba.

But she was one of them. By donning that uniform, Elise had announced her belief in CSS policies, her willingness to defend them with her life and her honor.

Roarke started for her, intensely aware of his cock, of the cruel hunger roaring through him. He knew he shouldn't go anywhere near her when he was in the demon grip of Nygaard's memory.

And he didn't give a damn.

Elise was intensely aware of Roarke's swift, silent approach, but she fought to ignore it. She was damned if she'd show him any fear.

He stopped. The nape of her neck prickled. It took every bit of self control she had not to spin in her chair to face him.

"How are your arms?" Roarke demanded, the question sounding almost reluctant. "You've been bound a long time."

She shrugged. "Numb."

He dropped to one knee behind her so suddenly she jumped. "Don't give me that look, I'm just decreasing the setting," he told her gruffly as she shot him a wary backward glance.

Elise eyed him, wondering if that really was a flicker of guilt on his face.

He worked over the cuffs in silence for a moment. Finally she heard a click, and some of the tension left her muscles. Feeling raced back on a river of pins and needles. She tried to pull her wrists apart. They still wouldn't budge.

Roarke's big hands closed over her arms and began to rub.

What now? "Captain Roarke..."

"I once spent a very unpleasant twenty-four hours in neurocuffs. Believe me, you'll thank me for this later."

"Somehow I doubt that, since you're the one who put me in the 'cuffs to begin with."

He laughed softly. "You've got a point."

"In any case," Elise continued firmly, wanting to get his hands off her, "I think I can withstand the pain."

"True," Roarke said, his strong hands rubbing and pulling, "but there's no point. Your suffering is the last thing I've got in mind."

She gritted her teeth. "Your hospitality is dazzling."

"Oh, it's my pleasure," he purred.

Finally he released her arms and stood. Before Elise could relax, he reached into the neat bun on top of her head.

"What are you doing now?"

"I want to see it down." Roarke found the clasp and opened it with easy skill. Her hair collapsed around her face in a cascade of cool blonde silk. He caught it in both hands with a rumbling croon of delight. Slowly, he drew his fingers through it, stroking, still making that guttural male sound in the depths of his throat.

Taking his pleasure the way he always did, Elise thought — without asking. Yet somehow she couldn't bring herself to protest. Each time Roarke's fingers moved, they brushed against her body, her neck, her head, the side of her face, in a constant, sensuous caress. The prickle returned to her nape, but this time from pleasure rather than fear.

"It's so soft. So fine." His tone deepened into a rumble. "Like the down between your thighs."

"Captain. . . ." She winced as her voice cracked.

"Surely you were expecting this."

"Barbaric behavior? I suppose I certainly should have."

"No — defeat." Lazily, Roarke caught up a handful of her hair and bent close to inhale the scent. His cheek brushed hers. She tensed. "You must have realized how thoroughly I had you outgunned."

Elise twisted her head, trying to draw her hair free from his grasp. He tightened his grip, not cruelly, but leaving her no doubt that he was in control. Slipping his free hand past her hair, he stroked the vulnerable length of her neck, the line of her jaw. His fingers felt warm, slightly rough. "Once I cornered you," Roarke continued softly, "it was a simple matter to strip away your defenses and render you helpless." Putting his mouth against her ear, he whispered, menace lacing his tone, "Then it was easy to…penetrate."

To Elise's horror, she felt arousal tighten low in her belly. Ignoring it, she demanded bluntly, "Are you planning to rape me, Captain Roarke?"

"Why, no, Captain Morrell. What I'm planning," His hot tongue flicked out and swirled around her earlobe, "is a ruthless," Roarke closed his teeth over the sensitive flesh in a gentle bite, "seduction."

His hand dropped smoothly to brush the tip of her breast. Even through the tough fabric of her uniform, she felt the sensuous temptation. Her nipple drew tight and eager.

"You're splitting verbal hairs, Roarke. You may get a response out of my body, but I'm still saying no. And that makes this rape." Her breasts were aching.

"Hmmmm. You have a point." He lifted his hand to touch the center of her throat at the top of her high uniform collar, then slowly ran his fingers downward between her breasts, along her tensed abdomen, right to the top of her pubic bone. As he triggered the invisible closure, her uniform split open with a whisper. "I suppose," Roarke purred, his hot gaze directed down at the arrow of naked white skin, "I'll just have to get used to being a rapist."

"If you think I'm just going to submit, you're greatly mistaken." Elise hoped he missed the husky note in her voice.

"No, you're hardly submissive, are you?" Moving in front of her, he took her shoulders in his powerful hands and lifted her straight up off the chair, then turned her around and gently, relentlessly forced her to kneel in the seat, half bending over the back. "In fact, I'm waiting for you to kick me in the teeth at any moment."

"What the hell are you doing now?" She wet her lips.

To her outrage, his teeth nipped her bottom. "Worshiping your magnificent ass." Taking it between his hands, he squeezed her cheeks, caressed the firm, muscled flesh with strong, possessive circular strokes.

"And I'm going to report *your* magnificent ass," Elise gritted. "I suspect the Rebellion high command would frown on this." She kicked back at him, but he grabbed her ankle in an iron clasp before her foot could connect.

"No doubt," he said coolly, releasing her leg, "But considering the length of time I spent being tortured by the CSS, I think they'll be more understanding than usual. And if not, I really don't give a damn."

"Is that what this is about? Vengeance?" Warily, Elise looked back over her shoulder at him.

"Wondering what nasty perversion I have in mind?" He dragged her back until his erection pressed against her bottom. "Don't bother. I've already had my revenge; I killed that sadistic CSSIntel bastard when I escaped. No, this is about pleasure. Mine," he rolled his hips, "and yours."

Despite herself, she felt a tingle of building arousal, a shameful, reluctant anticipation. He felt so…thick. She had a sudden, intense memory of his powerful body pinning her, his mouth suckling at her nipples as his fingers dipped into her wet core.

This time he wouldn't stop.

This time she'd get to have it all.

But she shouldn't want it.

He leaned closer, draping himself over her so he could reach into her open uniform. Tugging back one edge of her tunic, he liberated her right breast. She felt it thrust out into the cool bridge air, its nipple hard, shamelessly eager for his fingers. And he gave them to her, cupping her in delicious warmth before catching the stiff tip to pull and roll until Elise could no longer hold back a moan.

"You see?" Roarke murmured. "Pleasure. And you can blame it all on me. You're neurocuffed and defenseless, and I'm the nasty, dishonorable son-of-a-bitch rebel captain taking advantage of the situation to feed his own lusts. You can let yourself enjoy every luscious second."

She licked her lips. "What makes you think I'm enjoying this?"

Letting his back rest on hers, his strong thighs snuggling against hers, he reached one hand down her uniform and between her legs. A finger slipped easily into her in a long, slick glide. "Why, nothing, captain. It's obvious you don't care for my advances." The finger withdrew, then slid deep again. It was all she could do not to moan. "You're completely…cold to me."

A second finger joined the first, and he burrowed in and out of her until she shuddered. At the same time, his other hand resumed its torment of her breast. 'Cuffed, Elise could only rest her chin on the back of the chair and try not to moan as Roarke rolled his hips against her bottom.

"God, you're making me hot," he rumbled in her ear, using his thumb to stroke her erect clit. "Bound and bent over, ready to be mounted. And so creamy. This arouses you as much as it does me, you're just too stubborn to admit it. You'd rather deny both of us because I had the gall to defeat you in battle."

Elise sucked in a deep breath that almost became a whimper before she could stop it. She did desire him. Humiliating, but there it was. And why shouldn't she? His body was big and powerfully built, with strong, broad hands. He had a face as handsome as an ancient god's and wicked black eyes that knew entirely too much and promised even more, and a mouth that wove spells of sin and carnal pleasure. He was every dark fantasy she'd ever had.

But he'd blown the *Star Raker* halfway to hell, and he was going to put her and her crew in a Rebellion prison camp.

And he was not, damn him, going to win this one too.

She turned to give him a chill glare over her shoulder despite the pleasure he was wringing from her wet, ready flesh. "If you're going to rape me, do it and get it over with."

"Oh, I want to rape you, Elise. I want to strip you out of that ugly black uniform, bend you over your own captain's chair, and make you come so hard my engineering crew will hear you scream six decks down." Roarke's eyes narrowed. "And why not? Hell, if you want to play martyr, who am I to refuse?" With a quick pass of his fingers, he resealed her uniform, straightened off her, and padded toward his armor.

She twisted away from the seat back and struggled awkwardly to her feet, though her hands were 'cuffed behind her. Hoping her treacherously weak knees wouldn't dump her in the floor, Elise demanded, "What are you doing now?"

"Getting dressed." He shot her a nasty grin as he reached for the chest plate. "It's a tempting idea, but I suppose it would be tacky to actually screw you on your own bridge."

She set her teeth. "You suppose right."

"And your being paraded through the corridors by a half-naked rebel captain would make the situation a little too obvious to the crew. After all, we wouldn't want to set a bad example." Flexing his broad shoulders, Roarke picked up the heavy torso armor and shrugged into it like a coat. "But since you're so determined to be victimized, I'll just have to cooperate — discretely."

"Do you think this is some kind of kinky game to me?" Elise demanded, trying to ignore the play of tempting muscle as he suited up. "Yes, I'll admit you arouse me. You're a skilled lover. You could probably wring a response out of a neutronium bulkhead. But no matter what you do to my body, I won't willingly sleep with you. And if you force me, I will fight. I may not win, but you won't get any enjoyment out of it."

Roarke looked into her eyes, his own hard, level. "I'm aware of that, Elise. I've met you in combat often enough to know you're not the type to make it easy." Moving to tower over her in his armor, he flexed a gauntleted hand. "Fortunately, that's not a problem. With the suit, I don't have to hurt you to subdue you."

She glared up at him bitterly. "You're not going to leave me any dignity at all, are you?"

"Not if you refuse to give us both what we need, just to soothe your stiff pride."

"Why not? You've got a stiffness of your own you seem obsessed with."

He laughed. "Touche'." Reaching out, Roarke took her arm. "Now that you mention it, I think it's time we got started on that problem."

Elise growled, but she knew better than to attempt hand-to-hand combat with a man in armor.

Once again, Roarke held all the cards.

Chapter Three

Lifting her chin, Elise allowed Roarke to guide her to the bridge doors and out into the corridor. Glancing at his face, she saw he was watching her, his gaze hungrily flicking from her eyes to her mouth to the thrust of her breasts and back again. She felt her nipples tingle and harden.

Quickly redirecting her own gaze, Elise swore silently. How did he keep doing this to her? The man was her worst enemy, an arrogant rebel taking advantage of her status as his hostage. She was going to file a complaint with his Rebellion superiors. She was going to kick him in the balls the minute she saw an opening. She...

That pointed tongue flicking out to swirl around her hot, wet nipple. His mouth descending, engulfing the stiff peak, sucking, biting, pulling, until pleasure roared through her, drowning duty and honor and even self-preservation in a bright red flood of delight and desire.

She shook her head hard, infuriated. The bastard had the ability to seduce her even inside the privacy of her own mind.

It was embarrassing.

Stiffening her spine, she marched around the corner and down the corridor toward the door of her quarters. Jerking against Roarke's light hold, she managed to break it as she snarled at the key plate, "Captain Elise Morrell. Admit me." The door opened. She stalked through without looking back.

Taking a deep breath, Elise paused to regain control of her anger, aware of Roarke moving in behind her as the door slid closed again.

His gauntled hands caught her arms and quickly disengaged the muscle lock on her neurocuffs. Elise jerked and started to whirl, but it was too late. Dragging her arms over her head, Roarke clasped her wrists together to reengage the 'cuffs, then scooped her up and dumped her on the wide captain's bunk.

"What the hell?" Instinctively she tried to launch a punch at him, but her arms, locked in the neurocuffs, were pointed stiffly at the headboard.

"I'm not going to fight you, Elise," Roarke told her. "I won't hurt you even to soothe your pride. But I am going to take you. And if that means putting you in shackles, I'll do it." He reached down with one of those huge gauntlets, grabbed a fistful of her jacket, and ripped. The tough cloth shredded like rice paper, and the entire coat came off in his hand.

Elise stared at the ripped fabric in wordless shock. "Bastard!"

"I've always hated this outfit," Roarke told her, wicked laughter in his voice, as he reached down to grab another handful of cloth.

"That was my best dress uniform!" She aimed a kick at his head as he finished off her jacket.

"But black and silver is such a pretentious combination." He caught her booted foot in one hand, grabbed her pants leg in the other, and jerked. It split open, baring the length of her leg right up to her crotch. She slammed another kick into his ribs and winced as her heel glanced off the armor. Calmly, he pulled off her boots. "Besides, I'm a rapist. Ripping the victim's clothes off is half the fun."

Reaching into one of the pouches on his equipment belt, he pulled out a slightly bigger version of the neurocuffs and snapped one around her bare ankle. Elise tried for another kick but it was too late; he'd already activated it. Her entire leg went stiff and unresponsive.

"Roarke, I'm warning you," she snarled, "if you do this to me, I'm going to slit your throat!"

"Then I'll just have to keep you in bondage, won't I?" he taunted, as he stripped away the rags of her trousers and imprisoned the other leg in the second neuroshackle. Taking each ankle in hand, he positioned her with her legs wide apart in the air. "Not that I need an excuse."

Elise desperately wanted to change her shamefully open position, but she couldn't even twitch. She was immobilized — and completely naked except for a few scraps of black. "This is ridiculous."

"Not at all. You look like my favorite wet dream." Roarke's grin was astonishingly boyish, considering he'd just ruthlessly ripped her clothes off and bound her for forced sex.

"One of these days, Michael Roarke," she spat, "you're going to find out how *you* like it in shackles…"

His humor vanished as if cut off with a switch. "I already know the answer to that one. And an intelligent woman would not bring back that particular set of memories when she was naked, shackled and spread wide."

Seeing the sudden cruel black glitter in his eyes, Elise winced. He had a point. "Then I'll just have to settle for reporting you," she growled anyway, refusing to back down. "Your Starforce will bust your ass back to ensign."

He ignored that, busy with getting himself out of his armor. This time though, he didn't stop with the skinsuit, shucking his broad body out of it with as much ruthlessness as he'd ripped away her own uniform. He actually looked bigger without it, as though the suit had camouflaged his size.

Elise caught her breath at the width of his powerful chest, with its thick masculine pelt that flared from nipple to nipple in a broad cloud. Unconsciously her eyes tracked that pattern of soft hair, watching as it narrowed into a band to flow down over his hard, rippled belly. And down even further, pointing the way like a slim finger.

With a sinuous roll of his hips, Roarke freed his sex. It sprang outward, surrounded by the soft ruff. Elise blinked. His organ was bigger than she'd expected, even after feeling it through his clothes. The long shaft with its prominent veins looked almost too thick for its head, which was easily the size of a plum. It was also stone hard. That same obvious arousal pulled his furry dark balls tight, taut and full.

Roarke stood framed between her raised, spread legs like a stallion about to mount a mare, erection jutting, his hungry jet eyes locked on her face. His nostrils flared; Elise wondered whether he could actually smell the heat she felt trickling into her sexual core.

"Now lie to me," he rumbled, cutting the heavy, erotic silence. "Tell me again how you don't want me. Lie and call me a rapist. Or be honest with both of us and ask for my hands on you."

"You're an arrogant, egotistical bastard," Elise told him, her low voice too husky to be convincing. "And I'm not going to give you the satisfaction."

He smiled slowly. "You will."

Roarke reached out and caught her ankle as he slid a knee onto the bed. Slowly, watching her face the whole time, he leaned forward and parted his lips. His pointed tongue reached out, found a quivering tendon, and began to trace a wet, hot trail downward. Elise bit back a moan and closed her eyes, unable to withstand the combined raw eroticism of his hot stare and the feeling of him tasting her skin like a predator. She knew she should say something, make another pointless protest, yet the heavy mood of sensuality radiating from him was as good as a gag.

Roarke watched her, an urgent pulse pounding through his cock. Tatters of Coalition uniform lay on her skin like leaves, starkly black against her pale skin. She looked deliciously sensual, her breasts swelling, nipples stiff and dark, her hair a soft pale cloud around her flushed face. Her legs, wide apart in the air, revealed the pink petals of her sex, parted as though eager for his probing tongue and hungry prick. It was all he could do not to fall on her like the rapist she'd accused him of being.

But that wouldn't be good enough, Roarke told himself, clinging to the last shreds of his self-control. If he took her like that, so quickly, so selfishly, she could dismiss the experience — even if he wrung from her the climaxes he intended. He wanted something more. He wanted to brand himself on her senses, force her to admit she was as helpless in the face of this obsession as he was. He had to be something more to her than an enemy, more than a rapist. Why that was so important, he didn't know — and didn't particularly care. She was still going to submit to him, to his mouth and his hands and his cock. And he'd reward her with every jolt of pleasure he could wring out of her body.

That would be enough. It would have to be.

Roarke drew in a deep breath, drinking her scent as he grazed his lips down the long curving sweep of her calf. Her skin felt silken against his mouth. Discovering a sensitive spot behind her knee, he hesitated, biting gently at the muscle swelling there. Elise caught her breath. Roarke smiled and kept going, letting his hands explore the fine weave of tendon and muscle and bone in her strong thighs.

A trace of musk and salt teased his nostrils, and he inhaled deeply, savoring the evidence of Elise's growing arousal. He moved closer, edging his head between her legs, looking at the petals of her sex, half concealed by her soft bush. Lifting a hand, he stirred through the fine blonde hair with one finger, tracing the line between her delicate lips, careful not to push inside. Not yet, not yet.

"Pretty Elise," he murmured, drifting his finger along her mound, just brushing. "Do you know your danger, I wonder?"

Elise made a faint sound, not quite a gasp.

"Oh, maybe you think you do." Another brush of his fingertip, exploring the delicate textures of vulnerable female flesh and silken hair. "Maybe you're expecting me to fuck you like a pirate, brutally, not caring if I hurt you, out of revenge or selfishness or simple cruelty. But that's not the danger at all." He leaned closer, drinking the rich, sexual smell of her. "No, the danger is that now that I've finally caught you, I may never let you go."

She whimpered.

Roarke smiled and dipped his head.

She ought to make a comeback to that, Elise thought, feeling the muscles of her belly lace as she stared down at the crown of his dark head. She shouldn't let him think he was getting to her.

But Roarke's warm breath was gusting gently over her sex, and anticipation had stripped away any interest Elise had ever had in repartee. If he was trying to drive her mad, he was doing a good job.

Lick.

A single pass of his tongue along the edge of her outer lips, nothing more than a tantalizing promise. Roarke nuzzled closer and breathed deeply, blowing across her damp flesh. Then that long, lush tongue touched her again, pushing delicately inside to start slipping in and out, leaving wet, burning trails behind, lighting up her nervous system with starbursts of pleasure. He edged closer. She could feel his warm, muscled shoulders pressing against her legs, the brush of his short cropped hair against her inner thighs in a silken caress.

Instinctively Elise tried to bring her hands down to cover her sensitive, vulnerable sex, but her arms, locked in the neurocuffs, didn't even twitch. She could do nothing at all.

And he could do everything.

He'd found her clit.

His tongue circled it with wet, hot flicks, then slowed for leisurely sampling swirl. His teeth closed in a gentle almost-bite, followed by another flick of that skillful tongue. His lips closed to suck briefly, then opened again for another swirling assault.

She realized she was moaning and tried to stop.

A gentle bite.

Elise whimpered. Her hips began to flex. Pleasure curled in tight corkscrews in her belly.

His hands reached up, brushing along her sides to find her breasts. Rough fingers caught her nipples to gently pinch and roll the hard, tingling tips.

"Feeling raped yet, Elise?" Roarke rumbled, only his eyes visible as he looked up at her from between her legs. "Wondering what nasty revenge I've got in mind?"

"Bastard!" she gasped, unable to think of any other word.

"Of course. Are you thinking about what it's going to feel like when I slide inside?" He lifted his head, extending a pointed tongue. Licking slowly, he watched her, then paused. Her thighs twitched. "I'm hard and hungry, Elise. And soon, very soon, I'm going to take it all."

Suddenly, violently, Elise wanted him. Wanted everything he'd been threatening her with. She wanted to feel his massively powerful body pressing heavily onto hers, that long, thick erection digging into her hungry core. "Roarke..." she groaned, and swallowed.

He was sucking carefully on her clit now, his tongue flicking. Elise felt a burning pulse begin as her thighs started to twitch. She rolled her head back into the pillow, feeling it come.

Roarke stopped, though his strong fingers continued to pluck and play at her nipples.

"No! Roarke, please," she gasped, pride forgotten.

"Please what?" he rumbled. And licked.

"Please," she whimpered. "I need..."

He sucked, his mouth drawing at her needy flesh. She quivered. Lifting his head, Roarke pressed his cheek against the inside of her thigh and looked at her. "What do you need?"

"You...AH!...I need...you."

"You need me to do what?" He twisted one nipple with exquisite care.

"I need you to ...take me. Ride me. God, Roarke, please!"

"But I defeated you, Elise. I ran down your poor little ship with my big, ugly dreadnought and beat the hell out of it. And then I took you hostage and stripped you naked and bound you like a pleasure slave. Are you sure you want *me*?"

"YES!" It was a scream.

"Then *take* me." In a single, violent gesture that shouted of snapped self-control, Roarke heaved his big body upward. Hunger drew his features sharp as he reared back on his knees and took his thick sex in hand. He moved between her legs, braced a muscled arm beside her hip. Aimed himself. And thrust.

Elise threw back her head and screamed at the sheer animal pleasure of it, at the shattering sensation of that huge organ ramming into her, giving her just what she so desperately needed.

"Yes!" Roarke growled, coming fully down over her, staring into her face. "That's it, Elise. That's what I want from you. That's what I'm going to take."

He began to thrust, his powerful hips working as he stroked between her wet, clamping walls. She writhed under him, feeling the soft hair of his chest brushing her nipples, his hard belly rolling against hers as he rocked.

"God, Roarke," Elise moaned, "I've never felt..." The pleasure was building with every strong thrust, searing her core, winding her tighter and tighter until it seemed she was going to explode. Desperately she hunched up against him, wishing she could wrap her legs around his hips and drag him even deeper.

Roarke ground into her, circling his hips as he plunged until his sweat splattered her skin. His teeth clenched. His bunching shoulders blocked the light.

Elise writhed, unable to bear the strength of the pleasure drilling into her core. "Roarke!" she screamed, and convulsed as her mind flew apart in a silent, glorious detonation.

For a long moment Roarke lay over Elise, loving the way her full breasts pressed into his chest. Opening one eye, he saw the sweetly curved columns of her legs pointing into the air. "Inconsiderate bastard," Roarke muttered at himself, remembering that she was still neurocuffed. Sighing, he reluctantly dragged himself off her tempting body and up onto his knees.

Taking the 'cuffs from her ankles, Roarke eased her long legs to the bunk. The muscles were still quivering and jumping under her dewy skin, and he bent to massage them, savoring the silky feel of her calves and thighs under his hands. Even after the heated passion of the past hour, he felt a slow, warm tide of arousal. He was tempted to start again, but he knew it would probably make her sore after all they'd already done, so he hastily backed away to take care of the neurocuffs on her wrists.

Elise whimpered at the sudden freedom and stirred, a frown forming between her brows. Quickly, in case she should decide to get up, Roarke lay back down and lifted her sated body to drape it over his own.

"Roarke," she murmured huskily, trying to pull back from him.

He twined his arms around her drowsy nakedness and pulled her close. "Shhhh. It's been a long day. Sleep."

Elise made a grumbling sound and subsided. He knew that capitulation was a measure of both her satisfaction and her exhaustion, and grinned a little wolfishly.

Poor baby. He'd worn her out.

Her hair was tumbling over the back of his hand. Roarke reached up and stroked his fingers through it. It felt slightly damp, tangled, fine as strands of starsilk. She lay over him completely and deliciously limp, a sweet, intensely female weight. Roarke took her chin and tilted her head up. Her lips pouted, parted and rosy. Unable to resist, he bent his head and took them, brushing their moist, soft velvet with his mouth. He slipped his tongue inside to explore the slick surfaces of her teeth. She moaned, a muffled sound of pleasure and unconscious desire.

Roarke's arms tightened, pulling her close even as he drew away from those tempting lips. He wondered if she'd let him kiss her like that when she was awake. Afraid he knew the answer, he frowned.

Her breathing was deepening into sleep; it puffed warmly across his left nipple. Roarke forgot the moment's uncertainty and sighed.

He went to sleep more at peace than he'd been since the day he'd been captured.

Elise woke to the feel of Roarke's muscled chest pillowing her head and his hot erection pressing into her belly. She blinked her eyes, surprised at the heat that flooded her.

"You're awake." Arousal roughened his voice to a husky velvet drawl. With a twist of his powerful body, Roarke rolled her under him. She blinked as he

loomed above her, staring down into her face. Yet the urgent lust she'd come to
expect was absent from his eyes, replaced by something else, something...warmer.

Tenderness?

Lifting a hand, Roarke drew it gently through her hair, combing the pale
strands back onto the pillow. His absorbed gaze flicked over the tangled silken
mass, then came to rest again on her face. Slowly he lowered his head and
kissed her, a deep, languorous tasting. Surprised at the softness of his mouth,
Elise parted her lips. His tongue swept in to swirl around hers.

Within her something slowly dissolved, a bitter ice chip of rage and hate
melting beneath his surprising warmth.

Leaving her vulnerable.

Elise stiffened. She couldn't afford this. Not now. Not here, with her ship
and her crew and herself in his control. She had to stop. She wrenched her head
away, wincing at the sting as his teeth accidentally scraped her lip.

Roarke drew back and studied her, puzzlement at her withdrawal evident on
his face. "What?"

"Don't you think you've proven your point?"

Without moving, he seemed to pull away. "And which point is that?"

"That you could seduce me." She steeled herself.

"Ah, I see." His smile was very male. "Your pride again. You just can't allow
yourself to enjoy the moment."

His amusement stung, so she set out to sting back. "Oh, I did. But now the
moment's past."

Roarke arched a dark, brow, his expression taking on a predatory cast. "Is it?"

"Yes," Elise told him, forcing icy dispassion into her tone. God help her if he
started on her again. She'd never be able to resist him now that she knew what
he was capable of doing to her. "Don't get me wrong, you were skillful. In fact, I
think you're the best I've ever had. You seduced me with ease."

The lids lowered over those dark, hot eyes. "Darling, I didn't just seduce
you. I made you beg."

"But I've had a bitch of a day," she continued, though she could feel a blush
heating her cheeks, "and I need to get some sleep. If it's not too much to ask."

With an abruptness that startled her, Roarke sat up, his strong hands
grabbing her hips to flip her over on her belly. Before she could think to
struggle, Elise found herself up on her knees, her bottom in the air, the hot head
of his erection brushing her rump. His voice laced with humor and erotic
menace, Roarke purred, "And what if it is too much to ask?"

She couldn't show him any sign of reaction. "Unfortunately, I'm afraid I'm
far too tired to do you justice." Looking over her shoulder at him, Elise gave him
a distant smile. "Perhaps later."

Not at all offended, Roarke slowly rolled his hips against hers. "I could
change your mind..."

She kept her gaze steady, cool, disinterested. It took entirely too much work.

He stared back for so long she could feel her palms begin to sweat. Then,
casually, he broke the moment, his lips pulling into a wry twist. "But unfortu-

nately, I've got the duty. So you're off the…hook, as it were." Releasing her, Roarke rolled off the bed, then turned to quirk a brow at her. "For the time being."

Elise watched as he sauntered into the head for a quick shower, anything but the picture of a rejected and sexually frustrated male.

He hadn't bought it.

Damn.

And what was she going to do when he got off duty?

Roarke stepped under the stinging ice cold spray from the dozen tiny shower nozzles. God, that woman was stubborn. *What did you expect, you dumb bastard?* He endured the water pounding the length of his cock, instantly killing his erection. *You put her in neurocuffs and ripped her clothes off and screwed her. Was she supposed to roll over, smile sweetly, and swear her undying love? Maybe even admit last night meant as much to her as it did to you?*

And just what had last night meant to him?

Hell, he had no idea. Punching the soap dispenser, he let a handful pour into his palm, then scrubbed his hair brutally. The whole obsession with Elise had begun so simply, touched off by the encounter on Tyus. Nothing but a recurring dark, kinky fantasy of seducing the enemy ice queen and making her beg. Typical male bullshit, raw ego at work. But she'd been more of a challenge than expected in her ridiculous little ship, more clever, more elusive. He'd become intrigued.

In time, he'd become a lot more than intrigued — he'd become fascinated, obsessed, determined to have her. Until finally it wasn't a game anymore. He'd even begun to dream of her more often than he did Amin Nygaard. Dreams that were, God knew, a definite improvement over his usual torture-inspired nightmares.

And then there was last night. He'd seduced her just as he'd planned since those first two-dimensional male fantasies. And it had been the best sex he'd had in his life. He'd held her while she slept, woke with her in his arms. And she'd felt…precious.

Roarke considered the idea uneasily. It almost sounded as though she meant something to him, something more than a military victory that had morphed into a kinky bondage fantasy.

Jesus. Was he falling in love with Elise Morrell?

God, he hoped not. Conducting a romance with an enemy captain — particularly one on her way to a prison camp — would be practically impossible. Especially considering this particular captain was proud as a Deltan aristocrat and about as flexible as neutronium plate. Surely he wasn't that stupid.

But God, she'd felt so good lying in his arms this morning, warm and soft and sleeping, her long legs tangled with his...

At that last thought, Roarke groaned, leaning his head back until cold water pounded his face.

There was no doubt about it. He was screwed.

Roarke emerged from the head and prowled, magnificently naked, to his armor. Elise watched him dress, scanning his hard, angular features for any hint of emotion. This time she couldn't seem to read him.

Suited up, Roarke walked to the computer pad set into the wall and keyed it on. "Captain Morrell is not permitted to leave her quarters."

The pad beeped twice, acknowledging his orders. Elise knew he'd already had his computer expert reprogram the ship's network so that it would no longer accept the commands of any *Raker* crew member — especially her. Now not even the door would open.

He turned toward her. "I'll have somebody bring you something to eat. What do you want?"

"I'm not hungry."

Roarke hesitated, then shrugged. "Suit yourself." With that, he strode to the door and out into the corridor.

Watching the door slide closed behind him, Elise fought a wave of depression she didn't even try to understand. She'd gotten what she'd wanted; he'd left her without another mind-bending dose of his sensual attention.

It didn't matter anyway.

Fighting the mood, she stood up went to one of the closets set into the wall. Digging through it, Elise finally found what she was looking for: a thick white robe. She slid her arms into it, wincing a little at the soreness of her muscles, and tied the belt around her waist. Walking into the head, she paused, catching sight of her mussed hair in the mirror, and picked up a brush. Mechanically, Elise began to stroke it through the blonde tangle until she'd tamed it smooth.

God, she was depressed. If this was the price of fantastic sex, next time she'd pass.

And she looked like hell. Her lips were swollen, and there was something dazed about her eyes.

Forget it. She had work to do. Turning, Elise walked through the head doorway into the office that lay beyond it.

Dominating the room was her horseshoe-shaped private control center, with its inset vid screens and instrument panels. She sat down in the thickly padded cream chair and placed her palm on the ident plate. "Captain Elise Morrell. Access."

"Captain Morrell: access denied under the authority of Captain Michael Roarke," the computer told her.

Elise leaned back in her chair and closed her eyes. "Override code Ragnarok."

There was a brief pause as the virus she'd installed months ago swept through the operating system.

"Access accepted."

Chapter Four

With a flare of satisfaction, Elise watched Henry Voroninn's beefy glum face appear on her vid screen. His eyes widened. "Captain! How did you…"

"A little computer magic, Henry," she told him. In fact, it had taken her an hour of delicate, nerve-wracking work to contact him without setting off the safeguards Roarke's computer experts had planted in the *Raker's* network. Elise grinned impishly. "I didn't get this job by nepotism alone, no matter what Price says."

The big man frowned in puzzlement. "I thought they'd disabled all our security systems."

She nodded. "Except for the virus I planted."

"Roarke turned his back on you that long?"

"Actually, I wrote it several months ago. It seemed a logical precaution to take, with the *Liberator* breathing down our collective necks."

"Hhhmp." He looked more grumpy than pleased. "Wish you'd said something about this earlier. I've been pulling my non-existent hair out trying to come up with an escape plan."

"Sorry, Henry." Elise shrugged. "I just wasn't certain it would work. For one thing, I had to find an opportunity to launch it, which was far from a sure thing. And once I did, the chances were good that Roarke's counter-virus systems would defeat it. We got lucky." She grimaced as she stretched, absently trying to pull the kinks out of her spine. "God knows it's about time."

"But can they detect our communications? If Roarke catches you at this…"

At the thought of her captor's reaction, Elise felt a chill skate along the nape of her neck. Faking confidence, she smiled comfortingly at her second in command. "Don't worry about it. I designed this program to allow me to communicate with the crew without being detected. We should be safe. As long as neither of us patches into the bridge, anyway."

Roarke hunched in Elise's command chair, staring thoughtfully at the tips of his boots. Whether he liked it or not — and he didn't — he strongly suspected he was falling in love with Elise Morrell. Which presented him with a whole raft of problems, not the least of which was the lady herself, who was damned unlikely to indulge him. Then there was the problem of the Starforce High Command's reaction when he tried to keep her out of that prison camp.

If he wasn't so desperate, he'd be intimidated.

Still, he'd never backed down from a fight in his life, and he certainly wasn't going to start now. It was just a matter of convincing Elise she wanted him as much as he wanted her, while simultaneously convincing the High Command they *didn't* want her. It was all as simple as getting sucked out an airlock.

And probably about that pleasant.

The bridge doors slid open to admit Yolanda Boniface, who paused to eye him on her way to her station. "How's the captive?"

He snarled.

She gave him a cheeky grin. "That's what I thought."

Before he could manage a suitably annihilating reply, one of the vidcreens flashed to life, split down the middle as if for a bridge conference. Surprised, Roarke pivoted to stare at it, wondering why one of his crew would call in through the ship's intercom instead of using the radio implant.

"Okay, Captain, so we can communicate, " Henry Voronnin said as his face appeared on the screen. "What do we do now?"

Roarke jerked upright, knowing instantly that this conversation wasn't supposed to be happening. And he certainly wasn't supposed to be hearing it.

On the split screen beside Voronnin, Elise frowned. "That's a very good question."

"How did they do *that?*" Yolanda crossed quickly to the communications console.

"Bypassed the computer safeguards, probably. Do they know we're monitoring?" Roarke demanded, coming out of his chair to stalk closer.

Yolanda's narrow black brows drew down. "Doesn't look like it. We're patched in, but they're not picking us up."

"Good," he said, then shushed her so he could listen to Elise's plotting.

With a grin of pure homicidal cheer, Voronnin suggested, "Well, we could always release something lethal into the ventilation system."

"Suicide's counterproductive, Henry."

Her first officer gestured with a hand the size of a spacesuit gauntlet. "Who said anything about suicide? All our people are in their quarters. If we confine the gas to operations areas and the bridge, we won't put any of the crew in danger."

Yolanda leaned close to Roarke and whispered, "You're growling, Boss."

He stopped.

"Henry, the boarding party's wearing armor, and they have communication implants," Elise pointed out patiently. "The gas might kill a couple of them, but the rest would go to oxygen packs. And then we'd have a bunch of pissed-off troopers looking for revenge. I, for one, do not want to go up against armor bare handed."

Roarke clenched his gauntleted fists. "Isn't that a damn shame?" He was growling again. He didn't much care.

Elise tapped a finger against her computer console, thinking furiously. "If only they didn't have those communication implants, we might ..." Something flickered in her consciousness, and she stilled, trying to bring it into focus.

The plan materialized with all the speed and detail of something that had been brewing in her subconscious for hours. She snapped her fingers. "Communication implants. That's it! Henry, we can broadcast a sonic stun pulse right into their implants. Boom. They go down and out, and we've got an hour to retake the ship."

He considered the idea, then shook his head slowly. "I don't think that would fly, Captain, not if they're taking standard precautions and scrambling their communications. The implant computers will reject any signal that isn't in the right code, which means nothing of ours would get through."

"Henry, I'm telling you, this is the solution." Elise sat forward in her seat, unconsciously leaning toward him in her eagerness. "The *Raker's* computer could analyze a sample of their communications and decode it. It'll take time, but it's not as though either of us has a more pressing engagement."

"That's the God's truth." Henry meditated a moment. "Could work."

"Of course it'll work." She lofted a teasing eyebrow at him. "My plans always do."

"Except when they don't," he said drily.

Barely even registering the quip, Elise got down to business, her hands darting over her workstation console as she set up the program.

Watching her on the screen, Henry commented, "If this does go, it'll be our turn to take hostages. The *Liberator* won't fire on us if we've got Roarke."

"Mmmph."

"Then, once we're away, we take the whole lot of 'em to Elba. Let Roarke try playing his clever little games with CSSIntel."

"Elba?" Elise frowned uneasily, looking up at him.

He shrugged. "It's the only POW installation in the sector. We have to take them there; it's standard procedure."

"Right." She fidgeted, hating the idea. "Look, I don't know how much time I've got before he comes back. I'd better get on it. Morrell out."

For a long moment Roarke sat paralyzed, unable to believe Elise would even consider handing him over to those bastards in CSSIntel. Not after he'd held her in his arms this morning, relishing the tender sensation of her sweet, warm body against his.

Damn her.

Turning on his heel, Roarke headed for the nearest hatch. Over his shoulder, he barked, "Yo, find that computer virus and kill it. And send somebody after that bastard Voronnin."

Yolanda nodded and turned. From the corner of her eye, she spotted something white sitting beside the command station he'd left. "Hey, boss, you forgot your helmet…"

But the hatch had already closed behind him.

Elise stared at the vidscreen as the *Raker's* computer worked to crack the boarding party's radio code, but she couldn't concentrate. She couldn't seem to shake the image of Roarke locked up in a prison camp.

The last time they'd had him, CSSIntel had tortured him so badly he was still feeling the effects two years later. What would they do to him now, particularly considering he'd killed his original jailer to escape? Elise had an ugly feeling she already knew the answer to that one: they'd brutalize Roarke until he died, simply as an object lesson to the other prisoners. He wouldn't last a week, and his final hours would be unspeakable.

She wasn't going to do it. No matter what it cost her, she wasn't going to let those bastards have him. Even if it gave Scordillis the excuse he was looking for to break her, she was going to turn the boarding party loose on the first Rebellion planet she could find.

Elise scowled at the screen of her workstation as she considered the implications. It would mean the end of her career, the loss of her ship, every-thing she'd worked for so long. And yet, letting CSSIntel have Roarke would do something much, much worse.

That would strip away her soul.

She straightened in a burst of self-awareness. It wasn't just the principle of the thing, though she wouldn't have sentenced a dog to that hellpit. No, it felt a lot more personal than that. As if Roarke had assumed an irrational importance to her, despite the fact that he was the enemy commander who'd tried to kill her yesterday — and who'd successfully seduced her last night.

Because, neurocuffs notwithstanding, it had been more than a seduction. There'd been tenderness in the touch of his hands, his mouth, in the way he'd looked at her as he'd entered her body. And the next morning he'd held her like a lover. Elise could have withstood the rest of his arsenal: the wicked skill, the ridiculously arousing sexual threats, even the intelligence, the sense of humor, the lupine good looks, that strong, amazing body. She could have withstood it all, except for the possibility that he actually cared about her, that he saw her as something more than a target in battle and in bed.

But did it matter? She was still a CSS captain, and he was still the enemy. They...

Behind her the room hatch sighed open. "You've been a very bad girl, Elise," Roarke rumbled.

She turned her head barely in time to see him coming for her, his handsome face like stone.

Instinctively Elise tried to duck away, but in the armor he was far too fast for her. His big hands caught her by the collar and hauled her out of her chair. Before she could yelp a protest, Roarke stripped off her robe with one ruthless swipe. Elise swore, struggling, but a naked woman is no match for an armored man, and he was relentless. In seconds, he had her pinned to the bulkhead with the weight of his body while he banged a magnetic clamp against the wall over her head. Neurocuffing her wrists together, he caught them in the clamp's field.

"Roarke, what the hell do you think you're doing?" Elise spat, pulling uselessly at the neurocuffs, though she knew she wouldn't be able to break the clamp's magnetic grip; it was designed to hold several tons of equipment.

"We're going to have a little...talk." Roarke crouched to grab her ankles, fending off the kicks she directed at his head. He clicked neuroshackles around them and thumped a pair of clamps against the wall, then caught the shackles in the clamps.

"Do you chain all your bed partners, or is it just me?" Elise demanded between gritted teeth, subsiding in raw frustration.

"Just you," he said, his tone dripping honey. "Nobody else betrays me to CSSIntel before the sheets are even cool."

She stared at him, sick dread rolling over her.

"And yes, I did monitor your chat with Henry." He straightened to his full height, looming over her like an armored wall.

Elise straightened her own spine, trying to ignore the way the shackles spread her thighs. "If our positions were reversed, you'd have done the same thing."

He braced a palm beside her head and leaned close. "In the first place, I wouldn't work for the bloody CSS. I'm picky about who I do my killing for."

Knowing a threat when she heard one, Elise stared up into his handsome face, so close to her own. "You won't kill me."

A combination of irritation and reluctant amusement flickered over his face. "You're right, I won't. But that still leaves me a lot of room to maneuver." Reaching into one of the pouches on his belt, Roarke pulled out a thick black cylinder with rounded ends.

Elise felt her face go cold as the blood drained from her head. "Price'll be thrilled," she muttered hoarsely.

It was a neurowhip.

Cleansing anger flooded into her, flushing away the moment's fear. "Give me credit for some intelligence, Roarke. You and I both know you'd be the last one to use that thing on a prisoner."

"Now there — " He flicked one of the setting rings on the barrel with his thumb. "— is where you're wrong."

Before she could flinch, Roarke touched the neurowhip to her right nipple.

Elise cried out as intense sensation rolled over her, so hot and fierce it took her a moment to realize what she was feeling was pleasure. Shocked, she stared up into her captor's hungry eyes.

"Oh, yeeaaah." He gave her the smile the Wolf must have given Little Red Riding Hood. "Not only will I use this little toy on you, I'm going to enjoy it."

Still wearing that sensual carnivore's smile, Roarke lazily teased her nipple with the neurowhip. She gasped as phantom teeth nibbled gently on the pink bud.

"If you'll notice," he said in a mockingly pedantic tone as he ran the barrel gently over the curve of her breast, "the neurowhip has three setting rings, one for intensity, the other for the type of neuron being stimulated, a third for combination of stimuli you select. A readout tells you which settings you've chosen." His thumb flicked one of the rings, and she felt a delicate, arousing suction. "Though I didn't know about this particular group of settings until a certain female friend asked what I was doing with a sex toy in my quarters." His teeth flashed. "Evidently the neurowhip is a well-known piece of…equipment in some circles. Some enterprising CSSIntell agent must do a brisk smuggling business."

Again, he stroked the tube over her nipples, and another cascade of pleasure rolled over her. Adjusting the whip as he went, he raised the intensity until she clenched her eyes shut and groaned helplessly. It felt as though countless tongues were licking and sucking at her breasts, warmth and wetness and pressure flickering across her skin like flame.

"I've never used it this way. Hell, I've never used it at all." He watched her breasts tremble as she gasped. "This seems like a perfect time to experiment."

"Why?" she croaked, twisting in her bonds. Lush delight trailed the neurowhip as he ran it down her ribs. "I thought you were...AH!...angry..."

"Oh, I am." He drew an erotic circle around her belly button. "Not about the escape plot — you're right, I would have done the same thing — but I'm pretty pissed about Elba."

"I wouldn't have...I wouldn't have sent you..." She shuddered helplessly.

He heaved an exaggerated sigh. "Now, that's the problem with torture. You can never tell if the victim means what she's saying, or if she just wants you to stop." Leaning close enough to breathe in her ear, Roarke whispered, "Do you want me to stop, Elise?"

The whip was tracing a curving arc low on her belly, just above her pelvic bone. Any minute now he'd go lower, find her most sensitive flesh. She didn't think she could stand it if he touched her there. "God, no," she whimpered. "Don't stop."

Aching, Roarke watched Elise writhe, her white, deliciously lush body twisting in the neurocuffs. Her eyes were closed, the long lashes fanning against the curve of her cheeks. Her soft lips parted as she gasped. Her nipples were tight little points on her full, swaying breasts, and her hips made tiny, involuntary thrusts.

He was rapidly discovering just how uncomfortable it was to get a lead pipe erection in boarding armor. But he didn't dare take the suit off. If he did, he'd take her.

And then neither of them would know the truth.

Elise opened dazed eyes and looked around for Roarke through a haze of pleasure. She found him kneeling at her feet, running the neurowhip up and down the inside of her thighs. Even though he wasn't actually touching the erect nubbin between her legs, the back spill from the device was providing a wicked stimulation every time he brought it close.

Roarke looked up, his black eyes meeting hers, male and hungry, yet fiercely controlled. He was still wearing his armor.

Elise realized she wanted him out of it.

She wanted to see his glorious body naked, feel his hands, his mouth, his strong, warm strength. The neurowhip, intense as its stimulation was, couldn't give her any of that.

But he was trailing the device up her leg, closer and closer to her core. The sensations it wrung from her made her back arch.

"No, wait, not like...uhhh...not like that," Elise gasped.

Blessedly, Roarke stopped. "Don't you want to come? I can tell how…" His corded throat worked as he swallowed. "…hot you are."

"But I want…you. Take off the armor. Please, Roarke."

His lids lowered. "Why? What difference does it make?"

He wanted coherent thought out of her *now*? "It's cold."

"I can make it warmer." He flicked one of the setting rings.

"No!" His obtuseness was beginning to drag her out of her luscious fog. "I mean it's empty. Not like…not like when you touch me."

"But it's all the same thing. Just skillful stimulation of nerve endings. Isn't that what you said this morning?"

"It was more than that." She swallowed, licking her dry lips.

"You think so? Let's see…" Roarke leaned closer and opened his mouth. Elise tensed, staring down at his dark head, so close to her pubic mound. This time the wet, hot tongue she felt stroke into her curls was real. And it was his. Elise shuddered, desperate for him.

Roarke tilted his head back to look up into her face. "I wonder. If you close your eyes, can you tell the difference?" He lifted the neurowhip again.

"I don't want that thing. I want you." He was playing with her, dammit. She frowned, coming fully aware now, spurred by the restless blend of hunger and irritation he'd aroused so ruthlessly. "Is that what you wanted to hear?"

"Maybe."

"All right," she snapped. "Last night was more than sex, and we both know it. Take off that bloody armor, toss the toy out the airlock, and let's stop playing around."

Roarke's eyes flared with hot satisfaction as he tossed the neurowhip away.

Reaching for the shackles, he freed her legs with a couple of violent jerks. She watched impatiently as he grabbed the 'cuffs and liberated her wrists as well. Elise stepped away from the wall and helped him attack his armor, tugging off the awkward gauntlets, popping the pneumatic seal on his chestplate. Together they hauled the torso shell away from his muscled chest, flung it aside, and went to work on the lower half of the suit the minute he opened its catches.

"This isn't just sex," Roarke told her fiercely, pulling his legs free.

"I know that. Hurry and get that thing off." As he stripped off the last, unwanted barrier of the skinsuit, Elise shot him a cautious look. "What do you think it is?"

"Hell, I don't know. Bed?"

"No, here." She turned and bent over the desk. "It always made me crazy when you'd threaten to come into me like this."

"Me too," he growled, and moved up behind her. His big hands caught her hips and tugged her back. The smooth, rounded head of his erection brushed her bottom, lowered until it found her eager heat. He entered in a slick glide, filling her endlessly as she arched in pleasure.

"God, Roarke!"

"Yesssss!" He pulled her greedily against him, his hands going to her breasts to pluck and roll her hard nipples as he kissed her ear, the side of her neck, biting gently until she turned her face to his. Plunging his tongue into her mouth, he held his hips still. She didn't protest, wanting only to prolong having him within her.

They strained together like that, kissing slowly, awkwardly, their necks twisted, eyes closed. Elise felt Roarke shudder against her. "God," he moaned, "I want to drive into you, but it'd be over too soon. I'm too hot for you, I'd never make it last long enough."

Elise murmured an incoherent agreement even as she felt her own control eroding. Her hips rolled once, an involuntary thrust that buried his silken length a fraction deeper. She caught her breath. He felt so thick inside her, his body so strong around hers as he surrounded her with his arms and his chest and his powerful hips, cradling her in masculine power, in desire, in heat. No man had ever felt this way — as though he completed her, enhanced her, yet made her more wholly herself than she was without him.

She wanted more.

Teeth unconsciously biting her lip, Elise pulled away slightly, then drove back onto his width. He gasped. "Elise, don't. I can't..."

She thrust.

Roarke lost control. His powerful hands clamped into the curve of her bottom and dug in as he began to lunge, driving his long male shaft in and out of her. She quivered as ecstasy ignited in her core, searing brighter with each pistoning stroke.

"God, Elise, I need you," he groaned, "I'm not going let you go again, I'm going...to keep you, AH! Whatever it takes..."

"Yes!" She threw back her head as he pounded her, his hips slapping against hers. The pleasure blasted her every inhibition, her every vestige of control. "Yes, keep you..."

He grated something else, but he was thrusting so hard she couldn't make it out, couldn't comprehend anything beyond the fiery length digging inside her, giving her no mercy, offering no quarter from the brutal delight.

Detonation.

Elise convulsed in Roarke's possessive arms, screaming through her climax as her body tightened on his so ferociously he made a startled sound.

And came with a roar of pure male triumph.

When Elise next became aware, the edge of her workstation was digging into her belly, and Roarke was sprawled across her back, feeling heavy, sweaty, and utterly delicious.

"Mmmmm. That was..." She couldn't think of the words. Nothing seemed good enough.

"Yeah," he agreed blurrily. "Mmmm." After a long, languorous silence, he stirred. "I must be heavy." Gently he pulled away. She caught her breath as he left her. She realized she wanted to call him back, wanted his hot weight. Without him she felt curiously light, cool. And empty.

"I wouldn't have sent you to Elba," Elise said, suddenly desperate, though she didn't know why.

"Yeah," he said. "I just wasn't sure you knew it."

"What do you mean?" She pulled away from the desk, wincing a bit at the soreness in her muscles. It was an oddly satisfying ache.

"There's something happening between us, and it's not just war." He threw her a hooded black look. "I want more of you than what I can get by shackling you to the wall."

She grinned. "Though that has certain attractions I never would have guessed." Elise sobered. "But I'm not sure what either of us can do about it."

His expression turned wary. "What do you mean?"

Elise shrugged, making a helpless gesture. "We're on opposite sides, Roarke. If I don't manage to escape, I'm going to prison for the duration of the war. That doesn't sound like a particularly good way to start a relationship."

"I know that, I..." Roarke broke off, tilting his head as though listening to something. His dark eyes widened. "How did he get past the guard stationed in crew quarters?" he barked. Realizing he must be talking to someone through his radio implant, Elise grimaced.

"He didn't just walk through the bulkhead, Yo. I want to know what the hell..." Roarke broke off, eyes going narrow as he stared at Elise. "Forget it, I'm sure I know someone who can tell us. In the meantime, triple the guard and send out search parties. I want that bastard found, and I don't want any more *Raker* people getting loose!"

Elise stared at him, remembering she'd disabled Roarke's computer safe-guards — and the one man who knew she'd done it. "Henry."

"Yeah." He turned around and began hunting for his armor. "We'd better get dressed. And while we're at it, you can tell me how Voronnin got past the guards I had posted at the corridor junctions in crew quarters."

Frowning, she stood and made for a closet, stalling for time. She knew the answer, of course. Coalition ship designers were a cautious, paranoid bunch; there was an access tube that ran from the crew deck to the armory. A second tube was located just outside her quarters, also going to the armory. Nobody but senior ship's command staff knew about it. "Roarke, you know I can't tell you that. Regardless of whatever's going on between us, I have a responsibility to my crew."

He snorted. "Maybe, but not in Voronnin's case. For one thing, I don't think he feels much loyalty in return."

She frowned at him. "What are you talking about?"

"How do you think we monitored your transmission to him earlier?"

Finding a black one-piece ship suit, Elise pulled it out of the closet and put it on. "I assume you defeated my security program."

"Not quite, or he wouldn't have gotten loose." He grunted as he shrugged back into the torso armor.

One hand sealing the suit closed, Elise looked up. "What are you saying — that he betrayed me?"

"Wouldn't be the first time."

"I've known Henry Voronnin since we were in the CSS Academy. He's not the type."

Roarke sighed. "Remember that anonymous communication that led me to you on Tyus? Ever wonder where it came from?"

"What does that have to do with ...?"

"Who knew you were going out onto the beach, Elise?"

Elise felt her stomach sink. She'd called Henry before she'd gone for her swim that fateful night. "Anybody that looked out a window."

"He knew who you were, Elise. Even gave your ship registry," Roarke told her. "The only person who could have blown your cover was Voronnin himself."

Henry, a traitor? It couldn't be. He was the most genuinely decent person she knew.

It couldn't be.

Slowly, she moved to her desk chair and sat down. "But why?" The question sounded a lot more forlorn than she would have wished.

"Well, there's the fact that somebody with the CSS high command doesn't seem terribly fond of you. Not judging from the communique we got yesterday detailing your Superspace dropout coordinates. Hell, I met you expecting a trap — which it was, but not for the *Liberator*."

Elise stared at him, wishing that for once she'd been wrong about the CSS's capacity for treachery. "That wasn't Henry. He'd have been killed if you'd destroyed the ship. No, I think Admiral Scordillis himself was responsible for that one."

His eyebrows lifted. "A nasty enemy to have. Which gives Henry a motive." Roarke moved to lean an armored hip on the desktop. "If Voronnin knew the admiral was willing to go to those lengths to get you..."

"Then setting me up on Tyus would make sense. It'd be the only way to save the ship. And since that failed, and since we survived your attack..." She dragged a hand through her hair as pain clawed at her. "He must have patched us into the bridge hoping to goad you into killing me. With me dead, Scordillis would leave the crew alone. God, Henry."

And now he was on the loose. Headed for the armory. He couldn't get at the beamers — he'd need her voice command for that, the CSS having a pathological fear of mutiny — but he could get to the boarding armor. The armor wasn't locked down, because it had to be accessible to repel invaders even with the captain dead.

Which she might soon be, after Henry took the second access tube back to her quarters.

Elise lifted her head. "Roarke, you'd..."

The corridor door slid open, revealing two figures in black and gray CSS boarding armor. The visor of one of the suits slid back, revealing Henry Voronnin's familiar face, twisted in an alien expression of rage. "Damn you, Roarke, why won't you kill her? Are you that hot for her narrow little ass?"

"Henry," Elise growled, "you treacherous..."

Before she could open her mouth again, Roarke swept her out of her chair with one hand and tossed her into the corner. Her head struck the bulkhead with the force of his enhanced strength. Sparks exploded in a white-hot burst of pain.

Roarke dove after her, spinning to place himself between her and the mutineers. It was a risky move, literally backing himself into a corner, but he knew if he'd tried to defend her any other way, one of them would maneuver to his rear and take her. Triggering his radio implant, he barked, "Yo, get a crew down here! The goddamned escapees are in Elise's quarters!"

The smaller of the two promptly turned and rammed his fist into the bulkhead beside the door. Sparks showered. He turned and served the door to Elise's quarters the same.

"Your rescuers won't be getting in that way, Roarke," Henry told him over the sound of rending metal. "Not without a beamer torch and an hour's work, anyway." The big man edged toward him. "Let us have the captain, and we'll discuss this."

Roarke's lips pulled back in a snarl. "Go to hell."

"Be reasonable. There are two of us, and you don't even have your helmet. One good head shot, and your brains are all over the bulkhead. Either way, I'm going to kill her. Why die too?"

For a moment Roarke could see it: Elise, helpless in the merciless armored grip of these bastards. Rage scalded him. "Fuck you, Voronnin."

"I'll get her. One way or another." He was swinging his fist in a blurring roundhouse before his faceplate even had time to close.

Roarke blocked it away from his bare head and slammed out a counter punch. It struck Voronnin square in the chest, and he staggered, only to rear back and drive a kick right at Roarke's belly.

His first impulse was to dance aside, but Roarke caught himself at the last moment. He couldn't leave Elise unprotected. He swept down a block instead.

Too late. The booted foot hit him like an meteor. Even with the protection of his armor, the impact rammed into his belly with sickening force. Roarke gasped for breath, fighting to keep his feet and avoid being knocked into Elise, knowing he could easily crush her even as he tried to keep her alive.

Recovering his balance, he growled and shot two rapid-fire punches at Voronnin's faceplate. The assassin blocked the first, but the second staggered him.

Not daring to press his advantage for fear of leaving Elise vulnerable, Roarke stayed in his corner and waited for the next attack.

Woozily, Elise shook her head, blinking away the dancing gray spots that filled her vision. She must have blacked out for a moment. Something broad and hard was pressed against her, wedging her into a corner so tightly she could barely breathe. She heard Roarke curse viciously over a rhythmic series of crunches, the sound of something hard slamming and grinding into something that clanked and scraped with each blow. Still dazed, Elise pressed her forehead against what she suddenly realized was Roarke's armored back, and felt him shudder with impact. It was then that she recognized the sounds: hand-to-hand combat in armor.

Desperately she shook her head again, trying to make sense of the situation despite the hammer strokes of headache that made thought all but impossible. They were backed into a corner. It was the worst possible tactical position; Roarke couldn't maneuver at all. Why didn't he move, get room enough to defend himself?

The last of the mental fog burned away as she realized Roarke must be guarding her. Because if he didn't, Henry Voronnin would murder her like a child pulling the wings off a bug.

Looking up, she saw Roarke blocking punch after punch away from his head.

Damn. He couldn't keep that up. He was going to get himself killed trying to keep her alive. Stupid, quixotic...

What was she supposed to do without him?

Something hard closed around her ankle. Jerked, pulling her down and out. Elise yelled and grabbed for Roarke, but her hands slipped down the chill, smooth metal of his armor. She hit the deck hard, and her captor dragged her out of her corner, right past Roarke's leg, scraping off a layer of skin on his knee joint as she passed.

Roarke glanced down, saw what was happening and swore, grabbing for her, but a punch from Voronnin drove him back into the bulkhead.

A gauntleted hand closed brutally tight over her throat and jerked her to her feet. Elise gasped, fighting to breathe, clawing uselessly at the arm that held her. Gagging, she stared into the polarized plastic of her assailant's faceplate.

The visor slid back, revealing the smug, malicious features of Lt. Gloria Price. "Hello, Captain. Looks like I finally got you just where I want you."

Chapter Five

In frustrated rage, Roarke watched the second assassin drag Elise out of reach. He had to get her back before the bastard killed her.

Something blurred toward his face. He blocked it automatically, knocking aside yet another lethal Voronnin punch. Cursing under his breath, Roarke realized he'd have to take care of that treacherous son of a bitch first. Knowing he needed maneuvering room to do it, he lunged out of the corner, slamming a one-two combination into Voronnin's faceplate as he went by. The tough, armored plastisteel was designed to take a lot of abuse, but if you hammered at it long enough, it would give.

And that was just what Roarke meant to do.

He circled his hulking opponent, forcing himself to forget Elise's peril for the moment. It was difficult using martial arts techniques that called for agility in bulky boarding armor, but still he twisted his body into a powerful spinning kick targeted at Voronnin's skull.

With a roar of fury Roarke could hear even through the helmet, the big man grabbed his leg before the strike landed. Jerking straight up, Voronnin dumped him hard on his back, then stomped viciously down into his belly. Pain choked him, sickening and black. Voronnin drew back for another kick, but this time Roarke caught his boot. Clamping his other hand into his foe's knee, Roarke picked him up and hurled him away. Voronnin slammed into the bulkhead.

Rolling, Roarke sprang for him in a low, flat dive, managing to score another hard punch to the faceplate just as Voronnin landed a bruising kick between his ribs. But the helmet didn't give.

He just prayed Elise would still be alive by the time it did.

Black spots danced in front of Elise's vision as Price's ruthless grip cut off her oxygen. Even as she pounded the traitor's arms in an effort to break her hold, Elise realized she was deliberately spinning the assault out. In the suit, Price could have easily crushed her throat with one hard squeeze. Evidently she was enjoying herself too much to make it quick.

Elise's blows weakened as her strength drained rapidly. Even the pain was fading, drowned in a rising tide of darkness. With a sensation of mild surprise, she realized she was dying.

Abruptly the vicious grip relaxed. Wheezing, Elise choked down a gulp of air.

"Oh, Captain — I just remembered," the blonde said, malice in her cold blue eyes. Elise didn't stir, hanging limp as she concentrated on breathing. Price gave her a quick, hard shake. "Wake up, captain, you need to hear this. There's a message Admiral Scordillis told me to convey before you died. Are you still there?"

She managed a weak kick in the traitor's general direction.

"Good. Listen carefully now: your father is dead. The CSS had him assassinated a week ago. You're the last Morrell left alive. And soon…there won't be any of you."

Roarke managed to work his opponent into the same corner he'd just vacated, but he paid for it. Voronnin hammered a trio of blows into his torso so powerful the armor couldn't absorb that much force. Pain blasted hammered him, and something grated ominously in his ribs. Cracked, Roarke thought grimly. Perhaps worse. He tried to back away, but sensing his weakness Voronnin stalked him, drawing back his fist for another pile driver punch to the ribs.

Roarke automatically blocked — only to realize at the last instant the strike was a feint.

He looked up to see a huge fist coming right at his face.

Instinctively Roarke ducked, grabbing the arm as it passed overhead. Continuing the arc, he jerked forward and down. Voronnin went airborne and slammed head first into the bulkhead behind him. Plastisteel crunched. The assassin rebounded off the wall and slowly toppled.

Holding his abused ribs, Roarke cautiously moved close enough to see Voronnin's face. Through the shattered visor, his opponent's face was slack, eyes closed.

One down, Roarke thought grimly.

Elise stared at the blonde in stunned horror.

Obviously relishing her anguish, Price explained, "The Admiral suspected you might decide to step into your father's position with the Reform movement. That's why you've got to die." Smiling sweetly, she let go of Elise's throat so she could catch her by the shoulder instead. She drew back an armored fist that could shatter her captain's skull. "Any final words for the Admiral, Captain?"

Elise coughed. "Yes," she choked out. Her voice was barely a whisper, sandpaper rough. "Abort Omega Code Zero."

"What's that supposed to mean?" Price scowled, irritated. "If you're trying to stall…"

She broke off as her body snapped out to its full height, jerked rigid as though by invisible strings. Her hands fell away from Elise and slapped down at her sides. Price's eyes widened. "What?" Her head snapped back and forth in her helmet, but other than that, she didn't move at all.

She couldn't.

Despite the agony in her throat, Elise felt a feral grin slide across her lips.

"What's the hell is going on?" Price demanded, her voice spiraling into a screech. "What did you do?"

"I was…" Elise had to stop and swallow to get her abused vocal cords to work, but she still couldn't manage anything louder than a whisper. "…expecting something like this from you. A month ago I programmed your onboard suit computer to lock the armor down at my command." Watching fear swamp Price's eyes as the blonde realized just how throughly she was trapped, Elise felt her grin broaden. "You know, I do have a message for Scordillis. Tell him I resign." Slowly, she drew back her fist.

"Captain…!"

The punch landed squarely on Price's patrician nose. Blood spurted, accompanied by a satisfying howl.

"You have such a way with words." Roarke said into Elise's ear.

"I try." She redirected her triumphant grin over her shoulder at him.

Ignoring Price's nasal curses, he shook his head. "Here I was, desperately trying to finish that bastard Voronnin off in time to save you, unarmed and supposedly helpless as you are. I should have known better. You wouldn't be helpless stark naked in a tiger cage."

Refusing to subject her abused throat with any more attempts at speech, Elise smiled tightly.

Roarke frowned and put out a hand to lift her chin, tilting her head back so he could see her throat. "Let's see that…Elise, you've got her fingerprints branded into your throat. I'm amazed you can talk at all. Are you all right?"

"Fine," she rasped. As fine as she could be, anyway, under the circumstances.

He shot her a worried look, obviously doubting it. "Let me call my crew and see how they're doing with the door. We need to get you to a medic." Looking away from her, he said into his implant, "How are you coming with that laser torch, Yo?"

As Roarke talked to his people, Elise's attention fell on Henry, still sprawled unconscious on his back. His helmet faceplate was shattered into jagged chunks.

Taking a step toward him, she felt something roll under her foot. She looked down and saw she'd stepped on the neurowhip, lying where Roarke had apparently dropped it. Elise picked it up and absently began to twist the setting rings as she moved to stand over her former friend.

"What happened to you, Henry," she murmured. "And why didn't I realize it?"

His eyes opened. "You always did underestimate me."

His hand flashed upward and dug into the waist band of her coveralls. The next moment she was on top of him and his huge hand was wrapped around her head. Slowly, he began to twist.

Elise gritted, "Planning to break my neck, Henry?"

"Yeah." His grip tightened. "Sorry, Captain."

She rammed the neurowhip through the hole in his faceplate and activated it. He howled, his massive body arching under her, his hand tightening convulsively on her head. Teeth clenched, she held the whip where it was.

The deck plate boomed in her ear as something heavy hit the ground beside them. Fingers closed over Henry's, fighting to pry them away. Out of the corner of one eye, she saw Roarke's white, desperate face as he fought to keep Henry from twisting her head any further. Pain lanced up and down Elise's neck, and she screamed as the pain spiraled, her voice blending with Henry's bellow. She felt bone grate just as Roarke finally managed to jerk Voronnin's hand away, scraping off a layer of skin in the process.

Henry's bellow cut off.

"I should have killed that son of a bitch when I had the chance," Roarke panted into the sudden silence. Reaching down, he tenderly pulled Elise away from her would-be killer.

"S' okay," Elise rasped, looking down at Henry. His eyes were fixed, staring. Dead. "I thought neurowhips weren't supposed to kill."

"They're not" Roarke frowned at the body. "Though I do think I heard something about not bringing them in contact with the victim's head…" Glancing at the readout of the whip she still held, he flinched. "Not at that setting, anyway."

Elise looked down. All three readings were redlined. Horror wound tight in her. "Evidently," she whispered.

※>((ᐷ⊙)∂(ᐸ⅄

Elise made a soft sound. Roarke looked quickly over at her, scanning her as she lay on the regrowth couch a few feet away. He'd ended up in Sickbay with her when the medic discovered the interesting fractures in his ribs.

The desolation on her face tore at him. "You had no choice, Elise, you know that. He was going to kill you."

She shot him a blank look, as though it was taking her a moment to remember who he was talking about. At last she shook her head, pale strands shifting around her shoulders under the gold light cast by the medifield. "It's not that." Elise hesitated. "Roarke, the CSS had my father assassinated."

He blinked. "You're *that* Morrell?"

"Didn't you know?"

"The dossier I had on you was fairly sketchy."

She nodded, then fell silent again.

He studied her. Her face was too pale, suffering etching the delicate features and pulling her lush mouth tight. Yet her eyes were dry. "You've seen news stories then?" she asked at last.

"Yes."

"How did they do it?"

Roarke hesitated, then admitted reluctantly, "A sniper from ambush. I understand he died instantly. They're claiming a rival member of the Reformists hired the assassin."

"They would."

"I'm sorry, Elise."

"I know." She paused. "When the medic releases us, there's something I want to show you."

He nodded and allowed the silence to claim her again.

An hour later, they stood in a gravitylock and waited for it to cycle. Slowly, Roarke felt his body becoming lighter as the gravity in the cubical decreased until his feet left the deck altogether. The opposite hatch opened, and Elise pushed off, drifting out of the lock to catch at a padded perch in the tank beyond. Roarke followed more slowly, scanning the area with his habitual caution.

It looked just like the ZG tank on the Liberator. Designed to allow crew to practice zero gravity fighting skills, it was outfitted with a number of hoop-shaped perches that projected from the smooth, curving walls. Vid projectors allowed the occupants to program whatever background they chose for three-dimensional display on the tank walls; Elise had chosen a scene of the Earth from orbit. Roarke stared hungrily. He hadn't seen the home world since the war started, and he doubted he'd ever see it again. It was as chokingly beautiful as always, a lovely blue globe splashed with green and ocher, swirled with blinding cloud cover.

"Before we started this mission, while the *Raker* was still in orbit around Earth, my father came up for a visit," Elise said softly, "I brought him in here and had the computer relay a sensor image to the projectors. This is a recording of that image." Her voice dropped. "He said Earth had never been more beautiful to him, because he was seeing it from the deck of my ship. Since then, I've been coming here whenever I felt the need for his guidance. It makes…made me feel close to him."

"I can't think of a better remembrance." His voice was a bit too husky, and he cleared his throat. He felt a sudden, vicious desire to hunt Frank Scordillis down and kill him for her.

"My father thought the Rebellion was wrong, you know." Elise brought her feet around so she could perch on the handhold. "He believed the only real route to change was from within. Otherwise you just exchange one dictator for another."

Roarke scowled. "The Rebellion is a democracy, not a dictatorship. We've already ratified a constitution."

"I know." She let go of her handhold and hung in the air for a moment, letting herself float. "As much as I loved him, I've come to realize my father was wrong, about that and other things. Some systems are so corrupt they can't be changed. They simply can't tolerate anything but evil. If you try to change them, they'll kill you. And if you just go along, they'll corrupt you." Softly she added, "That's what happened to Henry. And ultimately, it's what would have happened to me."

"I think you're selling yourself short. Enemy or not, you've never been anything but honorable." Roarke grimaced. "Even when I didn't want to admit it."

She shook her head, the small movement causing her body to drift in the air until she reached out and grabbed the handhold again. "Since I'd become captain, I'd begun to finally see what the CSS was doing. Often I was appalled, it was so totally opposite everything I knew to be just. I considered resigning a hundred times, but I always rationalized my way into staying."

She shrugged. "I reasoned that my father's enemies would use my leaving the service to make him look bad, I reasoned that I was protecting the lives of innocent Coalition civilians, I reasoned that soon he would be president and the corruption would end." Taking a deep breath, Elise added, bluntly, savagely, "But the fact was I'd worked fifteen years of my life to win this ship, and I didn't want to lose it."

"Sounds to me like you were guilty of being human."

"Unfortunately that's no excuse." She put her slim foot into the hoop and gently pushed. Slowly, her unbound hair forming a swirling halo around her head, Elise floated upward. "But now that doesn't matter. I've lost it all anyway. My crew, my ship, my home. My father."

He looked up at her as she hovered over him, her body long and lush in the white coveralls he'd given her in lieu of the uniform she'd refused to wear any longer. "Elise…"

She was staring fixedly at the globe of Earth, its blue light washing her face in cool radiance. "Losing him…it's like when someone you love dies of a long, wasting illness. There's grief and pain, but there's also a kind of relief. Because it's over." Her eyes seemed to be growing larger, an effect caused by tears filling them, yet unable to fall. "I never realized how working for those bastards had eaten at me all these years. And without meaning to, he'd tied me to them." Impatiently, she dashed a hand over her face. The tears spun away, glittering in the earthlight. "But God, Roarke, it hurts."

Feeling helpless in the face of her grief, he pushed off from his handhold and floated to join her. "Elise…" Gently he caught her shoulders. She turned and flowed against him, wrapping her arms tightly around his ribs, the movement tumbling them both into a slow spin.

He felt her small, slender body shudder with pain. "They killed him. Roarke, the bastards killed him."

"I know, darlin'."

"There's no more of us left. Nobody but me. I'm alone."

"Shhh. You're not alone. I'm here." Gently, he kissed away one of the tears clinging to the feathered length of her lashes.

Suddenly her mouth was on his, desperate, fierce with a hunger that caught him off guard. Roarke stiffened in surprise, then began to kiss her back. Her tongue swept into his mouth, so possessive and eager he felt his cock harden. Her slim body strained against his. Instinctively he tightened his grip, giving her the strength and closeness she seemed to need so badly.

"Help me, Roarke," she whispered against his mouth. "Help me forget. For just a little while."

"Anything," he moaned as the tank spun lazily around them.

"We need to anchor," Elise said, her voice hoarse with a razored combination of choking grief and sudden, furious need. "Anchor us."

Instinctively Roarke reached out and snagged a passing handhold, then caught the one next to it with the other hand, bringing both of then to a sudden stop. Elise pulled back from him just enough to open the seal of her uniform, her mouth set in a line that trembled. He could only ache for her, even as his own hunger ignited as she wiggled out of the shipsuit. The clothing went sailing across the tank as she reached for Roarke's seal. Ruthlessly, she dragged at it until it opened, clawed it back until it was off his shoulders and pulled down to his elbows.

Elise began to nibble on the thick swell of his biceps, then licked her way up his arm and across his shoulder, biting and tasting as she went. After wrapping her legs around his thighs to anchor herself, she stretched up his body to pull the suit down to his waist. Roarke moaned as his erection pressed into her flat belly.

Her long, cool hands trembled as they traced the plates of his pecs, then explored the weave of muscle that lay over his ribs. He felt her breath gusting warm over his skin, the brush of her fine sexual hair against his right leg, and shuddered himself in raw, erotic pleasure.

"If you keep this up," Roarke said, his voice husky and rough, "I won't be responsible for my actions."

Elise straightened, her hands bracing her away from his chest even while she held on with her legs. There was a hypnotic, witchy sensuality about her as her long hair flowed around her head, her gem-green eyes glittering at him through a sheen of tears, her breasts with their darkly flushed nipples taunting him. "Surely the captain of the *Liberator* can muster more self-control than that."

"I'll try," he muttered hoarsely.

"Good." And, wrapping both hands in the fabric of his coveralls, she jerked them down. His stone-hard erection sprang free into the cool air. "Because I'm getting to the best part."

Elise stripped the suit the rest of the way down his legs and tossed it across the tank. For a moment she let go and allowed herself to float, studying Roarke as she considered the possibilities. He was stretched out, his hands locked around the handholds, muscled arms bulging as he held his powerful body taunt. It was a tempting picture — and just what she needed. What she had to have.

Forgetfulness. If only for a while.

Making love in zero-g was tricky. Unless one partner anchored the other, it was easy to go into a wild, uncontrolled spin or even bounce off one another altogether. It took strength and self-control to provide your lover with the strong, steady brace needed, not to mention a willingness to stay completely rigid. Roarke hadn't even questioned why he should be the one to anchor them, though she knew he'd probably prefer to be in control. He seemed to recognize what she needed.

Looking down the length of his body, Elise saw his erect shaft bouncing slightly in an invisible air current. She decided on the spot to reward him for his generosity.

Reaching out, Elise hooked an arm around his strong thigh and drew herself closer as she opened her mouth for the broad, purpled head. Roarke moaned in anticipation that would have made her smile at any other time. Now she just took him in without hesitation. The crown felt just slightly nubby as she swirled her tongue over it, then sucked it deeper inside. She grasped his hip, angled her body upward and sank, head first, down onto his erection.

Fellatio was the sole sex act that was actually easier in zero-g, since you could get into any position you needed to and suck as long as you wanted without worrying about muscle fatigue.

Roarke's back arched as he moaned in voluptuous pleasure. They drifted for a moment, then jerked to a stop as he remembered his task and grabbed hold of the hoops again. Slowly, Elise withdrew, paused to lick and bite gently at the crown, then took his organ even deeper. And so she played, first pulling her body closer by her grip on his hips, then pushing away again, over and over until he twisted in helpless pleasure.

"If this is payback for using the neurowhip on your nipples," he groaned, "it's damned effective."

She didn't answer, too intent on the moment, on the feel and taste of him. Forcing away the pain.

"But for you, I'm willing to suffer." His black eyes closed. "As long as you don't stop."

Instead of taking his shaft again, she pulled herself close to his groin and nuzzled his testicles. Sucking first one and then the other into her mouth, she tongued them, enjoying the shudder that ran through his powerful body. Returning her attention to his cock, she slowly licked up and down the shaft, then engulfed him for a few more long strokes down her throat.

"Elise." His voice had deepened into a rough growl. "If you keep that up, *I* won't be able to."

He was staring at her with that famished black wolf look in his eyes, and she realized his patience was eroding rapidly. But she wasn't ready for it to be over. Not yet.

Releasing his hard shaft, she worked her way over his torso, stroking the fascinating topography of his muscles, savoring the warmth of his skin. And his hooded eyes, flicking over her body in that predatory way he had.

"Elise, let me suck your nipples," he purred.

"I don't know," she rasped, a jolt of pleasure at the idea stabbing through her desperation. "You've been a very bad boy."

"Just give me another chance." His eyes hooded. "I'll show you just how bad I can be."

"Well, all right." She let herself drift up his body, touching him here and there as she moved. Taking hold of his powerful biceps, she presented a nipple to his mouth. "As long as you're very, very bad."

Looking up into her eyes, he lifted his head and curled out his long tongue for a slow lick of the hard pink tip. Pleasure lanced through her at the contact.

Then it was Elise's turn to moan helplessly as Roarke began suck and bite and lick at the stiff nipple. Desire coiled in a tight, laced ball in her belly. She twisted her torso to present the other breast to his mouth, and he obligingly, hungrily, closed his white teeth over it. His tongue flicked at his trapped captive until she writhed against him, the strength and hardness of his body madening her even more.

Suddenly Roarke released her. His dark eyes burned into hers. "Now." And he arched his back, thrusting his hips upward in invitation.

"Yes," she moaned, and hurriedly pushed herself down his body. Ravenous, desperate, Elise wrapped her legs around his hips, caught hold of his hot shaft, and lifted herself until she could aim it at her tight, creamy opening. Tightening her thighs, she grabbed his ribs and pulled until he sank into her, spreading her, filling her deliciously full. She shuddered.

"God, Elise…" Roarke twisted, pumping his hips to help her push his shaft deeper into her clamping flesh.

Driven wild by the force of her desire for him, Elise began to work, grinding her body against his, though she could scarcely bear the pleasure of the penetration. She could feel the muscle leaping under his damp skin as he struggled to both hold them still and provide a steady platform for her pleasure.

Gasping, she rode him, staring at his handsome, set face, watching the flex of tendon in his jaw as he fought to control his own passion. Forced to keep her strokes short, she circled her hips, letting his shaft gore her deliciously. Each flex and movement they made drove her pleasure that much higher, until her climax was just beyond the brush of her fingers, needing only one slight nudge…

"Elise!" Roarke groaned. "I have to…!"

His hands released the hoops and flew to her hips. Powerful fingers closed over her round buttocks, lifted her off his shaft, then drove her downward in one brutally deep thrust.

"Roarke!" she screamed, feeling it coming, bursting along her nerves in a firestorm. "I love you!"

He bellowed in triumph and release. Deep inside her, she could feel his thick cock jetting.

Later as they clung together helplessly, he whispered in her ear, "I love you, too, Elise."

Roarke floated in midair, relishing the feeling of Elise wrapped around him like a blanket, her body utterly limp, her skin damp and warm with pleasure. Her hair waved around them in the air currents, strands of fine silk shimmering in the blue recorded light of Earth. One of her long, slim hands was stroking his chest, combing through the ruff of hair in slow, sensual exploration. Her mouth was pressed against his breastbone, over his heart. He felt something wet against his skin he suspected might be another tear.

"What's going to happen now, do you think?" she asked, sounding sleepy.

"Well, you're not going to that damn prison camp, for one thing. Would you be willing to defect?"

"After what the CSS did? You'd better believe it." She bit gently at one of his nipples. He closed his eyes at the sharp pleasure. Resting her chin on his chest, she looked up at him. "I think I'm going to tell the crew what happened. All of it, including Scordillis' betrayal of us and Henry's assassination attempt. What they did to my…" She broke off. "My people deserve to know what the CSS really is."

"Will it make a difference?"

She shrugged. "Some of them will probably opt to stay in the service, either out of fear for their families or ambition, but I think those who can defect, will." Elise shot him a haunted look. "The real question is, will they be accepted?"

He nodded. "They'll have to undergo psyche evaluations to make sure they're not spies, but once their sincerity is confirmed, there'll be no problem. Frankly, the Star Force needs all the qualified ship personnel we can get." He hesitated, then added, "That goes double for you. There's always a certain amount of political infighting involved in who receives captaincies, so it will be difficult to get you a ship given your background. But you're too talented to waste, and I will fight tooth and nail to get one for you. And I should be able to pull it off, too." Roarke smiled grimly. "The high command still owes me one for Nygaard."

She pulled away and stared. "You'd do that for me?"

"Yes. I'm not saying what I get you will be much of a ship, but..." He broke off and shrugged.

Frowning, Elise reached out and caught his wrist. Weaving her fingers through his, she stared at their joined hands for a long moment. He waited patiently for her to speak.

"I want to avenge my father," she told him finally. "But you and I have just discovered each other. I don't want to leave you. And frankly, I'm not sure I have any interest in political intrigue just now. Of any kind. Not even to get another ship." She looked up at him, her green eyes vulnerable. "I don't suppose there's an open berth on the *Liberator*."

"I'm sure something can be arranged," Roarke told her, his voice rough with the knowledge that she was willing to choose him over another ship of her own. Twisting his mouth into a evil grin, he added wickedly, "In fact, I can think of several interesting positions I'd like to put you in."

"That sounds...promising." But her eyes had drifted to the image of Earth, hanging blue and white against the stars. He could almost feel the grief beginning to ribbon its way through her again.

"But for now," Roarke said softly, "I think I'd rather just hold you."

"Yeah." She wrapped herself around him again, her body warm and sweat damp. "I like that idea."

He drew her closer. He'd finally caught Elise Morrell.

And he planned to hold onto her for the rest of his life.

About the author:

*Angela Knight lives with her family on the East Coast. She's been writing for a few years and enjoys the outlet it provides. Her story, **Roarke's Prisoner**, was a labor of love and gave her the opportunity to combine her passion for science fiction and her love of romance in one story.*

Surrogate Lover

❧❦❧

by Doreen DeSalvo

To my reader:

Forbidden fruit is sweet, but forbidden love can be the sweetest of all. Enjoy a little taste.

Chapter One

The woman who opened the door was tiny, with honey-brown hair and huge blue eyes that dominated her waifish face. She looked him in the eye for a second, then nervously glanced away.

"You must be Dr. Ross," she said.

He smiled, even though she wasn't looking at him. "Call me Adrian. And you must be Sarah."

She nodded, then stepped back from the doorway. "Come in."

He shut the door behind him and followed her down the short hallway and into a room. Her bedroom. As if she expected him to get straight to work.

Before he could speak, she turned to face him. "Can I ask you a personal question?"

"Of course." She could ask, but if it was too personal, he might not answer. After all, he was here as a therapist.

"Are you married?"

"No."

"Do you have a girlfriend?"

"No."

She let out a breath in an audible rush of air. "Good."

"Why is it important to you?"

She shrugged and looked away.

"Sarah, if I'm going to help you, I need you to be honest with me."

"If you had a girlfriend, I wouldn't . . . I couldn't . . . it just wouldn't be right."

She couldn't even say the words, give the act a name. No wonder she couldn't enjoy it. "This isn't an issue of right or wrong, Sarah. I'm here to help you. All you have to do is concentrate on what feels good to you."

"*Nothing* feels good to me. Didn't Dr. Lansing tell you that?"

In a few minutes, he'd show her just how good she could feel. "No, she didn't." He moved to the bed and sat down on the edge. Before he could ask her to join him, she came over and sat next to him, not touching but close.

She gave a nervous little cough, as if her throat was dry. "You're not what I expected."

"What did you expect?"

She thought for a moment. "I don't know. But I didn't expect tall, dark, and handsome."

"I'm not that tall."

She laughed, a brief, quickly stifled laugh, as if she was afraid to let her feelings out. Typical. He patted her thigh reassuringly.

She turned toward him and slowly, cautiously, brought her hand up to rest on his shoulder. "I guess you want to get started."

He took her hand from his shoulder and lifted it to his lips for a gentle kiss. She didn't pull away, even though her hand shook. God, her tentativeness was sweet, and arousing more than his protective instincts. Surprising. He usually controlled his arousal, decided consciously when to let his body react. "We don't have to rush things. I'd rather wait until you feel comfortable. Until you're ready."

"I'm as ready as I'll ever be."

He'd heard that before. It meant that she wasn't ready at all. "Just relax. We don't need to do anything tonight, if you don't want to."

She raised her chin, looking like a brave martyr going to the guillotine. "I'd rather get it over with."

Get it over with? Good thing he didn't have an ego to bruise. "Let's talk for a while."

"Okay."

"I was born and raised here in San Francisco," he said, going into his standard small talk rap. "How long have you lived here?"

"Four years. I moved here for my job."

"What do you do?"

"I'm a graphic artist. Do we have to do this?"

The change in topic caught him by surprise, drove all of his standard lines out of his head. "Do we have to do what?"

"Chat like this, as though we just met at a party. It's bizarre."

She was right, but usually no one commented on it. Maybe she was more prepared for this than she looked. "We don't have to do anything. There are only two rules for our sessions together, Sarah. One is that you tell me if you're uncomfortable. You have the right to say no to anything."

He paused for a long moment, waiting for her to answer, waiting to make sure his words had penetrated.

"All right," she finally said.

"The second rule is that you tell me honestly what you're thinking and feeling, without censoring yourself."

"All right," she said again.

"So tell me, how do you feel?"

"Nervous."

He nodded. "So do I."

"You do?"

"Of course. We just met, but we're thinking about sharing something very intimate."

"But you've done this before."

"Not with you."

She swallowed. "I think I should tell you that I've never...." She trailed off.

Good lord, she couldn't be a virgin. That was one thing Dr. Lansing should have known to tell him.

"I've never done this with a stranger before," she finished.

Thank God. Deflowering virgins wasn't one of his specialties. He gave her hand a little squeeze. "With a stranger, sometimes it's easier to…" He searched for a euphemism, but came up blank. "…to enjoy sex."

She shook her head. "If I can't enjoy sex with a man I care about, how could I possibly enjoy it with a stranger?"

"And if you do enjoy lovemaking with a stranger, that must mean you're immoral?"

"Exactly."

"You're not having a casual fling, Sarah. This is therapy. I'm here to help you, just like Dr. Lansing."

A wisp of a smile touched her lips. "Sure. The only difference is that Dr. Lansing doesn't ask me to take my clothes off."

At least she felt comfortable enough to joke with him. He smiled back at her. "You can leave them on for now. I'd like to give you a backrub, if that's okay with you."

She looked puzzled, as if she couldn't imagine what a massage had to do with sex. But she nodded.

"Just lie down on your stomach." While she arranged herself, he walked to the door and turned off the bedroom light. The light from the hallway was bright enough to see by, but not harsh or glaring. Good lighting for a slow, thorough session.

He kicked his shoes off and sat on the edge of the bed near her feet. "I'm going to make you more comfortable." He lifted one of her feet and gently removed her shoe.

She twisted around and looked at him. "I can undress myself."

"I'm not undressing you." He took off her other shoe and dropped it to the floor. "Just relax. Nothing will happen without your consent, I promise."

She laid back down, and he crawled up the bed until he was kneeling beside her. He touched her back gently, so she wouldn't be startled, then rubbed her shoulders with long, even strokes. She wasn't as skinny as her bulky clothes made her look. She'd seemed dangerously thin, but he could feel supple muscles through her shirt.

He reached up to stroke her neck, pausing for a long moment to feel the silky softness of her hair, shimmering with golden highlights in the dim light from the hallway. "You have beautiful hair," he said, then almost bit his tongue. He never, ever, complimented a client on her looks. On her responsiveness, yes. On her technique, yes. But never on her looks. Looks were superficial, and had nothing to do with a woman's ability to feel passion. And nothing to do with his job.

"Thank you," she said softly.

He concentrated on his hands, tracing a pattern along her spine, massaging her with gentle, easy strokes, just to get her used to his touch. She sighed, a brief exhalation that he felt more than heard.

"Does this feel good?" he asked. If she'd admit to feeling any pleasure at all, that would be a good sign.

"Yes. But I'm worried about what you're leading up to."

"Don't worry about what's next. Just enjoy the massage."

"I'll try."

She did seem more relaxed than when he'd begun. Her muscles were less tense, more fluid under his hands.

She sighed again. "You're very good at this."

Even her voice sounded languid. A bedroom voice if he'd ever heard one. Time to move on.

He stretched out beside her, stroking her back with one hand. She opened her eyes and smiled at him, looking as satisfied as a woman who'd climaxed. He couldn't wait to see how she'd look when she did.

He touched the side of her face, letting his fingers stroke through her hair and tease her ear. She opened her mouth slightly, no doubt because her breathing had increased. He knew the signs.

"What are you thinking?" she whispered.

"I'm thinking about kissing you."

"Oh." She licked her lips quickly, nervously, drawing his attention to her mouth. A beautiful mouth, lips glistening and full, enticingly red even without lipstick. "Go ahead," she said.

He leaned towards her, then pulled back. What was he doing, giving in to his impulses like this? He was here for *her* pleasure, not his own. And before he kissed her, *she* had to want it. What he wanted was unimportant. Irrelevant.

"What's wrong?"

Obviously he'd been silent too long. He gave her a slow smile. "Nothing. I just want to fantasize about kissing you for a little while longer."

"Why?"

He leaned over until his lips were against her ear, and whispered, "Because fantasizing about it can be just as exciting as doing it." She trembled a little, but she didn't move away. He did, though, lying down beside her again.

She didn't say a word, and her eyes were wide.

"Are you thinking about kissing me?" he asked.

"Yes." Her tongue darted over her lips again. He wished she'd quit doing that — it distracted the hell out of him.

"And how does it make you feel?"

She gave a breathless little laugh, and the sound of it made heat rush to his groin. "Nervous."

"Don't be. I'm harmless. You can tell me to stop anytime you want." Even though his body wouldn't want to stop. Tonight it seemed to have a mind of its own. If she got any closer, she'd feel the proof, and no doubt be startled witless. He moved his hips away a few inches and forced himself to take slow, deep breaths. Calming breaths.

Time to get back to work. "Let's talk about fantasies," he suggested.

"Okay."

Great, she wasn't going to make this easy on him. But why did he expect her to?

If it was easy for her, she wouldn't be here with him. "Tell me one of yours."

She looked frightened by the thought. "I don't have any. When I think about sex, I think about the past. About past failures." She closed her eyes, no doubt trying to block out the painful memories.

"You won't fail me, Sarah. You don't have to worry about pretending with me, about pleasing me. You can concentrate on your own feelings and just ignore me."

She smiled. "Ignore you? That won't be easy."

He smiled back at her. All that humor and warmth, and a knockout to boot... she deserved all that life had to offer, including orgasm. Especially orgasm. He stroked her arm through her shirt. "You're hiding in these bulky clothes," he said. "I'm fantasizing about what your body looks like."

Damn, she looked frightened again. She must be ashamed of her body, trying to drown her figure in yards of cloth. He should have realized that. If he could just lose this damn erection, he'd be able to think more clearly, judge his words more carefully.

"I can see that you're beautiful, but I'm wondering about the details." To hell with his rule about not complimenting her on her looks. He'd do anything to wipe the insecurity from her eyes. A compliment was easy enough.

"For example..." He cupped her breast in his hand, molding it gently. "I can feel your shape, but I want to know what color your nipple is. I want to feel the texture of your skin with my tongue, see it glistening with wetness afterwards."

He teased her nipple with his thumb, felt it harden and rise in response.

She gasped, and her eyes widened. "That feels wonderful," she said, her voice full of surprise.

Excellent. She felt pleasure. She wanted him. That was the first step. Now he'd turn up the heat, take her all the way.

He kept stroking her, rubbing her shirt against her sensitive flesh. "Imagine how good my hand would feel against your bare skin," he said.

She closed her eyes and bit her lip, looking a little nervous and a little excited. Both responses were good. He could use the nervousness, make her feel naughty and daring. He moved closer, so that she'd feel his breath on her neck. "I could just reach up under your shirt and touch you," he whispered. "Would you let me do that?"

She nodded, but didn't say anything.

"Or maybe I'll push your shirt up instead, so I can watch my hand stroke your skin. Would you like that, Sarah?"

"I don't know."

At least she was honest. He backed off a little, moving his hand to the neutral territory of her collarbone. Why was his hand shaking? Because this woman was getting to him, with her big expressive eyes and her vulnerable smile. Not to mention her trim little body, which he could easily imagine underneath him, wrapped around him, on top of him. No wonder his hand was shaking.

She opened those big blue eyes. "Aren't you going to do it?"

Was that disappointment, or relief? "Not just yet."

She reached up and touched his head, and he felt her gently curling strands of his hair around her fingers. "Soft," she whispered. Then she closed her eyes and brought her lips to his, backing off after the lightest possible kiss. When she retreated he followed, pressing his mouth to hers, holding her head still while he brushed his lips across hers, feeling their soft dampness.

He felt her smile, and pulled back to look at her. "You lied," she said.

His brain was too clouded to follow that one. "About what?"

"Kissing you. It was better than fantasizing about it."

He smiled back at her, then closed his eyes and slowly, deliberately, kissed her again. She kissed him back with tentative movements of her lips that made his heart race. He couldn't stop himself from nipping gently on that full lower lip.

She gave a tiny little moan, a soft sound of desire that crumbled the wall that kept his own needs at bay. He devoured her, reaching into her mouth with his tongue, learning the tastes and textures of every crevice.

And she responded, pulling him close, closer, until his erection was pressed thickly against her leg. He moved against her, letting her thigh stroke his hardness, back and forth, in an agonizing, aching caress.

Air. Air. He dragged his lips from hers, gasping, and found them against her neck, nipping and teasing and sucking warmth to the surface. Somehow her hands were between them, struggling to open his shirt. He moved away just a fraction, enough to give her room. But she fumbled for too long, and he couldn't wait. He jerked open the waistband of his pants, yanked his shirttails out, and ripped his shirt the rest of the way open.

Her hands ran over his chest, shyly exploring, her touch so light that it almost tickled. She touched him as if he was the only man she'd ever been with, as if she wanted to please him but didn't quite know how. And suddenly all he could think about was teaching her, grabbing her hand and showing her exactly how he wanted her to touch him. What was wrong with him? He was here for her. To satisfy her.

He grabbed the bottom of her shirt and pulled it upwards, over her head. She lifted her arms to help him. He threw her shirt off the bed and turned to stare at her. Her breasts were gorgeous, barely big enough to fill his hands, but her areolas were huge, the largest he'd ever seen, soft and rosy around erect nipples. He fell on her like a starving man, suckling each breast in turn, and she wove her fingers through his hair, holding him close, wanting him.

When he finally lifted his head, she rubbed her damp breasts against his bare chest. He groaned. Who on Earth had labelled this woman frigid? Her previous lovers must have been selfish bastards.

She touched his hip, then slid her hand to the front of his pants and cautiously squeezed him through his jeans. He had to get out of these pants. He yanked the zipper down and pulled his pants to his knees, taking his briefs with them. Her hand closed around his erection, just holding him, and that simple touch nearly made him explode. He put his own hand on top of hers, guiding her, showing her the rhythm he liked. How long had it been since a woman had touched him like this? Ages. Years. Maybe never. He'd always been the one who did the pleasuring, the one who caressed his partner. Yet here was Sarah, thinking of his needs.

But she had needs too, and he knew how to satisfy them. He pulled out of her warm grasp and reached for the elastic waistband of her pants, pulling them off in one quick motion and clumsily taking her underpants with them.

Just looking at her body made his heart slam against his ribs. She wasn't skinny at all, but lithe and supple and petite. The nest of brown hair between her legs begged for his touch.

He laid down beside her, and she rolled onto her side to face him. Her eyes were closed, no doubt from shyness. What would it take to make her open them? He lifted her knee, wedging his thigh between hers to keep her legs apart, and let his fingers trace a slow trail from her breast to her stomach. When he reached between her legs and touched the damp flesh there, she gasped and bit her lip, but kept her eyes tightly closed.

Then her hand found him, curling around the tip of his shaft, and he couldn't take any more. It was all he could do to fumble through the tangled mess of jeans at his knees until he found a condom.

He slid the condom on, then he pushed her to her back, rolling over on top of her and finding home between her legs. His first thrust was sure and true, and he couldn't even stop to catch his breath.

Her muscles contracted around him, squeezing him, making him groan with the pleasure of it. Making him thrust blindly into her, mindlessly seeking release. And she was with him, matching his erratic rhythm, holding onto his shoulders like she never wanted him to stop.

But he couldn't wait for her. Too late to back off now, to slow down. Too late to bring her with him. He climaxed with deep, wrenching spasms, shuddering and swearing and feeling fierce, primitive satisfaction. So good. So unbelievably good.

Oh God, what had he done? To climax before his client — it was inconceivable. Selfish. Contemptible.

He'd make it up to her. There were other ways of making her come, and he'd try them all. Before the last wave of pleasure had ebbed away, he lifted himself to his elbows to tell her so.

But when he looked into her eyes, they were clear and calm. Passionless. She hadn't been with him at all. She hadn't wanted him. He groaned, and dropped his head to her shoulder. How had he let himself go like that? Here he was, half dressed, pants around his knees, while she lay naked beneath him, open and vulnerable. Used. He'd used her for his own satisfaction, and left her unfulfilled. How could he have done such a thing?

So much for a slow session. He'd never once asked her if he could undress her, touch her, enter her. She hadn't seemed to mind, but that didn't make it acceptable.

All he could do was start over, bring her to the boiling point again. And he wouldn't blow it this time. He framed her face in his hands and gave her a long, desperate kiss, twining his tongue with hers.

She made a choking noise, and pushed at his shoulders. He lifted his head. Her eyes looked troubled, frightened. God, was she frightened of him? "What's wrong?"

"Why did you kiss me like that?"

"I wanted to please you. We don't have to stop, Sarah."

"But I want to stop." Her voice trembled, as if she was about to cry.

"It can still be good, Sarah. Let me show you."

"No."

Damn, she'd almost shouted the word. He took a deep breath. "If you really want to stop…"

"I do. Please." She smiled, quivering and hesitant. "I think I've had enough for one night."

He couldn't bear another second of looking into her vulnerable face. He dropped his forehead to her shoulder. "I'm so sorry, Sarah."

"Why? It was very nice, Adrian."

Nice? God, she knew how to hurt a guy. Except he wasn't supposed to feel hurt. He wasn't supposed to feel anything beyond a general sense of satisfaction. He definitely wasn't supposed to feel the gut-wrenching pleasure that had just slammed through him, or the devastating sense of failure over leaving her unsatisfied.

He carefully disengaged himself and turned away from her to remove the condom. She handed him a tissue.

"Thank you." He wadded the condom up in the tissue and tossed it into the wastebasket, then turned back to her. She already had her shirt on, and was quickly putting on her pants, obviously eager to hide her body from him. He couldn't blame her.

He yanked his jeans up and fastened them, leaving his shirt hanging open. She sat down on the edge of the bed, fully dressed and looking everywhere but at him.

He reached out and touched her arm. "Next time will be better. I promise."

She looked at him then. "Next time?" She sounded surprised, as if she hadn't considered the possibility of a next time. And no wonder — after what he'd just done, she probably couldn't wait to see the last of him.

"Yes, next time," he said firmly.

She looked down at the floor. "I thought that since it didn't work this time…"

God, he'd never had this happen to him before. He opened his mouth, hoping his voice wouldn't shake. "You want to see a different therapist. I understand." He didn't like it, but he did understand.

"No, I just thought there wouldn't be any point in trying again."

She blamed herself. He couldn't stand it. "It was my fault. I let you down tonight."

She shook her head. He moved across the bed until he sat next to her, then wrapped one arm around her shoulders. "Entirely my fault," he insisted.

"No, it's just me. The cross I have to bear." She gave a bitter, choked laugh. "My mother always said I was the cross she had to bear. Look what she's cursed me with."

He could get the answers from Dr. Lansing, but he wanted to hear them from Sarah. Maybe she trusted him enough to tell him. Maybe he could help her through the pain. After all, he was a trained therapist. Even if he hadn't been acting like one lately. "What did she do to you?"

"You mean in general? Or what did she do to make me frigid?"

"Don't call yourself that." His own shout startled him. "That's a label. Don't make it stick to you."

"It's the truth."

He put his free hand under her chin and tilted her face up until she had to look at him. "You are a vital, passionate woman. You just have some bad experiences blocking you from seeing it."

Incredibly, she smiled. "You ought to be a politician."

"No need to insult me."

She smiled wider, and he couldn't resist her lips. He kissed her, just a quick peck on the mouth, as friendly and non-threatening as he could possibly make it.

When he backed off, she looked startled. "Why did you do that?"

"Did you mind?"

"Not really. But I don't want to try again tonight, Adrian."

As if he'd force her. "Kisses don't have to lead to sex."

She rolled her eyes. "I know that. But it is what you're here for."

"I'm here to help you," he corrected. "Sex is only part of it."

He took her hand in his. They'd wandered a long way from the topic of her childhood, but he couldn't think of a casual way to guide her back to the subject. If he asked outright, he'd sound like Dr. Lansing. And he didn't want Sarah to see him as just another therapist.

"What are you thinking?" she asked.

For an instant, he considered lying to her, saying something trite and shallow, something that wouldn't scare her off. But he would never want her to do that to him, to lie to him. "I'm wondering about your mother."

"Oh." She seemed to shrink away from him, putting distance between them. He pulled her back against him.

"You don't have to tell me if you don't want to. I just want to understand you better, that's all."

She took a deep, shuddering breath. "My parents were always mean to me. At best, they ignored me. Sometimes I misbehaved just to get their attention. They'd punish me, and I was glad to get the attention even though I resented them for beating me. I thought it meant that they cared."

She stopped, and he squeezed her hand reassuringly.

"When I was fourteen, there was a boy who liked me. We used to hold hands and walk home from school together. Kid stuff, you know?"

He nodded, even though she wasn't looking at him.

"One day when he dropped me off at my house, he kissed me. I kissed him back, or tried to. We didn't really know what we were doing, but I guess we both wanted to practice. My mother caught us. She dragged me into the house..." Her voice trailed off.

Adrian stroked her back, knowing that he couldn't really comfort her, hating himself for dredging up the pain that made her shoulders shake with silent sobs.

"She hit me, over and over again," Sarah whispered. "And she called me names…. She said I was a born sinner, conceived in sin, a constant reminder of her shame."

"I'm sorry," he said, helplessly.

"She locked me in my room for the entire weekend," Sarah went on, not seeming to have heard him. "They put bars on my window, and they locked me in my room every night. They took me out of school, claimed that they were teaching me at home. But it was just that they didn't trust me out of their sight. I'd barely even started to notice boys, but they were convinced I was sleeping with half of the town."

He rocked her in his arms, holding her gently, grinding his teeth in anger. What a wonder that she'd survived with her sanity.

"But the worst part," she went on, "is that I believed her. I was ashamed of myself. I thought I was the most wicked girl on the planet."

"But you weren't, Sarah. You were perfectly normal."

"I know that now. Well, I'm trying to believe it."

She reached out a hand, groping blindly towards the nightstand. He took the box of tissues and handed it to her. She straightened up to blow her nose, leaving him chilled where she'd been resting against him.

She glanced at him, then looked away. "I know I overreacted. I'm sure you've heard worse."

As if child abuse could be measured in relative terms. "Don't discredit your own pain. It's no wonder you have trouble with sex after an experience like that."

"I thought I could get over it on my own," she said. "It took me two years to run away, and I swore I'd never look back."

Alone and on the streets at sixteen? He didn't want to think about how she'd managed to survive. "Where did you go?"

"I had an aunt who'd never gotten along with my mother," she said. "She took me in, even managed to enroll me in school somehow."

Thank God she hadn't been totally defenseless. "Does she live nearby?" Where had that come from? He never asked patients questions that weren't related to their treatment.

"No, she died last year."

"I'm sorry," he said, hating the inadequacy of the words. Her lips looked pale and tense, her eyes red and watery. No wonder. First he'd jumped her, then he'd forced her to dredge up painful memories. He'd done nothing but cause her pain.

"Sarah?"

She looked up at him. "Yes?"

"Will you let me hold you for a while?"

She stiffened. "Sure," she said, warily.

Damn. "You can say no if you'd rather not. You won't hurt my feelings."

"No, I think I might like it."

He smiled reassuringly. "Would you mind if we lie down? It'll be more comfortable."

She scooted up the bed and laid down. He followed, careful not to crowd her or get too close. Gingerly, he put one arm over her waist.

"Adrian?"

"Yes?"

"I'm not sure how I should act with you."

"Don't worry about that. We just met. We need to get to know each other better."

Her brow furrowed. "But what sort of relationship are we supposed to have?"

"I'm not sure I understand."

"With Dr. Lansing, I know exactly how to act. She's the doctor and I'm the patient. It's hard for me to see you that way, because we've..."

"Because we've been intimate," he finished for her.

"Yes."

He'd always insisted on a purely professional relationship in the past. But Sarah needed to trust him before she'd open up and relax with him. A doctor-patient relationship would be too cold for her. "Why don't you think of me as a friend? Someone you can say anything to, without worrying about how it sounds." *And someone who's going to touch you and tease you as often as he can, until you whimper and moan and come apart in his arms.*

"All right." She moved closer to him then, actually leaning against his chest. He felt her hand brush his shirt open, then come to rest just over his heart. After what he'd done, she still wanted to be close to him. Amazing.

He should have held her after he'd come, but he'd been too disgusted with himself to realize that she'd needed comforting, not distance. If he made even one more misstep with this woman, he'd never forgive himself.

He kissed the top of her head, then rubbed her back, gently easing her closer.

"This is nice," she murmured.

"Wonderful," he agreed, even though the weight of his body was making his arm fall asleep. But Sarah seemed comfortable, and putting up with a numb arm was the least he could do for her.

Tomorrow he'd take her out. Someplace with enough privacy for a few furtive caresses, but where he wouldn't be able to lose control of himself. Once was bad enough. Especially since he still didn't know how it had happened. She'd enjoyed some of his lovemaking, and he'd read too much into her response, let passion cloud his judgment. It wouldn't happen again. Tomorrow everything would be business as usual, with his own needs held in check.

"Sarah?"

"Hmm?" She sounded drowsy, as if she'd almost been asleep. Asleep in his arms. She must trust him a little.

"Can I see you tomorrow?"

"Sure." Her voice was stronger now, more awake. "Same time?"

He pulled back a little, so he could see her face. "No. I thought we could spend the day together. There's someplace I want to take you."

"Where?"

So much for trust. "I'd rather surprise you."

"You have to give me some hint. I don't know what I should wear."

"Wear something casual. But make it a dress or skirt." *Something I can get my hands under.*

"All right."

He closed his eyes and slowly moved in for a kiss, giving her plenty of time to pull away. But she didn't. Her lips clung to his with shy enthusiasm, and he moved his mouth against hers, changing angles, applying just enough suction to seal her to him, experimenting with variations on the same gentle theme.

When they finally parted, she stroked his chest. "I can feel your heart beating," she said.

No wonder, since he could feel every pulse racing through his veins. "I could kiss you for hours," he admitted. Oh God, it couldn't be true. He closed his eyes in denial. He wouldn't let it be true.

Chapter Two

Adrian parked the car in a far corner of the parking lot, under a eucalyptus tree. He shut off the engine and turned to Sarah.

She stared out the window, looking skeptical. "Golden Gate Park? It's supposed to rain today."

And it looked like rain, overcast and breezy. But even so, the parking lot was full. Adrian took her hand. "A fifty percent chance. That means it might rain, or it might not."

She smiled and reached for the door handle. He pulled gently on her hand, stopping her. "Not so fast."

She turned toward him with a smile. "I was wondering if you were going to kiss me hello."

The woman would be the death of him. Didn't she realize how badly he'd behaved yesterday? How badly he'd lost control? He managed a weak smile, then gave her a quick kiss. Good. No fireworks this time, at least not for him. Today was for her.

"You're wearing too much," he said.

"Are you kidding? I was just wishing that I'd brought a coat instead of this sweater."

He winked at her. "I'll keep you warm." He wrapped his arms around her and hauled her fully against him, pulling her across the seat until she was almost in his lap. She giggled and leaned into him.

"You're still overdressed."

"You're crazy."

How could he broach the issue gently? "I want you to be conscious of your body today. Thinking about it every minute."

She shrugged. "I'll try."

"If you were wearing less, it would help."

"It's cold out. I'll freeze to death if I take off my sweater."

He took a deep breath, hoping she wouldn't balk. "I think you should take off something more intimate than your sweater."

"Like what?"

She was frowning, suspicious. Maybe just worried.

"Like your underpants."

She looked horrified. "Forget it."

"Why not?"

"It's perverted."

"Just think about it for a minute, Sarah."

Her jaw set in a stubborn line. Well, he'd known this wouldn't be easy. He leaned closer to her. "Just imagine how sexy you'd feel."

"Sexy?" She sounded incredulous.

He reached up and curved his hand around her delicate neck, stroking her jaw with his thumb. "Why don't you try it right here? Just for a minute. Here in the car, just the two of us."

She hesitated, biting her lip. Then she shifted in the seat and fumbled under her skirt. He kept his gaze locked on her face, even though he wanted to look. But if she caught him staring at her panties, she'd probably get embarrassed. And he probably would, too.

She carefully smoothed her skirt back down. Her hands were empty. She must have left her underpants on the floor.

She glanced at him, then away, obviously shy. "Now what?"

"How do you feel?"

"Embarrassed."

And he hadn't even peeked. "That's okay."

She shot him a wry smile. "I understated it. I feel like I'm about to *die* of embarrassment."

"I'm the only one here, Sarah. And I've certainly seen you in less." Why on Earth was he reminding her of that? Their first coupling could only be a bad memory for her.

"But this is different," she said.

He nodded, acknowledging her feelings. "Do you feel self-conscious?"

"Yes."

He put a hand on her thigh, mere inches from her sex, and felt her legs tighten and squeeze together, reminding him of exactly how tightly they'd cradled his hips last night. He bit his tongue, hard — hard enough to ward off his lurid thoughts — and moved his hand the barest fraction of an inch, subtly stroking her leg, hinting that he might move higher, hinting that he might move underneath her skirt. "Is this so horrible?"

"No," she breathed, almost moaned. "No, it doesn't feel horrible at all." She trembled.

Time for the next step — getting her out of the car. "You're tingling, aren't you?" He kept his voice low, soft, seductive. "Imagine feeling this way whenever we touch. Whenever we accidentally brush against each other. Imagine how much we'll want each other by the end of the day. You won't be able to think about anything else. Neither will I." Hell, he couldn't think about anything else right now.

She shook her head, vigorously. "You can't possibly expect me to walk around like this all day. It's not decent."

Worrying about decency was keeping her in chains, keeping her sexuality locked up in shame. But he couldn't tell her that. "No one will know but us," he said instead.

She still looked skeptical. Would she make him force the issue? "Trust me," he said. "I know what I'm doing." Ha. After last night, she had plenty of reason to doubt that.

She bit her lower lip, obviously wavering. How could he tip the scales? "You won't really be exposed."

"But I'll feel exposed. I do already."

"Think of it as a fantasy." He bent to whisper in her ear, building the fantasy for her. "You're exposed, but no one knows it. When I touch you, I'll think about it. You'll think about it. You'll feel daring and excited. But to everyone else, we'll just be touching casually."

"I'll be embarrassed."

He moved his hand again, delving between her legs just a little. Her eyes widened. "How does this make you feel?" he asked.

She swallowed. "Nervous."

"Nervous about what?"

She licked her lips. "I don't know."

She felt more excited than nervous — he could see it in her eyes. But now wasn't the time to make her admit it.

He gave her leg a gentle pat, then lifted his hand away completely. "That's strange," he commented. "I don't feel nervous at all."

"You aren't the one with your underwear around your ankles."

He grinned. Just when he thought she was running scared, she came up with a joke. But she did look a little frightened, and after what he'd done to her last night, he just couldn't force her to go through with this.

He took her hand. "Sarah, I think you should give this a chance. But if you don't want to, I won't make you."

She swallowed. "I'll do it."

He could have kissed her for being so brave. Instead, he bent down and picked up her panties. Pink panties. Plain pink satin, too feminine for words. He stuffed them into his jacket pocket. A little public nakedness would do her good, help her see that she had nothing to fear from letting her passions out. And maybe it would keep her as off-kilter as he'd been last night. If she became really uncomfortable, he'd let her sneak into a restroom and put them back on. Maybe.

They got out of the car, and Adrian walked around to Sarah's side, where she struggled with the door.

"There's a trick to it." He jiggled the door until it snapped into place, then took Sarah's hand.

"What kind of car is this?" she asked.

"A '57 Chevy. I bought it in high school. It's the only car I've ever had." Enough about the car. He smiled down at her, feeling sheepish. "Don't let me get started on my car. It's one of my obsessions."

"I can see why. It's a great car."

Sweet of her to humor him. He couldn't resist planting a light kiss on her forehead. They walked hand-in-hand through the parking lot, then followed the path that led down to the lake. The park was crowded for such a cloudy day. A few hardy souls were picnicking on the grass, but most were circling the lake, either jogging or sauntering aimlessly.

He and Sarah joined the saunterers, but she stopped after a few steps to admire a flower bed.

"Aren't they gorgeous?" She leaned over to smell one, giving him a great view of her rear end, her dress pulled tight and molding every curve. Damn, he could tell she wasn't wearing anything underneath it.

He reached over to pick a flower for her, but she slapped his hand away.

"Don't you dare!"

"I just wanted to give you one."

"If everyone here picked one, there wouldn't be any left. Leave them for other people to enjoy."

"Yes, ma'am."

As they stood there, smiling at each other, he noticed two men a short distance away. Sarah saw them too, and abruptly dropped his hand.

They were staring at her, practically drooling. God, she must hate that, must feel like a piece of meat. He put a protective arm around her shoulders. The men smiled at each other, then smirked at Adrian. He bent his head and planted a loud kiss on Sarah's mouth. She laughed out loud, God knew why, but she seemed to find his protectiveness amusing. Out of the corner of his eye, he saw the two creeps walk away.

"Honestly, Adrian, they were only looking."

How could she be so blasé about it? And why was he angry? If she didn't mind complete strangers checking her out, that was a good sign. A very good sign. "You're absolutely right. There's nothing wrong with just looking."

She grinned at him. "I'm surprised you're not used to it."

Confusion made him stop and digest that. They weren't talking about the same thing at all. "What?"

She laughed. "Come on, are you trying to tell me it's never happened before? You're a gorgeous guy, and this is San Francisco."

"They weren't looking at me."

"Of course they were. I'm surprised that you're so easily threatened."

His masculinity wasn't easily threatened. His sanity, definitely. When he'd thought those men were checking Sarah out, he'd felt angry and possessive and primitive. He'd felt something suspiciously close to jealousy.

❦

Sarah bent over for the dozenth time, inhaling the scent of yet another ornamental flower. Coming here had been a lousy idea. He was damned tired of making sure no one was checking out her ass.

Sarah was having a great time, seemingly oblivious to her lack of underwear. So much for keeping her off-kilter.

Maybe he wasn't trying hard enough. He'd kept his touches light and casual, mainly just holding her hand. Selfish of him, really. He should be teasing her, tormenting her, doing his level best to get her hot.

He just didn't want to torment himself at the same time. Self-preservation. What a coward.

When she straightened up, he put an arm around her waist. She looked surprised, but not uncomfortable. And not excited, either.

He leaned down and kissed the back of her neck. "You taste delicious."

She jumped, and moved away a few inches. He put his hands on her hips, gently suggesting she stay close to him.

"Someone will see!" She sounded terrified, as if her parents would torture her again for indulging in a little necking.

"See what? Me kissing you?"

"Yes."

"There's nothing wrong with this, Sarah."

"I know. But I can't help feeling ashamed. Especially in public."

"Do you see that couple on the bench across the lake?"

She nodded. As he watched, the couple kissed, gently and unhurriedly, their passion obvious even from this distance.

"What do you think when you watch them kiss?"

"That they're very lucky," she answered.

"So it's okay for them to touch each other? To desire each other?"

She sighed, sounding exasperated. "I know, I know, it's okay for me to feel that way too. It's natural and normal and wonderful, and I shouldn't be ashamed of it."

"And it's easier said than done."

She turned and looked up at him, surprise written on her face. "How did you know?" Before he could answer, she spoke. "Dumb question. You've probably known a hundred women like me."

That stunned him. Speechless, he could only shake his head.

"Dozens, then."

"I've never known anyone quite like you, Sarah."

Her face fell, and she looked ready to cry. Damn, he'd only meant to compliment her. "What's wrong?"

"Someone else said that to me once."

"Someone else?" he repeated, like an idiot. Another man. Why did that surprise him? She was sweet and pretty and charming. Of course there was a man in her life. He swallowed, forcing himself to be calm. "Does he know about me?"

"No."

No wonder she didn't want him to touch her in public. "Are you worried that he'll find out?"

"No. We're not seeing each other anymore."

He didn't want to know, but he had to ask. "How long has it been?"

"A few months."

"Did you love him?"

"I thought so."

Poor Sarah. He wrapped his arms around her, holding her close. She nestled her head against him, a gesture of trust that made his chest swell with warmth.

"We broke up over…well, I'm sure you can guess."

The bastard. What kind of man dumped a woman who obviously needed support and encouragement? No doubt he'd wanted her to climax just for his own vanity. "Don't dwell on it," he commanded.

"I can't help it. He's the reason I went to see Dr. Lansing in the first place."

Great. She wanted to get better, then go chase after the creep. He'd remind himself of that whenever he started feeling too attached to her. And he definitely didn't want to hear any more about this ex-boyfriend. "Let's walk."

They wandered a little further along the shore, until they reached the wooded side of the lake. It was colder under the trees, but no one else was nearby. A little privacy at last. Adrian stopped.

Sarah pointed at a group of people lounging around a picnic table about a hundred feet away, just at the water's edge. "Look. A boat race."

It looked more like a bunch of children sailing cardboard boxes, but he didn't argue with her. The kids were jumping up and down, yelling, and Sarah watched them with a smile on her face, looking carefree and happy.

A lovely woman.

No. A client, a patient. Unavailable. A woman with a life that didn't include him. A woman with an ex-boyfriend she wanted back.

Yes, that was more like it. His only place in Sarah's life was as a therapist. He'd help her discover passion, then let her move on, and he'd pat himself on the back for another job well done. That would be the end of it. That *had* to be the end of it. And the sooner he got her off his hands, the better.

Adrian smiled. If she hadn't been standing so close, he might have slapped himself. That's what Dr. Lansing had told him to do whenever he found himself getting too involved with a patient. He'd never needed the advice before.

He looked at the kids again. The parents were rounding them up and heading for the parking lot, a few holding bags over their heads.

"It must be raining," Sarah said.

He glanced up at the thick canopy of leaves above them. "We'll stay fairly dry here. Let's wait it out."

She nodded, but crossed her arms over her stomach. A gust of wind rustled the leaves overhead, and she shivered.

"Cold?"

"A little."

He moved to stand behind her and folded his arms over hers. The top of her head fit perfectly under his chin. He dropped a quick kiss on her golden hair. "Guess what I'm thinking."

"I can imagine."

"I'm thinking that no one can see us." He bent his head again, giving her neck a little nip.

"Adrian!"

She sounded breathless, excited, the way he'd been longing to hear her say his name. "I could kiss you, and no one would notice."

"I would."

He laughed. "I hope so." He ran his hands up her arms, then back down, slipping them around her waist and pulling her back against him. She'd feel his erection, but so what?

She jiggled her backside against him. "Is that a gun in your pocket?"

"No, I'm just happy to see you." Quickly, before she could object, he passed a hand over her breast.

"Adrian, stop!"

"Why?"

"Because. We're in public."

He glanced around. Most everyone had left when the rain started, and now there were just a few stragglers in sight, at least fifty feet away and heading for the parking lot. "There isn't much of the public left." He ran his hands over her abdomen, over her thighs.

She trembled. "Please, Adrian."

"I thought you'd never ask." He should respect her wishes, give her some space, but his hands, his selfish hands, closed over her breasts. She gasped.

"Tell me what you're feeling, Sarah."

"I feel excited."

"So do I." Stroking her breasts, feeling the hard pebbles of her nipples, remembering how they had felt in his mouth — she drove him to the breaking point, just standing here letting him touch her. No practiced caress had ever made him hotter. And she'd get just as hot this time.

"You've been driving me crazy all day," he said hoarsely.

"I have?"

"Yes. I kept thinking about you, naked under this skirt. About how easily I could reach underneath it and pet you."

She arched her back, pressing her breasts against his hands. Just as suddenly, she pulled away. "Let's go."

"Why?" He knew damned well, but he wanted to hear her say it, needed to hear her say it.

"Because we're in public. And it's raining."

"And?"

Her brow furrowed. "I don't know what you want me to say."

"Why else do you want to leave?"

"Because I want to be alone with you."

Ah, that was closer to an admission of desire. "And when we're alone?"

Hurt settled on her face, and she bit her lip. "Don't you want to…to go to bed with me?"

As if she couldn't tell. "I'm more interested in what you want, Sarah."

"Oh." Mercifully, the hurt cleared from her face. "I want that too."

He gave her a leisurely, gentle kiss. A reward, though it punished him to keep the kiss soft. He wanted to force her lips open, lay her down in the cool,

damp grass and find out just how hot she could burn. Patience. She wouldn't
burn if he rushed her. This time he'd keep things slow, keep her hot. "Tell me
how your body feels."

"Excited," she said.

"What else?" He ran his lips over her neck, then bit gently.

She cried out, a short sound that she quickly stifled.

"That's it," he encouraged. "Tell me how good you feel."

"I feel…oh…"

His fingers plucked gently at her nipples, hard little points budding
against the fabric of her dress. "Imagine we're alone, on your bed. What
would you want me to do?"

"I'd want your mouth on me." Her voice had dropped to a whisper, but he
heard it.

"I'd want that, too." He bit his lip, hard, to distract himself. This time he'd
make her want him until she was desperate to come. "Did I tell you how beautiful your breasts are? How good they felt against my tongue?"

He stopped to catch his breath. His own fantasies were driving him crazy. He
needed to focus on hers. "Did you like that?" He felt her nod, and bent low to
whisper in her ear. "What else did you like?"

She didn't answer. But she squirmed against him, rubbing that delectable
ass of hers against his erection. He choked back an agonized moan.

"Tell me, Sarah." She was silent. He'd fill in the blanks for her. "You liked me
suckling your breasts. What else did you like?"

"I liked your kisses," she admitted.

"My kisses excited you?"

She nodded.

He brushed her hair aside and planted a wet kiss on the back of her neck,
then gave her a gentle nip for good measure. "These kisses?"

She nodded again.

"What else did you like?"

She twisted away, turned to face him. "Why are you making me say these
things?" she demanded.

"Because it turns me on. Doesn't it turn you on, thinking about the things
we did together? About the things we could do together?"

"A little bit."

No doubt she got a little excited, then panicked and stopped herself. All he
had to do was get her past the panic stage. "That's not quite fair," he said. "It
turns me on a lot."

She opened her mouth to respond, but a gust of wind made her cry out
instead as a cold mist of rain soaked them both. She pressed against him full
length, but too late. Her back was soaking wet, her clothes dripping. A cold
shower — just what she needed to douse the fire he'd been carefully stoking.

He started to shrug off his jacket, but she shook her head. "Don't bother.
I'm already soaked to the skin."

He grasped her hand. "Come on, let's make a run for the car."

He ran out from under the trees, leading Sarah by the hand. A fine sheet of rain hit his face, light but chilled by the wind. They'd both be drenched by the time they got to the parking lot. He picked up the pace, felt Sarah tugging on his hand, and slowed again, matching her stride.

They'd walked quite a distance around the lake, and the rain seemed to come down faster every minute. When they finally reached the wooded path that led to the parking lot, the wind turned to a gentle breeze, and the rain dripped in slow, erratic drops from the trees. He slowed down to catch his breath. Sarah panted behind him, looking wet and miserable. Damn, he kept forgetting how tiny she was. He'd rushed her, forced her to keep up with his own longer legs.

He stopped and held her against him. She shook with cold, drew deep breaths. He had to get her to the car, but he couldn't drag her there. He held her until she caught her breath, then looked down into her wet face. "Ready?"

She nodded.

"Let's go." He led her the rest of the way down the path, walking fast but not running. When they reached the edge of the parking lot, the cover of trees ended, and the wind blew a gust of rain into his face.

Sarah tugged him forward, and he followed her as she ran. His car was the last one left in the lot. He fumbled in his pocket for the keys, had them ready before they reached the car.

He unlocked her door first and got her inside, then hurried around the car and let himself in. The rain beat a noisy rhythm against the roof. Sarah was shivering, running her hands over her bare arms. Her soaking wet sweater lay in a heap at her feet.

He had to get her warm. He turned the key in the ignition and put the heater on full blast, then shrugged off his jacket. Too wet to do Sarah any good. He threw it in the backseat.

His shirt was dry, and he had a T-shirt on underneath. He quickly stripped off the long-sleeved shirt and handed it to Sarah. "Here. Put this on."

She started to put it on over her wet dress. He reached out a hand to stop her, and felt the goosebumps on her cold skin. "It won't do you much good if it gets wet."

She looked up at him, and he could read the awareness in her eyes. If she took her dress off, she'd be naked. At least until she got his shirt on.

He looked away, took his hand off her arm and put it on the steering wheel. There wasn't much he could do to give her privacy, but he didn't have to drool over her while she sat there freezing.

Out of the corner of his eye, he saw her slip her dress over her head. She had a bra on today. A pink one, the same color as the panties in his jacket pocket. Lord have mercy. She sat there freezing, as disinterested in sex as she could possibly be, but the cold shower had done nothing to ease his own arousal. Unfortunately.

He turned his head further away, looking blankly at the rain dripping down the outside of the window next to him. He could still hear her, though, and imagined her slipping those slender arms into the sleeves of his shirt, buttoning it up to cover that pink satin bra.

"Adrian?"

He wouldn't look at her, wouldn't embarrass her. "What?" he asked, without moving an inch.

The touch of her cool, damp hand on his forearm made him start.

"Won't you be cold without your shirt?"

"No," he said, more harshly than he should have.

Her hand left his arm. Had he hurt her feelings? He turned to her then, saw her biting her lower lip.

"I'm sorry, Sarah."

"It's all right."

"No, it isn't. I shouldn't take my frustration out on you." Actually, he shouldn't even be feeling frustrated. He had better control over himself than that. Usually.

"I'm frustrated, too," she said softly.

Had he heard her right? The rain was making an awful racket on the roof of the car, but he'd swear she'd admitted to being frustrated. Her cheeks looked a little red, as if the admission had caused a blush. But no, they were probably just red from the cold.

He reached out and caught her hand, which felt only a little cool now. Why couldn't he think of anything to say? All he could do was stare at her face, and try not to stare at those luscious bare legs.

Her cheeks grew even redder. "I must look like a drowned rat," she said.

Was she serious? Her hair was curling into thick waves as it dried in the blast of air from the heater, and she looked delectably waifish in the long folds of his shirt. And that blush on her cheeks...what tantalizing thought had caused it? "You look beautiful."

She smiled ruefully. "I'm sure my makeup has all washed off."

"You don't need any."

She sighed, and her fingers toyed with the hem of his shirt where it lay against her thigh. But she didn't say anything.

He rested his arm along the back of the seat, brushed her damp hair with his fingers. "What's wrong, Sarah?"

"For a moment there, in the park, I almost felt..."

What had she felt? Excited? Frustrated? Happy?

"Sexy," she finished.

He hadn't been able to keep his mind off of her, had barely kept his hands decent, and she'd only felt sexy for a moment? He'd been doing a terrible job. "You *are* sexy."

"Yeah, right. That's why you've barely looked at me since we got in the car."

That cynical tone stung him. He never wanted to hear it again, not from her.

"I thought you were cold and wet and miserable," he said. "I was trying to give you a little space. A little privacy."

She studied his face, as if trying to gauge his sincerity. "I'm still a little cold," she said.

Was that an invitation? He'd take it as one. They moved at the same moment, and she was in his arms, her mouth damp and cool against his.

He wouldn't rush a thing, not this time. He kissed her slowly, thoroughly, expertly, holding back the urge to taste her with his tongue, to press her chest against his. He gave her lingering kisses, gentle nips, soft murmurs of encouragement.

And when she started gasping against his mouth, out of breath, he trailed kisses across her jaw, along her collarbone, as far as the gaping neckline of his shirt would let him. She tilted her head back, giving him better access to her neck, and he used it, used his lips to tease her skin, to explore the hollow at the base of her throat.

She sighed, although with the noise of the rain he could barely hear it, and he felt her fingers weave through his hair, cradling his head.

"I think this was a teenaged fantasy of mine," he said against her neck.

"What?"

Ah, he'd almost forgotten to use fantasies, even though she was fulfilling one for him. "Kissing a half-dressed woman in my Chevy, in the rain." He grazed his teeth over the soft skin of her neck, letting his tongue trail along behind. "Wondering how far she'll let me go."

"How far do you want to go?"

All the way. He was more than ready. His traitorous body hadn't cooled off since he'd held her in the park, before the rain. *Mind over matter.* But if that didn't work, he'd make damn sure he kept his pants on. He wasn't going to blow it this time.

"This far?" He moved his hands to her breasts, touched them through the big shirt, felt her nipples rise behind her bra. Irresistible. He lowered his head and took one in his mouth, sucking strongly, using his teeth so that she'd feel him even through all that fabric.

"More," she moaned.

She sounded so desperate, so demanding. She wanted him. He knew it.

He slid to the middle of the seat and lifted her onto his lap so that she faced him, her thighs straddling his. She didn't protest, and her eyes were closed, but he could still read the desire on her face. He reached for the top button on her shirt and undid it, then the next, his fingers clumsy. No hurry. He wanted to stretch out the moment, to give her time to savor the anticipation.

Slowly, so slowly, he spread open the shirt. Sarah seemed to be holding her breath, waiting for his touch. And he wouldn't disappoint her. He stroked her breasts lightly, tantalizingly, through the satin barrier of her bra. She strained closer, seeking more contact. Her bra hooked in the front, and he undid the clasp, then brushed the fabric out of the way. Her breasts were as beautiful as he remembered, with the same large, velvety areolas. So beautiful.

When he kissed her breasts, she caught her breath. When he licked, she sighed. And when he took her in his mouth and suckled, she gave a tiny little cry, almost a moan. She wanted him. Only him. When she climaxed for the first time, his arms would hold her. Soon. Very soon.

He stroked her back, her arms, surrounding her with his touch as his mouth lavished attention on her breasts. She moved against him, urgently, as if she wanted more but didn't know exactly what.

He knew. But he wouldn't give her more, not yet. Before he moved on, before he stepped up the pleasure, he wanted her aching for him, wanted her body to need him so much that her brain couldn't interfere. He panted against her chest, let her feel his hot breath on her sensitized, wet skin.

She squirmed in his arms, gasping, pleading without words. Almost ready. Almost. Gently, carefully, he put his right hand on her thigh. Her hands moved suddenly, going straight for his jeans and struggling to undo the snap. Not this time. No way. He grabbed her hands and moved them to his shoulders. "Not yet," he said. And then, before she could object, he reached between her legs and gently touched her.

She jerked and stiffened. Had he rushed her again? No, she felt hot and wet against his hand. Obviously ready, physically at least. But mentally?

He stroked her gently. She made no protest, offered no encouragement. "You feel so good," he said.

Still no response. He lowered his mouth to her breasts, tasting them again, and she came alive, moving rhythmically against his hand, showing him exactly what angle she liked, how much pressure she needed. Here? No, *here*. Like this? Yes, just like that.

And when she finally grew tense and still, he didn't stop, didn't skip a beat. Any second now. "Yes, yes," he murmured against her breast, encouraging her. She cried out, the sweetest sound he'd ever heard, then shuddered and trembled for endless, precious moments, taking her pleasure from him, giving her pleasure to him.

And finally, she collapsed against him in exhaustion.

Adrian hid his smile against her breasts. His groin throbbed, his body ached for release, his head filled with the enticing scent of Sarah, of her arousal. But he was satisfied.

Sarah had climaxed. It was enough. For now, it was enough.

Chapter Three

She stirred after a while, and shifted so that he could see her face. The sun had nearly set, and he could barely make out her features. She looked dazed and happy.

"Is it always that good?" she asked.

Her curiosity made him smile. "Yes. Sometimes it's a little different, but always good."

"Different how?"

"Different depending on lots of things. Your position, how long you've been excited, how tired you are."

"Would it feel different with you inside me?"

His mouth went dry. She still sat across his lap, knees spread, her breasts easily accessible behind the gaping folds of his shirt. And she had no idea how much he wanted to open his pants and thrust up into her. "Yes," he managed to croak.

She leaned forward, until her hair brushed his cheek and her lips rested against his ear. "I want you inside me," she whispered.

He pushed her shoulders back, and searched her face. Her eyes looked clear and bright. No passion, just residual satisfaction. She'd said it just to please him. Just because she could tell how damned horny he was. Just because after last night, she probably thought he was a rutting beast who couldn't last an hour without coming.

"I'll wait until you're ready again," he said.

She frowned. "That doesn't seem fair to you."

She tempted him. Thank God she wasn't trying to seduce him, or he'd cave in like quicksand. But he couldn't use her for his own pleasure again. Never again.

"I don't mind," he said. "I want to wait."

"Why?"

She sounded plaintive, as if she really didn't understand. If he wasn't careful, if he bruised her ego, he'd undo all the progress she'd made today. He touched her face, gently cupping her jaw. "I do want you." Understatement of the year. "But more than that, I want to please you."

"And I want to please you."

He bit back a sigh. "I know you do. But unless you really wanted me, I'd feel like I was using you. And it's a little too soon to make you want me again."

She still looked puzzled, but she shrugged and smiled at him. "Whatever you say. I feel too good to argue with you."

"You look good, too." And she did, with her eyes shining and her hair spread around her face in a wild cloud.

She smiled wider. "I feel like I've finally broken free of my parents."

"No more shame?"

She laughed and kissed him, full and wet. "The next time we're in public together, I'll give you a great big kiss."

Her voice sounded strong and confident. Too confident. He'd better set her expectations to a reasonable level. "I'm glad you're feeling more comfortable about public displays of affection," he began. God, he sounded like a prude. Like a wooden therapist, not a living, breathing man who had just made the woman in his arms cry out with pleasure.

But he couldn't take the words back now, even though Sarah was looking at him as if he'd just grown a second head. He cleared his throat. "It may take a little more practice before you have an easy time reaching climax."

Her smile didn't dim. "I don't know about that. I think I've found the secret."

"Secret?"

She shook her head, and dropped her gaze. "I can't tell you."

He should insist. As her therapist, he should use whatever technique she needed to help her. For his last patient, he'd actually impersonated Brad Pitt. Oh God, could Sarah have been thinking of another man? She'd kept her eyes closed. Maybe she hadn't wanted to see him, to ruin the fantasy.

It shouldn't bother him. Hell, he'd done the same thing himself at times. He would not be jealous of Sarah's fantasies. If he started thinking of her as his exclusive woman, as his lover, he'd have to quit seeing her.

And he couldn't quit now, not when she was so close. She'd had her first climax, and he needed to build on that milestone, to make her comfortable with her passion.

She shifted her weight, lifted herself off of his lap and sat next to him on the seat. "My legs were falling asleep. And I'm sure yours were, too."

They had been, but he hadn't noticed. He put an arm around her shoulders, and she turned to look at him. Her mouth met his, and he let her lead, let her deepen the kiss, let her tongue steal out to touch his lips, then dart away.

After a few moments, she sighed against his mouth and moved away.

He opened his eyes. Her face was turned away from him, but something in the set of her shoulders, the arch of her neck, told him she felt sad. And just a moment ago she'd been laughing. What had he done?

"What's wrong, Sarah?"

"Nothing."

She even turned and looked at him, smiled at him. But her eyes held sadness. He'd get to the bottom of this. "Is something bothering you?"

"No."

"Please, Sarah. Be honest with me."

"I kissed you, and you didn't kiss me back."

"I thought I did."

"Well . . . you didn't seem very interested."

He held back an exasperated sigh. Here he was, trying to cool off, and kissing her wasn't helping. "Just because I wasn't aggressive, that doesn't mean I didn't enjoy the kiss."

"Are you going to make me blurt it out?" she said, frustration ringing in her voice. "I want to make love again."

Her signals sure were subtle. From that tentative kiss, he was supposed to figure out that she wanted to make love?

"And not just for your sake," she added.

The defiance in her voice made him smile. "Do you honestly believe that I'm going to put up a fight?" he asked.

"I thought you might."

He gave a deep, theatrical sigh. "I'm just afraid you'll wear me out."

She chuckled. "You have only yourself to blame. Now that I know how good it can be...I want to practice."

Practice. She was practicing on him. Practicing for another man. Thinking of another man while she satisfied her curiosity with a mere therapist.

He wanted her to think about him. Only him. Not Brad Pitt. Not some worthless ex-boyfriend. Him, Adrian Ross. Not her therapist, but her lover.

Now there was a fantasy.

Just for tonight, he'd indulge himself with one harmless fantasy, pretend that they were lovers in truth. He'd take her home with him, make love with her in his bed, on his couch, in his shower. But if he did that, if he allowed her into his private life, he'd be crossing a dangerous line, breaking an ethical code he'd sworn to uphold. No, he couldn't even have this one fantasy. He'd take her back to her own home, keep things safe, protect them both.

He opened his mouth and said, "Let's go to my place."

≈⚬⟨⚬⟩⚬≈

By the time they got to his house, the rain had stopped and the sky was pitch black. Adrian pulled into the garage and turned off the car, then reached into the backseat and grabbed his soaking wet jacket.

"Don't forget your dress," he said as they got out of the car.

He crossed the garage and threw his jacket into the dryer. Sarah put her dress in too, and he shut the dryer and turned it on.

He led her up the narrow flight of stairs to the door, jingling his keys nervously. Hard to believe he'd actually brought Sarah home. No doubt he'd regret his impulsiveness later, but for now, he'd enjoy having her with him. She wouldn't need him much longer. Tonight might be all he ever had.

He opened the door to the house and switched on the light. When he paused, Sarah bumped into his back.

"Sorry," she said breathlessly.

He turned and pulled her into his arms, kissing her with the passion he'd been restraining all day. She pressed herself against him, reaching up to pull his head down, to seal their mouths more tightly.

He let his hands move down her back, over the sweet curve of her ass, not quite covered by his shirt. Irresistible. He hauled her up against him, and she gave a squeak of surprise, breaking their kiss and holding onto his shoulders for balance. He lowered her back down until her feet touched the floor, loving the way her body slid against his.

Whoa. He forced himself to take a deep breath. If he didn't slow down, he'd end up taking her against the wall here in the hallway. Not a bad idea, but he wanted the next time to be special, not a hurried frenzy of lust. And he'd already promised himself the shower, the couch, and the bed.

He moved back just a fraction, just enough so that he could see her face. Her eyes slowly opened, looking up at him with a dazed expression.

"I can't believe how excited you make me," she whispered.

"I know the feeling." Great, he'd said it out loud. He'd better watch himself. He could live with making Sarah part of this fantasy, but only if he was the one who paid the price. If she got hurt, if she became attached to him, he'd never forgive himself.

She tugged on his shirt, and he let her pull it over his head. Then she lowered her face to his chest, rubbed her cheek against his skin. She sighed, the barest hint of breath. "Now that I know I can do it, I'm not afraid to let myself feel."

"I'm glad." He stroked her hair, tangled and damp from the rain. "You still have a ways to go, though."

"I know." He felt her smile against his chest. "I'm looking forward to it."

So was he. And he couldn't wait another minute. "Come on."

He took her hand and led her upstairs to his bedroom. She didn't hesitate, and when they were inside she laid down with him as though they'd been lovers for years. As though she belonged here, with him.

She kissed him softly, briefly. Then again. And a third time. Hesitant kisses. Innocent kisses. He kissed her back, just as cautiously, but he cupped her face in his hand, stroking her, gently holding her mouth to his. She felt so delicate, and her kisses were so fresh and sweet, she could almost be a virgin.

And he'd treat her like one. He'd make slow, sweet, burning love to her. No skillful, practiced caresses, no thrusting kisses, no lustful demands. Just ardent gentleness.

Each move he made was slow, cautious. He kissed her all over her face and neck, endlessly, brushed his lips across hers in gentle strokes. Such soft, soft skin. No one could kiss like her, with those shy, tentative little movements that made him wild to please her.

He touched her breasts through his shirt for long moments, waited an age before he reached underneath the fabric to touch her bare skin. When he finally pulled the shirt off of her, he kissed her breasts softly, suckled gently, and her fingers slowly wove through his hair, as if she didn't know where else to put her hands.

He stroked her from her hair to her feet, slowly, slowly memorizing the texture of her skin, the shape of her body. Her skin looked flushed, felt hot, and she shifted restlessly under his hands. If only she would open her eyes.

He slid down and nuzzled at her thighs, felt them tense for an instant, then part. What he wouldn't give to taste her. But no, he had to move slowly, couldn't startle her. He used his hand, his fingers, set a teasing, tempting rhythm. And he waited, waited until she moved impatiently, urgently, until she wanted more, needed more. Then he touched her sex with his mouth, kissed her, and she writhed beneath him, moaning, desperate.

He couldn't bear to tease her any longer. He knew her body well, better than she did, and he used that knowledge to push her straight to the edge. But he wanted more from her than this, more than just a quick climax. He stripped his pants off in record time, almost forgetting the obligatory condom.

She held her arms out to him as he rose above her, welcoming him. But she seemed so tiny beneath him. He felt like a big oaf, crushing her, smothering her. He wanted to give to her, not dominate her.

He rolled onto his side, taking her with him, drawing her leg up over his hip. She moved against him, aligning her body with his, slowly, slowly taking him inside. *Look at me.* He rocked his hips in a slow, steady rhythm, watching her face. Her lips parted, her breath came in short, swift gasps, but she kept her eyes closed. He brought his hands to her breasts, teasing them. Ah, she liked that. Her hips met his thrusts, quickening the pace.

Suddenly she hid her face against his chest, and her whole body shuddered and trembled as her climax hit. He felt the convulsions along the length of his body, and as all her tiny feminine muscles contracted around him, he closed his own eyes and rode the wave himself, pouring everything he was, everything he hoped to be, into the milking heat of her body.

He held her close as his heartbeat slowed to normal speed. Even coming down with her felt like pure bliss. But she pulled away from him, and even though she didn't move far, he hated the distance. He'd wanted to stay inside her for just a little while longer. Hell, he wanted to stay inside her forever.

When she touched his cheek, he opened his eyes, found her gazing at him with a dazed expression on her face. He probably looked about the same. But he couldn't think of a thing to say, and he couldn't look away.

She stroked his cheek, his neck, his chest, tracing a slow path down his torso. He caught her wandering hand and brought it to his lips for a kiss, then teased her delicate little fingers with the tip of his tongue. She gasped, but she didn't pull away. He kissed and nibbled and tasted until every inch of her hand had been touched. Just kissing her hand turned him on. Unbelievable. In another minute, he'd be ready to make love to her again.

He held her hand against his chest, rubbing at the dampness his mouth had left. His own hand covered hers completely. "You have such tiny hands," he mused. Damn, he'd better keep a lid on those loverlike comments.

She moved away a little, and he looked into her eyes. She looked serious. Anxious. Maybe she wasn't ready for more lovemaking, and didn't know how to tell him.

He patted her hand reassuringly. "What is it, Sarah?"

"I don't know exactly how to say it. But I want to thank you."

Gratitude? God, he didn't want gratitude from her. "You don't have to thank me."

She smiled, a little feebly. "I know you're just doing your job, but you've helped me so much, and it…it means a lot to me."

Just doing your job. She said it so casually, as if he didn't have any feelings at all. As if she didn't expect him to. As if she didn't want him to. "I'm glad I've helped you." His voice sounded hollow. He swallowed, but the painful lump didn't ease. "I want to make you happy. I want you to *be* happy," he corrected, before she got the wrong idea. Before she realized he'd told the truth the first time.

"And now I have a shot at happiness," she said. "Thanks to you."

Happiness with some other man. A man who wouldn't have to let her go. Someone like that damned ex-boyfriend of hers.

"You were right about fantasies," she said.

He froze, feeling as if his heart had skipped a beat. He didn't want to know. He really didn't. "What were you imagining?" Good, his voice had sounded casual, almost teasing.

"You'll think I'm silly."

"Never."

"I imagined that it was my first time," she said softly.

Thank God she hadn't imagined another man. Well, maybe she had. Maybe that was why she'd kept her eyes closed. But at least she hadn't told him so. "You should have let me know earlier. I could have helped."

"Helped? How?"

He wasn't about to admit his own fantasy, so similar to her own. "I could have played along. Treated you gently, calmed your fears, moved more slowly."

She looked surprised, as if the thought of sharing her fantasies with her lover had never occurred to her. "You would do that for me?"

"Of course." *It's part of my job.*

She gave him a sweet smile. "You're a wonderful man, Adrian."

"Thanks." What else could he say? If, by some wild chance, she was becoming attached to him, he shouldn't encourage her. But God, how he wanted to. He wanted to haunt her dreams, to fill her mind at every waking moment, to make her compare every man she saw to him and find them all lacking. He wanted her to feel bound to him, the way he felt bound to her. When had he become such a selfish bastard? Her needs were all that mattered. And he needed to let her go, let her find a man she felt more than gratitude for.

But not yet. He'd let her go, but not just yet. He'd give himself the rest of the night. The shower. The couch. Maybe he'd keep her here all night, wake up beside her in the morning. She wouldn't get much sleep, though. Not with a selfish bastard like him.

Dr. Lansing was with a patient when Adrian arrived. He sat down in the deserted waiting room and picked up a magazine, gazing blankly at the pages while he thumbed through it. He tried to read a page, but his mind refused to concentrate. He tossed the magazine back down. No sense in pretending.

He stood up and paced around the room. What could he say to Dr. Lansing? Falling for a patient was the worst thing a therapist could do. He hated to disappoint her, knew she'd be furious with him. But as Sarah's primary therapist, she needed to know. And if he told her, there wouldn't be any way he could go on seeing Sarah. Once Dr. Lansing knew, he'd have to give up all these crazy fantasies of having a relationship with Sarah.

The door to the inner office opened, and a tall young man came out. He nodded as he passed Adrian on his way out of the waiting room.

Adrian took a deep breath. This felt like facing a firing squad. Confession had damn well better be good for the soul.

He walked into the inner office. Dr. Lansing sat behind her desk, writing in a small appointment book. She didn't look up.

"Good morning, Adrian. I'll just be a moment."

"Take your time, Dr. Lansing." He sat down in one of the chairs facing her desk. How could he tell her? This woman had known him through all his years of college, had been his mentor. Hell, even after all these years, he still called her Dr. Lansing.

She put her pen down, then took off her reading glasses and looked at him. "What's the matter, Adrian?"

She'd always been able to read him like a book. How could he put this delicately? "I've been having a small problem with Sarah."

She frowned a little, looking concerned. "What's the problem?"

"I seem to have lost my objectivity about her."

"Lost your objectivity? How?" Her voice was gentle, probing.

"I think...I seem to have... I think I'm in love with her," he blurted out.

Her frown cleared, and incredibly, she smiled. "That isn't unusual, though, is it? You always fall a little in love with your patients. It's what makes you such a good therapist."

"No. No, this time it's different. I've crossed over the line." He raked a hand through his hair.

"Have you discussed your feelings with Sarah?"

"God, no. I haven't been that stupid." He'd come close, though. Last night had been hellish.

"Then how have you crossed the line?"

She looked so sympathetic, but it wouldn't last. Not once she knew. He took a deep breath. "I've been treating her like she's my lover. Like she's my girl-friend." Might as well lay it all out. "When I'm with her, I've been indulging my own private fantasies."

"Does Sarah know?"

He shrugged. "I haven't told her anything, but she must realize that I'm treating her differently than all my other patients."

Her eyebrows shot up at that. "How could she know? You're the only surrogate she's seen. And really, Adrian, as long as she doesn't know, there isn't much harm in it."

He couldn't believe this. "Didn't you hear me? I've been taking advantage of a patient. Using her to satisfy my own needs."

"Have you satisfied her needs as well?"

He felt heat rise in his face. Damn. Discussing intimate acts with Dr. Lansing had never embarrassed him before. "Yes."

"And?" That encouraging tone made him want to tell her everything, every detail.

He forced himself to meet her gaze, resisting the urge to duck his head like a naughty child. "She's able to climax," he managed to say.

"Easily?"

God, yes. "As easily as most women."

"Then you've done your usual exemplary job," she said. "Sarah's overcome a difficult problem, with your help."

She made it sound so simple. Just another exemplary job. So why did he feel torn up inside? "I don't think I can let her go," he admitted. "This morning, I tried to tell her that she didn't need to see me anymore. I just couldn't do it."

"How does Sarah feel about you?"

If only he knew. Well, he did know, he just didn't want to admit it. "She's fond of me. I think it's the usual case of misplaced affection. Mild transference, nothing more."

"Then you know what you should do."

He nodded. "Let go. For her own good." And he would let go. For her. Even if it damn near killed him.

"Do you think she'll be hurt when you tell her you can't treat her anymore?"

No more than he would. Probably a lot less, actually, since she had the ex-boyfriend to fall back on. "I'll minimize the damage. Let her down gently. I've done it before." But he'd never felt this way before. For Sarah's sake, though, he'd force himself to do it.

Dr. Lansing picked up a notepad. "Why don't you act like this is just another case. Tell me about Sarah's progress. Give me a report."

She wanted a report. Somehow, he had to force himself to get clinical. Focus. Detach himself. "The first orgasm was a breakthrough for her. Once she realized she was physically capable, the mental barriers didn't work anymore."

Dr. Lansing nodded while she wrote. "I suspected as much. Do you think she'll have any difficulty with other partners?"

Pain hit his chest, a fiery, burning sensation. Like a corkscrew in his heart, piercing, twisting deep. The thought of Sarah with another man…the thought of another man seeing those beautiful breasts, touching them, kissing them…oh God. Maybe she'd keep her eyes open for him. Maybe she'd want to see his face while they made love.

"Adrian?"

He coughed, covering up the dryness in his throat, the dampness in his eyes. "No," he choked out. He coughed again. "No, she knows what she needs. But she might be too shy to ask for it." And an insensitive creep might not take the time to discover what she needed.

"I'll encourage her to be more vocal. Any residual shame issues?"

"No. Although she is experimenting with fantasies, and some of them might trouble her." And he wouldn't be there to show her how fulfilling an active imagination could be.

"I'll talk to her about the fantasies." Dr. Lansing laid down the notebook and looked at him. "I think you should talk to me again. After you say goodbye to Sarah."

"There's nothing to say. I'm quitting. You won't have to worry about me."

She kept that non-committal therapist expression on her face. "Don't make that decision while you're upset. You're too good of a therapist to quit."

He clenched his hands. Was this some kind of test, like the ethics scenarios she'd given students in her classes? "I've committed a breach of ethics. How can you even suggest I continue to see patients?"

"Being a surrogate is a difficult form of therapy, Adrian. It's surprising that this didn't happen sooner."

Ah, but he hadn't had a patient like Sarah before. "I've taken advantage of a patient. A vulnerable patient. A woman who trusted me with her emotional health."

"And you've done nothing but help her," Dr. Lansing insisted. "Sarah has problems with guilt and shame, but emotionally she's very strong. I think she has a great deal of ego strength. Besides, she doesn't know how you feel, and you aren't going to see her in an unprofessional capacity. No harm done."

No harm done. At least not to Sarah.

"Just take some time off," Dr. Lansing went on, in a tone that ordered more than suggested. "Finish writing that book of yours."

"I will." He stood up. "Thank you, Dr. Lansing."

She looked surprised. "No need to thank me, Adrian."

"Anyone else would have demanded my head on a platter."

"You seemed determined to hand it to me. But what would I do with it?" She walked around the desk, and he held out his hand to shake hers.

She took his hand, then pulled him into a light hug. Surprised, he stiffened for a second, then relaxed and hugged her back.

When they released each other, she was smiling. "You're a good therapist, Adrian. In a little while, you'll have everything under control again."

"I hope so." More than hoped. He prayed so.

Chapter Four

Adrian glanced up at the clock. The hands had barely moved. Still ten more minutes before Sarah would arrive.

He pushed his chair away from the desk, stood up and paced to the window. Might as well watch for her, since he couldn't get any work done. The street below was crowded, a sea of people, some milling about aimlessly, some walking quickly, trying to dash around the window shoppers.

He caught a glint of golden hair across the street. Sarah. Amazing that he recognized her instantly, especially from this distance, from this far above her. He watched her check the addresses of the buildings she passed, then cross the street. She'd be out of sight when she got closer. He leaned against the window, trying to keep her in view for as long as possible.

She'd be here in a minute. He should pretend to work. Or at least sit down, so that he couldn't take her in his arms. No, he wouldn't do that. Never again. His relationship with Sarah was over. In his mind, he'd already given her up. Now all he had to do was tell her.

He sat down behind his desk and picked up a pen, as if he'd been writing in the folder that lay open on his desk. But he stared at the door, waiting.

A soft knock came. He stood up, then sat back down. He couldn't open the door for her. If he did, she might hug him, and then he wouldn't be able to let her go.

"Come in," he called.

She stepped inside and closed the door behind her. "Hi." She smiled at him, a soft, shy smile. A smile he'd never see again, not after today.

He kept a smile on his face, even though his jaw ached from the effort. "Have a seat."

She crossed to the desk slowly, giving him plenty of time to notice the way her loose, long dress swayed around her legs as she walked. What he wouldn't give to see those legs bare again, to spend just one more night wrapped in them. No. No, he had to tell her. He had to. Now.

She sat down in one of the client chairs facing his desk, hiding those luscious legs from his view. "I didn't know you had an office."

Did she think he did all of his work in bedrooms? In cars? He'd asked her to come here on purpose, hoping that the impersonal surroundings would help him let go. But all he could do was stare at her face, trying to imprint her image on his mind. He wished he had a picture of her. Something tangible, something besides memories. God, he had to stop torturing himself like this.

"You're probably wondering why I asked you to meet me here," he began. His voice sounded wooden, lifeless. Impersonal. Impersonal was good. Maybe he could convince himself that there was nothing personal between them.

She nodded. "When I left your house, you didn't say anything about getting together."

And she hadn't wanted to mention it herself. When they'd said goodbye this morning, he'd noticed her hesitation. But he hadn't had the guts to break things off then.

"Things were rushed this morning," he said. "You had to hurry home and get ready for work. I wanted to talk to you when we had more time." And when he had more strength.

Her eyes widened. "Talk to me about what?"

"About you." He'd rehearsed this scene, he knew what to say. All he had to do was spit it out. "You've made a lot of progress."

"Thanks to you."

He'd ignore that. If he answered, none of his rehearsed lines would work. "In fact, you've made so much progress that you don't need to see me anymore."

"I don't?"

She looked surprised, but not hurt. She didn't look hurt at all. "You're a passionate woman," he said, continuing the speech. "You've proven that to yourself. You have control over your sexuality now."

She nodded. She didn't look thoroughly convinced, but she nodded.

Two more lines. Just two more lines to say. "You should continue to see Dr. Lansing, though. She can help you with any other issues that come up."

She gazed at him blankly for a moment, as if she didn't realize he was finished. Finally she spoke. "If I have…if I have problems, can I see you again?"

How could he say no? But if he said yes, he'd spend the rest of his life waiting for the phone to ring, waiting for her to call. And letting her go once was bad enough. No way could he go through this again. "I'm afraid not. I'm going to take some time off and finish a book I've been working on."

Her lip trembled a little, and she bit down on it. If he made her cry, he'd never forgive himself. He should have told her more gently. Should have been more concerned for her feelings instead of his own. "You don't need to see me anymore, Sarah."

Her hands were clasped tightly in her lap, a small sign that she was upset. But she nodded, and her chin rose a fraction, as if she wanted to face the future bravely. "What's the book about?"

Couldn't she just leave? Sitting here making small talk with her, craving her, kicking himself for being a fool in the first place…it would just give him more memories, more things he had to forget. "It's a self-help book for people who are having sexual problems."

She smiled at him. "Aren't you afraid the book will put you out of business?"

If she could smile like that now, knowing she'd never see him again, he obviously hadn't meant a thing to her. "Not really. I've decided not to work as a surrogate anymore."

"But you're so good at it."

Easy for her to say. "I might try counselling couples instead. I've done some work in that area." And couples were safer. With a couple, he could keep his distance, keep himself from getting too involved.

"When will your book be out?"

"I don't know. Maybe in a year."

"I'll look for it."

He forced a smile. "I'll send you a copy." By then, he just might be over her.

She glanced down, then back up at him. "I guess this is goodbye."

Just a few more minutes. He had to hold himself together for a few more minutes. "I'm glad I got to know you." That was the polite thing to say, his standard farewell to a client line. But he usually said it with more warmth. The tight rein he'd been keeping on his feelings made him sound cold, uncaring.

Her eyes looked a little wet, and he saw her swallow. *Please, Sarah, don't cry. Don't make my last memory of you be the sight of you in tears.*

She smiled. "I can't thank you enough for what you've done for me," she said.

She sounded like she had herself under control. Like she hadn't been ready to cry. Maybe he'd imagined it, projected his own misery onto her. "I'm glad I could help. When's your next appointment with Dr. Lansing?"

She glanced at her watch. "In an hour."

"Good." She could talk to Dr. Lansing if she was upset about not seeing him anymore. But she didn't seem upset. She seemed calm. Collected. Rational. As if she wouldn't even notice if she never saw him again.

She stood up. He did too, and quickly reached across the desk to shake her hand. She ignored his outstretched hand and walked around the desk.

Her arms slipped around his waist, and she hugged him tightly, almost fiercely. There was nothing he could do but hold her. Her body fit so perfectly against his, her cheek rested so trustingly against his chest. He brushed his lips against the top of her head, so lightly she probably couldn't feel it. He'd never forget how soft her hair was. He wouldn't forget anything. The herbal scent of her hair, the light warmth of her body pressed against him . . . he'd never forget, even without this last embrace imprinted on his brain.

She pulled away, and looked up at him with another of those gentle smiles. "Thank you."

Gratitude again. "You're welcome." Any other response would have stretched out the conversation, kept her standing here, next to him, making more tortuous memories for him. He couldn't take much more. In another minute, he might break down and tell her...tell her what? That he thought he was in love with her?

He pulled his hands from her waist and took a step back, breaking all contact with her.

And she turned and walked away. He watched every step as she went to the door, then left the office. She never looked back at him.

Go after her. The command came from somewhere deep in his subconscious. Compelling. Tempting. Pointless. There was no future for him and Sarah.

Whatever they'd had between them, it was over. She felt nothing but gratitude for him.

He sat down and stared at the clock. There was no way he could get any work done today. He'd wait fifteen minutes, until she was long gone. Then he'd leave. And try to find some way to fill up all the empty hours.

❦

Adrian slung the wet towel over the shower rod, then reached behind the bathroom door for his robe. Sarah. She'd worn this robe. Just last night, she'd sat on his couch, looking pale and golden and waifish in all these yards of black terry cloth, combing the tangles out of her wet hair after their shower.

He put the robe on, rolling the sleeves back down to their full length. Everything reminded him of Sarah. There was no escape. He'd gone for a long, bruising run after he left the office, hoping that the physical exertion would clear his mind. But he'd caught himself comparing the sky to Sarah's eyes. And somehow he'd ended up in Golden Gate Park, standing in the parking lot where she'd had her first taste of fulfillment, hearing her breathy little sighs and soft, shy moans as though she was in his arms again, aching for him again. She never had told him what her secret fantasy was. Now he'd never know.

He walked downstairs, to the living room. More memories here. Memories of Sarah in his robe, and then out of it, stretched along this couch, her eyes shining with passion.

He turned away from the empty couch and pulled a record from the shelf at random. Great. Roy Orbison, singing all about loneliness. That suited his mood just fine. He put the record on the turntable and threw himself on the couch, resting his forearm across his eyes. The music drifted over him, as sorrowful and melancholy as he felt.

The memories would fade with time. They had to. He'd give himself the rest of the night to wallow in misery. Tomorrow, he'd drown his sorrows in work, let the book become his life.

The doorbell rang. Sarah? No, it couldn't be Sarah. He was crazy to even imagine that. He got up and walked to the hallway, then looked through the small window in the front door. God, it *was* Sarah. Had she missed him? Been thinking about him? No, that was just wishful thinking. Any feelings she had for him were based on gratitude. Clients had chased him before, refused to accept the end of their relationship. He'd treat Sarah the same way.

He opened the door. "Hi."

"Hi," she said. She looked a little nervous, but she was smiling. "Can I come in?"

He couldn't handle this. Not again. Not tonight. Once had been bad enough. He'd take control of the situation, have it out right here. He wouldn't give an inch. And he certainly wasn't going to let her inside. "I don't think that's a good idea."

Her eyebrow rose a notch. "Don't be silly." She brushed past him and walked in.

So much for taking control. He closed the door. When he turned, Sarah was headed down the hallway, and he followed. She wore a slinky little blue dress, one that barely covered her ass and looked like an oversized tank top.

When she got to the living room, she smiled at him over her shoulder. "Cool music."

"Thanks."

She wandered over to the shelves that held his records. She'd noticed them last night, but now she studied them as if she hadn't seen a record before. "Don't you believe in CD's?"

Why was she here? To talk about his record collection? "Sure, for newer music. But I collect oldies, and I like having them in the original format."

She turned to face him. The dress was cut low over her chest, practically down to the nipples, so low that he could tell she wasn't wearing a bra. And the blue color did wonders for her eyes. Seeing her like this, when he'd finally resigned himself to giving her up...it was torture. "Sarah, why did you come here tonight?"

She looked a little surprised by the question. "Well, I..." She gave a nervous little laugh. "I wanted to see you."

How many times did he have to go through this? "I can't see you anymore. I told you this afternoon."

"You said you couldn't see me as a therapist."

"Right."

"That I didn't need any more sex therapy."

"Right."

She moved closer, until he could almost feel the heat radiating from her body. Or maybe it was his own body heat. His temperature seemed to be soaring.

She smiled up at him. "I don't want to see you as a therapist."

This couldn't be happening. She couldn't possibly mean it. He took a step back, away from the temptation of being within reach. But seeing her in that dress was tempting, too. "Listen to me, Sarah. I can't see you anymore. Not at all."

"Why not?"

"Because I'm your therapist."

Her smile widened. "Not anymore."

Why did she have to make this so difficult? Every nerve in his body wanted to hold her. "But I *was* your therapist. I could never have a different relationship with you."

"Never?"

He couldn't lie. But he had to. "No, never."

"But if you'd met me some other way, you could?"

"But I didn't meet you any other way. You were my patient."

She laid a hand on his chest, gently, barely resting it against him. Just having her touch him in that simple way, through his robe, drove him crazy. He wanted to hold her so bad, to haul her into his arms and bury his face in her hair.

Her smile was soft, teasing, beautiful. "What if you met me again, a year from now?"

He gripped her arms, pulling her hand away from his chest. "You aren't going to wait a year. You're going to get on with your life. Find a man to share it with. Forget about me."

She slipped her hands behind his neck and pressed her body against him. "Will you forget?"

Blood thundered in his ears. To have her this close again, offering herself to him...no, he couldn't let her do it. He stepped back, and she let him go, her hands falling to her sides.

"Sarah, what you're feeling right now...it's only temporary." He ran a hand through his hair. "You feel grateful to me. That's normal. But you need to find a man you feel more than gratitude for."

"I feel more than gratitude for you, Adrian."

He shook his head. "That's temporary. You don't really want me."

"I do want you." She sidled up against him again, and wrapped both arms around his waist. Somehow his hands ended up on her back, holding her close. "Let me show you how much I want you," she murmured. She used her face to push his robe apart, and he felt her lips move across his chest. "Just give me one more night."

He'd pay for this later. When her feelings for him wore off, he'd regret this. But he couldn't resist her any longer. He took her face in his hands and kissed her deeply, achingly. To hold her again, kiss her again, when he'd thought she was gone for good...he felt like a condemned man who'd just been given a reprieve.

She wriggled against him, as if she couldn't get close enough. She really did want him. His desperation faded, and he eased his grip on her. They had all the time in the world. She was here, in his arms, and she wasn't going anywhere. She'd come to him, sought him out, even after he'd let her go. She wanted him. And nothing on Earth would make him let her go again. He brushed his lips over her face, lightly, lovingly.

They slid to the floor together, stretching out side by side. He touched her face, outlined every beautiful feature. Her fingers mirrored his, stroking his own face. She seemed to be memorizing him, as if she felt the same sense of rediscovery that he did.

She kissed him, deep and sweet. Her teeth caught gently at his lip, setting fire to nerve endings all over his body, making him moan against her mouth. She pulled away, and he opened his eyes. She was looking at him, watching him, with lust and need written on her face. He'd never seen her look so desirable.

She caught his gaze, and smiled. "What are you thinking?"

He cupped her cheek. "That I want to look into your eyes when we make love."

She turned her head and kissed his hand. "Do you ever fantasize?"

"Sometimes. But just being here with you feels like a dream."

She quickly dropped her head to his chest, as if she wanted to hide her expression from him. "I have to fantasize," she said softly.

She sounded like she was confessing to murder. "There's nothing wrong with that," he assured her. He stroked her hair, cradling her head against him. "Tell me your fantasy."

She shook her head.

"Let me help you make it real." Whatever she wanted, whatever she needed, he'd do it. Gladly.

She took a deep breath. "I've been imagining that you're in love with me."

He felt like his heart had stopped. "You don't have to imagine that." He moved until they were face to face, until he could see her eyes. "I do love you, Sarah."

She closed her eyes for a brief moment, then opened them. Her lips trembled. "Say it again."

"I love you." Adrenaline surged through him, a heady burst of freedom. He could finally say those words. He almost laughed, but he kissed her instead. "I love you," he whispered, against her lips.

She kissed him back, eager, frantic, until he was gasping for breath. She seemed wild, almost delirious, as if his words had freed all the passion in her soul. As if she couldn't hear them enough. "I love you," he said again. He tried to hold her, to soothe her, but she pulled away and spread burning kisses down his chest. Her hair fanned across his skin, and he looked down, loving the sight of his hands tangled in all that golden hair, the sight of her lips on his chest.

Her hand moved down his body, over his robe, searching, finally touching his aching hardness. He moaned, and tried to pull her back up for a kiss. But she resisted. "Let me," she said. "Let me please you."

An offer he couldn't refuse. He couldn't even believe she was here, let alone taking the lead. For the first time, they were making love, really making love, as lovers, as partners. He wanted to take it slow, savor every second. She spread his robe open, and her hand caressed his hot skin. Next time. They'd take it slow next time.

He felt her hair brush against his stomach, moving lower, lower. And then the moist heat of her mouth enclosed him, an unbelievably erotic caress. A mist settled over his vision. So good. Too good. He pulled her away, and she made a small noise of protest. "Easy, love," he murmured. "I can't take much more."

She rose above him, her smile as tempting as Eve's, her legs straddling his hips. That sexy dress was so short, he could see that she wasn't wearing any underpants. Shocking. Thrilling. And she used her nakedness, stroked his hardness with the soft, wet heat of her sex. He groaned. She smiled, and teased him more.

The dress covered too much of her. He tugged at the hem, trying to lift it. She leaned forward to help. He pulled it over her head, dropped it somewhere on the floor. His hands fell to her thighs, and he let his gaze devour her. She was so beautiful. Naked and unashamed, flushed with desire. And her eyes were open, looking down at him, watching him.

As she moved to sit up again, she angled her body so that his erection pressed inside her, deep inside her. She felt so hot, so wet — oh God, he wasn't wearing a condom.

He should stop her, protect her. But she laid a hand on his chest, distracting him. "It's all right," she whispered. She moved then, her body swaying in a slow rhythm that took his breath away. And she watched him, through half-closed eyes, watched him panting for breath as she drove him higher and higher.

He'd bring her higher, too. He reached for those beautiful breasts, touching, teasing, until she cried out. With one hand he stroked gently downwards, down to where their bodies were joined. When he found her sweet center, she sobbed with pleasure. She closed her eyes then, but he saw the passion on her face, saw the need build, saw the glorious, fierce pleasure of her release. And he let himself go, let the wild, hot convulsions of her body take him over the edge.

She collapsed on top of him, still trembling with aftershocks. He held her close, stroked her back, her hair, waiting for his own heart to calm down, gasping for breath. He could stay like this forever.

What had she done to him? Her sudden passion, her aggressiveness, had transformed him. She'd claimed him, branded him. He felt utterly possessed. Utterly satisfied. And for the first time in his life, he wanted to ask a woman to marry him.

No, it was too soon for that. He'd wait a few months, make sure she didn't feel pressured. Give her a little more time to get used to all the changes in her life. No hurry.

He couldn't ask her to marry him right now, but he could say this. "I love you so much."

She froze. "You can stop now."

"Stop what?"

"Stop playing along with my fantasy."

He went cold. Had this all been a fantasy to her? He rolled over, settling her beside him. She couldn't hide now. But he couldn't read anything from the shuttered expression on her face. She'd never said that she loved him. She'd said that she felt more than gratitude for him…maybe she'd meant lust. But if she didn't love him, why would she fantasize that he loved her?

He struggled for words. "Sarah, I…"

She put her fingers against his lips, stopping him. "You don't have to explain. I understand."

That made one of them. He took her hand and moved it away from his mouth, held it against his chest. "Good. Maybe you can explain it to me."

She bit her lip, obviously troubled and confused.

Now he'd really have to spill his guts. And not knowing how she felt about him made it all the worse. "You don't believe I'm in love with you."

Her eyes looked misty, and she blinked a few times. "It's okay. I know you just said it to make me happy." A faint glimmer of hope shone in her eyes, tentative and fragile. "Didn't you?"

Later, much later, he'd hassle her for thinking he could lie about something so important. "I didn't lie," he said. "I really do love you, Sarah."

The tears spilled over then. She ducked her face against his shoulder, and he cuddled her close. She loved him. He knew that now.

He wouldn't make her say the words to him. When she was ready, she'd tell him. He could wait. "Well?" he demanded.

She laughed, and pulled back until he could see her smile. "Of course I love you. Why do you think I came here tonight?"

"To seduce me?"

She blushed, just a little. "What on Earth gave you that idea?"

"The scandalous dress you were almost wearing. And the underclothes you weren't."

She blushed full force. "You taught me that one," she protested.

He kissed the end of her nose. "I'm not complaining."

She kissed his nose in return. "You're a very good teacher."

He stroked her hair back from her forehead, just because he could, just because he wanted to relish touching her. "And you're my top student. My only student, from now on."

"I'm glad," she said, simply. "I just wish you didn't already know it all. I'd like to teach you something."

He laughed. "Don't worry, love. I'm sure you'll think of something."

She snuggled against him, and pulled the loose side of his robe over them both. Under the sheltering folds of fabric, he felt her nip gently at his earlobe. "You better believe it," she whispered.

He did. After all, she had plenty of time. Like the rest of their lives.

About the author:

A lifelong daydreamer, Doreen DeSalvo sold her first short story at the age of eight. Her payment was a candy bar. Over twenty years later, her passion for writing — and chocolate — remain. She currently lives in a Victorian house in San Francisco with the man she fell in love with as a teenager. Having experienced her own personal fairy tale, she can think of no career more rewarding than writing romance.